MARGARET
LAZARUS DEAN

THE TIME
IT TAKES TO FALL

Simon & Schuster

New York London Toronto Sydney

SIMON & SCHUSTER
Rockefeller Center
1230 Avenue of the Americas
New York, NY 10020

SIMON & SCHUSTER and colophon are registered
trademarks of Simon & Schuster, Inc.

For information about special discounts for bulk purchases,
please contact Simon & Schuster Special Sales:
1-800-456-6798 or business@simonandschuster.com.

Book design by Ellen R. Sasahara

Manufactured in the United States of America

1   3   5   7   9   10   8   6   4   2

Library of Congress Cataloging-in-Publication Data

Dean, Margaret Lazarus.
The time it takes to fall / Margaret Lazarus Dean.
p.   cm.
1. Space flight—Fiction. 2. Challenger (Spacecraft)—Accidents—
Fiction. 3. Space shuttles—Accidents—Fiction. 4. Florida—Fiction.
5. Domestic fiction. I. Title.

PS3604.E1535T56 2007
813'.6—dc22   2006052213
ISBN-13: 978-0-7432-9722-6
ISBN-10:   0-7432-9722-9

For
CJH

What does it say that an egg recites poems that are utter nonsense
in the face of trying things? Of course, we know he was cracked

by his own faith in balance. When the horses and men returned home
from their assembly job, they were too numb for words, they had
    no stories

to tell their children, they spent the evening in silence.

    —Jennifer Metsker

When the shuttle lifts off, all of America will be reminded of the
crucial role that teachers and education play in the life of our nation.
I can't think of a better lesson for our children and our country.

    —Ronald Reagan, announcing the Teacher in Space Program, 1984

PROLOGUE

I T IS ONE OF MY FATHER'S MOST FIRMLY HELD BELIEFS THAT
American interest in spaceflight ended all at once and for no good
reason in 1972. But surely that can't be accurate. I've always imagined a long fall, a slow waning, a slipping out of love with the idea of
men bouncing on the moon, defying gravity, the fire and the rockets.
I was born just at the end. As my mother labored in the basement of
a hospital in Titusville, the last men ever to walk on the moon, Gene
Cernan and Jack Schmitt, climbed back into their lunar module with
the last samples of moon rocks, stowed their space suits, and prepared to return to Earth.

My father first came to the Space Coast in 1965, when caravans
of young families were still descending upon central Florida, unpacking their children into new subdivisions smelling of fresh lumber and
the swampy traces of marshland recently drained. He was drawn
here by the hiring frenzy in those years when Congress gave NASA
more money than they asked for, when NASA was meant to win a
war made entirely of metaphor. I try to imagine what it was like to
live here then; I like to think of a time when all Americans believed so
fervently in such an innocent idea, that getting to the moon first
would settle something once and for all. I like to imagine people
invoking the name Cape Canaveral, its syllables implying a power
almost magical. The families huddled around their TVs, eagerly

watching my hometown, the marshes and sable palms of central Florida glowing green with their anticipation.

Congress withdrew funding; work was stopped. The Saturn V rocket my father had already helped to assemble, intended to send Apollo 18 to the moon, was shipped to Houston instead and tipped unceremoniously onto its side to rust in a grass field for bored, sweating tourists to pace around and for children to attempt to climb. Entire departments at NASA were closed, thousands of workers fired. So many people left central Florida in the early seventies that whole subdivisions emptied, drained of families as quickly as they had filled. My father, a technician with only a high school education, miraculously survived the purge. Congress had approved funding for NASA's next project, the space shuttle, and my father was chosen to work on it.

I learned to recognize the space shuttle from pictures long before I ever saw the real thing: snub-nosed, covered with heat tiles, black on its belly and white on its back. The point of the shuttle was its reusability; the Apollo vehicles had all been abandoned in space or burnt up in the atmosphere, but the plane-shaped Orbiter was designed to fly, come back, and fly again. My father brought home a plastic model of the Launch Vehicle: the Orbiter mated with a rust-colored External Tank, and a pair of refrigerator-white Solid Rocket Boosters that would help lift the shuttle past the Earth's atmosphere.

My earliest memory of the space shuttle is of the very first launch, of the Orbiter *Columbia* in 1981. It was the first of four test flights, flown by veteran astronauts from the Apollo era, to demonstrate the system's capabilities. No manned spaceflight had launched since the Apollo mission the month I was born, and now I was eight. I had been waiting all my life to see a spacecraft take off from the Kennedy Space Center. I remember the shock of leaving the house in my nightgown in the middle of the night, riding to the Cape with my father in the dark on clogged roads, the red brake lights ahead of us blinking like a swarm of insects.

As my father and I got closer to the Cape, cars slowed and pulled over anywhere to get out and spread picnics on the grass. I watched them as we crept by, rows and rows of families eating sandwiches and fried chicken in the middle of the night. At a NASA checkpoint, a man in a little booth leaned out to squint at my father's badge, then nodded us through. We parked across the Banana River from the launchpad. The Launch Vehicle looked so small that I was disappointed; I'd imagined standing at the base of the stack, gazing up at it the way you look up at a skyscraper from the sidewalk. I'd wanted to feel the shuddering heat of ignition on my face.

"Don't be disappointed, Dolores," my father said. "This is as close as anyone is allowed to get." He explained that even the technicians piled into vans and drove three miles away just before ignition, in case of an accident. It wasn't until years later that I understood that an explosion on the launchpad would be like a nuclear blast.

When the countdown started, people all around us picked up the chant: *Fourteen. Thirteen. Twelve. Eleven.* The sun had just started to come up, bringing back the colors—the green of the grass, the red of our car—that had all been grays in the dark. At *six* the Solid Rocket Boosters ignited, the rockets my father had worked on, and at *liftoff* the stack slowly pulled itself up, inch by inch, until the pink cloud forming underneath it illuminated the whole landscape, the light of the rockets spilling out across the water, lighting up each tiny wave, each blade of grass, like day. The rumble I felt and heard later, the pressure in my chest, each of my hairs set to vibrating as if the Earth and everything on it were an instrument the shuttle strummed on its way into orbit.

"The Solid Rocket Boosters are dropping off now," my father told me two minutes later. "They'll fall into the ocean. Workers in boats will pick them up and tow them back to be used again."

After five minutes, my father described the External Tank dropping off and burning to nothing in the atmosphere. By then the Orbiter traveled alone, a tiny point at the top of the sky, indistinguishable from any star.

My father said, "Now *Columbia* is in orbit around the Earth. The astronauts are looking out the windows and seeing black sky with stars."

Somehow, this was the first I truly understood there were men on it, living people now in space, floating weightless, free of the grasp of gravity. They would travel millions of miles before this simple mission was over. I felt a surprising sting of jealousy. Standing out there on the banks of the Banana River in the first light of dawn, I imagined how those astronauts must feel. They had escaped the planet and now were watching its surface move unhurriedly like the credits of a movie, like something beautiful and harmless, their homes passing every ninety minutes underfoot. That was when I first understood how desperate I was to be there too.

Columbia glided in for its fourth landing at Edwards Air Force Base in California on the Fourth of July. My father and I watched it together on TV.

The President spoke, looking out happily over a field of people, all of them frantically waving little American flags. "The fourth landing of the *Columbia* is the historical equivalent to the driving of the golden spike which completed the first transcontinental railroad," Reagan read from the podium, then looked off inspiringly into the sky. "It marks our entrance into a new era. The test flights are over. The groundwork has been laid."

My mother, walking by with a load of laundry in her arms, muttered, "Then why do you keep cutting NASA's budget?"

But I loved the way the President spoke, slowly and warmly, savoring each word. I was full of hope for the future of the space shuttle, though I was in a position to know better. My space notebook was crammed with evidence: all four test flights had been plagued with technical problems, slowdowns, and near-disasters. But listening to Reagan speak, I believed the groundwork had been laid. I believed I would fly in space someday. I would have waved a little American flag if I'd had one.

While *Columbia* was wheeled away, Reagan pointed dramatically toward the end of the runway, where *Challenger,* the recently completed second Orbiter, was affixed to a 747, awaiting transport to Florida. *Discovery* would be completed in a couple of years, *Atlantis* after that.

"*Challenger,* you are free to take off now," the President said. It was the wrong language—NASA would say "*Challenger,* you are go." But the crowd cheered happily, and it did take off; the 747 gathered its mechanical might and tilted off the ground, and the camera caught a profile of it there in the sky, the silver plane with the smaller black and white Orbiter clinging to it, like a baby animal to its mother.

I took notes on the President's speech in my space notebook. I had documented each test flight—the preparations, profiles of the astronauts, pictures of each launch and landing. My father asked to see the notebook, so I handed it to him.

My mother walked by again, barely glancing at the TV. She had been impervious to spaceflight all my life, since Apollo 18 had been canceled. She was proud to live on the Space Coast and proud that my father worked for NASA. But going to launches required getting up in the middle of the night and waiting four hours in the car; she always said it wasn't worth the hassle when the launches were likely to be canceled anyway.

Flipping through my notebook, my father looked proud and amused at first, then serious, then finally he closed it with a frown.

"I'm going to be an astronaut," I told him.

"Did you know that the missions to the moon could have been flown without any astronauts at all?" he said. "Every moment from ignition to reentry was fully automated. All of it could have been controlled from the ground. Some engineers argued against including a human crew at all. If you really want to be a part of NASA when you grow up, you should be an engineer, not an astronaut."

"*You're* not an engineer," I pointed out.

"No, but I could have been," he said. "And you could too."

But even as a child, I understood what he didn't seem to: that the whole point was to see men in space, men on the moon, men walking on a surface farther from their homes than anyone had ever been, planting their flags and driving their lunar buggies while their pretty young wives waved and cried back on Earth.

The shuttles launched, one after another. When I was there to see them close up, they were thumb-sized things struggling their way into the sky on a pillow of steam. When I didn't go to the launch, I looked outside for the bright vertical streak, too bright and fast and upright to be a plane. When the shuttles returned, the double sonic boom startled me, the Orbiter breaking the sound barrier first with its nose, then with its wings. I kept track of the launches: which mission was being assembled or loaded, which was moving out to the launchpad, which one scheduled to launch, delayed, in orbit, reentering the atmosphere, landing, or in processing again.

When the shuttles launched, everyone celebrated: bars served free drinks, kids were allowed to miss school to watch our fathers' accomplishments appear on the national news, and for a time, our fathers were happy. But when the launches were delayed, everything moved into a strange sort of limbo. People in from out of town extended their hotel reservations, grew weary and then contemptuous of central Florida, looking around as if they were being held here against their will. A launch that was supposed to have gone up one morning but wouldn't attempt again until the next made us all feel we were living in a day that didn't count, a day between parentheses. The fathers looked out windows, confused and distracted, refiguring their plans. We could see them shuffling Orbiters and manifests in their minds, feeling for temperature and wind, thinking through contingencies. Sometimes I caught my father whispering to himself: *If not tomorrow, then not till Sunday. If windy on Sunday, then not till Tuesday.* The fathers were somehow tinkering with time itself, it seemed to me. Time would not move forward properly until after they had fixed the flawed parts, tested them, reinstalled them, and fired the shuttle off successfully, sending a vertical column of steam into the air to announce: Here. Start the clocks. Begin again.

OPERATIONAL

1.

MY SISTER DELIA AND I WERE SPLAYED ON THE FLOOR IN FRONT of the afternoon shows when we heard the familiar slam of our own car door. We ran to the window. It was only three o'clock. My father had never come home from work early; often, in the push to prepare one launch after another in a continually quickening schedule, he worked late and didn't come home during daylight hours at all.

We watched him walk up the path toward the front door. He was a large man with a round soft belly and a calm face. When he opened the door, he looked surprised to see Delia and me standing there. He nodded and smiled at us.

"Hi, Dolores," he said to me, then, "Hi, Delia."

My mother emerged from the kitchen, where she had been repotting a plant. She looked as alarmed as we were to see him home in the afternoon. Her brown eyes searched his face.

"What's going on?" she asked. "What are you doing home?" Her hands were covered with potting soil halfway up her forearms. She clasped them together. My mother was beautiful, with wild black hair and big brown eyes, but worry distorted her face into something like anger.

"It's what we expected," my father said. His voice was flat, as if reporting that we needed milk. He turned his hands up to her, showing her the pink palms.

"Why are you home, Daddy?" Delia asked. Everyone ignored her; she was four.

"There's been a slowdown with the Main Engines. It has nothing to do with the boosters. But until this gets straightened out, there isn't much for me to do." My mother watched his face closely as he talked, moving her lips slightly as though she were trying to speak along with him.

"Why are you home, Daddy?" Delia asked again.

"Shut up, Delia," I said.

"Don't talk to your sister that way," my parents said together.

"They can't just put me on the next launch," my father explained to my mother. "The payload people need some time to catch up. It's just for six weeks or so. Maybe two months. Long enough I'll have to find something else. But temporary."

My father looked down at Delia and smoothed her hair. He and my mother still made the mistake of thinking we didn't understand their talk, that we knew only what they explained to us. This was still true of Delia, for the most part, but I was eleven.

My mother sat down and began to cry. She covered her face, forgetting the dirt on her hands. Delia crawled into her lap and patted, patted, patted her shoulder.

"It's okay," my mother cooed to Delia through her tears. Delia pried my mother's hands from her face; her forehead was smeared with dirt. Her eyes and nose were red, but she forced a smile.

"Everything's okay," my mother repeated. She sniffed and dried her face with a dish towel, Delia still staring up at her with wide green eyes.

"I've already got some leads," my father said, his hands in his pockets.

My mother shook her head and scoffed quietly.

"What kind of leads?" I asked. They both looked at me.

"Why don't you girls go and play in your room?" my father said.

Delia and I went into the room we shared while he and my mother kept talking, her voice high and quick, his low and quiet. We both tried to listen but couldn't make out any words. I pulled out the space notebook I'd been keeping since the first launch. The most recent entry read:

STS 41-D, *Discovery*.

Launch attempt June 25, 1984, scrubbed due to computer problems.

Launch attempt June 26 aborted at T minus 4 seconds because of a Main Engine failure, the latest abort ever. Launch put off for two months so *Discovery* could be rolled back to the Orbiter Processing Facility. The faulty Main Engine was replaced.

Launch attempt August 29 delayed because of more computer problems.

Launch attempt August 30 delayed 6 minutes because a private plane intruded into NASA airspace.

Launch, finally, at 8:41am.

Judith Resnik became the second American woman to fly in space and the first person of Jewish heritage.

My father took me to this launch.

Judith Resnik had been my favorite astronaut since I'd first seen her on TV the day the seven women astronauts were chosen, leaning on a split-rail fence in a slightly forced pose, all of them smiling. The astronauts were about my mother's age, dressed in blouses and slacks, their hair fashionably styled into wings. Judith Resnik, in close-up, had a round baby face, a bright and innocent look. Her voice, her way of speaking, carried just the tiniest thread of friendly sarcasm. She seemed impatient with the silliest of the questions: *What do you think it means for a woman to finally travel in space? Are you aware of the dangers involved? How will you feel if you are chosen to be the first American woman astronaut?* She answered these questions with a tilt of her head, a sly smile. I'd hoped she would be the first, but Sally Ride had been chosen, the year before.

Delia pulled out her crayons and flipped through her pad of construction paper, looking for a clean page.

"Why is Daddy home?" Delia finally asked, selecting a crayon and scribbling.

"He's laid off. He can't go to work for a while, so he has to get a different job," I explained.

"Why?"

"Why what?"

"Why can't he go to work?"

"The point is . . ." I said in my best adult voice, "the point is he'll go back there soon." Hearing myself say this, I immediately felt better. It sounded true. "It's not like he got fired. It'll be like nothing happened at all."

"Okay," Delia agreed. She seemed comforted and started drawing in earnest, but after a minute she pointed out softly, "Mom cried, though."

"Yeah," I said. "She didn't understand at first. She overreacted. It's just for six weeks."

Delia scribbled. I waited for her to ask what *overreacted* meant, but she didn't. I'd been explaining things to Delia since she'd been born, and I always told her the truth. Since her life coincided almost perfectly with the years the space shuttle had been flying, I'd been explaining the shuttle to her all along. *Those are the rockets and that's the tank. The astronauts sit in the nose part, there. Those are the three Main Engines. One of them could fail, but not two.*

After a while, Delia stuck her head out in the hallway and yelled, "Can we come out now?"

"Yes!" my mother yelled back.

When we came out to the living room, my father was watching the news. Delia curled up next to him on the couch. I found my mother doing the dishes. She had dried her eyes.

"What's going on?" I asked.

"It's not something you have to worry about, okay? It's just for a little while. Your father's very smart. He could do lots of things. Besides, it's just for six weeks." She fell quiet as she scrubbed at a pan. A few minutes later, she said quietly, "This happened before."

"When?"

"Before you were born. Whenever NASA runs into hard times, they lay off people like your father first. It was hard, but in the end they needed him to come back, so everything worked out okay."

"How long did it take?" I asked.

She looked up toward the ceiling, as if calculating. She blew her fuzzy black bangs off her forehead, then looked down at the pan again. She seemed to have forgotten the question. "Don't you worry, okay? We'll figure everything out."

My father found another job, repairing machinery at an appliance factory. His first day of work, my mother saw him off as always, made his coffee in the same mug, so Delia and I were falsely comforted.

"Good luck," my mother said quietly as she kissed him goodbye.

"Ready?" he asked me.

"Ready," I answered. We said goodbye to Delia, who was waiting for her ride to preschool.

All the way to school, my father talked about the math I would be learning this year. It was one of his favorite topics.

"Soon you'll be getting into real algebra. Multiple variables, the quadratic equation. The concepts you'll learn this year are the foundation for calculus. Everything you learn in the future will build on this." I couldn't help but feel a little proud. All of the women astronauts were either doctors or physicists.

We pulled up in front of the Palmetto Park Middle School, a large, rambling, low-slung building framed by mature and symmetrical palm trees. Three weeks earlier, I had started seventh grade.

"Do you need lunch money?" my father asked. He heaved himself up in his seat to reach the wallet in his back pocket, making the seat squeak and crunch. More than kisses or other signs of affection, that motion embodied his everyday, responsible love for us. He handed me a dollar, then kissed me on the cheek.

I walked up the steps and through the big set of doors, where kids were milling around talking and yelling, some of them wandering into the building as if by accident. Inside, I breathed the smell of industrial cleaners mixed with dust, paper, cooked food, and the bodies of hundreds of adolescents.

I knew only about half of the kids in my class. The kids who had gone to the district's other elementary school seemed alarmingly more mature. They wore more stylish clothes and spoke to each other more harshly. They also had a leader, Elizabeth Talbot, who wore designer jeans and T-shirts with the names of bands I had never heard of. From the first day I'd laid eyes on Elizabeth, I simultaneously hoped she wouldn't notice me and hoped she would choose me as her best friend. So far, she hadn't noticed me. Today she sat between Toby and Nathan, writing something on their notebooks that made them all laugh in low, scornful tones.

I took a seat near my friends from Palmetto Park Elementary, Jocelyn and Abby. Jocelyn had always been pretty, and this year her fluffy blond hair was growing out from an attempt to fashion it into wings. Abby was not as beautiful as Jocelyn, but looked more put-together than the rest of us. She wore her black hair in a glossy cap, and her blue pants matched perfectly the blue stripe in the rainbow on her shirt. Both of them watched Elizabeth Talbot's every move.

At recess on the first day of school, when Elizabeth Talbot went from person to person, pointing at each of us and demanding, "What's your dad do?" Abby had said, "Accountant," Jocelyn had introduced herself and added, "Firing room," and I had answered, "Dolores Gray. My father works on the Solid Rocket Boosters." It went without saying that everyone's father worked for NASA.

Now I found it difficult to imagine my father going to work in a factory, so I pictured him at NASA instead. Once, before the fourth test launch of *Columbia,* he'd taken Delia and me into the Vehicle Assembly Building and showed us the tools he worked with, the elevator that took him up to different levels so he could work on different parts of the rockets. He introduced us to his boss, who peered at us through his thick glasses as if we might suddenly pounce and bite him. Mostly, my memory of NASA was of the candy machine down the hallway, the feel of the quarters clinking into it, and the candies that Delia and I chose, brightly colored sour disks. The crunch of sugar between my teeth, the smarting saliva feeling, and Delia's tongue afterward—blue, and green, and pink.

Four launches took off successfully in 1983, then three more already the year I was eleven, 1984. My father had said his layoff would last for six weeks to two months; maybe he would be back in time to work on the flight scheduled for November 7, and no one would ever have to know.

After lunch, we straggled out to the courtyard, where everyone stood around listlessly, looking each other in the eye and then looking away, as adults do. Jocelyn, Abby, and I sat on a low wall. As we talked, I looked around and counted under my breath: twenty-five kids. Of the thirteen I knew, ten had parents who worked for NASA. As far as I knew, none of them had been laid off. Then again, how would I know?

Across the courtyard, Elizabeth Talbot stood talking with some boys, her arms crossed over her chest. Her father had designed some part of the oxygen system in the space shuttle's crew cabin. One of the boys threw a ball to her, and she caught it nonchalantly, without looking, and tossed it back.

A few days later, Mr. Jaffe frisbeed fat newsprint booklets onto our desks. A loud moan broke out: standardized tests. We took them at least once a year. This one would take all afternoon. We opened our test booklets to a reading section and began when Mr. Jaffe said, "Now." Secretly, I liked these tests. I liked filling in the newsprint bubbles completely with a sharpened pencil. I liked the tense hush and the rustling sound of pages turning, the occasional scrubbing of erasers. Half an hour into the hour-long section, I finished the last question and closed my test booklet. I looked around the room at the other kids, still working. Abby scratched her way through a long division problem. Nathan hunched over his desk, clutching a shock of sand-colored hair at his forehead. Next to him, Toby sat with his eyes squinted shut, slowly filling his cheeks with air until they ballooned, then slowly leaking it out.

On a scrap of paper, I drew a picture of an astronaut in a space suit. A few seconds later, Eric Biersdorfer closed his text booklet and laid his head on his arms. I stared at him in disbelief: no one had ever finished as quickly as I did.

Eric had gone to a private elementary school, so no one knew him. So far, he had sat by himself without trying to talk to anyone. He was tiny, the smallest boy in our class. I watched him to see what he would do next, and it seemed that he really was done; he pulled a *Choose Your Own Adventure* book from his pocket and held it open under his desk so that Mr. Jaffe wouldn't see. Then he raised his head suddenly and met my eyes. He looked at the closed test booklet on my desk and then smiled at me. The surprise of it traveled all the way to my feet. We sat, not looking at each other, but staring into mutual space with our ears on our elbows, until the other kids finished and Mr. Jaffe called time.

My father couldn't take me to the next launch because he had to be at work at the appliance factory before dawn. He'd been working there for only three weeks, but already this felt dangerously long; I worried that NASA would forget him and hire somebody else when his work needed to be done again.

I went outside while the sun was still coming up, casting a strange blue light onto the houses and trees in my neighborhood. I wasn't sure which direction to look for *Challenger,* and I started to think I'd missed it, when I caught sight of it over our garage, a tiny bright light scoring a white vertical streak onto the sky. I counted two minutes and then I thought I could see the Solid Rocket Boosters fall, but I couldn't be sure. My father had assembled one of those boosters before he was laid off.

Later, I wrote up the launch in my space notebook.

STS 41-G, *Challenger.*
Launch October 5, 1984, at 7:03 am, no delays.
This is the largest crew of astronauts ever to fly (seven). Two of them are women (Sally Ride and Kathryn Sullivan), and this is the first time two women have flown in space together. Also the first time a Canadian citizen (Marc Garneau) has flown in space.
Sally Ride lifted a satellite out of the payload bay using the Remote Manipulator Arm. Kathryn Sullivan became the first woman to do a spacewalk during a 3-hour EVA (Extra-Vehicular Activity). She and David Leestma simulated the refueling of a satellite in the payload bay. "I love it," Sullivan said as she floated through the airlock.
My father didn't take me to this launch.

I didn't write in my space notebook about my daydream of this mission, my fantasy of what it must have been like to live on a spacecraft. What it must have been like for Kathryn Sullivan to spend three hours pulling on the layers of the EVA suit, the thin under layer laced with tubes of water to cool her, the tough pressurized outer layer, the gloves and helmet. What did she think about, getting suited up, knowing that she would be the first woman to venture out of a spaceship on a tether, to float alone in the blackness of space?

On the afternoon bus, the only open seat was next to Eric Biersdorfer. As I sat down, keeping as much space as possible between my body and his, Eric didn't look up or say anything. His head rested against the window, and he held a book open against the back of the seat in front of him.

After a few minutes, Eric suddenly set his book on his knee and looked out the window.

"I don't read books written for children," he said. "They're too boring."

He told me about the books he'd been reading, and I noticed that he had a slight stutter when he got excited. It occurred to me to try to find out whether his father worked for NASA, but I didn't. I just listened to the talk as it spilled out of him, fascinated that such a person could exist where I did.

Delia and I woke early on school days, when the sounds of talking, running water, and our mother's radio station burbled through the door. We shuffled out to find our mother sitting at the kitchen table in her robe, with the newspaper spread out, chewing on Delia's green crayon. Delia ran over and sat on her lap, crinkling some of the papers.

"Hi, girls," my mother said without looking up.

"What are you doing?" Delia asked, excited. She liked projects.

"Your mom's going to get a job and make some money," she said. She looked up at us, her brown eyes hopeful and energetic.

"What do you think about that?" she asked us, looking from me to Delia and back again. It was a real question.

"Good idea!" Delia said.

"Who's going to take care of us?" I asked.

"You girls are big enough to let yourselves in when you get home and fix your own snacks. We'll get a key made for each of you. You'll wear it on a ribbon around your neck so you don't lose it."

"What kind of job?" I asked. "Where would you work?"

"Maybe SeaWorld!" Delia cried.

"That's ridiculous," I told her. "She's not going to work at Sea-World. That's not the kind of job she wants."

"Thank you for the suggestion, Delia," my mother said warmly. "But I've decided to be a secretary. I'd like to work in a nice office and answer phones for an important businessman. What do you think?"

I thought of the women I'd seen on television, dressed in dark suits and lipstick, clicking through offices in high heels, whispering important messages into the ears of silver-haired men. The offices were always dark wood, and it always seemed to be cold outside; I assumed that these offices only existed in the north. But my mother seemed so inspired by this idea, I wouldn't have dreamed of discouraging her.

"That sounds perfect," I said.

We didn't hear about the job idea again for a few days, until the morning I came out of my room to find my mother in the kitchen dressed up in a white blouse and a frilly pink skirt I had never seen before. Her hair, usually a fuzzy black cloud, had been smoothed into a tiny bun on the back of her head. The blush on her cheeks made her look eager or embarrassed. She wore high-heeled sandals with pantyhose; I could see the seams across her toes.

"You look nice, Mom," I said.

"Thank you, baby," she said. "Do you think I'll get hired?"

"Of course," I said. "What's the job?"

"It's working for a doctor's office, checking in patients and filing records. I talked to the doctor himself yesterday. He said mostly he just wants a friendly person at the front desk when people come in. I told him, 'That's me!'" Her voice quickly rose into a nervous laugh, as though she were talking to the doctor all over again.

"How do I look?" she asked. "Would you hire me?"

"Definitely," I said. "I'd pay you a million dollars."

When I left, she was crouching over to apply her mascara in the hallway mirror, stretching her mouth into a long distorted shape like a fish.

At recess, Eric and I sat on the steps and watched Elizabeth Talbot kick around a soccer ball. She controlled it with her feet the way the boys did, curling her cleat inward to steady it, then drawing back to kick it precisely with the side of her foot. The six weeks my father was supposed to be laid off were almost up. I expected him to get a call any day. Elizabeth jogged over to where a group of boys were talking; we watched her retie her ponytail as she discussed a Dolphins game with them. Somehow, she didn't have to try at being better than everyone else.

"I wish I could play soccer like her," I said to Eric. This wasn't exactly what I meant, but I wanted to broach the subject of Elizabeth. I wondered what Eric thought of her.

"You could if you wanted to," he pointed out.

"Not like her," I said.

Eric shrugged. "I don't see why not," he said finally.

My mother got the job. That night, she told my father all the details—the questions the doctor had asked her, the responsibilities that would be hers. She still had her work clothes on and, wearing them, she held herself more upright, speaking in complete sentences.

"Look at you," he said, holding her at arm's length. "All dressed up."

"I'll have to dress like this all the time now," she pointed out. "I'll need some more good work outfits."

"This is full-time?" he asked.

"Oh yes," she said. "Full-time."

They stood holding each other's arms, forming a closed circle. It always made me a little anxious when they did this, that they would forget me entirely. It was one of my earliest memories, seeing my parents kiss on the lips when my father got home, briefly but with force; I saw their lips change shape in profile pressed against one another, and it had seemed a strange and slightly violent thing to do. When they hugged in the middle of the room, I stood next to them with a hand on each of their legs, waiting for them to remember me.

The first day of my mother's job, she woke early to shower and do her hair. When Delia and I wandered out to the kitchen, my mother was already dressed with her makeup on.

"Well, good morning," she said. "I have a surprise for you."

She slowly clicked open her change purse and pulled out two keys, then placed them carefully in our palms as though they were valuable. I turned mine over in my hand, examining it. It was silver, brighter and shinier than my parents' keys. Its teeth were sharp, brand-new.

My mother found some ribbon and strung the keys on them, then tied the ribbons around our necks like medals.

"Remember to keep these under your shirts," she said. "You don't want to advertise to strangers that you'll be home alone."

"Why not?" Delia asked. My mother gave me a quick warning look.

"It's just a secret," my mother said. "So keep it under your shirt."

She spent a few minutes showing us how to unlock the door from the outside, then how to lock it again from the inside. We were not to answer the phone or open the door to anyone. We were not to leave the house or use the stove.

All day I checked and double-checked to make sure I had my key and that it was hidden from sight. The tip scratched my chest, just at the end of my breastbone. I felt the weight of the key around my neck with everything that I did.

As I got off the bus in the afternoon, I became convinced that the key wouldn't work in the door, or that someone would see us and break into the house. Delia was standing on the corner, swinging her key by its ribbon.

"Put that away," I hissed. "Everyone can see." Delia looked at me as if I were crazy. No one was on the street. She slipped her key into the lock and swung the door open.

A few hours later, my mother breezed through the door in her high heels. She set down her purse and kissed us hello.

"How was it?" I asked.

"Well, there's a lot to the job. You'd be surprised all the things I'm supposed to keep track of, all at the same time. But Dr. Chalmers said I had a great start for my first day."

By the time my father got home, the three of us were watching TV with our feet on the coffee table. My mother was slumped in a chair, still wearing her work clothes, her eye makeup smudged around her eyes. Delia sang along with a commercial, caught up in its exuberance.

My father looked from my mother to the kitchen to my mother again. My mother had usually started dinner by now, but she made no move. He went into the kitchen, which was still dirty with dishes from the night before, and began opening and closing cupboards. Curious, Delia and I followed him in there. He stood facing the refrigerator with his hands on his hips, thinking.

"Where does your mother keep the macaroni and cheese?" he asked. We both pointed silently at the cupboard. Everything he did— choosing a pot to boil the water in, adding the milk, straining the noodles—was slightly different from what our mother did.

"You're doing that wrong," Delia said triumphantly as he dropped a chunk of margarine onto the macaroni. "You're supposed to cut it into little bits."

"Oh," he said. "Well, this will work anyway." We watched as he stirred, trying to get the margarine to melt, for a long time. He added the orange powdered cheese, then spooned it into a bowl for each of us.

"That's it? Just macaroni and cheese?" Delia asked.

"This is dinner," my father said. "It's a perfectly nutritious dinner."

"But where's the meat?" I asked. "Where's the green vegetable?"

He gave me a look.

"I'm just kidding," I said. "We like macaroni and cheese. Right, Delia?"

"Yeah," admitted Delia. We carried our bowls out to the living room; my mother accepted hers with a coo of surprise. Then we ate together in front of the TV.

Within a month, my father took over doing the laundry, throwing everything in together on the wrong settings, so all of our clothes became discolored and misshapen. Clutter built up in the living room, piles of newspapers and mail and apple cores and dirty socks and homework papers. I decided to clean: I picked up everything off the living room floor, dragged out the vacuum cleaner, and untangled the cord. Then I noticed Delia in the doorway, watching me, her eyes wide.

"Why are you staring at me?" I yelled over the noise.

"What are you doing?" she yelled back.

"What does it look like I'm doing? I'm cleaning this disgusting room." But she kept staring, and soon I felt it too: the exhaustion and hopelessness of this task. Even once I finished this job, the other rooms would still be a wreck, the dishes still dirty, the kitchen floor still sticky underfoot. I turned off the vacuum and left it standing in the middle of the floor, the cord snaking across the carpet. None of us had ever thought about the fact that my mother did these things; none of us knew what to do now that she wasn't doing them.

Through the rest of October, sometimes I played with Jocelyn and Abby in the courtyard, but more often I sat on the steps near Eric but not close enough to attract attention. We watched the boys in bright colors clump together, separate, regroup. There were groups now, kids who stuck together in the lunchroom and in the courtyard. There was a sort of order to things.

Eric made no special effort to keep quiet, or to keep out of people's way. He was tiny and pale. Paleness itself was unusual enough in Florida, but Eric was *very* pale, a translucent pale, blue pale, veins showing through his skin. He said things: in class, and in the courtyard, he talked, and not quietly. He used words that I knew but would never have used with other kids: *inevitable, mitigating, askance.*

Eric's eyes were watery and icy gray. He had the oversized, serrated teeth of a kid just growing in his adult set. And that awful haircut: his hair seemed almost designed to accentuate his ears, and how can I describe those ears? They were both huge and elegantly shaped, more intricately whorled than most ears. They did not seem, as some large ears do, to be made of some type of molded rubber. Eric's ears seemed to be made of skin—delicate white skin with thin scarlet blood vessels running through. I was only eleven, but I knew it was strange for me to find Eric's large ears so lovely. I knew large ears were supposed to be laughable, but Eric's ears, like everything else about him, seemed untouchable.

Eric Biersdorfer and I had a nice balance: we were both good at social studies and science; he did better in language arts, and I did better at math. I had always liked doing schoolwork; I took pleasure in the dogged satisfaction of scratching through a math problem step by step and getting to an answer at the end that was right, not negotiable or disputable. The first thing we did after we came in from lunch was check our homework from the night before, reading down the column of numbers while Mr. Jaffe gave out the correct answers in his slow, serious voice. Every checkmark I ticked down the margin—correct, correct, correct—seemed to affirm my idea of myself as good at math, smart in that way that not many others were smart.

One afternoon, I went inside before everyone else to find Mr. Jaffe stapling a brightly colored calendar to the corkboard. When he turned and saw me watching him, he gestured at it dramatically. "This is an o-fficial calendar from the National Aeronautics and Space Administration," he announced.

"Oh," I said. I approached it to look more closely. "Where'd we get it?"

Mr. Jaffe flipped the calendar over. On the back was a color portrait of a big jowly man with silver hair and pink cheeks. The man was dressed in a suit and standing in front of an American flag and a model of the space shuttle, smiling in a fatherly and false manner. Under a round seal was an extravagant and illegible signature. Under the signature, the man's name was printed in all capital letters. It said: RANDOLPH R. ("BOB") BIERSDORFER, DIRECTOR OF LAUNCH SAFETY.

I flipped the calendar over to the front again and studied the photo for that month: *Columbia* lifting off from the 39-A launchpad. Black-bellied, attached to its red External Tank and its white rockets, the shuttle pointed its black nose up against the blue sky, showing us its American flag tattoo. White and pink steam billowed under it. In the background you could see the Vehicle Assembly Building, where my father had worked all my life until September.

When Eric came back in with the rest of the kids, he saw the calendar, met my eyes, and looked away. None of the other kids seemed to notice it. But Eric seemed irritated with me, as if this new and troublesome fact—his father's being the boss of everyone else's father—were somehow my fault.

"Why are you acting so weird?" I asked him finally, when no one else was around. Involuntarily, I looked at the calendar at the back of the room over his shoulder.

"It's just better when people don't know," he said. "I just wish my dad would stop giving out the stupid calendars, that's all."

I touched my key where it rested under my shirt. If I were in his place, I thought, I would let everyone know in some accidental way that I was better than they'd thought I was. Eric probably lived in a bigger, nicer house than anyone. Those clothes he wore, which looked so nondescript on him, were probably expensive brands, and knowing that made them look a little better to me. But Eric would never tell anyone about his father. Eric wanted to be left alone at school, and it seemed that it hadn't helped him, at his other school, to be so different and also to be the son of a rich, powerful man, the boss of the other fathers.

STS 51-A, *Discovery.*
Launch attempt November 7, 1984, canceled due to wind shear. (What is wind shear?)
Launch November 8, 7:15 am.
Anna Fisher was on board. She is the third of the women to fly and the first mother in space. She used the Remote Manipulator Arm to grab two broken satellites and put them into the payload bay.
My father took me to this launch.

The trick with launch attempts was to pace yourself, not to get too excited all at once, because just as likely as not the attempt would be scrubbed. My father and I packed food and crept outside in the middle of the night, then parked and waited for hours. The tourists and first-timers never understood the waiting. They wore themselves out with anticipation, clapping and hollering at the vehicle squatting on the launchpad; then they shouted with rage when the weather turned, or an instrument read outside the acceptable range, and the calm voice of the public affairs officer came on the speakers to announce that the launch attempt had been called off.

While we packed our things to leave after the launch was scrubbed, I looked up at my father and thought of asking him about his NASA job, when he might go back. But he just gave me his quick nod and smile, and I decided not to.

When we arrived home, my mother was standing in her bathrobe, the phone to her ear, her voice high and formal. My father got to work unpacking the groceries we'd bought on the way home. But Delia and I watched her, trying to figure out who could elicit such a charming phone manner.

She hung up the phone and looked at me.

"That was Mrs. Biersdorfer," she said.

My father pulled himself out of the refrigerator.

"Did you know that your daughter is friends with Bob Biersdorfer's son?" she asked him.

"Bob Biersdorfer's son," Delia said conversationally, hugging a box of sugar cereal she'd pulled out of a grocery bag.

My mother turned to me. "Why didn't you tell us you were friends with Bob Biersdorfer's son?"

It had never occurred to me to tell them; school and home were two separate universes. My father stood with his hands on his hips, looking from her to me.

"She's invited to the ballet in Orlando next Saturday," my mother told him. "Their family has season tickets and *Bob* can't make it." She used his name heavily, not quite sarcastically. "The son said he wants to invite her. She'll have dinner over there afterward. At the Biersdorfers'." All three of them looked at me.

My mother gave me a big smile.

"You may have gotten your daddy his job back," she whispered, excited.

"Deborah," my father murmured quietly.

"What? She'll have dinner over there. You'll go to pick her up, he'll invite you in for a beer…"

My father stooped into the refrigerator again, sniffed a moldy cantaloupe, and handed it to Delia to toss into the garbage.

"This is an *opportunity*," my mother added, and the way she pronounced the word, it sounded longer than when other people said it, broad and long-ranging, with hills and valleys, secret spaces. "Right, Dolores?"

"Right," I answered quickly, not sure what I was agreeing to.

"You have to learn to use your connections," she said, this time speaking to my father. He rummaged loudly through a grocery bag.

"Okay," my father said when my mother didn't look away. "All right okay all right."

2.

I TOOK A BATH WHILE MY MOTHER WENT THROUGH MY CLOSET, trying to find something I hadn't outgrown that I could wear to the ballet. I washed my hair and wondered why I had such a feeling of dread. Eric Biersdorfer had invited me to the ballet: fine. Eric's father was the man who could get my father his NASA job back: fine.

Then I saw what it was: the faces of Jocelyn and Abby, the two of them huddling so their shoulders touched as they always did, leaning together; they could see me where I sat in the tub. They laughed as Eric and I took our seats together in the theater, all dressed up. Jocelyn and Abby would tell Elizabeth Talbot, and what then?

Once I was washed and dressed in a pink sundress that was too tight in the armpits, my mother stood me in front of the full-length mirror in their bedroom and brushed out my hair. Delia lingered behind us. My mother had promised Delia she would do her hair too, even though she wasn't going anywhere.

"I want you to be very polite," my mother said, yanking my head back a little with each brushstroke. She was fixing my hair in a bun on top of my head, a style I thought too little-girlish.

"Maybe a ponytail instead," I said casually. My mother didn't seem to hear me.

"I want you to say please and thank you, and don't stare at people, and answer when someone speaks to you. Will you do that?" she asked me. I tried to nod, but couldn't—she held all of my hair tightly in one hand.

"Yeah," I said.

She glanced into the mirror to meet my eye. "It's important," she said.

"Important," Delia repeated.

"I know," I answered, and looked right at my mother's reflection. I gave her a big smile to show how I would act. "Thank you, Mrs. Biersdorfer!" I piped in a little-girl voice.

My mother laughed. "You've nearly outgrown that," she said, looking at my dress.

"Yeah," I agreed. "It's tight."

My mother finished pinning my hair into place and sprayed it with her hairspray.

"We should get you some training bras next time we go shopping," she said.

"*Training* bras," I repeated with disgust. "I'm only eleven."

"I know, but you're starting to get a little something here." She reached out to touch, with her forefinger and thumb, one of the swollen bumps of breasts just starting to form on my chest.

"*Mom,*" I protested, and knocked her hand away.

She gave a bemused smile. I felt a horror that she had not only created these breasts by calling them to my attention, but had also made them laughable.

"I don't need a bra yet," I said petulantly.

"*Sensi*tive," she chided. "Whatever you say, baby."

She stood behind me with her hands on my shoulders, surveying her work. I looked just the way she wanted me to, young and sweet, excited to see the ballerinas and emulating them a bit with my high bun and strappy dress.

"How does your sister look?" my mother asked Delia.

"Pretty," she answered perfunctorily.

"I'm so proud of you, baby," my mother whispered in my ear. She was proud, I could tell, but she was also nervous for me; they went hand in hand.

Mrs. Biersdorfer pulled up at our curb in a large shiny car and stepped out gracefully, keeping her knees together. From the doorway of our house, my mother and I watched her pick her way politely up our weed-strewn walk. Bigger than my mother, louder than my mother, Mrs. Biersdorfer wore her makeup aggressively, like a mask: the rouge and mascara were what you saw, not the face underneath. Her colorless hair was curled and poufed large. Her blue suit was stiff like a uniform.

"Hello there," she said, wiggling her beige nails at me, before turning to my mother for the obligatory pleasantries. While she and my mother chatted, I found Eric in the backseat of the Oldsmobile and slid in next to him. He grinned when he saw me, turned red, and clunked his head against the window. He was dressed in a gray seersucker suit with a white dress shirt and a red bow tie. His hair was wet and looked as though someone had recently been attempting to comb it into submission. But Eric's hair wanted to be vertical. He wore penny loafers with his suit, with athletic socks that bunched out at his ankles.

I still felt the dread I'd felt in the bathtub, but once I saw Eric, I was glad he had asked me to the ballet. He was taking a great risk by doing this, even if he didn't realize it. And now that we were here in the car, it didn't seem to be as much of a danger; in fact, it seemed like the most natural thing in the world for us to go to the ballet together.

Mrs. Biersdorfer got into the car and pulled away from the curb without looking back at us. Eric looked out his window. I looked out my own. The neighborhood and its green leaves and street signs fell away to reveal the freeways, wide and fast, and the shiny structures of Orlando.

The main character of the ballet was danced by a woman who kept changing tutus. She was dark and had an angry look. The way her hair was pulled down at the sides emphasized her nose, which was long and had a bump in it. She took in a breath, raised her arms, and slowly toed the floor like a horse, flexing every muscle in her leg. I was conscious of Eric breathing beside me. I heard every rustle he made, every rustle I made, like we were communicating in code. I watched the main ballerina's partner: he wore as much makeup as she did, and the white of his outfit, draped over his shoulder and exposing one nipple, picked up purple and green from the lights. He stepped backward out of the circle of light in three steps, his feet turned out—toe-heel, toe-heel, toe-heel, then stopped, his back foot perfectly pointed against the floor, a look of perfect longing for her on his face, and he watched her dance all over the stage.

The house lights came on. We blinked, got up, and made our way out to the lobby.

"Would you like anything?" Mrs. Biersdorfer asked me. I shook my head mutely, then remembered my mother and the chirpy way I'd practiced saying "Thank you, Mrs. Biersdorfer!" Already I'd let her down. I should have asked Mrs. Biersdorfer for something so I could thank her for it charmingly.

Eric asked for peanut M&Ms, and his mother bought them and a drink for herself before drifting off to mingle with other important adults. Eric made a game of throwing and catching the candies in his mouth.

"Do you want one?" he asked.

"Sure," I said, holding out my hand.

"Then you'll have to catch it," he answered. He tossed another and caught it in his mouth before I could grab it. Cackling, Eric shoved handfuls of M&Ms into his pockets, and I pinned him against a pillar, grabbing for them. I could feel his thin body, the delicate rack of his rib cage, and it felt like a body long familiar, though I'd never touched him—though, I realized, I'd never really touched anyone before. And it was all wrong, to be touching him, and I stopped laughing and pulled away, horrified. Oblivious, he danced with triumph, thrusting his fists in the air.

"Don't be a dork," I said quietly, so quietly I couldn't be sure he had heard me. I looked around the lobby. Eric's mother was elaborately extricating herself from a circle of hairsprayed women, kissing cheeks. I didn't belong here with Eric—I belonged at Jocelyn's or Abby's, or kicking a soccer ball around with Elizabeth Talbot.

Eric ate the chocolates smugly. After a while he finally offered me one, and at first I ignored him, but then I took it and ate it without meeting his eyes.

"What?" Eric said.

"Nothing," I answered. We went back into the theater for the second half of the ballet.

When we went outside, the sun was low and pink in the sky. As we walked to the car in the parking ramp, Eric skipped and twirled, curving his arms the way the dancers had. His mother gave him a hard look. "What?" he said, but he stopped. After that, no one spoke.

Eric's family lived close to Orlando, only ten minutes or so from the performance hall. In his neighborhood the houses were large and made of gray brick, with a lot of space between each one, great distances of perfectly manicured grass. Mrs. Biersdorfer pulled the car into a garage that opened automatically as we approached it.

"I hope Livvie kept everything warm for us," she said.

In the uncomfortable silence that followed, I asked, "Who's Livvie?"

Mrs. Biersdorfer snapped her head in my direction, as if she'd forgotten I was in the car.

"Livvie works with us," she said. "She's our housekeeper."

Eric looked steadily out his window. His mother shut off the ignition, and he made no move to get out of the car. Mrs. Biersdorfer got out, shut the door behind her, and went into the house without looking back at us. Eric and I sat in the backseat for a moment, not moving. With the air-conditioning off, the car was quiet, the ticking of the engine the only sound.

"I'm sorry about her," Eric said suddenly, gesturing toward the driver's seat. His face started to redden, and he met my eyes for only the shortest second before he looked away.

"You shouldn't be sorry," I said, embarrassed for him. "It's not your fault."

"Well, anyway," Eric said, and he fumbled with the door handle for a moment before opening his door. I followed him into the house, which was cold from air-conditioning and had a slightly musty smell. The furniture was sparse, all angular chairs facing one another. The living room had a high ceiling, open to the second floor. I didn't know anyone else who had a house with a second floor.

"Come on," Eric said, and led me up the stairs.

Eric's room was large, almost as big as my family's living room.

The walls were painted a pale sky blue that darkened toward the ceiling, where the blue became black, dotted with silver stars. Everything was neat in a way that seemed vaguely military—the bed was made, no toys or clothes in sight. Nothing gave him away. I wondered whether the room was always like this, or whether he had cleaned because he knew I was coming over. Even his books were pushed way back on their shelves into the shadows, making it hard to see the bindings. Eric stood in the middle of the room, still wearing his suit.

"You're very neat," I commented. Eric nodded. He stood stiffly with his hands in his pockets, looking almost angry.

"What do you want to do?" he asked. "Do you want to play a game? I have Scrabble and backgammon."

"Don't you want to change out of your suit?" I asked. "I'll wait out in the hall."

Eric seemed to consider this. "No, that's okay," he said finally. "You have to wear your dress. It wouldn't be fair." He pulled a backgammon board out of his closet and we sat on the floor to play. By the time his mother called us for dinner, Eric was already winning. He looked up impatiently.

"I'm not even hungry," he said. "Are you?"

"Kind of," I said. In fact, I was starving. The smell of roast beef had become stronger since we had been playing, making my stomach rumble.

"Well, let's go, then," Eric said. I followed him down the stairs to the dining room. I had assumed that Mr. Biersdorfer would be home for dinner, and I had also expected to see Livvie, the mysterious housekeeper. But only Eric's mother was in the dining room, sitting at the head of the table. Eric and I sat across from one another, unfolding linen napkins onto our laps.

"Did you both wash your hands?" Mrs. Biersdorfer asked.

"Yeah," Eric lied for us. We ate silently. I tried not to watch Mrs. Biersdorfer, but it was difficult not to: she did everything slowly and deliberately. Her plate was neat at all times, each forkful of food organized and well balanced before she carefully placed it in her mouth without disturbing her lipstick. Then she chewed slowly, looking off at a point far away. Only after she had swallowed and taken a sip of wine did she turn her attention to her plate again to organize another forkful.

Eric kept his head down and ate quickly, picking up little bits of food: a dab of potatoes, a few peas, a sliver of meat. I had expected this dinner to be different from our dinners at home—better food, no TV—but the silence was strange. It embarrassed me, made me feel that I should speak but also that I should be as quiet as possible, that I should be the quietest of all.

After ten minutes, Eric put down his fork and sat back forcefully. He looked at his mother, then at me. Then he crossed his arms across his chest and looked down at the table.

"Did you get enough to eat?" she asked without looking at him.

"Yup," he said, then looked at me. "Are you done?"

"Eric, let her finish," his mother scolded.

"That's okay," I said. "I was done." I put down my napkin and stood. Mrs. Biersdorfer looked up at me, surprised, then looked back down at her plate. For an awkward moment I stood there, knowing I had done something wrong but not sure what.

"May we be excused?" Eric said, sliding himself to one edge of his chair. Clearly we weren't supposed to stand without permission. I never would have guessed that.

"You may," said Mrs. Biersdorfer.

We were halfway up the stairs when Eric stopped and turned back.

"Oh, um," he said with a false offhandedness. He rifled through his hair with a hand. "Did you say thank you?"

"What?" I asked, my pulse quickening.

"You should say thank you for dinner," he said, gesturing at the dining room door. Of course: thank Mrs. Biersdorfer for dinner. The most obvious opportunity to thank her for something, and I'd missed it. But how could I go back in there now just to thank her?

"I'll meet you upstairs," Eric said. He stood watching me until I turned to walk back down the stairs. I felt a weird anger toward him then. I had never had my manners criticized by another kid before. Yet I also felt ashamed because clearly I didn't have any manners. I never knew what to say to adults like Mrs. Biersdorfer, so I said as little as possible.

I paused at the door to the dining room, not sure what I would say when I went in. I stepped inside thinking that Mrs. Biersdorfer might have left. But she was still there, standing at the head of the table folding napkins, while a large black woman in a shapeless beige dress loaded our plates onto a tray—Livvie.

"Thank you for dinner Mrs. Biersdorfer it was really good," I blurted, all of the words running together. Both women looked up at me, then briefly at each other. I had meant to address Mrs. Biersdorfer, but I realized I was still staring at Livvie. Livvie picked up her tray and pushed through the swinging door to the kitchen.

"You're welcome, Dolores," Mrs. Biersdorfer said. "We're glad you could join us today." She gave me a tight little charity smile, and it occurred to me for the first time that Mrs. Biersdorfer thought I was poor, *underprivileged,* that she thought of taking me to the ballet as offering me an opportunity I would never have had without her generosity. Even the food, her smile said, was better than I usually got, a rare treat.

"Can I do anything to help clean up?" I asked.

"Oh no," Mrs. Biersdorfer said. "That's very kind of you, but we'll take care of it. You run along and play with Eric. What time is your father planning to pick you up?"

"I don't know," I said. No one had told me any of the details, yet now I felt stupid that I didn't know. I felt a sudden fear that my parents would forget me, that there had been some miscommunication between them—maybe my mother thought my father was picking me up, he thought she was, and I'd be stranded here until late at night, imposing on the Biersdorfers.

"Well, I'm sure he'll be here before too long," Mrs. Biersdorfer said with another tight little smile. She disappeared into the kitchen.

Upstairs, Eric sat on his bed, still wearing his suit, reading a book. We got back to our game, and only a few minutes later we heard the door open downstairs. I assumed my father had arrived to pick me up, but the booming male voice was nothing like my father's. Eric lifted his head from the game and held his face up like a dog catching a scent.

"My father," he said.

"Should we go down?"

"Why?" Eric asked.

We went back to backgammon, and it seemed like a long time before the doorbell finally rang again. That time, I heard the singing notes of my mother's polite voice.

"What's wrong?" Eric asked.

"It's my *mom,*" I said. But he couldn't understand that my father was supposed to pick me up—the whole plan my mother had worked out in her mind, with Mr. Biersdorfer inviting my father in for a drink, then helping him get his job back. I could imagine what had happened at home: her trying to coach him on how to behave, as she had with me; her growing conviction that he would decline any offer of a drink, that he would not make small talk, but just gather me up and go. I could imagine her deciding not to trust him with this opportunity, deciding that she would have to come over and charm the Biersdorfers herself.

Eric and I sat nervously, expecting to be called downstairs at any moment. But minutes went by, and nobody called us. We put the game away and stood near the cracked door, listening. We could hear our mothers talking to each other, though we couldn't make out the words.

"Do you get along with your parents?" I whispered. Really what I wanted to ask was why he had invited me to the ballet—whether he'd asked me because he wanted to be my friend, as I had thought at first, or whether, like his mother, he wanted to offer an opportunity to someone less privileged.

"What do you mean?" Eric asked. "Do you mean, like, do we fight?"

"I guess," I said. "Or, like, are they mean to you?"

Eric thought for a minute. "They're older than other people's parents," he said finally. "They got used to not having kids around before I was born." He fell silent for a while and we both strained to hear what was going on downstairs. I wondered whether Eric's parents had told him this story, or whether he had figured it out on his own.

"I ran away from home once," he whispered. I gave him a skeptical look, but he stared back at me steadily.

"Where did you go?" I asked.

"To my old school. I climbed in an open window."

"Did you *walk* there?" I asked, incredulous. I was trying to picture

Eric hiking through the suburbs of Orlando, a sleeping bag under his arm, his most treasured possessions in a knapsack.

"I took a cab," Eric said. "I was only there for a few hours. My parents figured out what happened and called the cab company for their records."

I tried to imagine the punishments that might befall me for doing such a thing. I would have no idea how to summon a cab, what to say to the driver, or how much money to give him.

"Did you get in trouble?" I asked.

"They came and picked me up. They told me not to do it again."

"Dolores!" my mother's singsong social voice rang out from the bottom of the stairs.

"Yeah?" I called back.

"You ready to go, baby?"

"Come on," Eric said. Downstairs, my mother and Mrs. Biersdorfer were standing in the living room looking up at us. My mother was wearing one of her work outfits, a green dress and white jewelry, even though it was Saturday. She was smiling and flushed under the gaze of Mrs. Biersdorfer.

Through the dining room door, which was open just a crack, I heard the clinking of glass. A warm yellow light seeped out. Something moved and resolved itself into a man's thick arm, the white sleeve rolled up, a glinting watch. I heard the sound of a glass of ice rising and falling. Above the arm, I saw a sliver of pink face and silver hairs.

"Are you ready to go, baby?" my mother asked. I nodded.

"It was really *so* nice of you to invite her," my mother sang to Mrs. Biersdorfer. "She's never been to a ballet before. This was quite a treat, wasn't it, Dolores?"

"It was fun. Thank you, Mrs. Biersdorfer." I tried to sound like my mother, to give my voice the lilting tone hers had.

"I'm glad you could join us, dear," Mrs. Biersdorfer said. Her eyes flicked from my mother to me as she spoke. "We're looking forward to seeing you again."

Eric waved from where he stood on the third stair.

"'Bye," he said, looking suddenly embarrassed.

We pulled the heavy door closed behind us. I didn't see our car, but my mother took my hand and led me confidently down the sidewalk. Soon I saw it, parked a few houses down.

"What a handsome woman Mrs. Biersdorfer is," my mother said, still using her theatrical voice. "And what a lovely home. It was decorated by a professional. I could just tell. Everything was just . . . perfect. The husband was awfully nice, too. An old-fashioned gentleman."

"I didn't meet him," I said, and I was surprised to learn that she had.

"I got the feeling they might have liked to ask me to stay longer. But, of course, dinner was already over."

"You were there a long time anyway," I pointed out.

"Yes, well. Did you hear her say she'll be seeing us again soon? I think that's a good sign maybe they want to socialize with us. You know, D, this could be really important for your father."

"I think she was just being polite," I said. "Isn't that just something people say? It doesn't mean she's really going to call us."

My mother's brow furrowed for the slightest moment.

"You are the most pessimistic child I've ever met," she said. "You're just like your father. Sometimes people say that and mean it, and sometimes they don't. We'll just have to wait and see."

When we got home, she told my father about her encounter with the Biersdorfers in detail, acting out all the parts. She seemed to remember everyone's exact words.

"He's a real old-fashioned gentleman," she said of Mr. Biersdorfer again. My father listened quietly. When she finally finished telling him about it, she watched him for his reaction.

"Well, that's great," he said. He gave a quick nod, patted his thighs, and stood up to turn on the TV.

My mother didn't mention the Biersdorfers again for the rest of the evening or the next day, and by Sunday night it seemed she had forgotten about them completely. Now and then, I felt a tiny sharp feeling in my chest, and I knew it was about Eric and what would happen if anyone at school found out we had been together. I never should have done anything as ridiculous as going to the ballet with him. When I saw him on Monday, I decided, I would be polite but distant. In this way I would save us both.

But on Monday, Eric wasn't in school. Mr. Jaffe said that he was sick, and it couldn't have happened at a better time. When I got on the bus that afternoon, I realized how much I had made a habit of sitting next to Eric; that would have to stop too.

Just as the bus was pulling away, it jerked to a stop for someone running toward it. Elizabeth Talbot, panting and smiling, pink-cheeked, climbed on and sat next to me.

I thought of my space notebook at home in a desk drawer, its embarrassing pages packed with all the details and specifications of my uncoolness. My heart beat rapidly and I couldn't think of things to say, but Elizabeth simply looked at me, opened her mouth, and started talking. She told me all about her soccer game on Saturday, the white piping on her new green uniform, the goal she had scored against an eighth-grade goalie. When she got through that, she told me about an old movie she'd seen on TV about a lady who pretended to be another lady, maybe her sister, in order to get a man to fall in love with her. He did, in the end, but Elizabeth was principally preoccupied with a scene in which the woman plucked her eyebrows down to almost nothing. Then she cut her long hair short so that it curled all over her head. After all that, she put on a lot of makeup and then she looked completely different. Elizabeth smoothed the tips of her fingers across her brows and down the sides of her face, her eyes closed. She said, "First she pulled her eyebrows with the tweezer, then she cut her hair with the little silver scissors. And then she was so pretty, she was like a totally different person."

Elizabeth sat with her eyes closed as the bus bumped us along. Then she opened them and looked at me. She said, "I know who your boyfriend is."

Horrible. How could she know already that Eric and I had been together? She began to hop in her seat, a soft little hop as if she had to pee.

"Oh?" I said, as if bored to death. "Who?"

"You know who I mean," she said, still hopping. "Eric Biersdorfer. He likes you."

"Oh," I said nonchalantly, my heart pounding. "Him."

Elizabeth hunched in close to me, cupping her hand to her mouth, our shoulders touching.

"Did he tell you?" she whispered. I couldn't believe it. Elizabeth Talbot. It was like we were best friends.

"Oh yeah," I said, still casual as hell, although a tiny point of heat had started in my chest with this lie.

"What did he say?" she demanded, wrinkling her nose, eyes huge.

"Oh, you know," I sighed. "Just, you know. That he likes me."

"Oh my *God,*" Elizabeth said, throwing herself back against the seat. "Eric *Biers*dorfer."

I knew I should stop there, but I couldn't. "His father's got a really important job at NASA, you know."

"Oh yeah?" she asked, bored. I was losing her attention.

"And . . ." I paused until she turned to me, still not sure if I would say it or not.

"You won't believe this," I said, lowering my voice, hunching toward her. "He invited me to the ballet last Saturday."

Elizabeth's mouth fell open. "You mean, like a date? Did you go?"

"My *mom* made me," I said, mock traumatized. This was acceptable: her expression filled with sympathy.

"Did he come to your house? Did he come up to the door?" she asked.

"He stayed in the car."

"Did his mom drop you off there, or did she come in?"

"She came too."

"Did he sit next to you?"

I rolled my eyes and nodded.

"Did he try to hold your hand?" She was almost whispering. "Did he try to kiss you goodnight?"

I looked over my shoulder dramatically before answering. "I don't want this to get around," I whispered. "I don't want it to be any harder for him than it is." I was surprised to hear myself speaking this way. Elizabeth blinked several times rapidly in anticipation, her lips parted.

"But let's just say that he wanted to."

Elizabeth went insane with delight. Squealing, she smacked both hands over her mouth and practically flung herself out of her seat.

When she regained control of herself, she said his name again. "Eric Biersdorfer."

Elizabeth asked me questions about Eric all the way to her stop. As the bus pulled over, she said, "Come over to my house. My mom will drive you home before dinner."

I knew my mother would be home early that day, so Delia wouldn't be home alone. As I followed Elizabeth down the aisle and climbed off the bus, everyone watched us, taking note.

Elizabeth's house was big, with salmon-colored stucco and a row of palmetto trees lining the yard. The front door was ajar, and as soon as we walked in, Elizabeth's mother called to her from some faraway room. We stood in the living room, which was all white wicker and chintz. Everything looked so perfectly placed it seemed no one had ever sat. I thought about my own living room, cluttered and grungy.

"Dolores is here," Elizabeth yelled back. Mrs. Talbot appeared in the doorway, a tiny energetic woman with kind eyes and a huge smile. She was wearing old clothes smeared with pink paint and a kerchief on her head.

"Dolores!" she cried. "It's so nice to meet you! You're in Elizabeth's class with Mr. Jaffe, right?"

"Yeah," I croaked. This seemed like a rudely brief answer, but I couldn't think of anything more to say. I kept feeling I'd lost my key, but every time I checked the ribbon around my neck, it was still there.

"We're painting Elizabeth's room," she said. She held out one arm to show me a thick smudge of paint, bubblegum pink. "You like the color?"

"It's nice," I said. In fact, I thought the color was too girly, but I was impressed that Elizabeth could choose any color she wanted, even such a bright and impractical one. All of the walls in my family's house were white.

"You girls must be starving," Mrs. Talbot announced. She fixed us cheese sandwiches and Cokes, then disappeared to finish painting. Elizabeth and I ate at the kitchen table while Elizabeth demanded more details about the ballet—what I wore, what Eric wore, what kind of car his mom drives. I told her again that his father was high up at NASA, but again that didn't seem to mean anything to her.

"If they're so rich," she said, "why does he dress like such a hick?"

I was afraid that when the subject of Eric Biersdorfer ran its course, I wouldn't be able to think of other things to talk about and Elizabeth would grow bored with me. But I needn't have worried; Elizabeth was capable of supplying conversation on her own, out of whole cloth. By dinnertime, when Elizabeth's mother reemerged to drive me home, Elizabeth asked me to a sleepover at her house that weekend. The best part of this, I thought, was that now Jocelyn and Abby would have to look up to me.

Eric never said anything bad about me to anyone. I'm sure of that; he had no one to talk to. But I talked about Eric. At the sleepover in Elizabeth's basement, I sat up in my sleeping bag, talking, conscious of the girls' eyes on me, my face flushed with the attention, and I told my new friends made-up stories about him: that his mother was not really his mother, but his stepmother; that he was beaten for minor offenses; that he wet his bed at night. None of them asked how I had come by this information. They just listened, silently, as I told it, and believed me.

When Eric came back to school, it took him a while to gather how much things had changed. He came over to my desk between language arts and math and asked what had happened the days he'd been gone, whether he'd missed anything. I shrugged without looking in his direction.

"Dolores," he said, "s-s-*some*thing must have happened."

When I wouldn't meet his eyes, he asked me what was wrong. I didn't answer, and he kept asking, saying my name again and again. Finally he went back to his own desk.

In the courtyard, he sat alone on the steps, and he remained there for months, sitting curled up with a book, as he had in the first days of school. Throughout the rest of the semester, I worked myself into a position that I hoped would be unshakable, where I could never again be in any danger of unpopularity. I knew that any compassion for Eric would threaten my fragile position, so I avoided speaking to him or even looking at him, and I tried to believe I was doing it to save Eric as well as myself.

We still assumed my father would get his job back soon, but week after week passed without word. My mother was so sure our encounter with the Biersdorfers would cause NASA to rehire my father that she talked about it as a certainty. My mother believed that if she only demonstrated her confidence about my father's rehire, the universe would reward her by arranging for it. Only once, over dinner, was my father moved to point out that his rehiring was not inevitable.

"It's just that there are rules determining these things, who gets called back and in what order," he explained.

"It's been months," my mother pointed out brightly. "Surely you're at the top of the list."

"It's not necessarily that simple," my father said.

My mother made a face at me over his shoulder.

"Always so pessimistic," she said. "We'll see." Even then, she seemed to know something he didn't.

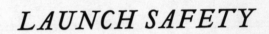

LAUNCH SAFETY

3.

ON MY BIRTHDAY, A FEW WEEKS BEFORE CHRISTMAS BREAK, MY mother took me shopping and bought me two new outfits. Then, at her insistence, we went to the lingerie department.

"Try these on," she said, handing me two size-A bras, one white and one pink. "I think you've already moved past the training kind."

"Why are they padded?" I asked.

"All the A cups are that way," she said as we moved toward the dressing rooms. "I guess they assume that if you're an A you must want a little more."

"Well, I don't," I said. My mother stayed outside the dressing room while I closed the door and untangled the bra from the hanger.

"Do the boys say anything to you?" my mother called through the door.

"What do you mean?" I asked, struggling to figure out the bra's clasp.

"You know. About your—development."

"Mom, please," I begged. I somehow felt that if no one talked about my development it wouldn't really exist. I slipped off my shirt, shivering in the air-conditioning, and put on the bra.

"When I was your age, I had nothing. I worried about it all the time." Reluctantly, I opened the door to show her.

"We need to adjust it," she said. "Turn around." Her fingers were cold on my back as she shortened the shoulder straps. Then she squared my shoulders in front of the mirror.

"Perfect fit," she declared.

"It feels weird," I said.

"You'll get used to it," she said. I wanted to squirm away, but she was still holding my shoulders.

"Look at you," she said. "All grown up."

"Okay," I said impatiently. "Can I put my shirt back on?" Something about the feeling of the bra straps and the chill of the air on my skin made me want to cry. I knew my mother meant to compliment me, but I didn't want to look this way. I would have stopped if I could.

After the holiday break, things settled into a new order at school. Every day after lunch Eric sat on the steps alone. Elizabeth and Jocelyn and Abby and I sat on a wooden bench in the center where we could keep an eye on all activity in the courtyard. Everyone understood this bench to be ours and left it free for us even when we weren't there.

We clustered around Elizabeth, listening to her talk. Her tastes were simple, and she returned to the same themes every day: her accomplishments as a soccer player, TV shows she followed, clothes she had seen in magazines and how long they might take to make their way to central Florida. These topics had at first seemed exotic and mature to me, and though I still found them intimidatingly foreign, they had become boring through repetition. Our talk had become a contest between Jocelyn and Abby and me, all of us jockeying to win Elizabeth's favor with our knowledge and sophistication, to make her laugh.

After lunch as we filed out to the courtyard, Elizabeth was acting restless. Jocelyn, Abby, and I knew what was coming.

"Look at Dierdre and Jason over there in the doorway," Elizabeth whispered. "Are they, like, boyfriend and *girlfriend*?"

"Ew," I said quickly. "Jason smells like rotten eggs." It was important to me to establish my distance from this type of boy-girl behavior because I knew all three of them must remember the weeks I had sat that way with Eric. The girls had never mentioned it, but they could be holding on to it for future use.

"Jocelyn, go tell Dierdre to come up here and talk to us," Elizabeth ordered, and we watched as Jocelyn marched across the open area of the courtyard. Dierdre raised her head, sensing trouble, as Jocelyn made her way toward the doorway where she and Jason were sitting. We watched Jocelyn speak to her, watched their two heads turn at the same moment to look up toward our wooden bench. Dierdre, talking, shook her head once, and at first I thought she was refusing to come over to us. My heart beat with fear for her, but then she stood up and brushed herself off, and I watched the two of them move slowly across the courtyard. Dierdre stood in front of Elizabeth, waiting to be addressed.

"Dierdre," Elizabeth said in a businesslike manner. "Is Jason your boyfriend?"

"Nnnno," Dierdre said carefully.

"Then why are you holding hands with him?"

"We weren't holding *hands,*" Dierdre said, turning red. "We were just sitting over there." She turned and pointed at the doorway, as if the location had been the only issue. "We were just sitting." She looked not angry, but frightened.

"Are you aware that Jason smells like rotten eggs?" I asked.

Dierdre squinted at me, confused.

"We just wanted to know if you were going together," Elizabeth said lightly. "It looked like you were getting pretty serious."

"We were just *talking,*" Dierdre insisted, but now her face had softened as though she might cry. Elizabeth looked Dierdre up and down slowly, chewing her lip as though making a decision. Deirdre waited, apprehensive but patient. She looked like she would wait forever.

"You can go," Elizabeth said finally. Dierdre waited briefly for something more, bewildered, then walked away. She headed toward a clump of girls sitting on another bench, in the opposite direction from the doorway she had shared with Jason. I knew she would never speak to him, in the courtyard or anywhere else, ever again.

As soon as she was gone, we all burst into giggles.

"Rotten eggs!" Elizabeth squealed, and looked at me with

approval. We laughed for a long time, long after we were actually amused, just to make sure Dierdre heard us. Across the courtyard, Eric sat on the steps. He had a book open on his knees, but his pale face was tipped up. He'd watched the whole scene. We made eye contact for a second; once he saw I was looking at him, he went back to his book.

That night I couldn't sleep. I lay awake reading a new space shuttle book I had found in the library; the pictures of the space shuttle were mostly ones I had seen before, but I was fascinated with a section in the back filled with photos and brief biographies of all the astronauts. I loved finding a woman's face among all the men, reading her place of birth and high school graduation year and where she went to college and graduate school, just like the others'. Imagining her as a college student, a high school student, a Girl Scout, made me feel that I could grow up to be like her.

Long after I'd assumed everyone was asleep, I heard the door to my and Delia's room slowly creak open. I shoved the book under my pillow and pretended to be asleep as my mother crept into the room. She sat on the edge of my bed in her pink robe, picking at her chapped bottom lip. Each tiny tug vibrated the bed frame. She sat for a long time. I didn't open my eyes and tried to keep my breathing even and regular. Finally she spoke.

"Dolores," she whispered gently. I opened my eyes, faked disorientation, and gave a stretch.

"Hey, D," she said. "You awake? I want to ask you something." I studied her face in the gray light: she hadn't been crying, but her face was tight, pinched with anxiety. "What was the name of your little friend? The Biersdorfer boy?"

A heartbeat of dread went by. My father had been laid off for four months now. I had gone to the ballet and thought about nothing but myself; I had done nothing to get my father his job back. My mother studied me, her eyes intent, as if what I said next would be crucial, could break her heart.

"Eric?" I whispered.

"Eric," she repeated emphatically, in a voice that meant she had been trying to remember all day. "When was the last time you played at Eric's house?"

"I've only been to Eric's house that once," I said. "After the ballet." Wouldn't she have known if I'd been there again? "I only go to Elizabeth's or Jocelyn's or Abby's."

Her forehead wrinkled.

"That ballet was the only time," I said. "Just that once."

"Well, *whenever* you went," she said, suddenly exasperated. "When was that?"

"That was a long time ago. That was in the fall," I said. "I haven't really seen him much since then."

I started to get an uncomfortable windy feeling in my chest, a feeling that I would come to have often, later, as a teenager: the feeling of having been caught doing something thoughtless, selfish, destructive—having quite literally forgotten the existence of other people—my mother or Delia, this friend or that—in the elation of doing something I wanted to do, being who I wanted to be, someone slightly cooler than my normal self.

"Aren't you still in the same class with Eric?" she asked.

"Well, yeah," I said. "But we're not really friends anymore." My heart pounded twice, three times, four, as I waited for her response. But I was surprised to find that, at this moment, it was more important to me to maintain my distance from Eric than to please my mother, more important to be who I was with Elizabeth than with her.

"Well, I want you to do something at school tomorrow," she said. "I want you to talk to Eric, and I want you to tell him that our family wants to have his family over for dinner. We should get to know each other, if you and he are going to be friends."

She patted me on the arm and kissed my forehead.

"Okay?" she asked. Her face had suddenly become so open and hopeful, I couldn't bear it.

"Okay," I agreed. She smiled and kissed me again before creeping out of the room, leaving the door cracked the way Delia liked it.

Mr. Jaffe taught us vocabulary words during language arts, and instead of listening I worried about when I would talk to Eric. I decided that the best time would be during math. We sometimes worked on problems in groups, creating enough chaos to cover a conversation. But when math came, we did an activity where we each worked quietly at our desks.

At lunch, Elizabeth supervised us so closely there was no hope of getting away.

"Does your father work for NASA?" Elizabeth asked me that day, apropos of nothing. My heart stopped. She scrutinized me closely, waiting for me to answer.

"Yes," I lied. I fiddled with my key on its ribbon around my neck.

"Is your father an astronaut?" she asked.

"No," I said, my face getting warm.

"I know he's not," she announced. "I was just testing you, to see if you would lie."

Hearing the word *astronaut* escape her lips, seeing the snarling way she said it, filled me with fear. If Elizabeth ever saw the growing pile of space shuttle books in my room, saw into my fantasies in which I cast myself in the role of Judith Resnik, that would be the end of me. I would become the next victim of her blood sport.

"What exactly *does* your father do for NASA?" she asked. Her face scrunched with impatience, waiting for me to answer.

"He works on the Solid Rocket Boosters," I said, trying to keep my voice even. I scanned my brain for any way she could have learned that my father had been laid off. "He assembles the rockets."

"Oh, so he's a technician."

"That's right," I said warily, knowing I was being tricked into something but not sure yet what.

"So," she said with satisfaction, "he's not an engineer."

"What's the difference?" Abby asked.

"The technicians are kind of like mechanics," Elizabeth explained loudly for the benefit of all, happy to have been asked. "They didn't go to college. The engineers are the experts. The make the decisions and design the space shuttle. The engineers are the bosses of the technicians." She studied me, waiting for a reaction. I shrugged to hide my panic.

"My father's an engineer," Elizabeth added.

"Who's the boss of the astronauts?" Abby asked.

"The engineers," Elizabeth said. "The engineers tell them what to do."

"My dad's an astronaut, kind of," Toby offered from his end of the table.

"Oh, is he?" Elizabeth asked sweetly. Jocelyn and Abby giggled.

"He is, kind of," Toby said. "He works with them, to get them trained and stuff? And he told me once that if any of the astronauts gets sick or something that my dad will probably go instead."

"You're lying," Elizabeth said curtly. "The astronauts live in Houston, and so do their trainers. They only come to Florida for a few weeks before the launch. Your dad's probably a janitor or something."

"No, he's not, he drives the crawler transporter," Toby backpedaled. The crawler transporter was the massive tank that carried the assembled Launch Vehicle from the Vehicle Assembly Building to the launchpad at one mile per hour; we all fantasized about driving it.

"He probably cleans up after the astronauts when they live in quarantine before the launch," Elizabeth finished. "He probably mops the floors."

Toby was silent. He would be made to pay, maybe for a long time, for his lie.

In the courtyard, Elizabeth, Jocelyn, Abby, and I took up our usual position on our bench. While Elizabeth talked, I watched Eric sitting on the steps and thought about what my mother had asked me to do. His body was pulled up into a shrimp shape, the book on his knees inches from his eyes. The wind moved his shock of hair to the left, then right, then left again. I'd told my mother I would ask him and his family to dinner, but I could see no way to stand up from the bench, cross the courtyard in front of everyone, approach Eric, and speak to him.

Eric looked up and held his head high in the air, as if sensing something. He scanned the courtyard and went back to his book. A few moments later, he looked up again. He could sense me watching him, thinking about him, even though he couldn't see me. He looked left and right. Then he closed his book, put it under his arm, stood, and walked into the school building. This was my chance.

"I'll be right back," I said. "I have to go to the bathroom."

"So go," Elizabeth said impatiently.

The school seemed gloomy and dusty inside as my eyes adjusted to the light. I ran down the hall to our classroom. Mr. Jaffe was in there alone grading papers at his desk, and he looked up as I came in and then left just as suddenly. Where was Eric? I stood for a long time in the hallway, not quite believing that I was going to do what I did next.

Quickly and without knocking, I walked into the boys' bathroom. It was a mirror image of the girls', except for a row of low white urinals lined up on a wall where our bathroom bore only a dull, scratched mirror. I squatted to look for feet in the stalls. There were none.

I was about to leave when I noticed that all of the stalls' doors hung open at just the same angle, casting just the same shadow, except for the last one, which was closed. I could imagine him in there, his feet on the seat, hunched up with his book on his knees. I walked to the door and knocked on it once. "Eric," I said loudly.

I heard a startled crash from within the stall. "Jesus *Christ,*" Eric said, his voice shaking. He took a moment to reposition himself. "Dolores?"

"Yeah," I said. There was a long pause while Eric waited for me to say why I was in the boys' bathroom knocking on his stall. I didn't say anything.

"What do you want?" Eric finally asked, not unkindly.

"My mom wants to invite your parents for dinner," I said. But that wasn't right; Eric was invited too. "I mean, your family. Your mom is supposed to call my mom to set it up. Okay?" I spoke as quickly as I could, feeling a warm rush of relief as I did: I was about to be finished with this impossible task. Eric was quiet for a moment.

"Why?" he asked.

"What do you mean, *why*?" I was finished delivering my message; now I wanted to leave.

"Why does she want to have us over?"

"Oh. I guess . . ." I tried to remember my mother's exact words. "She thinks we're friends, so I guess she thinks . . . that our families should be friends."

There was a long silence in the stall. I'd blushed hard as I said the word *friends,* and I was glad that Eric couldn't see me.

"Why don't you just tell her?" Eric asked calmly.

"Tell her what?" I asked, though I knew what he meant.

"Tell her that we're *not* friends. That you don't speak to me anymore." His voice was matter-of-fact, free of sarcasm or malice. Hearing his voice, I couldn't understand why I had stopped speaking to him, why we weren't friends anymore. What had happened? I had made a choice, but I couldn't recall why. I remembered a force, powerful and compelling, but now that Elizabeth was my friend she seemed not to represent this force at all, but to be just a bossy twelve-year-old girl.

"I'm speaking to you right now," I told Eric. "I'm not communicating telepathically, am I?"

"Yeah," Eric said. "Well." After a long pause, he spoke again with a tone of finality: "I'll tell my mother."

I tiptoed to the door, checked the hallway left and right, and slipped out of the boys' bathroom as if it were on fire. As I walked back to the classroom, I was proud of myself. I had done what my mother had asked, and it seemed that I would get away with it—no one had seen me speaking to Eric.

When everyone began pouring back into the classroom, Eric walked in with them, his book under his arm. He put the book in his desk, opened his social studies book, and turned the pages rhythmically, never looking in my direction.

STS 51-C, *Discovery.*

This launch was scheduled to be *Challenger,* but *Discovery* was substituted because *Challenger* had heat tile problems.

Launch attempt January 23, 1985, canceled due to cold weather. The overnight temperature got down to 18 degrees. (Why can't the shuttle launch below freezing?)

Launch January 24, 1985, at 2:50 pm. The Backup Flight System failed at External Tank separation, and the crew had to fly manually. During reentry, the BFS started 8 seconds late, but worked correctly otherwise.

This was the first mission dedicated to the Department of Defense. The mission goals and payload are secret. Ellison Onizuka became the first Japanese-American to fly in space.

My father took me to this launch.

My mother took that entire week off from work to prepare for dinner with the Biersdorfers. On Monday she had all of the carpets steam-cleaned, so when Delia and I got home we were confined to a narrow plastic path that led from the door to our room. She brought us our dinner in there, and we weren't allowed to come out all evening. When the carpets were dry, we saw the next morning, they were two shades lighter than they had been all our lives, and plusher. They gave under each step we took in a way that reminded us of luxury.

Tuesday she hung new drapes in the dining room and touched up smudges on the walls with paint. When Delia and I came home that afternoon, we found her in the back yard refinishing the dining room table.

We went to the glass patio door and watched her. She hadn't noticed us yet and worked unselfconsciously. Her face was surprisingly ugly when she didn't think anyone was watching her—her forehead tight, she squinted meanly at the table, moving her lips now and then. She wore yellow rubber gloves up to her elbows and a set of pink pajamas. Our father had shrunk them in the wash, and now the sleeves came to just past her elbows, and the bottoms strained over her hips. The top with its lace edging was now streaked with red wood stain in a way that seemed obscene. Her hair escaped from its ponytail in frizzy black drifts that hung in her eyes and swayed with the rhythm of her work. We watched her, watched the way she concentrated, her whole body following the back-and-forth of the brush's strokes, the stray pieces of hair following.

"What is she doing?" Delia whispered, though the patio door was closed.

"She's painting the table," I said. "So it'll look nice for Friday."

"When is Friday?" Delia asked.

"Today is Tuesday," I said. "Tuesday Wednesday Thursday Friday." Delia lifted her eyebrows slightly in a look of hopelessness, never taking her eyes off our mother.

"Three more days," she said.

Wednesday our mother scrubbed the kitchen and bathroom with toxic-smelling powders and sprays. Delia and I found her standing on a chair in the kitchen, sweeping the ceiling with a broom. Dust rained down onto the counters and appliances and floor, everything she had just cleaned.

"Shit," she swore softly. "I should have done this part first."

"Can I help you clean, Mom?" I asked.

"No, thanks, baby," she grunted, taking a swipe at the ceiling fixture. "You and D go and do your homework."

When she was finished, the kitchen didn't exactly gleam—the linoleum and the chipped white appliances were too old to shine. But the kitchen had an orderly feeling to it that I'd never experienced before. She had thrown away the collection of empty containers that clustered on top of the refrigerator and had taken down all of the drawings and notices from the corkboard. It was nearly empty now, with only a cluster of pushpins in the corner and the index card entitled EMERGENCY NUMBERS. The corkboard made me oddly proud of my mother—it implied an ability to organize, a spartan sense of order.

Thursday she cleared away everything in the house that was old, tacky, or otherwise unsightly. This phase of the project was the most transformative. When I got home from school that day, I felt as if I were walking into a sitcom set for a show about our family. Elizabeth's house had this sense of reality, and Jocelyn's, and Abby's on the days the maid had been there. Eric's house had had it. I was surprised to find that this quality didn't come from the nicer things—bookcases, new furniture, plants—that those families had, as I had always assumed. The feeling came from a lack of clutter, from simplicity. Gone was the pile of bills and mail from the side table. Gone was the pile of shoes in front of the door. The laundry that never quite seemed to get folded from the uncomfortable wingback chair was gone, and so were the old magazines piled near the couch, their covers warped or torn off. Homework and discarded sweaters and dirty plates and a stapler that I remembered being on the coffee table for months, gone. The comfortable mess of our living room, all of the marks of my family's past, our chaotic life together, all gone.

I'd always avoided having Elizabeth over, always making sure our plans were for her house or Jocelyn's or Abby's instead. But now I wanted Elizabeth to see this house, for her to think that we lived this way all the time.

When my father came home, we watched him approach our mother where she stood in the kitchen, stirring the margarine into a bowl of macaroni and cheese. He kissed her on the back of the neck. "This place looks great," he murmured into her hair. "You're a miracle worker."

She smiled up at him. They felt it too: this housecleaning was not just a temporary effort but a permanent change. I was filled with pride for her. We heard our mother humming as she finished putting together the macaroni and cheese, and she served it not in front of the television, where we usually ate, but around the table, from matching dishes. She poured Delia and me matching glasses of milk in actual glasses, not plastic cups. Delia watched her glass coming toward her with an enraptured look, as if the milk were something she had seen advertised but didn't quite believe she deserved.

When Delia and I went to our room, we found just inside the door ten or twelve grocery bags, all full to the top. It took me a moment to recognize the bags' contents as the junk that had been in the living room.

"Dolores," Delia cried softly. She took a step back, frightened. We looked at the bags without touching them. At the top of one rested a shoe; at the top of another, my math book. A coffee cup lined with mold, an ashtray half full of gray powder, a paperback book, bent and marked with a footprint. Delia looked like she might burst into tears. I felt it too. We had thought our new clean house had transformed us, but the junk still existed. There was only so much our mother could do.

Friday, our mother spent the morning at the beauty parlor and then began to cook. When Delia and I got home in the afternoon, we found her in the kitchen chopping onions. We oohed and made her do a slow turn for us. Her hair had been straightened and then waved into large, smooth curls. Her bangs lay organized and sprayed into place across her forehead. A light frost of pale blue glittered on her eyelids, and heavy black lines outlined her lashes. Her skin was an even, matte pink color. When she stopped turning, arms outspread, she held her artificial smile carefully, trying not to let her lipstick touch her teeth.

She was beautiful. I looked at Delia, who was gaping at our mother. I knew she felt the same way I did: that this new mother was glamorous, more exciting than the mother we were used to, yet we didn't know this mother or how she might treat us.

A number of cookbooks lay open on the counters, and all after-noon, while Delia and I watched TV, we could hear her swearing softly as she flipped through them. She hadn't cooked much since starting her job, and I couldn't remember seeing her cook from books at all, trying to do everything perfectly and neatly. I snuck into the kitchen to see what she was doing. She was still chopping onions, but they were getting away from her, sliding under her knife so that they were cut at strange angles, strange geometrical shapes, and all crazy sizes. She picked through the piles with her lacquered nails, scooping out the ones that didn't look right to her and throwing them away. I could tell she didn't want to be watched, and I slipped out before she noticed me. The next time I checked on her, she was washing out measuring spoons while a sauce crackled angrily in the bottom of its saucepan.

"Dammit," she said. "D, could you turn that off for me?"

I turned off the burner. A black crust was beginning to form around its edge.

"*Dammit,*" she said again, more distinctly this time. "That'll prob-ably taste like ashes. I guess I have to start it over."

"What are you making, Mom?" I asked.

She sighed. "A number of things."

"What do you mean?"

"Well, it's not like when we just have a regular family meal together and we're having hamburgers and that's all we have. It's more like when you eat at a fancy restaurant. First there's the cocktails, then the appetizer course, then the main course, and each one is a different food. It's complicated."

"What's the main course?" I asked, although I could tell this conversation was peeling away the feeling of elegance and exactitude that she had been cultivating all week, the feeling that she needed to keep about her like a borrowed shawl if she was to bring this off.

"The main course is meat," she said. "Now let me get this mess organized, okay?"

I left the kitchen as she scraped the sauce into the garbage.

I was in charge of dressing myself and Delia in the last hours before the Biersdorfers arrived. I brushed Delia's hair into two ponytails and tied red ribbons around them. We put on the dresses my mother had laid out for us: Delia wore a red dress with a white lace collar, her only fancy dress, and I wore a white dress my mother had bought me for my birthday. I understood how my mother wanted us to look: neat and girly, matching. We both brushed our teeth and washed our faces. Delia drooled a glob of toothpaste onto her red sleeve, and I scrubbed at it with a washcloth. She stood passively, watching her eyes in the mirror as I jerked and jostled her.

"What is this?" Delia asked.

"What is what?"

"Tonight. What are we doing?"

I knew it had affected her, seeing our house change.

"It's a dinner party," I said. "You know that."

"Yeah, but what is that?"

"It's—you know—a *party*. We'll eat dinner together. The grownups will drink wine." I didn't really know either.

"But why is it a *party*?" Delia demanded. Every party she had ever been to had been a children's party, with balloons and cake.

"It's not, really," I admitted. She seemed disappointed. I kept rubbing at the toothpaste as we talked, and the stain became paler, then invisible. I scrubbed until long after I couldn't see it anymore.

We heard the front door opening and my mother's high company voice welcoming the Biersdorfers. We cracked our door and stood there for a minute, listening. Our mother's voice warbled, outlining a shape of gaiety. My father's low voice rumbled under it in a polite cadence, probably offering to take their coats. My mother's heels clipped to the end of the hallway leading to our room.

"Girls!" she called, her voice sounding almost frantic. "Our company is here!"

Delia's eyes widened a bit in fear at the sound of our mother's voice. I stood in the doorway and held Delia's hand, breathing quickly.

"She's calling us," Delia said, and pulled gently toward the door.

"Wait," I whispered, "Just a second. It will be better if we wait a second." I wanted to put off going out there until things had calmed a little.

"She's calling us," Delia said again, and for the first time I could remember, Delia pulled her hand from mine. I remember the rubbery way it slipped away from me, skin from skin, and then her small red back upright as she walked away from me.

4.

MR. BIERSDORFER SAT IN MY FATHER'S RECLINER. ERIC HOVERED behind it in the shadows, shifting his weight from foot to foot. He looked up briefly as I came in, then looked away. He was wearing the same bow-tie outfit he'd worn to the ballet, and it was getting to be too small on him; his wrist bones poked out past the sleeves.

Eric's mother was perched at one end of the couch; my father sat at the other. My mother was nowhere in sight, and the kitchen resonated with clinking noises. Delia leaned against my father's leg while he absentmindedly patted her back. There was nowhere left to sit; I stood in the doorway to the dining room.

I had only ever seen Mr. Biersdorfer in his picture on the calendar. In real life, he looked older and angrier. His hair was thinning at the front, and his eyes, a light blue, were small and dull. He looked at me, then at Delia, but when no one said anything to us, he looked away.

"Eric, aren't you going to say anything to your friend?" Mrs. Biersdorfer asked without interest.

"Hi," Eric said without looking at me.

"So Frank," Mr. Biersdorfer said. "What's a man got to do to get a drink around here?"

"I thought my wife was getting some drinks, but maybe she's busy with the canapés," my father said in a jovial voice I had never heard him use before. "What can I get for you?"

"If you've got any scotch in there I wouldn't turn my nose up at it." His voice made me jump every time it went off. "And my wife looks like she could use a glass of white wine."

Everybody watched as my father disappeared into the kitchen. Then Mr. Biersdorfer slapped his hands against his knees and looked around the room as if for the first time. We all looked around with him. I'd been so proud of our living room earlier in the day, but now that the Biersdorfers were here, everything seemed shabby and second-rate. The carpet was drab and worn, the furniture discolored and lumpy. The curtains hung limply from their rack. I tried to imagine what the Biersdorfers might say about our house as they drove home. I watched Mr. Biersdorfer, trying to decide what his exact words might be, and his eyes caught on me.

"Hello, little girl," he said to me. I'd already come to the conclusion that he was the sort of adult who ignored children entirely, so I was astonished when he addressed me.

"Hi," I said very quietly, almost whispering.

"You must be Dolores," he said.

"Yeah," I answered. We stared at each other for a long moment. Then he looked away in stages, and wound up staring at the kitchen door. My father burst through it a moment later holding two squat glasses and handed one to Mr. Biersdorfer. My mother followed him carrying a full glass of red wine.

"I'm so sorry," she gushed to Mrs. Biersdorfer. "I know you wanted white, but I only have red tonight because we're having beef!" By the time she got to the end of her sentence she sounded more angry than apologetic. I knew she felt tricked by the request for white wine.

"Red is just fine with me," Mrs. Biersdorfer said. "I actually prefer red." She picked it up and took a small sip.

"Delicious," she pronounced. My mother gave a tense smile and disappeared into the kitchen again. She reemerged almost immediately carrying a tray of pigs in a blanket, and circled the room with them. After we had each taken one, she seemed unsure of what to do with the tray.

"Here, let me take that," my father said, popping up again. "You sit with our guests for a few minutes."

My mother reluctantly sank into his seat on the couch. I watched

Mrs. Biersdorfer nibble at one of the pigs in a blanket carefully with big horsey teeth.

"Well, I'm just so glad we could finally all get together," my mother started. "Dolores has told us so much about you." Eric's eyes darted to me for a second. He seemed to be considering whether this could be true. Of course it wasn't, but I blushed imagining what Eric might think I'd said about him.

"Well, we were glad to know that Eric found a friend at Palmetto Park," Mrs. Biersdorfer answered. "This school has been a hard adjustment for him." Eric glowered at his mother.

"What's Frank cooking up for us in there?" Mr. Biersdorfer asked.

My mother pinked. "Oh, he's just getting things organized," she said. "I've already done all the cooking. Everything is almost ready."

"I was about to wonder," Mr. Biersdorfer said with a laugh, just as my father appeared in the doorway.

"I said, I was just about to wonder, Frank," Mr. Biersdorfer called to him. My father raised his eyebrows in polite confusion. "I was just about to wonder who does the cooking around here, you or your wife!"

"All the best chefs are men," Mrs. Biersdorfer said quietly.

"My wife says all the best chefs are men!" said Mr. Biersdorfer as my father drifted into the room, unsure of where to stand. "But I can't boil an egg without help. I must not have been given that talent!" Mr. Biersdorfer smiled broadly around the room as if he had made a joke. My mother beamed back at him.

"Shall we all come to the table?" my father asked timidly.

"Oh! Well—okay," my mother stammered quietly, giving my father a quick glare. She clearly felt that this announcement was one she should have made herself. My father looked at her and gave a little shake of bewilderment, his hands turned up.

We all wandered into the dining room and took our seats. Mr. Biersdorfer was at the head of the table; Mrs. Biersdorfer was on my left. My mother took her seat closest to the kitchen door while my father slipped into the kitchen again. The table was covered with a new white tablecloth, the creases from the package still sharp. I wondered why she had gone to the trouble of refinishing the table a few days ago if she was going to cover it up. Our places were set with my parents' wedding china, a pattern of blue flowers I'd only seen a few times. At the center of the table wobbled a single silver candlestick with a half-burnt purple candle in it.

Eric was seated across from me. Delia sat next to him and stared up at him, her mouth slightly open. Eric pretended not to notice and scowled at the candle. Mr. Biersdorfer cleared his throat over and over again.

He picked up his empty glass and rattled the ice. "Could use another one of these," he said quietly.

My mother didn't seem to hear. Mrs. Biersdorfer subtly shook her head no without looking at him.

"Maybe later," he said. My mother heard this: her head snapped up, and she studied his face, trying to understand what this meant.

My father appeared in the kitchen doorway, balancing a platter of meat surrounded by potatoes and carrots. Mr. Biersdorfer let out an appreciative holler. My father crouched at Mrs. Biersdorfer's elbow.

"May I serve you?" he asked.

She examined the tray. "Of course," she said skeptically. "What is it?"

"Standing rib roast," my father answered. ". . . But it's not really standing anymore. It seems to have sort of fallen over. But it'll taste the same."

"It'll taste the same," my mother repeated quietly. My father circled the table, serving everyone. My mother watched Delia and me, making sure we remembered not to start eating until the grown-ups did. I held my hands in my lap. Delia held her fork in her fist and stared at Eric, leaning forward so far her chin almost touched her food. When my father finally sat down, we all began to eat.

"This is delicious, Deborah," Mrs. Biersdorfer said after a few minutes.

"Yeah, it's good, Mom," I added. This was the sort of thing I'd thought my mother wanted me to say, but she didn't seem to hear. No one else said anything for a long time. Eric coughed quietly and swallowed hard. Somehow, this tiny movement called everyone's attention to him.

"Eric," my mother ventured. "It was so nice of you to invite Dolores to the ballet. She'd never been before. She loved it. She came home asking to take ballet lessons!"

This was a lie, but none of us were about to point that out. As she spoke, Eric developed unhealthy-looking red blotches on each cheek. He let a second go by, unsure how to answer, then simply nodded at her miserably. When it became clear he wouldn't answer, Mrs. Biersdorfer looked over at me.

"Are you taking class?" she asked.

"No," I said. Mrs. Biersdorfer looked at my mother.

"It was just a thing of hers," my mother said, using her manicured hand to brush away the importance of this thing. "If she watches gymnastics on TV, she wants to take gymnastics. When she sees a shuttle launch, she wants to be an astronaut. If she sees men working at a construction site, she wants to do that too!"

"They need to begin the training very early," Mrs. Biersdorfer said. "I'm a patron of the Orlando City Ballet. Some of the dancers started when they were three. If you don't have the foundations by eleven or twelve, well, then professional dancing is out of the question."

As she spoke, Delia started to kick a table leg in a slow, annoying rhythm. She was staring at Eric, as she had been since she had first laid eyes on him. No one said anything to her, but we all watched the purple candle vibrating in the center of the table every time she kicked.

Mrs. Biersdorfer continued to talk. "Their bones need to grow a certain way, the joints. And they need to develop the ankles. The ankles need to be strong enough to go *en pointe* by thirteen. Otherwise, it's out of the question."

"Oh, is that so?" my mother asked pleasantly. "I never knew that." She was more comfortable in this type of conversation. She knew the right sorts of things to say. Delia kept kicking, but my mother didn't seem to notice.

"Oh yes," said Mrs. Biersdorfer. "I met a dancer from one of those little places in the Soviet Union, Slovakia or Slovenkia, something like that. She grew up in a one-bedroom apartment with thirteen people. Sometimes they didn't have enough to eat, but she took class every day with a prima ballerina from when she was three. Every day! Sometimes she gets stuck *en pirouette,* like Baryshnikov. Her balance is so perfect she just keeps going around and around and she can't get down!"

"Delia!" my mother hissed suddenly. Delia froze, and the kicking stopped. Mrs. Biersdorfer pursed her lips and took a sip of her wine.

"Well, maybe we should look into signing you up for some lessons," my mother said to me. We both knew she had no intention of doing this.

"Where would you recommend she start?" my mother asked Mrs. Biersdorfer.

"Well, there is a very fine school in Orlando. Many of the dancers in the OCB teach there. But it's rather expensive, I'm afraid." She paused for only the tiniest second. "But they *do* have some scholarships for promising youngsters," she offered. We all thought that over for a minute.

"You'll have to write down the name of it for me before you go," my mother said. Either she was doing a good job of hiding her reaction or she didn't realize that she had been insulted. My father did, though. His face had gone bright red, and he suddenly cleared his throat and asked Mr. Biersdorfer a question he seemed to have been saving for an emergency.

"I read about the issues on 51-C," he said. "Sounded pretty serious."

"Oh, don't even say '51-C' to me," Mr. Biersdorfer answered, clearly relieved to have a topic on which to hold forth. "Well, right from the beginning, as you know, it's been a nightmare. We've never had to swap one Orbiter for another."

My mother realized the men were talking NASA business, and looked back and forth between my father and Mr. Biersdorfer eagerly.

"I read that there was also a high helium level during the countdown phase," my father added politely.

"That's right. Then, on top of all that, the BFS didn't take over at separation."

"Backup Flight System," I whispered. Eric looked up at me for a second, then looked down at his plate again.

"Luckily, it was nominal during reentry," Mr. Biersdorfer said. "Could have been bad."

My father gave a professional grunt of amusement and shook his head slowly.

"I'll tell you honestly," my father said. "When I read about this mess in the paper, I said to Deborah, 'I sure hope my team had nothing to do with this.'"

Mr. Biersdorfer's hearty laugh thinned to an uncomfortable cough. "Heh heh, no," he said. "Your team did a hell of a job on this launch. Everyone knows what a nightmare those SRBs have been from the beginning, and your team has kept us flying despite all that."

My mother beamed at the sound of praise. Her hair had gone limp over the course of the evening, and a few of the curls had flattened completely. She watched Mr. Biersdorfer, her cheeks flushed from the wine, her eyes sparkling in the candlelight.

"That joint rotation problem is one of the biggest messes we ever had to deal with," Mr. Biersdorfer said, leaning toward my father. "Because the specs say one thing, but if the rocket doesn't look like that, you can throw those specs right out the goddamn window! Because you got to keep in mind, it was the contractor that fucked it up! Excuse me, kids."

Mrs. Biersdorfer frowned.

"I'm sorry for talking shop at the table, ladies," Mr. Biersdorfer said to my mother. "But Frank here ought to know that his team did a hell of a job!"

"Well, I sure am glad to hear that," my father said quietly.

"And I sure feel bad that your team was rewarded the way they were for their efforts, I'll tell you that too!" Mr. Biersdorfer was shouting so loudly now I could feel the sound resonating in my fork.

My father cleared his throat and looked down at the table, nodding.

"I'll tell you another thing, Frank, this situation won't go on much longer like this either! We're going to need your skills again real soon!"

My mother sat up straight, smiling at Mr. Biersdorfer. She brought her hands together into a single, silent clap. My father didn't move or respond.

"What are you doing these days, Frank?" Mr. Biersdorfer asked. "Just taking some time with the family?"

"I've got a situation out in Titusville," my father said. "I like to keep busy. I like to stay challenged."

"Well, that sounds great," said Mr. Biersdorfer. "I tell you, when we need you again, we might not be able to get you back!"

This was met with a silence that seemed to vibrate in the room. My father didn't move but smiled tightly at his butter knife while turning it over and over on the tablecloth. An uncomfortable long second went by.

"Oh, he wants to come back," my mother said finally, in a tiny voice. Surprisingly, Mr. Biersdorfer heard it.

"Well, great!" he said. "Because we're going to want you back real soon!"

My mother served coffee and encouraged Mr. Biersdorfer and my father to continue talking in the living room while she and Mrs. Biersdorfer cleaned up in the kitchen. I was embarrassed to think of Mrs. Biersdorfer scraping food into our garbage can when I knew she didn't have to do those things for her own family. I wondered whether I should have told my mother that the Biersdorfers had a maid; if she'd known, she might not have let Mrs. Biersdorfer help in the kitchen. But it was too late now.

Eric followed the men into the living room and plopped himself forcefully onto my father's recliner. Delia curled up on the couch next to my father like a dog and went to sleep. There didn't seem to be anything for me to do but talk to Eric.

"Do you want to see how that chair can recline?" I asked him.

"No," he said.

"Do you want to see my room?"

He paused, staring angrily in the direction of our fathers. He didn't want to see my room any more than I wanted to show it to him, but we both wanted to get away from the others.

"Okay," he agreed, and followed me out of the room. Halfway down the hall, I remembered the bags full of junk, but by then it was too late. I led him into my room and turned on the light. The room was extremely messy, even without the grocery bags piled by the door. Eric walked in carefully, trying not to step on books and clothes. He went to the bookshelf over my desk and squinted at the spines, his head cocked to one side.

"Are these all the books you have?" he asked. Most of them were about the space shuttle.

"Yeah."

I thought of trying to explain this, but I couldn't think of any excuse for owning so many space books. He pulled a book off the shelf and flipped through it: *The Space Shuttle Operator's Manual.*

"Your sister seems really different from you," he said after a while, without looking up from the book.

"I know," I answered. "She's retarded." Eric could be a terrible snob about intelligence, and I wanted to set myself apart from Delia.

"No, she's not," he said, scowling. "She's just younger than you. That's not the same thing as being stupid."

"I was smarter than that when *I* was five," I said.

"No, you weren't."

"How do you know? You didn't know me. I could already read chapter books when I was five." Eric didn't respond to this, but I could hear his response anyway in my head: *Just because you could read chapter books doesn't prove you're smarter.*

We settled down to read. Eric lay stretched on his stomach on the floor. A couple of times, I thought to show him my space notebook, to see what he would think of it, but I decided it wasn't worth the risk. Eric had read almost thirty pages of *The Space Shuttle Operator's Manual* by the time his mother called for him.

In the living room, the Biersdorfers were putting on their coats. "We so enjoyed finally getting to meet you all. We must do this again sometime," Mrs. Biersdorfer was saying. My mother smiled, her face flushed, and my father slipped his arm around her waist in a showy way I had rarely seen.

"I hope we can do that," my father said. "Deborah and I enjoy it when our kids introduce us to new friends."

Eric put on his jacket and followed his parents out the door. I could see the white edge of my book sticking out of his pocket. When he had asked whether he could borrow it, I worried that he might return it at school where Elizabeth might see, but I said yes anyway. I was flattered that I owned a book Eric wanted to read.

The next morning, my mother slept in. My father and Delia left for the grocery store, and after they had been gone awhile, my mother wandered out of their room sleepily. She seemed to be in a good mood. She went into the kitchen and fixed sandwiches for us from the leftover roast, and we sat down together to eat. I watched her as she sipped her coffee: her eyes were still smudged with black from her trip to the beauty parlor, which now seemed so long ago. Her hair had given up its straightened shape and curled itself into the same cloudy frizz I had always known. She chewed sleepily; I waited for her to talk. She ate half of her sandwich and took a sip of her coffee before she spoke.

"Did you notice her shoes?" she finally said. I shook my head no.

"When we were neatening up in the kitchen, I asked her where she got them and guess what she said. *Paris.* Can you imagine that? He takes her to Paris to buy shoes."

"They probably didn't go to Paris *just* to buy the shoes," I said, aware that I was sounding bratty. I couldn't stand hearing her speak of the Biersdorfers so reverentially. "Maybe they were there for a vacation anyway."

"Well, I'm sure they were," my mother said. "That's not my point."

"She's not very nice to Eric sometimes," I informed her. "She yells at him when he didn't do anything."

"I did notice that *he* drinks too much," my mother agreed. "He killed nearly a half a bottle of scotch. He's a nice man, though. He said to me on the way out, 'Deborah, that meal was certainly a treat. Sometime you'll have to teach my wife how to make that cobbler. She's no good with desserts.'"

"Really?" I asked. That must have been before Eric and I had come out to the living room.

"So I said, 'Well, I'll be happy to give her the recipe anytime.' And he kissed my hand."

"Really?" I asked again. I hadn't seen anything like that.

She thought before speaking again.

"Well, of course, they owe us dinner now, at their house. But I did hear him saying that this is a busy time for him at NASA, though, so they might not be able to do anything for a while. Maybe we'll see them at one of your school assemblies."

"I don't think we have any assemblies coming up," I said, relieved.

"Well, maybe you and Eric will play together soon," she said. Her voice was tinged with that nervousness she'd had the day before, and the sound of it made me tired and scared. "Has he invited you out again or anything like that?"

I sighed loudly instead of answering.

"All right, don't get sniffy. I'm just asking. Are you and Eric in any activities together at school?"

"What do you mean?"

"Like after-school activities or anything like that?"

"No," I said. "I never see him after school. He's in my class but we don't talk to each other that much. We just went to the ballet that one time but we aren't really friends *at all.* Okay?"

My voice was like a voice I had heard Elizabeth use with her mother. I usually didn't dare speak to my mother this way, but I was desperate to make clear to her that I wasn't friends with Eric, that I wouldn't be her go-between for this project involving the Biersdor-fers. I was afraid of how angry she would be as I spoke, that she would explode and cry and that I would spend the rest of the day in my room, sorry that I had told the truth. But instead, her face took on a playful little smile as I spoke.

"Oh, I know that type of boy," she said. "He gets all standoffish once you know he's sweet on you."

"What are you talking about?"

"He obviously has a crush on you, baby. He asked you out to the *ballet,* he dressed up in his best little *suit . . .*" Her voice made my skin prickle.

"His *mom* made him wear the suit," I protested. "His mom proba-bly made him *ask* me to the ballet." I felt airless and desperate.

"Okay," she said, waving her hands in front of her face in defense. "Whatever you say."

I felt hot tears of humiliation pushing themselves into my eyes anyway. I hated her changing Eric in this way: I'd had my own idea of him, of the complexity of his existence and of our relationship, and now he had been reduced to her crooked version of him. She had changed Eric forever into a boy with a crush, a boy interested in my body, with weird animal longings. I would never be able to talk to him normally again.

5.

I USUALLY WENT GROCERY SHOPPING WITH MY FATHER AND DELIA on Saturdays, but the following Saturday my mother had suggested a different plan: my father and Delia would go to the grocery store while she took me shopping for school shoes. As soon as the two of them left, she sprang into action, showering and laying out a nice dress and matching shoes. She took a long time putting her hair in rollers, lotioning her skin.

"Where are we going?" I asked skeptically. She was putting on mascara, leaning into the mirror over her dresser wearing only panty-hose and a bra. I knew she had heard me because her breathing quickened, but she didn't answer.

"Come here," she said when she was done. She held my chin in one hand and stroked mascara onto my lashes with the other.

"You don't need it," she observed. "You have your daddy's long lashes." Her voice was warm and low, and I let myself be lulled by it.

"Don't blink," she said, and used her fingertips to hold my eyes open until the makeup dried.

We climbed into the car. She drove too fast, weaving excitedly from lane to lane, giving me instructions all the while.

"When we get to the store," my mother said, "I'm going to give you some money, and I want you to pick out some nice school shoes. Something nice and sturdy. Brown. Not sandals, but lace-ups."

"Where are you going to be?" I asked. Children didn't go into shoe stores alone to make purchases, I knew, and I felt she should know too. Fitting new shoes had always been an interaction between my mother and the shoe salesman, usually a middle-aged man. I tried to imagine talking to the shoe salesman myself as he knelt on one knee with the metal foot measurer. It seemed ridiculous.

"I have some things to do on my own," she said. She lit a cigarette in a series of snappy gestures that told me not to ask any more questions.

She parked in front of the shoe store, got out of the car, and started to walk away briskly, as though she were alone. But then she stopped herself and came back, digging through her purse, and handed me a twenty-dollar bill.

"I'll meet you right back here in an hour," she said, pointing at the sidewalk.

"Okay, Mom," I said. I had decided to be agreeable, but she had stopped paying attention to me. I watched her walk away along the row of stores, her gait quick and off-balance, wobbling slightly in her high-heeled shoes.

In the brightly lit shoe store, I picked out a shoe that I thought would please her, a simple lace-up brown leather with thick soles. The man who measured my feet didn't seem surprised that I was there alone, so I relaxed a bit and let him slide the stiff shoes onto my feet. He had big droopy eyes and called me "honey." When he instructed me to, I walked around the store, my feet feeling wooden and alien.

"How do they feel?" the salesman asked, and when I didn't answer, he knelt in front of me. I heard the whistling sound of his breathing through his nose as he pressed down hard on the leather of the shoe, feeling for my big toe.

"Perfect fit," he declared. He got up, grunting, and led me to the register to ring up the shoes. I unfolded the bill, and he gave me three dollars' change. He wrapped up my old shoes, graying white sandals, in the new box with tissue paper.

When I stepped back out on the sidewalk, hardly anyone was around, only a few women shopping in pairs or with small children. There was no sign of my mother. I walked slowly up and down the row of stores carrying my shoe bag, looking in the windows. I stopped at a jewelry store to look at rings sparkling in their boxes, then at a bakery where giant chocolate chip cookies were displayed in the window decorated with frosting, like cakes. *Go Gators,* said one, its green frosting faded by the sun. Another said *Liftoff,* with a crude outline of an Orbiter in white and black frosting, pink frosting flames coming out of the base. The day was hot and getting hotter; if my mother didn't come back soon, I would have to find an air-conditioned place to wait. But then how would she find me?

I had the sudden horrible feeling that too much time had gone by, that I was supposed to be meeting my mother somewhere right that minute, that she had been waiting for me for a long time, growing angrier and angrier. If I was keeping her waiting right now, she would be steely and hurt for the rest of the day.

I wracked my brain for an exact memory of her instructions to me, where we were supposed to meet. She had said *right back here,* pointing at a particular square in the sidewalk, but I couldn't remember which one. I convinced myself that she must be waiting somewhere else, somewhere she thought she had told me to be—out at the car, maybe, or in another store, in the nail shop where she sometimes had her nails slicked red by the wide chatty manicurist, or the restaurant at the end of the row of stores where we had dinner sometimes.

I walked by the nail shop first. I cupped my hands around my eyes to see in: the store was nearly empty, the only customers two teenage girls with their feet in soaking tubs. The lady who did my mother's nails recognized me and waved from her station. I waved back before moving on, feeling panicky.

I finally ventured into the restaurant. It was dark inside and cold with air-conditioning. I spotted my mother immediately, not at one of the tables where we usually sat, but in the bar area, perched on a tall stool. She was facing my direction but didn't seem to see me. She sat with her legs crossed off to one side, smoking, listening intently to what her companion was saying, a man with his broad white-shirted back to me. For a nonsensical moment I thought he must be my father, that somehow my father had come here instead of going to the grocery store. But even as the thought presented itself, I knew it to be wrong; this man had dark gray and silver hair, not brown like my father's, and he pushed himself back confidently against the wood of his chair. My father would never have sat like that; he would slump forward trying to take up as little space as possible.

My mother raised a tall thin glass to her lips and drained it. When she set it down again, the smile she gave the man was slow and odd, a smile I didn't remember seeing before. Her companion raised a short glass of amber liquid, and it was by the way he shook the glass to rattle the ice that I recognized him as Mr. Biersdorfer.

I turned around and pushed out the glass door of the restaurant. What I felt at first was relief that I hadn't done anything wrong, that it was my mother who was late, not me, that she wouldn't be angry when we found each other. The presence of Mr. Biersdorfer was a secondary matter. It actually made an odd kind of sense, at least on the surface—it explained my mother's dress, her makeup, and her nervousness.

I waited for what seemed like forever, but I didn't mind waiting now, now that I knew it wasn't my fault. When she came out, she would be apologetic. She might even take me shopping for new clothes to make up for it, or take me out for ice cream. I sat on the curb admiring my new shoes, turning them this way and that, considering what Elizabeth Talbot would think of them when I wore them on Monday.

When my mother finally came rushing out of the restaurant, her heels clacking loudly on the sidewalk with each step, she waved at me, though I was looking right at her.

"D!" she called to me happily. The few people who were around turned to look at her. She came over to me, took my arm, and squeezed it.

"Have you been waiting long?" she asked, leading me toward the car.

"Yeah," I said. Didn't she know how long I had been waiting?

"Did you get some nice shoes?" she asked. I held out one of my feet in response, and she looked but she didn't seem to see it.

"I saw you in the restaurant," she said to my shoe. My heart stopped for a second. "Did you see who I was with?" she asked brightly. I wasn't sure what the best answer to this question might be. I could truthfully say no, I thought; I hadn't actually seen his face.

"Your friend Eric's dad," she answered herself, holding the car door open for me. She looked over her shoulder briefly, but the sidewalk was empty except for an old lady in a pink pantsuit. We climbed into the car, which was hot as an oven.

"Why did you meet him here?" I asked hesitantly. I wasn't sure I actually wanted to know. She looked around for him again before pulling out of the parking lot.

"You can't mention any of this to your father," she said, ignoring my question. "He would never understand this, D. If he asks you about today, you just tell him I was helping you pick out your shoes, that we were shopping together and went to a lot of different stores, and, ah . . ." Her face got a faraway look as she concocted her story. I hated when she did this, when she tried to tell me what to say—she always put things too childishly for me, in simple naive words that I would never use.

"Just tell him that we were shopping the whole time and then I took you out for an ice cream."

"He's not going to ask," I pointed out.

"No, you're right," she agreed. "It would never occur to him to ask how I spent *my* day." Some train of thought caught her, and she drifted away for a minute, looking toward the sky. Then she seemed to snap awake, adjusted herself in her seat, placed her hands more firmly on the steering wheel.

"Anyway, no one could blame me," she said in her summing-up voice, a tone that was meant to shut down any further questions or discussion.

"Blame you for what?" I asked, knowing that, whatever it was, she wouldn't say now. But then, a few minutes later, she did answer.

"Blame me for taking things into my own hands," she said finally. I knew she thought she was being mysterious, leaving just enough unsaid.

The phone rang while we were all watching TV. My father answered. I didn't listen to what he was saying until he said, "Oh!

Well! Dolores would really enjoy that." My mother and Delia both looked at me when he said my name. He listened for a while.

"Uh-huh. Uh-huh. Well. It's awfully nice of you to *invite* us." He was using an oddly loud voice.

I went and stood by his elbow. He ignored me.

"Who is it?" I asked loudly. He put his finger to his lips, his eyebrows raised to say, *This is serious.* My mother was watching his face too.

"Well, that would be real nice," my father said, his voice vehement and sincere. "It sure is *nice* of you." He listened for a long moment, nodding uselessly. "Okay," he said. "Okay, *great.* See you then. Buh-bye."

When he hung up, he didn't look at me but at my mother, and a weird expression played around his mouth, proud and hopeful.

"That was Bob Biersdorfer," he said, and for just a moment I thought my mother's face betrayed fear. But then she was smiling too.

"He wanted to invite us to the next launch," he said, "51-D. It's a couple of months away."

"When?" my mother asked. She drew the word out to show her disbelief.

"April twelfth."

"The next launch," my mother whispered. And if she'd known this would happen, her face did not betray it.

6.

The Biersdorfers' Oldsmobile pulled up in front of our house at five A.M., just as the sun was coming up. The launch had been delayed forty-five minutes, so we hadn't had to leave at four as we'd planned. Delia and I watched out the front window while Mr. Biersdorfer walked up our front path. He wore green plaid pants and a pink polo shirt stretched taut over his belly. He rang the bell, and as he waited for someone to answer the door, we watched him place his hands in his pockets and look straight up at the sky, revealing a wobbly pink neck.

"Who is that?" Delia whispered. She hadn't been invited to the launch; my father had told her she was too young. This infuriated Delia because she had turned five a few days before. She still wore the sparkly cardboard birthday hat around the house sometimes.

"You know who that is," I answered. "It's Mr. Biersdorfer."

"Eric's father?" she whispered.

"That's right," I said.

I tried to picture him sitting across that little table from my mother in the dark restaurant, that broad white back, but weeks had gone by, and the scene had become vague. I tried to imagine what his reaction would be if I yanked open the door and announced, *I saw you with my mother*. He would look right at me, see me and consider me for the first time, his face forming an expression of shock or horror. The thought made my heart race with fear. I stood motionless.

My father emerged from the bedroom carrying his shoes. He was wearing a polo shirt too, but his was green and didn't stretch quite as much over his stomach. Mr. Biersdorfer rang the doorbell again.

"What are you doing?" my father asked quietly, bewildered. "Why don't you answer it?" He kept his voice down because my mother was still sleeping. Delia and I stared back at him, neither of us moving, while he struggled his shoes on and opened the door himself.

"Good morning," my father said, and shook Mr. Biersdorfer's hand.

After bellowing his greeting to my father, Mr. Biersdorfer shouted, "Hullo!" staring at a spot three inches above my head. After a second, I deduced that he was talking to me.

"Hi," I answered.

My father edged us out quickly; my mother had instructed him not to let Mr. Biersdorfer in because the house was a mess. Delia watched us go.

I could see the top of Eric's head through the backseat window. He appeared to be studying our neighbors' mailbox; he didn't look up as I climbed in next to him. He continued staring out his window at birds, buildings, and eighteen-wheelers, all the way to the Cape. I couldn't see his face at all, so I watched his hand resting on the black vinyl of the seat between us, white and limp.

We drove to the Space Center, our fathers talking about current events and weather the way adult men do when they don't know each other well, careful to agree about everything. Through my window, I saw the yellow morning sun lighting up the edges of the same green hanging trees I always saw, the same marshy places, the same shafts of light and wavering stripes on the street I'd always seen, my whole life. Halfway to the Cape, I saw the construction site I remembered seeing when I was little, when my father used to take me to his work on weekends. It was still a rectangular pit in the ground, a skeleton of beams and cranes rising out of it, tiny workers moving on them. To my surprise, Mr. Biersdorfer noticed it too: he pointed at it suddenly, almost hitting my father in the nose.

"Have you heard anything about that development?" Mr. Biersdorfer asked.

"No. What's it going to be? Office complex?"

"Shopping center," he said. "I invested in a couple of these projects in St. Pete. Very lucrative. But this one has some kind of curse. First they started digging on some kind of protected wetlands or something—they had to stop work for almost two years while they haggled that out with the EPA. Then some of their funding fell through. The president of the bank ran off to Venezuela with all the money, apparently. I guess it's back on track now."

My father grunted agreeably. "It might be nice to have a shopping center right here," he said.

"More and more new families moving in," said Mr. Biersdorfer. "Good time to invest."

Eric fidgeted, rolled his eyes, then looked out the window again. I watched the hole in the ground as we passed it: it seemed impossible that those workers could make of it an actual building, a building like all the other buildings already finished, that people could walk into and spend the day in. Right now it looked like some sort of oversized jungle gym, bare beams surrounded by machines.

As we got closer to the Cape, the traffic thickened as cars pulled off into the breakdown lane or onto the grass. We crawled past, watching people get out of their cars and stretch, spread picnic blankets on the ground and on the roofs of their cars. At the main entrance to the Space Center, Mr. Biersdorfer rolled up to a red-gated entrance and showed a man in a uniform a badge in a folded leather wallet.

"Good morning, sir," the man in uniform said, and the gate opened.

Mr. Biersdorfer enjoyed playing host, narrating what we were seeing around us. Eric stared out his window, never moving his head to follow his father's pointing finger. But I was thrilled to be at the Cape again. I knew much more than I'd known last time I was here about what was accomplished in each building, why each was located where it was in relation to the launchpads, why each was designed the way it was.

The parking lots were full, even the parking lots past the security checks. Mr. Biersdorfer pulled the Oldsmobile into a space marked RESERVED—DIRECTOR OF LAUNCH SAFETY. "One of the benefits," he said with unconvincing modesty.

"I wouldn't mind watching the launch just from right here!" my father said, and when I looked out the window, I saw what he meant: we could see the whole stack from where we sat in the car.

"Well, it's going to get even better in the viewing area," Mr. Biersdorfer said. "And they've got some cold drinks up there too!"

"Sounds good!" my father agreed loudly.

Mr. Biersdorfer directed his look at me for the first time.

"So what do you think about the launch?" he asked me. "Pretty exciting, huh?"

I stared at Mr. Biersdorfer, unsure of what to say to him. The fifth of the six women, Rhea Seddon, would be flying today. She was a doctor and would be conducting medical experiments on herself and the rest of the crew.

My father cleared his throat and spoke for me.

"Dolores follows the astronauts' careers," my father announced, to my horror. "Which of the women is it flying today, honey?"

"I don't know," I mumbled when they all looked at me.

"Well, she's not your favorite one anyway, right?" He turned to Mr. Biersdorfer. "Dolores likes Judith Resnik best," he supplied. "She could tell you where she went to college and what color her eyes are."

"Really," Mr. Biersdorfer said, looking at me as if I were about to supply this information. When I didn't, he spoke again. "Judy Resnik. She's the first—ah—Jewish person in the program."

"Oh, is that so," my father murmured.

"We're sending up a U.S. senator for the first time today," Mr. Biersdorfer went on. "He's quite excited about going, they tell me. He's on the Space Appropriations Committee."

"Well, as long as he went through all the training programs," my father said neutrally. In fact, the decision to send a senator had infuriated him. The night we'd heard about it on the news, he'd explained to the TV that the space shuttle was not a carnival ride.

The viewing area was just a set of bleachers. The Launch Vehicle stood on the other side of an expanse of sand and water. People in the stands watched it as they talked to each other, the way people talk while looking at a TV, even though it wasn't doing anything yet. Birds flew by once in a while. A large digital clock placed in front of the viewing area counted down.

"That clock isn't quite accurate," Eric said, startling me. "It's counting hundredths of a second, but it isn't quite accurate. The one they've got in Launch Control is accurate. That one costs millions of dollars."

We looked at the countdown clock together. The numbers were orange, five feet high, against a black background of barely visible outlines of 8, like a clock radio display. The hundredths-of-a-second column ran crazily, smoothly, through its numbers.

"The astronauts are already strapped into the crew cabin," I said.

"Yeah. Probably."

"Have you seen a lot of launches from here?"

"Yeah," he said. "All of them, pretty much."

I waited a long, dangerous second. "Do you want to be an astronaut when you grow up?" He looked out over the ocean, so long that I started to think that he hadn't heard me.

"Do you see that little green hill out there?" he asked, pointing at the horizon behind us. I didn't see anything.

"Out there," Eric insisted. "Past those buildings." I shook my head. He dropped his arm in annoyance.

"Well, there's a hill. Okay? A species of pelican lives on that hill. Every time the shuttle takes off, the pelicans get freaked out by the noise and the vibration. And every time it lands, the sonic boom scares them. I read that they might die out completely."

"Why would they die?" I asked. "Just because of the noise?"

"The noise *scares* them," he repeated, scowling. "They get confused. They forget how to take care of their babies and they forget how to mate."

"I don't see why they should *die,* though," I said. "Can't NASA move them? Can't they just put them in a zoo or something?"

Eric shook his head, hard; his face was starting to turn red. "They can only live in that *one place,*" he said, "that's their *habitat.*" As he spoke, I could imagine him hunched over the newspaper as he read it, scowling at the page, indignant. I was happy and relieved that Eric was talking to me, and for a minute I considered agreeing with him, just to make friends with him again. But I found that I couldn't. It was more important to me to be loyal to NASA, my future employer.

"Are you saying they should stop the shuttle program just because of some birds?" I asked carefully.

"Why not?" he said. "If it's doing more harm than good?"

I stopped for a moment, thinking about what my father would say. I looked over to where he stood. He was leaning his ear toward Mr. Biersdorfer's mouth and nodding vigorously.

"Because I think exploring space is worth certain sacrifices."

"Well," Eric said, his voice full of scorn, "you'd fit right in here, I guess."

"What do you mean?"

"They came to just the same conclusion that you did. 'Oh well. A whole species extinct forever just so we can go to space and service some Japanese satellites. Oh well. Too bad.'"

"Maybe they're trying to find a solution," I said, and that sounded right: that's what my father would say. "They've got the smartest people in the world working for NASA. Maybe one of them is working on how to solve the problem."

"Well, they're not," said Eric. He had crossed his arms over his chest. "Just take my word for it. They're not."

I looked around at the other people in the stands, their sunglasses making them look like a field of bugs. Mr. Biersdorfer continued yelling technical terms at my father, who continued nodding and smiling vacantly. The shuttle on the pad looked permanent, like a building, like something that wasn't going anywhere.

In front of me, a woman I hadn't noticed before bounced a baby on her shoulder.

"They *told* him he could take it," she was saying, adjusting her sunglasses. "They allot some extra space for each of them, an extra container or whatever, for personal items like that."

"Did he say why he wouldn't take it, then?" her companion asked. She wore the same style of sunglasses.

"Well . . ." the woman with the baby hesitated, the way people do when they're deciding whether to talk behind someone's back or not. "He didn't really *say* this, but he might not have wanted to bring a baby toy, I guess. You know, it's all these military men. How would he feel bringing this little stuffed animal, this little giraffe, into space? With all these military guys!"

"Still," the other woman said. "If it's for Jeremy. Surely he could tell them, *This is for my seven-month-old baby boy,* and they wouldn't say anything more about it."

"Well, that's what *I* thought," said the baby woman. "But it's his first mission. He wanted everything to be perfect."

Her hair was limp and mousy brown. I could see only a thin edge of her face not covered by the sunglasses when she turned toward her friend—her face was flushed and blotchy from the heat, and she kept blowing long bangs out of her eyes. She wore a loose pair of denim shorts and a white T-shirt that looked like it had been washed a million times—it was so thin I could see her bra underneath against her skin, the flesh of her back bulging out slightly above the strap. The baby goggled over her shoulder at me, his face a little cauliflower.

"That's an astronaut's baby," I whispered to Eric. I felt stupid as soon as I'd said it, but he looked up with interest and asked quietly, "How do you know?"

"She was talking about what her husband was allowed to bring on the mission," I whispered, and Eric studied the side of the woman's face, as I had been doing.

"Wouldn't it be strange to know someone on it?" I asked.

Eric nodded. "It's strange enough that there are *people* on it," he said. "When you think about it, they're basically strapped onto a couple of missiles. That's all it is."

"Yeah, well, my father puts those missiles together," I pointed out.

Eric looked over at my father, and I watched his face. I couldn't tell whether he was impressed, but I thought he might be. He might respect someone who actually worked on the machines, rather than someone like his father, who just made decisions.

"I'm going to go someday," I said then. I was surprised to hear myself say it. Eric didn't answer, didn't take his eyes off the space shuttle.

"Don't you believe me?" I asked.

"I'm just not sure why you'd want to," he said. "The astronauts are basically just guinea pigs. They just press the buttons that the engineers on the ground tell them to press."

"Yeah, but they get to go to *space*," I said.

I wasn't as interested in exploring space as I was in the flight itself: the speed, the weightlessness, the gadgets and everyday life lived in a spaceship, the domestic details. I longed to wear that headset, to hold that tiny microphone expertly to my mouth and report things to Houston, rattling and chanting numbers in their complicated language. To say the words they said: *telemetry, capcom, go at throttle up*.

"Well, they're not exactly *exploring*," Eric pointed out. "They're just in low orbit. The same orbit over and over again. It just doesn't seem worth all of this." His gesture took in the launchpads, the stands, all of the buildings surrounding us.

"I mean, so you're going to space," he went on. "So you ride to space strapped to a big firecracker. It's not like you've *accomplished* anything. It's not like you've solved any of the world's *problems*."

"Well, I'm going to go," I said. He didn't answer.

"Don't tell anyone, okay?" I said.

"What?"

"Don't tell anyone at school about, you know, what I just said," I stammered.

Eric shook his head and snickered.

"What?"

"Who do you think I'm going to tell?" Eric asked. "Who do you think I talk to at school?"

"I don't know," I said, exasperated. "I don't keep track of what you do."

"You do *too* know," Eric said quietly, in a way that made me shiver.

After another long silence, I asked, "What are you going to be when you grow up?" I didn't know what else to ask him.

Eric shook his head. I feared that he wouldn't answer me, but then he spoke.

"I don't know," he said. "Not an astronaut."

"An engineer?" I asked. "A scientist? You could solve that problem with the pelicans."

"No," he insisted. "I'm going to do something that has nothing to do with any of this."

We both considered that for a minute. He'd sounded so indignant, so dismissive of the shuttle, of everything around us. But I had to strain to think of other jobs.

"Maybe I'll be a teacher," he said.

"Yeah," I agreed. "You'd be a really good teacher."

A hold is built into the countdown at T minus nine minutes, a pause to let Launch Control resolve any minor problems that have been discovered without having to race the clock. Eric and I and our fathers knew this pause was coming and were prepared for it, but all around us a shout of exasperation went up when those giant orange numbers stopped moving. The newcomers always seemed to feel they were somehow being cheated, that NASA had failed.

I began to get a bad feeling about this launch, the feeling that something disastrous was going to happen. The last launch, which had also been *Discovery,* had had so many problems—what if they hadn't all been fixed right? I imagined the Main Engines, with their millions of parts, greasy, nicked, worn, abraded, melting—it might take only one malfunction to kill them all. The whole thing would become a fireball right on the launchpad, shock waves of fire and heat billowing out toward where we stood, right before our eyes, and this woman with the baby would scream and cry for her husband. The astronauts, strapped into the cockpit, must feel the same dread I was feeling now—the certainty that something had not been fixed correctly, that something had been forgotten, overlooked.

We had been hearing voices over the loudspeakers since we arrived, the voice of the official announcer, and voices of the men in Launch Control. Here in the VIP stands the speakers were bigger and more expensive-looking, and so the voices were richer, brighter, easier to understand than they were through the little speakers nailed to trees and telephone poles in the public viewing area. Now the voices began running through their final checkout: "Flight?" "Go." "Capcom?" "Go." "Range Safety?" "Go." "Booster?" "Go." "Flight surgeon?" "Go." The voice on the loudspeaker called for our attention, and when the clock read T minus ten seconds, he began to count down aloud: *Ten. Nine. Eight.* His voice was slow and deliberate. *Seven. Go for Main Engine Start. Six. Main Engine start. Five. Four.* He counted in a thrilled but confident voice. The concrete trench under the ship turned red and orange, an effect I had never been able to see from across the river. All sorts of new details were visible here. Heat ripples made everything waver. The whole stack bucked in place: it was trying to get away, but something was holding it back.

"And *lift*off!" the announcer insisted. "*Lllllllift*off!"

And it did lift off. Slowly, impossibly, the whole Launch Vehicle—Orbiter, Solid Rocket Boosters, External Tank—lifted as one, the pieces of the tower reluctantly retracting to let it go. The stack shuddered and lifted ridiculously slowly. It continued to rise, faster now, and a plume of white smoke hung in the air, tracing a path through the sky. We watched the shuttle go up and up, and our heads tilted back hard, our mouths gaping open. I wanted to be up there, lifting off; I wanted to be Rhea Seddon, to be the one everyone was watching with such awe and emotion. The astronaut married to this woman with her bra strap and her cracking lips and her stained baby blanket, a man who had kissed this woman standing right in front of me, was on that spaceship, wearing a helmet and talking to Houston. He was tearing straight up into the sky faster than sound. He and Rhea Seddon and five others were going to space and leaving us all behind.

The shuttle became smaller and smaller until it was a point like any airplane, scoring a white trail onto the blue sky, except upright rather than horizontal. The noise died away and people were still cheering, the clapping dying out the way it always does, sounding a little disappointed. The astronaut's wife in front of me cried a little. Her friend looked uncomfortable and patted her on the back quickly, saying, "Oh, he'll be fine, he's having the time of his life." The astronaut's wife nodded and sniffled.

Some families around us started to pack up their things to leave. But Eric and I still watched the tiny point of light, our heads tipped back; we waited for the Solid Rocket Boosters to fall off, then for External Tank separation, then for Main Engine cutoff. We watched until long after the shuttle had disappeared. Even though he scorned the space shuttle and claimed not to want to be an astronaut, I knew he was feeling the same awe.

On the way back to the car, Mr. Biersdorfer paused for a moment in talking to my father about congressional budget hearings.

"What did you think of that?" he shouted at me and Eric.

"Cool," said Eric dismissively. Mr. Biersdorfer turned his attention to me. I took in a breath, but found that I couldn't say anything. I realized I had been crying.

"Are you okay, honey?" Mr. Biersdorfer asked quietly, stooping down to see my face. That made me like him a little more. All three of them were looking at me now. I was as surprised as anyone that the launch had made me cry—it was the beauty of it, but also the frustration of being left behind, being left on the ground. I looked at my father, afraid of what he would think of me, but he put his arm around my shoulders and handed me a crumpled tissue from his pocket. We started walking back toward the car. I avoided looking in Eric's direction.

"I remember I misted up a little bit at *my* first launch," Mr. Biersdorfer said, his old loud self again. "Now, that was a Mercury test, and let me tell you I had something to cry about because it blew up on the launchpad. It was unmanned, of course," he added quickly.

"This isn't my first launch," I pointed out.

"Oh." Mr. Biersdorfer straightened up, surprised. "No, of course not."

The men went back to talking about the same boring things as before, and Eric and I walked on silently. We climbed into the car, and Mr. Biersdorfer turned on the air-conditioning full blast. After a brief lull in their conversation, we heard Mr. Biersdorfer say, "I know Eric is going to miss Dolores and the gang at Palmetto Park next year."

My father murmured knowingly, but a moment later, he seemed to realize that he didn't know what Mr. Biersdorfer was talking about.

"Where is Eric going?" he asked.

Mr. Biersdorfer glanced over his shoulder at me for the briefest second. "We're moving Eric to another school. We've all agreed that Eric would be a better fit in a different environment."

Eric forgot his resolution to stare out the window and turned to look at me. A moment later he turned back, but during that second of eye contact, I saw him again as a whole person: his icy gray eyes, his dangerous intelligence, his cold love for me. All along, I'd thought somehow that what I was doing to him didn't count, that he somehow didn't feel it because I didn't actually want to hurt him—everything I'd done, I felt I'd been forced to do. But what if he had felt it? What if I had hurt him?

My father looked at me kindly for the rest of the day. He liked that I'd cried, that I'd been enthralled by the launch—he thought I'd been moved, as he was, by the power and perfection of the machine.

When we got home, he told my mother proudly about everything that had gone on. She wanted details, wanted to know everyone's exact words. I started to understand, listening to them, that they both assumed it had been Eric's idea to invite my father and me to the launch, not Mr. Biersdorfer's. I wanted my father to know that Eric never would have chosen to invite me anywhere, that it must have been Mr. Biersdorfer. I knew this would make them happy if they knew it, give them hope that Mr. Biersdorfer liked my father enough to pull strings for him, but I couldn't think of a way to tell them. Any way that I could bring it up would have to involve my telling them that Eric hated me now, and why. And I could never tell them that.

That night, I entered the launch into my notebook:

STS 51-D, *Discovery*.
April 12, 1985. Delayed 45 minutes for bad weather. Launch at 8:59 am.
Payload of STS 51-E was combined with 51-D (51-E was canceled due to inertial upper stage problems). Rhea Seddon is on this flight. She will conduct medical experiments. Also on board is Jake Garn, a US senator from Utah. He is on the Space Appropriations Committee.
I saw this launch with my father, Eric Biersdorfer, and Mr. Biersdorfer, the Director of Launch Safety.

My mother took me back to the same strip mall. She didn't make as elaborate an excuse to my father this time, just told him we needed some things and slipped out after dinner. In the car, she rolled down the windows and sang along with the radio.

This time she left me in the bookstore—I was in Young Adult and she was in Self Help—when I saw her slide a book back onto the shelf and move toward the exit, pulling her purse strap higher on her arm. She wasn't gone long this time, maybe forty-five minutes, and when she came back, she wanted to buy me an ice cream. As she drove, I watched her face: it seemed she wasn't about to tell me where she had been and who she had seen. She smiled to herself while we ate our ice cream, hummed quietly, talked about clothes she wanted to buy for me, for herself, for Delia. We couldn't get really good things here in Palmetto Park, she pointed out. Maybe we should try Titusville, or even Orlando.

"Why are we doing this tonight?" I asked.

"What do you mean, baby?"

"Why are we here? Why did you take me out?"

"Oh, just to get out for a bit," she said mischievously. "Just to have fun."

"Why couldn't we bring Dad and Delia?" I asked.

"Just the two of us," my mother answered, and gave me a wink. It was true that I enjoyed having her to myself; it gave me a feeling of grown-up sophistication and cheer. Two girls out on the town. I couldn't help but be drawn in by it, even if I knew there was another layer underneath.

On the last day of school, Elizabeth invited us to a slumber party at her house the following weekend.

"I don't think I can," I lied. "My grandparents will be visiting."

"Can't you get away even one night?"

"I shouldn't. I haven't seen them for years. But you guys have fun without me."

"That's too bad," Elizabeth said, putting on an exaggerated sad face. I was amazed, as always, that a lie could change everything so easily. The girls went on making their plans without me.

As they did, I watched Eric Biersdorfer across the room. He cleaned out his desk, piling handfuls of crumpled homework papers on the floor. Now and then, he came across something he wanted to keep, smoothed it, and carefully placed it into a folder. When he was finished, he threw out the pile of trash, slipped the notebook and a few books into his backpack, and zipped it shut. He took no notice of me watching him, or pretended not to. When the bell rang, I followed him as he walked calmly through the hallways clogged with screaming kids. I almost called out his name to say goodbye, but I didn't, and instead I stood watching as he passed through the front doors for the last time, and climbed into his mother's Oldsmobile waiting at the curb.

LAUNCH DELAYS

7.

THE FIRST WEEK OF JULY WAS TERRIBLY HOT, AND OUR AIR-conditioning broke. In the days before it could be fixed, we hardly slept; we just lay in our swampy dark beds waiting for a breeze. My mother worked late several nights in a row that week, one night so late that she was still gone when my father and Delia went to bed.

Now that I never saw him anymore, I thought of Eric all the time. He had a way of shrugging before he started to write something, just a quick jerk of the right shoulder up to his ear, which made him seem to be dedicating himself completely to whatever he was about to write, as though shrugging off the world and its constraints entirely. Sometimes I found myself doing his shrug, a bit self-consciously, in remembrance of him. His gray eyes, the freckle just under one of them, like an exclamation point. His sandy brown hair, the way it stuck up in the back. The way he licked the front of his teeth before saying something important. The sour milk smell of his breath, his jerky way of walking, his girly way of crossing one leg over the other, jiggling the top foot unself-consciously. He was the only boy I knew who would do that.

Sometimes I could hear his voice in my head, his thin reedy voice with the slight lisp, the way some of his s's slurped quietly in the back of his teeth. His habit of sniffing often while he listened to me, watching my face thoughtfully with no pretense toward wavering, no uncomfortable glancing away.

Only in my room at night, when I had already been lying awake for hours thinking nonsensical thoughts, could I think my most private thoughts of Eric. What if he were my boyfriend, what if I loved him, and I didn't even know it? Only in the dark, divorced from the realities of my day-to-day life, could I think about Eric's body, thin and pale, with those ears, those blue veins in his skin, those gray eyes that saw me, the only eyes that saw me the way I wanted to be seen.

I had been reading my space notebook in bed for a long time when I heard my mother's key rasp in the lock. I tried to arrange myself into a convincing sleeping position. Her steps moved slowly up the hallway, and I heard her stop at our open door. I could see her clearly by the streetlight that shone in my window—she wore her work clothes, a skirt and blouse and stockings, her high-heeled shoes dangling from one hand. I could tell everything about her mood, about her day, from the way she rested her hip against the door frame, from the sound of her breathing in and out. Her eye makeup was smudged around her eyes, and her hair stood up on top of her head; as she looked in at me, she raked through it with her fingers absentmindedly. But she was happy. Something had gone well today. Any second now, her eyes would adjust to the light and she would see me, see that I was still awake.

My heart pounded. She blinked at me, her head tilted to one side. Then she put her pinky finger delicately into her left nostril. She pulled it out again and rubbed it slowly against her thumb. She still couldn't see me—the streetlight must have been in her eyes.

"Mom," I whispered. Even as I said it, I wondered why I wanted to let her know that I was awake; just a moment before, I had been afraid that she would be angry.

She wasn't sure she had heard anything at first. The fan whirring in the corner dampened the sound. She dropped her arm to her side and tilted her head, extending her right ear into the room a little.

"Mom," I whispered again, a little more insistently this time. She squinted and leaned herself into the room, trying to make out my face. I sat up in bed.

"What are *you* doing up?" she whispered. I felt relieved when I heard her voice—she wasn't mad.

"I couldn't sleep," I lied.

"When did your dad go to bed?"

"A long time ago. I heard him snoring."

"Oh," she said. "Good."

"What time is it?" I asked.

"After one. You should have seen all the work I had to do, D. It was a disaster. I don't know what Dr. Chalmers would do without me. And I have to be back in there at nine tomorrow."

"You should get some sleep."

"Yeah, I know. The thing is, I'm so keyed up from working, I'm not really sleepy either. And it's so hot. You want to go for a walk?"

"Okay." I swung my legs out of bed. We'd never gone for a walk at night before, or during the day, for that matter. I followed her down the hall, through the living room, and out the front door. I was still in my nightgown and bare feet. Outside, the air was loud, with all the neighbors' air conditioners humming, the sounds of cicadas, the cars groaning by on the freeway in the distance. I felt an urge to run, and so I did: I ran barefoot down the middle of the street in my nightgown, the warm night silky on my skin. I looked up to see the stars, but the streetlights almost blocked them out. I could see only a few, shining dimly.

"Come walk with me," my mother called, holding out her hand. I knew she wanted us to stroll slowly down the sidewalk hand in hand, admiring the flowers in people's yards. I wanted to keep running, but I went to her anyway. Her hand was warm and moist, and she swung our arms together as we walked.

"What a beautiful night. Doesn't it smell delicious? Must be those azaleas." I hadn't really noticed the smell, but she was right—a low, warm scent, not flowery, but sweet.

"Isn't it nice to just go for a walk like this, just the two of us?" She tilted her head back and closed her eyes, breathing in deeply. This was the mother I wanted: calm, happy, carefree.

"Things are going to change soon, D," she said. "Things are going to get much better for us. We've been going through a rough time for a while now. But soon it's going to be over." I waited for her to say more; I could tell she had more to say. But instead she stopped silently in front of a neighbor's flowering bush.

"Aren't these pretty," she said, and plucked one. She held it under my nose so I could smell it. Then she tucked it behind my ear. She fussed with my hair, arranging it around my face.

"So pretty," she said. Then she said, "Can you keep a secret, D?"

I nodded.

"Your father is getting his job back," she whispered, leaning in close to me, her eyebrows raised.

"How do you know?" I asked her. My father had been laid off for ten months now. He hadn't said anything about it all evening, hadn't acted especially happy, or different in any way. "Why hasn't he told us?"

She didn't seem to hear me.

"I knew everything would turn out okay," she said, smiling. "I knew we just had to be patient. You and Delia will be able to get everything you need. Everything you want. And your parents won't be so worried all the time. We'll all be happy again."

"When did he find out?" I asked.

"You can't say anything to him about it, D." She was suddenly serious, her voice low and hard. "You can't say anything to Delia either. She's too young to keep it quiet." She took my hand and started to walk, this time more briskly. We turned a corner, and I was surprised to see our house, dark, in the middle of the street. I'd lost track of where we were. I noticed anew how different our house looked from the others: We didn't have any flowers in our yard, as most of our neighbors did, and our grass grew every which way, creeping into the spaces between the sidewalk squares. Our house looked impermanent and shabby—the white paint was peeling, the wooden trim had detached itself in places and hung limply. Drips of rust streaked under the drainpipes. I wondered how the other houses stayed so perfect. It seemed as though my father was always working on something, fixing something on the house or mowing the lawn, but it didn't seem to make any difference—his work somehow just didn't count as much as the other fathers'.

"Daddy will want to tell you himself, so you'll have to act surprised," she said, not taking her eyes off the house. "I just wanted to tell you because you were lying awake worrying. I wanted you to know that everything is going to be okay."

We crept quietly into the house and she kissed my forehead as I got into bed.

"Sleep tight, baby," she whispered. "And don't forget—act surprised!"

I crawled into bed, still smelling the azalea smell on my hair and nightgown. I rolled over to go to sleep. My left hand was still warm and sweaty from her touch.

In the morning, my father asked what time she'd gotten in.

"Oh, about one," she said breezily. "You should have seen what a madhouse it was there."

"Did you go out again?" he asked. "I thought I heard the door a second time."

"No. Well—I opened it again just to make sure it was locked. That must have been what you heard." When he turned the other way, she winked at me.

"Did you check the mail yet today?" she asked, getting up and going to the door. She came back sorting through a pile of envelopes. She chose one and handed it to my father. He set down his coffee and ripped it open. When he unfolded the letter, we all saw the NASA seal, the blue circle with stars, showing through the paper. His eyes moved quickly over the letter, back and forth, and we all watched them as if the pattern of their movement would tell us what he was reading. He blinked a couple of times, nodded in a satisfied way, refolded the letter, and slipped it back into its envelope.

"What is it?" my mother asked, leaning forward. A manic smile was starting to spread on her face.

He held up the envelope. "It's from Lerner," he said. "They're reinstating my position."

"Oh my God!" my mother cried softly, jumping to her feet. "Does that mean you're back for good?" She went around the table and put one hand on his shoulder to steady herself as she read. Tears appeared in her eyes. She was completely convincing. I wondered, for a moment, whether I had imagined our walk the night before. Maybe it had been just a dream, like a premonition.

"My benefits and seniority will carry over like I was never away," he said, pointing out a part of the letter to her, then turning to look up at her face. She beamed at him. He wiped his eyes with his napkin, and my mother said, "Oh, Frank!" and she threw her arms around his neck. Delia ran to them and hugged them, and then I did too. We all danced around the kitchen table, clasped in one giant hug, my mother pink-cheeked and laughing, as if something funny kept happening over and over again. My father looked at my mother and smiled when she smiled, and hugged back when she embraced him again.

"What do you think, D?" he asked me.

"It's great, Daddy," I told him.

That night we went out for dinner, and we were the perfect happy family I had always wanted us to be. Of course, I knew something was wrong. For the rest of the day, I turned it over and over in my mind: *She knew, she knew,* and examined it from every possible angle. Our walk, and what she had told me, couldn't have happened. So in the way children can do, I decided that it *hadn't* happened, and put it out of my mind. It was easy: I was full of hope for a new era just about to begin. I believed in sudden changes, a small thing setting off a chain of events that would make my family happy, our lives normal, immune to criticism from anyone.

8.

JUDITH RESNIK FLOATED AROUND INSIDE THE CREW CABIN wearing a polo shirt and shorts. Tanned and healthy, she executed a somersault, her limbs brown and slightly shiny, reflecting the light. Her dark brown curls floated around her head, reaching out toward the camera. Judith Resnik clowned with the other astronauts; spinning themselves in weightlessness, they all smiled and made faces for the camera. The idea of having a woman on a spaceship was still new and strange, and though the other astronauts made a show of not treating her differently, their eyes were drawn to her; each of her movements became somehow symbolic and exaggerated. She didn't seem to mind it. She was fearless and far from home, spinning carelessly in her stocking feet.

The morning my father went back to NASA, the TV showed old footage of Judith Resnik on *Discovery*. She would be flying on another mission at the end of the year, a mission with a schoolteacher who had been chosen through a much-publicized competition. My father had already registered his opinion of this Teacher in Space idea; he scorned it only marginally less than he had the senator in space. But since he'd found out he was going back to work at NASA, he'd stopped yelling at the TV.

My mother was busy cooking eggs and bacon, and Delia sat at her place, an expectant look on her face. My father came in smiling, smelling of aftershave. Everything about him was clean, pressed and neat. We all stared at him as he walked across the room and took his seat at the table. He wore a white short-sleeved, button-down shirt, just as he always had before he was laid off. He put a paper napkin over his belly as my mother spooned eggs onto his plate.

"Should I pack you a lunch?" my mother asked. "Or do you think Lerner and the guys will want to take you out?"

"Oh, we'll probably go out," my father said, sipping his coffee, and from the way they smiled at each other, I could tell that this answer made them both happy.

"What will you be working on?" she asked. "Do you know?"

"They're just starting assembly on 51-J. But the next one is sched-uled to launch three weeks later, so they might put me on that one."

"Wow, they're getting closer and closer together, aren't they?" she asked happily.

"Yup. Someday soon they'll be taking off once a week."

"Unbelievable," my mother said. "Isn't that amazing, D?"

"That won't work unless they can start launching from Vanden-berg too," I pointed out, putting a forkful of eggs into my mouth. This was something my father usually enjoyed discussing, the pros and cons of a second launch site, but today they both looked at me with annoyance.

My father began a detailed description of the upcoming launch schedule—which cargo might fly on which missions using which Orbiters. My mother asked questions and expressed happy surprise at the answers. Delia and I watched as they spoke, fascinated. A week ago my mother wouldn't have been interested in hearing about the manifest schedule, but now she took in every detail.

My father kissed Delia and me goodbye. His hand on my chin was cold. Delia and I stood in the doorway and waved as they walked out to the car. He opened the passenger door for her, and before she stepped in, we saw him slip his arm around her waist and kiss her on the mouth. They kissed for a long, strange minute, his hand smoothing down her back over and over. We watched, even though we knew we were letting out the air-conditioning standing in the open doorway like that. Delia's head tilted to one side, and she squinted at them, confused.

"They're just kissing," I said. Delia looked at me as if I were crazy.

THE TIME IT TAKES TO FALL

I'd been thinking about the way they'd embraced like that when I was little, how I'd hated it, feeling left out. The closed circle of their bodies, no room for me.

Our parents climbed into the car and pulled away. We watched until they turned the corner and disappeared.

The house behind us seemed very quiet and empty all of a sudden. I felt left behind in a way I normally didn't when they were gone.

"Dolores?" Delia asked.

"Close the door," I said. "You're letting all the air-conditioning out."

"How did Daddy get his job back?" She was still looking down the street in the direction where the car had driven away.

"Delia, shut the door," I told her again. "What do you mean, how? His boss wrote him a letter and he opened it. You remember that morning when he got the letter and we danced around, don't you?"

Delia closed the door slowly, looking unsatisfied.

"No, I mean—why? Why did he get his job back?"

"What do you mean, why? Because he's smart and he's a good worker."

"No, I mean—" Delia huffed with frustration. She couldn't articulate her question, whatever it was.

"Let's go to the pool," I whispered, and that cheered her up.

Delia and I had been walking to a pool in our neighborhood, even though we were under strict instructions never to leave the house. It was a long walk, but we cheered up once we drew close and heard those bright splashes and the plasticky sound of the diving board reverberating.

We passed through the locker room where the women and girls changed. As always, Delia stared at the teenage girls turning their narrow backs to the room, showing the indentations at their kidneys, like places where someone had pushed two thumbs in. The moms struggled into their suits, their heavy, stretched breasts pointing toward the floor.

At the poolside, Delia and I claimed two chairs, laid out our towels, and watched the teenagers. They rubbed themselves with tanning lotion, already seemingly dying of boredom. They were unspeakably cool. I remembered looking up to Elizabeth in this way, and before that Jocelyn and Abby, believing them to have important knowledge I lacked, that I would never be able to understand. But now, compared to these girls, it seemed obvious that Elizabeth didn't know much at all. She was still just a child like me, and knew only how to mimic the knowledge these kids had.

One girl I especially admired had a purple suit and chin-length curly hair. I watched her spread lotion carefully over her legs and arms, then spray a bottle of lemon juice onto her hair. I wanted to try bleaching my hair with lemon juice too, but I feared that my mother would notice and ask too many questions.

A boy in orange board shorts and bleached blond hair spread out his towel near the girl with the purple bathing suit. He was often here, always wearing those same board shorts, and always commanded a lot of attention.

"Ladies!" he shouted, loud enough to get the attention of everyone on our side of the pool. "It's time for tan line inspections." They all giggled while he moved up the row of girls one by one, demanding that each one move a strap or lift an edge of her suit. He checked off their names on an imaginary clipboard, muttering notes to himself: "Coming along nicely," or "Needs more baby oil." For one pale girl, he pretended to scribble and murmured, "No discernible color whatsoever."

"Oh, come on, Josh," she said with a laugh. "It's not my fault. I'm out here every day. I've just got no melanin in my skin."

"Claims she has no magnatonin in her skin," the boy in the orange shorts added solemnly to his notes. "Clearly a ploy to escape punishment."

They all laughed. He pretended to throw her into the pool, but instead cannonballed in himself. I watched him as he hovered there in the air, his knees drawn up and his ankles crossed in front of him. He was impossibly comfortable with himself, I thought—the opposite of me. He never had to worry about doing the wrong thing, because whatever he did, by definition, was exactly right.

I watched him swim across the width of the pool toward the edge where Delia and I lay, the wavering bright orange of his trunks visible underwater. When he hauled himself out of the pool, he cracked a smile, and at the same time he happened to look right at me. The surprise of the eye contact flooded me with adrenaline so fast I nearly shuddered. He kept his eyes on me, his blond bangs soaked brown and dripping into his face.

He jutted his chin in greeting or confrontation. I became aware that I was smiling; I had been laughing at his clowning along with the others. He kept watching me, wearing an expression I couldn't identify—amusement, maybe, not quite contempt. He turned on his heel and did a chicken walk back in the other direction, to the teenagers' area.

"Dolores?" Delia asked. "Who is he?" She was looking up at me.

"Shut up," I said distractedly. My heart was beating quickly and I felt hot. I was probably blushing.

I was careful not to look in the teenagers' direction for the rest of the afternoon. Whatever had happened, I didn't want to ruin it. I reran the moment over and over in my mind. Whatever the meaning of his look, it had been a look. He had seen me. I tried to imagine what he had seen: a girl laid out on a towel, wearing a blue bathing suit, her nose and shoulders sunburned, her hair wet and tangled. It occurred to me that the way I saw myself might not be the way I actually looked at all.

Delia ran to get her bathing suit as soon as our parents left the next day. Instead of pulling out my old, stretched-out suit, probably still damp from the previous day, I walked down the hall to my parents' room and started pulling open my mother's dresser drawers. At the bottom of one, I found her black two-piece. I pulled off my pajamas and slipped it on. People always remarked on how tiny my mother was, and I'd known I was catching up to her, but I was still shocked when the suit fit perfectly.

I stood in front of the full-length mirror on the back of their bedroom door, looking at myself, and I was both curious and slightly horrified by what I saw: my head, my same old round boring head with the same stringy brown hair and the same sunburned face, perched atop a body that filled out this bathing suit. I examined myself from every angle and came to the astonishing conclusion that I looked good in it.

My mother had been commenting on my breasts for a while now; just the day before, she had complained that I had outgrown the size-A bras she had bought me just months before. I hadn't wanted to tell her; I didn't want to hear her teasing, but I also had a nonsensical hope that wearing a too-tight bra would keep them from developing any further. Now this bikini showed everything I had been trying to hide. I adjusted the straps, trying to get used to the way the top fit. If I was going to walk past the teenagers' area wearing this suit, I had to look confident in it. I bent over and shook the cups to create cleavage, as I had seen my mother do.

"I'm telling," Delia said from the doorway. She'd been watching, for how long I didn't know.

"What?" I said, trying to sound nonchalant. "I'm just trying it on."

"That's Mom's," Delia said. "You shouldn't be in here."

"Then you shouldn't either," I said. "Get out." I put on my shorts and T-shirt over the bikini. We left the house, checking and rechecking to make sure we had our keys, and we trudged to the pool together, squinting in the morning sun.

At the pool, Delia looked at the bikini thoughtfully as I pulled off my clothes, but she didn't say anything more about it. The teenagers were all there, lined up like a jury, surveying the moms and the kids in the pool with bored absorption, as if performing some elaborate equations based on what they saw. I laid myself out in tanning position while Delia joined some younger kids in the shallow end. Soon they were all splashing around together playing Marco Polo. I closed my eyes against the sun, which burnt red through my eyelids.

My father returned home from work that evening carrying a huge fruit basket wrapped in red cellophane.

"What's that, Daddy?" Delia asked.

"It's a fruit basket," our mother said, her voice pleased and expansive. "Who sent it?"

My father put the basket on the dining room table and went into

the kitchen. I looked at the card. It read: *Welcome back and best wishes!*
R. Biersdorfer. In my mind, Eric rolled his eyes. My mother took the
card from me and tucked it back in the basket.

"What's it say?" Delia asked, but no one answered her, and she
didn't ask again. "Can I have a fruit?" she asked my mother.

"Maybe after dinner," my mother said. That night, it sat at the
center of the table as we ate. No one had much to say, and our eyes
kept falling on it.

"Did you see Mr. Biersdorfer today?" my mother asked.

"No," my father said, sounding mildly surprised. "We work in different buildings."

"I know—I just thought you might have run over there, to thank
him."

"I'll send a note to thank him for the fruit," my father said.

"For the *fruit*," my mother repeated scornfully. "I think you have a
lot more to thank him for than the fruit."

My father was quiet for a minute. He looked at me, then at Delia,
showing each of us a little reassuring smile.

"I don't think I necessarily have anything more than that to thank
him for," he said carefully to my mother.

"Fine," she said to her plate. "If you know something I don't
know."

"What would I know that you don't?" my father asked. "I don't
know anything."

"Never mind, Frank," my mother said. She got up and started
clearing dishes even though the rest of us were still eating.

"There's no secret," my father said. He had to raise his voice to be
heard because my mother was running water in the kitchen.

Delia and I stared at him. The look on his face was different from
any I'd seen on him before. He wasn't irritated, tired, sick, impatient,
or excited. My father looked hurt, I recognized suddenly. He didn't
understand why she was angry. I felt a strange fear: he didn't see why
she was angry, and I did.

"She just wants you to be grateful," I told him quietly.

"I am," my father insisted, his voice high-pitched with bewilderment. "Of course I'm grateful. Lerner didn't have to call me back first,
but he did."

"Not to Lerner," I said. "To her."

He looked over his shoulder toward the kitchen, where my mother was still moving around.

"To her?" he repeated. I'd hoped he had some idea what I was talking about, that this prodding would stir him to an understanding. But his expression was completely innocent, completely blank.

"I've always been grateful to your mother," he said, still careful to keep his voice down.

"Okay, Daddy," I said. "Never mind."

I couldn't help staring at him now, at the way his glasses shifted slightly on his face as he chewed the rest of his dinner. He thought he had been proven right all the times he said he should just wait patiently to be called back to work. I had been in the habit of thinking of my father as some kind of large appliance with no weaknesses or vulnerabilities, but just in that moment, I had realized that he was alive, capable of suffering, the way I had occasionally, when I was little, had the sudden certainty that a stuffed animal was sentient.

The fruit basket stayed where it was, untouched, for the next few days. We ate our meals around it, arranging our plates and bowls so as not to touch it. By the end of the week, it had begun to smell, and my father took it out to the trash.

9.

THAT SUMMER, I FELT ONE ERA OF MY CHILDHOOD END AND A NEW ONE begin. The era before, when my father didn't work at NASA, was over and quickly came to seem like something I had made up. In this new era, we were proud of my father again, my parents bought us things, and the house was cleaner and more organized, its surfaces more solid, more reliable. Delia and I came home and kicked off our shoes, let our bags drop to the floor, flung ourselves onto the couch.

I asked for new things and got them. We all acted as though we were rich now: my mother bought a dining room table, new curtains, and had the couch reupholstered. She bought herself dresses, shoes, a new purse; she had her hair straightened at a salon. Delia and I each got new sheets for our beds, new clothes. We ate out three nights in a row; my mother had taken to coming home and declaring, "I'm just too tired to cook!" It gave us a giddy feeling to hear this, a lifting feeling of freedom and indulgence to hop into the car and ride through the humid evening, the sun setting pink and orange, knowing that we'd be able to order whatever we wanted—large Cokes, big entrées, not just from the kids' menu.

"Are you too tired to cook?" Delia took to asking excitedly as my mother got home. She learned to ask for dessert, and she loved to watch our parents put up a brief but pleasant struggle before acquiescing and ordering sundaes, cakes, puddings, in exchange for the promise that she'd let them have a bite.

This new era brought with it a privileged sensation, a feeling that I would be taken care of. I could do the things Elizabeth and Jocelyn and Abby did at home, that kids on TV shows did—complain and roll my eyes and take my parents' generosity for granted.

I watched my parents, studied their faces and their movements as they went about their daily routines. My mother had never mentioned our walk, the secret she had told me. I watched them when they were together, scrutinizing them for signs of strain, my mother still in her work blouse and lipstick, telling a story about a filing problem at work, my father grunting amiably.

I tested my father once as we drove to the grocery store.

"Don't you think it's weird?" I asked him. "Months and months went by and they didn't need you, and now suddenly they need you?"

"The work flow is very complicated," he said in a voice that let me know he was about to explain this complication in its entirety, a voice like the beginning of a long paragraph.

"But still," I interrupted him. "Don't you think it's weird that right when you met Mr. Biersdorfer you got your job back?"

"Well, it wasn't *right* when I met him," my father pointed out. "There was quite a lapse in between. But even if it was, I don't think you should deduce too much from that. Correlation is not causation."

I gave him a look.

"D, I understand that from your perspective it seems like you and Eric brought us together and then this happened. You and he might even have planned on that, talked about how this would happen, right? And I really appreciate your thoughtfulness. But the fact is, this would have happened even if you never met Eric, and they never came over, and we never went to that launch that day."

"Okay," I said. "Okay."

At night I kept myself awake in the dark listening for sounds of arguing in their room. When I heard murmuring, I strained to make out the words, imagining that he had finally confronted her about the times she said we were shopping, about some sign that she'd known about the job before he had. But the volume of their talk never increased; I never heard crying or yelling. Soon the talking would stop and the house took on the humming feeling it had when everyone in it was asleep but me.

In the silences, my imagination could work more freely: I thought they must be whispering horrible things to one another, or packing up for one of them to go. Delia and I might wake in the morning to find one of them gone for good. But in the mornings they were always both still there, wearing their normal puffy morning faces, doing their normal morning things.

My father took me with him to the Cape for the next launch, STS 51-F. The launch was delayed an hour and a half due to a computer problem, but my father and I were good at waiting. We brought food, drinks, books to read. We listened to the radio. I no longer felt the old dread that something might go wrong; by now I had seen so many flights take off safely, it no longer seemed so dangerous. I secretly looked for Eric, sensed that he might be just behind me at a launch, just outside my peripheral vision. Of course, I knew he would be in the VIP stands with his father where we had sat for the launch of 51-D, nowhere near the public viewing area where my father and I parked. While we waited, my father charmed a man from Ohio with a red beard by telling him that more astronauts had come from his state than any other. He told the man to look for NASA to really come through in the next year, that 1986 would be a breakthrough year for the space shuttle, that there would be more launches than ever, including the Teacher in Space mission. If the shuttle could launch enough satellites, he said, it might even be able to pay for itself. My father began a detailed description of the fee structure for cargo on the space shuttle, which the man with the red beard seemed to find fascinating. He was dressed in jeans and a white dress shirt; he was sweating profusely. But he seemed happy to be talking with my father. He nodded seriously as my father gestured at the Vehicle Assembly Building. After a while, he pulled out a little notebook and took notes.

"What's that gravel path?" he asked my father, pointing toward the horizon.

"That's the crawlerway," my father answered. "Once the Launch Vehicle is assembled, it rolls out to the launchpad on a crawler, like a tank. I'm sure you've seen pictures of it. They used the same ones for the Apollo spacecraft. That's the path the crawler uses."

"They have to build it with special gravel," I told the man. "So it won't get crushed."

"That's right," my father said. The man smiled down at me.

My father went back to telling the man about the cargo planned for upcoming missions. He was so engaged in his conversation that he barely paused for the final countdown and liftoff.

"Cleared the tower," my father observed as the Launch Vehicle passed the top of the launch tower. "Right now is the most dangerous time, because the Solid Rocket Boosters can't be shut off. If something goes wrong with them, there's nothing anyone can do."

The man from Ohio didn't take his eyes off the rising Launch Vehicle, but he cupped a hand behind his ear to show my father he was still listening. My father narrated the whole sequence of events, as he had done with me when I was little—the Solid Rocket Boosters dropping off, the External Tank separating and burning up in the atmosphere.

When the applause had subsided, people around us began packing up. The man from Ohio kept watching with us as the tiny point moved up in the sky. The speakers crackled a volley of alarmed-sounding talk. I understood only one term: ATO. Abort to Orbit.

"What happened?" the man from Ohio asked my father. I looked up at him too. This had never happened before.

"One of the Main Engines must have failed," my father said reluctantly. "When one shuts down too early, the spacecraft can still reach orbit, but a lower one than planned."

"Is it dangerous?" the man from Ohio asked.

"Oh no," my father said. "It's one of the things they plan for."

I looked up at my father again, surprised. It wasn't like him to misstate the facts, and it was certainly a misstatement to say that an Abort to Orbit wasn't dangerous. Just the fact that a Main Engine had failed—a first—opened up a new world of possible disaster.

"Could I get your number?" the man from Ohio asked a few minutes later, when he was ready to leave. "In case I have any more questions?"

"Sure!" my father shouted, then patted himself down showily. The man produced a pen, and my father scribbled our number on the back of a scrap of paper. The man handed my father a card.

"You can call me too," he said. "In case you think of anything else. You know, about the abort." He waved goodbye as he made his way back to his car. I squinted at the card as my father slipped it into his wallet: Rick Landry, Cincinnati *Observer*.

"Reporter," I said. My father grunted. I wasn't sure whether he'd known that all along, whether the man had mentioned that he was a reporter at some point when I wasn't listening.

"Will the shuttle really be able to pay for itself next year?" I asked.

"Could be," my father said. We sat in standstill traffic for a long time, and while we waited he told me about a problem with the Solid Rocket Boosters, the joints between the parts not fitting right. My father was still high from the attention the man from Ohio had paid him. So many times in the past few weeks, I'd tried to lead him to the truth about my mother and Mr. Biersdorfer, but today I wanted him to remain innocent. I listened while he talked and talked about his work.

There was a long line of cars waiting to get out of the Space Center, and when we reached an intersection my father turned left onto an empty street. He gave me a wink, and I realized we were heading toward the Vehicle Assembly Building, the first time I would see it since his rehire. The VAB had not been open to the public since 1980, when the first solid fuel was used, because the fuel was toxic. The tour buses now disgorged their contents into the parking lot, where visitors gawked at the building from afar and took in statistics— nearly four Empire State Buildings could fit within, if sliced up; Yankee Stadium could be installed atop the VAB with an acre left over for parking.

My father proudly presented his badge to a guard at the door, then hooked his thumb at me.

"My daughter," he said, and gave the guard a hopeful look, a what-do-you-say-buddy look. "She wants to work for NASA when she grows up." I watched him, fascinated. I wasn't used to my father putting on a performance like this, trying to appeal to a stranger, the way my mother would.

The guard moved his eyes from my father to me. I stood up tall. Luckily, I looked old for my age. The guard gave my father a conspiratorial smile and nodded.

"You stay close to your dad, now," the guard said sternly. I nodded obediently, blushing. "Don't let her get near any of that area where they're working with solid fuel," the guard warned.

"No, we're just going to walk through," my father said. "We won't get near anything."

But the solid fuel was exactly what he wanted to show me. Once in the building and away from the guard's gaze, my father led me right up to the rockets, let me get close enough to smell the grease and propellants. We stepped back to take in the spectacle of the External Tank mated with the Solid Rocket Boosters for 51-I. I stood with my head tipped back to see it, tipped back farther and farther, until I noticed, far above us, hanging from the ceiling, a spread white form, huge. An Orbiter, supported by a yellow lifting sling, hung from a beam. I had been in the Vehicle Assembly Building many times before, but I had never seen anything like this. The name was spelled out on the side in letters as tall as me, black letters on white tile: *Discovery.*

"Pretty impressive-looking, isn't it?" my father asked. I nodded. I was trying to think of something else to say when my father said, "You can see where the explosive bolts attach."

I looked at my father out of the corner of my eye. He didn't have his head tipped back as far as I did; he was still looking at the rockets. I could tell he was about to begin explaining to me how the explosive bolts worked, whether I wanted to hear it or not. I wanted to get a closer look at *Discovery,* but to my father, the rockets were the only important part of the system; that was what he had brought me here to see. He would never understand that the Orbiter, the part that carried the astronauts and the payload, the part that came back to Earth, was the only part anyone really cared about. The Orbiter was what I pictured when I thought about my future and what I saw in my dreams. I turned away while he was still gazing up, hands jiggling the change in his pockets, a satisfied look on his face.

We took an elevator up to one of the moving platforms so we could see the explosive bolts more closely. The platform was fifteen stories off the ground, and I walked up to the edge, only a chain preventing me from falling.

"Careful," my father said. He pointed out a small sign near the metal bars that attached the rockets to the External Tank. It read: CAUTION: EXPLOSIVES.

"If those bolts don't give right when they're supposed to, the SRBs would burn up in the atmosphere with the External Tank," my father explained. "And that would be a waste. At the same time, they can't come off *too* easily, because if they came off before the shuttle reached orbit, well, that would be real bad, as you can imagine."

"They would crash and die," I said.

"Well, the Orbiter wouldn't reach its orbit."

"They would die," I said again.

"They could do an RTLS," he said, then snuck a sideways look at me.

"Return to Launch Site," I said. "Turn the Orbiter around and glide in."

"That's right," he said, rubbing my shoulder blade.

On the way home, as we waited for our lunch at a family restaurant, he told me more about the joint rotation problem he'd mentioned in the car, the impingement and erosion. He drew a diagram on a napkin with a ballpoint pen. As he talked, he kept adding to the diagram, shading things in, labeling. He sipped his coffee as he worked.

"So at ignition, when the fuel starts to press out, here"—he drew a few quick arrows on the inside of his rocket in the drawing—"the joint rotates like this, instead of like this."

He held his two hands together in the air, his fingers touching, to demonstrate how the connection between two pieces of the rocket bent outward rather than inward, as they had been designed to. "So when the hot gas pushes against the joints, it gets into the cracks, just for that millisecond. That's called impingement. And when the gas actually scorches the O-rings, that's called erosion."

"And that's bad?"

"Could be," he said. "Theoretically." He still held his hands up, the fingertips touching each other. A shaft of sunlight hung in the air over our booth, lighting up the dust particles, lighting up half of my father's face. It was a compliment to me, I knew, that he was telling me about the impingement and erosion, and not the man from Ohio. Mr. Landry was a civilian, a taxpayer, one of the people whose impressions of NASA must be carefully manipulated to emphasize the positive, a message of efficiency and cost-effectiveness. But I was an insider. I was one of the privileged.

"I think you'd be good at this kind of thing," he said. He blinked up at me expectantly. I wasn't sure what he meant.

"Do you like this kind of thing?" he asked, gesturing at the napkin. "Solving puzzles? Figuring things out?"

"Yeah, I guess," I said. I didn't see what the drawing on the napkin had to do with solving puzzles.

"Did you know that you got the highest scores in math on the standardized tests in your school?" he asked.

"No," I said. How would I have known unless someone told me? He was silent for a moment, letting the information sink in. I felt not pride exactly, but a sort of satisfaction, a pleasant warm weight in my chest, at the idea of being the smartest.

"Your scores were in the ninety-ninth percentile," he said. "Do you know what that means?" I shook my head no.

"That means that if you rounded up a hundred kids from all across the country at random, one of them, *at most,* will be as good at math as you."

He looked at me for a response. I struggled to keep my face blank. I thought about beating out those ninety-nine kids for a spot in the astronaut corps. My father was proud of me, not just for doing well in school, but for the hope I implied for the future. He hadn't had the money to go to college, so he'd had to settle for being a technician rather than an engineer. But I would earn scholarships. I would set myself apart from the others.

"They're starting a new Gifted and Talented program in the school district," he said. "Have you heard about that?"

"No," I said. I wondered how it was my father knew something about my school that I didn't know yet.

"The program will start in the fall. Some of the students will skip ahead and take classes with higher grades. I spoke to your principal, and he agrees that you could start at the high school next year, at least for science and math."

"*High* school?" I repeated. "But that's in a different *building*."

"Well, it's only across the street," my father pointed out. "You might still take some of your other classes in the middle school. We'll see how it works out."

I'd often daydreamed about changing schools as a way to escape Elizabeth Talbot, but the fantasy had been hopeless; without going to a private school, which I knew my parents would never be able to afford, there was no other school to go to. But here: high school. A daydream I hadn't even thought to dream.

"Starting this fall? Like, a month from now?"

"That's right," my father said. "Of course, it's completely up to you. It depends on whether you think you can handle the work."

In my mind, I walked out the front door of Palmetto Park Middle School and crossed the street to the high school. Elizabeth and Jocelyn and Abby ran to the windows to watch me go, and the rest of our class clustered behind them. The wave I gave them was affectionate, a bit pitying. I saw myself walking through the hallways in the high school, my hair French-braided, wearing lip gloss. By the time Elizabeth and Jocelyn and Abby got there the following year, I would have already made friends and wouldn't need them anymore. I would be Gifted and Talented. I would have a quiet maturity to me; people would be drawn to it.

"I'd have to leave my friends," I said. I wanted to seem reluctant, to be talked into this.

"Well, it might be a hard adjustment," he said, clearly quoting something the principal had said to him. "But sometimes you have to make a decision. Sometimes you have to decide what's more important to you, your friends or your education."

I nodded thoughtfully. He gave me a satisfied smile and went back to his coffee. Somehow that had decided it. Before we left the restaurant, I took the napkin with my father's drawing on it and put it in my pocket. We rode home together in amiable silence.

As I always did, I cut out all the newspaper articles about the launch we'd seen and wrote up a summary in my notebook.

STS 51-F, *Challenger.*
Launch attempt July 12 aborted 3 seconds before launch due to malfunction in a Main Engine.
Launch July 29, 1985, 5 pm.
Five minutes, 45 seconds after liftoff, the number one Main Engine shut down prematurely, causing an Abort to Orbit. *Challenger* still reached orbit, but one lower than planned. This is the first abort after liftoff and proves there are still major problems with the Main Engines. If that engine had failed 30 seconds earlier, *Challenger* would have had to attempt a Transatlantic Landing abort and try to land in Zaragoza, Spain.
On this flight, the crew did a "Carbonated Beverage Dispenser Evaluation." Coke and Pepsi both wanted their drinks to be chosen for future space shuttle missions, but the astronauts said that both tasted bad because they were warm (no refrigeration on the space shuttle) and fizzed excessively.
We met a reporter from Ohio who was covering the launch for his paper.
My father took me to this launch.

10.

My mother drove unevenly, smoking and looking in the mirror at every red light. She was wearing a new outfit, a short purple skirt that fluttered around her knees and a white blouse. It was so hot that my mother's curls had already collapsed. We both fanned our thighs with our skirts.

"Where are we going?" I asked.

"I told you," she said. "I need to run some errands."

"What kind of errands?"

"A few different things," she said distractedly. "Different places."

She pulled down the visor and grimaced into the mirror, checking her teeth for lipstick.

"Why did you get dressed like that?" I asked. "Are you meeting someone?"

She sighed loudly.

"I wish you wouldn't do this to me today," she said in a quiet, defeated voice. "I don't know how you decide which days to hassle me, but could I please put in a request for not today? I've just got too much to deal with."

I wanted to say Mr. Biersdorfer's name then, just to see how she would react—just ask her, point-blank, whether she was going to meet him. But there was a limit, it seemed, to how bratty I was willing to be.

She turned into the parking lot at the strip mall and pulled up at the curb instead of parking. She took the car out of gear but didn't shut it off; she opened her purse and handed me two twenty-dollar bills.

"What are you doing?" I asked. "Aren't you going to park?"

"I want you to get your new jeans while I do some other things."

I was amazed at her ingenuity. I had told her the day before that I wanted a new pair of jeans—I'd been laying the groundwork for a much longer campaign, but she'd figured out how to use the jeans to make this outing go more smoothly.

"Why don't you come with me?" I asked.

"Dolores." Her voice was just at the edge of something hard. "I have so much to do today. Please go in here and buy your jeans and whatever else you need, and I'll be back for you in an hour. I just don't have time to do everything with you today."

I hated the way that, even though I knew she was lying, she could still use this exhausted-mother tone and make me seem the unreasonable, difficult one.

I took the money and climbed out. I watched her car turn around and drive back out of the parking lot, its falling whine so familiar. She drove fast with the windows open, braked hard at the turnout to the street, her taillights coming on. She'd forgotten to look for oncoming cars, and the long honk of a truck dopplered away as she pulled out behind it.

I bought my jeans quickly, then went back outside and sat on the curb. I thought about how things had changed. I had wished for my father to get his job back, and he had; I had wanted to get away from Elizabeth and her clique, and now I would be going to a new school. Elizabeth had been disappointingly nonchalant when I called to tell her I wouldn't be coming back to middle school. My parents had agreed I could take all my classes at the high school for one semester to see how it went. I had hoped Elizabeth would be impressed, but after asking for a few details about the Gifted and Talented program, she hadn't betrayed any opinion one way or the other.

Sitting there on the curb, I wished that Eric Biersdorfer and I could go to a launch together. We would talk amiably about the books we'd been reading; then, just as the shuttle cleared the tower, he would take my hand. No confrontation, no awkwardness. But thinking of Eric made me think of his father, and I couldn't help but imagine that Mr. Biersdorfer was with my mother somewhere right at that moment, smiling at her with his large jowls, red-cheeked, laughing, his alcohol breath subtly flavoring the air. He was looking at my mother, his eyes glittering, and she was smiling back at him, her satisfied smile, the one she wore when she felt she had accomplished something.

A man appeared in front of me, a stocky man in a blue guard uniform. His skin was light brown with dark freckles like poppy seeds.

"Hey, how are you today?" he said happily. He seemed genuinely pleased to see me.

"Fine," I squeaked. I felt disoriented to be pulled out of my thoughts, as if I'd been sleeping.

"Hey, is someone here with you?" he asked.

I stared at him blankly.

"Like your mom or dad?"

"Oh—my mom," I lied, nodding. He smiled and nodded back, a look on his face like, *Of course, silly me.*

"Uh-huh. And where's your mom right now? In there?" he pointed at the clothes store behind me.

"Yeah," I said, rattling my shopping bag so he could see I'd bought something. "I'm waiting for her."

"Okay," he said, nodding again. "It's just I noticed you been sitting here for a while now. I just wanted to make sure you were with somebody. An adult."

"I'm twelve," I said, suddenly feeling talked down to.

"Oh, I can tell you're not a little kid. It's just regulations. Minors must be accompanied by a parent and all that."

"Well, my mom's here," I said. "She's just slow."

"Hey, that's okay," he said, smiling broadly. "There's no rush. But if you want to cool off, you might want to wait inside. You'll probably be more comfortable. It's nasty out here."

The guard took a dozen steps down the row of stores and stopped with his back to me, looking out across the parking lot with his arms folded, like a lord surveying all that he owned.

I got up and dusted myself off carefully. I went into the store, nervous that someone inside would ask me the same questions—

why I was back here after having made my purchase, who I was with. But the woman at the cash register just smiled vaguely at me. I found a place to sit in a window where I would be mostly hidden by a rack of clothes. Every once in a while I looked expectantly toward the dressing rooms, pantomiming waiting for my mother. None of the other salesgirls seemed to notice me.

A while later the guard wandered by again, digging a pinky finger in his ear. He caught sight of me in the window and smiled; he pulled the finger out and waved at me. I waved back. What kind of life was it, I wondered, to be a guard, to walk around just making sure people felt safe? I wanted to ask him whether he'd ever had to deal with any actual criminals, whether he'd had to run anyone down. He didn't have a gun, just a walkie-talkie.

When my mother finally pulled up, I looked around for the guard before I ran out to the car; I didn't want him to catch me in a lie. But he was nowhere in sight.

"Hi, baby," my mother said in a tired voice as I climbed in. "Let's see your jeans."

I clutched the bag tighter in my lap. "What time is it?" I asked.

"I don't know," she said, distracted. "Five or so."

"How long was I there?"

She squinted at me. "What do you mean?"

"How long did you leave me sitting there?" I pushed.

She finally understood that I was challenging her. She looked straight ahead, squared her shoulders.

"I don't know," she said. "Maybe half an hour."

"It's been *way* more than half an hour," I insisted. "It's been *hours*. You left me there *all afternoon*."

My conversation with the guard, his assumption that children should always have adult supervision, had emboldened me.

"It hasn't been nearly that long," she said curtly. "Maybe forty-five minutes. We should get you a watch so you can keep better track of time."

"Okay, get me a watch," I said nastily. "I'll ask Daddy for one. I'll tell him I need to keep track of how long you leave me alone with nothing to do while you drive off somewhere else."

My mother fell quiet and pressed her lips together. My throat felt tight, the tears threatening to erupt. I wished I could feel as bratty as I sounded, but I didn't. Even now that I'd come this far, if she admitted she'd done something wrong, apologized, I would have stopped.

"You listen to me," she said in a low voice. "This is none of his business. It's none of his business if I need to drop you off while I run some errands. Mothers do that all the time, for your information."

"What other errands did you run?" I challenged her.

"I had to take the vacuum cleaner to get fixed, for one thing."

"Why couldn't you have taken me with you?"

It was remarkable how easy it was, undoing her. All you had to do was speak the truth.

"Why, Dolores? Why today?" she asked desperately, checking her side mirror before changing lanes. "Do you have some sort of internal calendar that says, *Victimize Mom today*? Or is it just that you can tell I can't take it today? Is that how you choose?"

"I know what you've been doing," I said. "I know who you've been seeing."

For a second she didn't react, and I thought she was about to explode in rage, but instead she spoke again in her low voice.

"I want you to stop talking like this. If you try to talk to your father about this, you will be very sorry. Do you hear me? You'll be sorry if you say that. I don't know what he would do if you told him a vicious lie like that."

"Yeah right," I said. "I've never seen him get mad in my life."

"Well, you'll see him angry if you say something to him like this. Believe me. If you tell him a nasty vicious lie about me that he knows isn't true."

"But it's *not* a lie," I insisted, and for just a moment I was confused. Maybe I was lying; maybe I had made it up? Maybe I hadn't sat alone for as long as it had seemed.

"Where is the vacuum cleaner place?" I asked. I thought if she could say right away, then I'd believe her, at least enough to drop this. But she didn't seem to hear me.

"You'll see," my mother said. "You'll find out." She didn't say anything else for the rest of the car ride home. In a way I had to admire her for sticking to her story even when challenged, for believing in the force of her own imagination.

When we got home, my mother greeted Delia and my father breezily, then disappeared into the kitchen to start dinner. My father sat in his regular place on the couch, nodding once at me happily before going back to his magazine. I felt a surge of anger. He was ridiculous, laughable in his ignorance of what went on around him in his own house.

"How was it?" he asked happily, without looking up. He liked us shopping now that he was back at NASA; it made him feel rich.

"How was *what*?" I shot back.

"Shopping," he said. "Did you get anything good?"

"We didn't shop," I said. I was standing near the corner of the couch, and now I swayed on my feet a bit with surprise at what I had done. I hadn't expected to tell him. I felt a high, giddy satisfaction with myself.

But he didn't react. I counted to ten. He was still reading. It made me want to pinch him.

"We *didn't shop,* Daddy," I insisted.

"Didn't shop?" he asked a moment later, his voice rising only slightly with indulgent curiosity. "I thought you were going to the shopping center." When he finally looked up, it wasn't at me, but toward the kitchen doorway. My mother stood there, drying her hands on a dish towel.

"We *did* go there," she answered in a light voice. "Dolores got the jeans she wanted. Just the right brand. Didn't you, D?" There was no threat in her voice, no edge, no strain. She smiled at me, a little mom smile. It was so convincing that again I doubted my story myself. Maybe we *had* been there together; maybe she *had* been in the dressing room when I talked to the guard.

"Oh, that's good," my father said absently, already going back to his magazine.

I thought of the guard's freckles, his sympathetic eyes. That guard didn't think I should be alone. I pictured him standing with his hands on his hips. I tried to imagine what would have happened if I had told him the truth when he asked me where my mother was. I thought about how I'd say it: *My mother drops me here and goes off to meet someone. She doesn't come back for hours.* His face would change as I told it—first surprise, then concern, then outrage. *It's a good thing you told me,* he would say, nodding, already looking around, getting ready to take action, to call someone. Change my life forever. *You did the right thing.*

It was the guard's reassuring voice in my mind that made me cry with a sudden desperate pity for myself.

"What's wrong, D?" my father asked, bewildered. He looked back and forth from my mother's face to mine. She was regarding me now with flat hatred.

"Go to your room," she said after no one had spoken for a while.

"What is this about?" I heard my father ask when I was halfway down the hall. "What's going on?"

I heard her voice join his immediately, almost overlapping, but I couldn't make out the words.

I went into my room. I wanted to believe that I had only day-dreamed the lie. But I remembered the fading sound of her car engine, her sudden brake lights as she sped out and elicited the whining honk from that truck. That was something I should never have been able to remember, the feeling of watching her driving away.

I thought I heard the moving, underwater sound of their fighting that night, low voices and an occasional bump or small crash like a wooden boat moving through water. I crept out to the living room where I might hear them better, waited until my eyes adjusted and I could see the hulking shapes of our furniture. Their words were no clearer. I lay on the couch, a scratchy afghan pulled over me. Their murmuring might have risen to yelling, or maybe I was moving in and out of sleep and didn't know what I heard. Maybe this will be good, I thought; maybe they will talk and come to some understanding. Maybe she will cry, explain, and they'll make up, and we'll have no more of this muddy confusion between them, no more of the days and nights when they drift through the house like separate ghosts, Delia and I the only ones able to see both of them at once. They'll forgive each other, and forgive me, and then we'll be able to live all one story at once, without secrets, without having to forget things.

But in the morning, my mother was gone.

EROSION

11.

"YOUR MOTHER'S GONE ON A TRIP," MY FATHER SAID THE NEXT morning while pouring his coffee. "She'll be back before too long." Then he turned to face us and nodded once, a gesture I had come to recognize as his way of trying to get us to accept something without discussion. I could remember many times when he had nodded at my mother this way after telling her bad news—that the garage would take a week to fix our car, that the plumber couldn't come until Thursday, that he had been laid off—her face going limp with annoyance or anger or disbelief, and his brief nod, with this curt smile, silently begging her to accept what he had said and not ask questions or get upset.

"What kind of trip?" I asked skeptically. "She didn't tell us she was going on a trip."

"Your mother just needs some time to herself. She gets worn out taking care of us and taking care of the house and working every day. She needs . . . some time to herself." His voice strained to make this sound normal, like something they had agreed upon long ago and had simply forgotten to tell us about.

Delia watched me, waiting to see whether or not I would accept this.

"But why would she go on a trip without telling us?" I demanded.

"Dolores, please," he said, in exactly the same tone my mother used when I had asked too many questions. But then he added, "It was a last-minute decision."

Once he was gone, I went into my parents' room to see what was missing. Most of my mother's things were still there, but her battered plaid suitcase was gone, as were her black high heels, a green dress that she wore to work often, a red blouse, her pink robe. All the things she liked the best. I pulled open her top drawer, and most of her underwear was gone; all that was left were the old, overwashed pairs. Her hairbrush was gone too, her favorite perfume, her cold cream, her makeup bag.

My mother saved everything: the buttons and little rings of thread that come with the tags of nice clothes, every letter that anyone had ever sent her, every photograph, even ones that were blurry or overexposed. She had a drawer stuffed with every note my father had ever written her, even short loveless notes: *BE HOME LATE TONIGHT. DON'T FORGET I'M ON SECOND SHIFT TOMORROW.* She saved broken jewelry, old hair elastics that had lost their elastic, old makeup, mascara tubes and eyeshadow cases, the plastic scuffed and cracked, the colors leaking and blobbing together. She kept a carton of her brand of cigarettes in her bottom desk drawer, and when I pulled the drawer open, I was surprised to find the carton still there. She liked to have an excess, a stash, saved against some possible shortage or emergency. She liked the feeling of plenty, the feeling that this need of hers, like many others, would never be made undignified by having to go unmet.

I tried to imagine her packing all of these things in the middle of the night. How had she chosen them; what sort of trip had she been imagining? And what would my father have been doing while she packed? Did he try to talk her out of it? Did he try to help her pack? It was hard to imagine him choosing things, holding up items questioningly and folding them into the suitcase for her when she nodded yes. But it was equally hard to imagine him just standing by while she packed to leave him.

Delia stood in the doorway watching me.

"*Where* is Mom?" she asked, as if our father had told us and she just couldn't remember the details.

"He didn't say where," I reminded her. "Just 'on a trip.'"

My father had never lied to me before. He probably thought this wasn't a lie, that because she had in fact traveled somewhere, she *was* "on a trip." She was, in fact, tired from working and taking care of us. It was amazing how little he thought I knew of their lives. It had been my tattling about the shopping that had started all this, but still he assumed I knew nothing about the truth.

Now Delia watched me go through our mother's things. I knew she wanted to ask me a question, but she was still figuring out what it should be.

"What do you think Mom is doing right now?" Delia asked. She backed into the closet, letting the sleeves of my mother's clothes fall over her arms like a shawl.

"I don't know," I said. "Dancing. Having a fancy meal."

"Yeah," Delia agreed. "That sounds good."

"She's probably thinking about us," I lied. "She's probably wishing she took us with her."

"Yeah," Delia said noncommittally, caressing the sleeve of a silky blouse. I wasn't sure whether she noticed that some of the clothes were missing.

"She's probably at SeaWorld," Delia volunteered.

"No, Delia," I said. Sometimes it seemed that she misunderstood things on purpose.

"I'm going to tell you the truth," I said, though I wasn't sure yet whether I should. "I know where Mom is."

"Where's Mom?" Delia whispered.

"She left Daddy to be with another man."

"Oh," Delia said.

I didn't tell Delia what I imagined: my mother had driven to a hotel by the highway as soon as she left us, to a place prearranged with Mr. Biersdorfer. A fine hotel right on the beach, a high-rise with an elegant restaurant on the top floor where my mother could go for dinner, wearing the black high-heeled shoes missing from her closet. I tried to feel happy for her. I knew this was what she'd always wanted.

"What man?" Delia asked.

"Mr. Biersdorfer," I said. I wasn't sure whether she would remember him from the dinner party. She looked confused.

"Eric?" she asked after a minute.

"No, not Eric. Eric's father. Daddy's boss."

"Oh." She thought this over. "What is Mom doing with him?"

"Look, Delia," I said slowly. "Sometimes a wife doesn't want to be with her husband anymore, so she finds a new boyfriend. She leaves her husband and her kids if she thinks she'll be happier with her new boyfriend."

"Is Mom a wife?" Delia asked after consideration, squinting a bit as she always did over questions of vocabulary.

"Yes," I said. "Mom is Dad's wife."

"Okay," Delia said. "And Dad is her husband." I could tell she didn't understand at all.

"Look, Delia, never mind. Don't tell Dad I said anything, okay?"

"Okay," she agreed contentedly. This was one thing I liked about Delia: she enjoyed having secrets with me, and she kept them well.

That evening my father got home late but in a good mood.

"What should we do tonight, girls?" he asked cheerily. "We can do whatever you want."

"Can we go out for ice cream?" Delia asked, trembling with excitement.

"We can get ice cream if that's what you want. We have to get a real dinner first, though. Let me just change my clothes and make a phone call."

But then he was gone for a long time. Delia and I didn't notice for a while because we were watching TV. At first we hoped he would take his time so we could see the end of *The Cosby Show*. But then it ended and *Family Ties* began. When that was over, I crept to the hallway outside their bedroom door, trying to hear something. I only heard his low murmur.

"Are we still going for ice cream?" Delia whispered when I came back.

"No," I whispered. "I don't think so."

We made peanut butter sandwiches and ate them in front of the TV. When it got dark and he still hadn't gotten off the phone, I picked up the extension in the kitchen. I heard my father's voice, low and urgent. There was something strangled and bellowing about it—I almost thought he was laughing, and a confused moment went by before I realized that he was crying. I had never heard him cry before. It was a strange sound, mostly breathing, but also voiced, as if he were saying something without words. I must have made a sound, because my mother spoke.

"Dolores?" she snapped.

I hung up. My father was still on the phone when we went to bed.

12.

MY MOTHER WAS STILL GONE A WEEK LATER, AND WE HAD HEARD nothing from her. The house was empty without her, stale and stagnant. She had always been easily bored by routine, and though I had often wished she would be more predictable, now that my father was taking care of us, I missed her imagination. My father never had sudden inspirations to take us to the toy store or to the beach; he never changed his mind. He cooked the same things over and over, asked us the same questions, watched the same shows, and put us to bed at the same time with the same words: "Okay, girls, time to hit the sack."

My mother had always been a presence, even when she wasn't in the room; she left her clothes draped across chairs, magazines open on the sofa arms, her high-heeled shoes resting on their sides in a pile near the door. With her gone, everything froze into position where it had been the day she left. None of us felt qualified to move anything. Delia took to holding a pink felt slipper of my mother's in her lap while she watched TV. She shoved her fist into the toe and wore it that way for hours, absentmindedly waving her arm around like an amputee.

On Saturday Delia and I woke up to find my father vacuuming, having dragged all of the living room furniture out the patio doors into the back yard.

"What are you doing?" I yelled over the sound of the vacuum, but my father didn't hear, just waved at me happily, and it was like a bad dream I often had, where I was drowning in full view of one of my smiling parents, who only smiled more broadly and waved when I screamed for help. When he saw I was crying, he crouched over me, pink-faced and out of breath in the newfound silence after he shut off the machine's roar.

"What is it?" he kept asking me, and when he got no answer he asked Delia, who didn't answer. "D, what's wrong?"

I tried to calm myself and tell him, but I knew I could never explain. Seeing everything cleared away, seeing the patterns on the carpet where our furniture had always stood, the darkened rings around the flattened circles and squares—it was like seeing somebody naked. His doing this was like him saying that my mother had never been here, that she was never coming back. After a while, my father gave up trying to comfort me and turned the vacuum back on, running it over and over those places where the dirt would never come out.

On Monday after my father left for work, I pulled out the phone book from where we kept it in a drawer next to the fridge. While Delia looked through the cupboards for a snack, I looked in the phone book under *D* for *Doctors*.

"Who are you calling?" Delia asked.

"No one," I answered, flipping through the pages. It had occurred to me that wherever my mother had gone, she probably hadn't quit her job. She must still be going to work every day. She had instructed us long ago never to call her there except in an emergency; because part of her job was answering the phone, she couldn't tie up the line talking to us. But that day it had occurred to me that Dr. Chalmers's office would be listed in the phone book, like any other business.

And there it was, in tiny type, squeezed between Dr. Chall and Dr. Chamber. The words *Family and Pediatric Care* just after his name, with a phone number. I memorized it and closed the book. When I went into the living room and sat with Delia in front of cartoons, she didn't look up or say anything.

All afternoon, I repeated the number in my head. I'd thought when I first looked up the number that I would call right away, but seeing Dr. Chalmers's name in print had chilled me, the way it was listed with the names of all those other doctors I didn't know, a row of stern men in white coats who didn't have time for the likes of me, a child whining for her mother. And what if, when I called, someone other than my mother answered? What would I say? I could say, *I'm looking for Mrs. Gray,* but then what if the person said, *Why?* or, even more intimidating, *What is this regarding?*

My father came home and fixed us hot dogs and canned beans for dinner. Delia prattled on about something she had seen on TV; I kept waiting for her to ask about our mother, but she didn't.

Later that night, while my father put Delia to bed, I went to the phone and dialed. It was long after dark. The line rang twice, and then a heavy mechanical click sounded in my ear. The light hiss of a tape started up.

"Hello," my mother's voice said, and my heart leaped up even as I understood from the formality of her tone that this was not my mother but a recording my mother had made, probably during those first self-conscious weeks at her job.

"You have reached the medical offices of Dr. Albert Chalmers," my mother's voice said. "Our offices have closed and we can't be here to take your call, but please leave a message after the tone. If this is an emergency, please hang up and dial 911. Thank you."

The tape was full of tiny pauses, places where my mother gathered her breath, or where she reached the end of a line someone had written out for her, maybe Dr. Chalmers himself. When she reached the word *we,* I could detect the tiniest thrill in her voice, a sound surely inaudible to anyone who didn't know her well. Her voice contained all the excitement and promise of the new job, the pleasure she'd taken in speaking in a professional capacity. I hung up without leaving a message.

The construction site that Mr. Biersdorfer had pointed out by the road, the structure that had been slowly accreting layers of gray, then pink, then stone, was finally finished.

We saw the mall from afar as we approached it on the night of the grand opening—the lights playing over it, the massive building squatting there like an alien ship that had just landed by the side of the road. We parked and got out of the car. The night was warm and close, a humid haze forming itself around each of the lights. When we reached the entrance, ten tall glass doors flanked by palm trees, my father pulled one of the handles, a long glass cylinder. We heard a whooshing sound, the air-conditioning blowing like its own weather system. The air inside felt cool and dry and smelled somehow northern, a spicy cleanness, high and sharp. And inside: pink marble, glass, chrome, and light as far as the eye could see, up three levels of stores, all the way up to the skylights, and more palm trees.

Hundreds of people I had never seen before walked the corridors, wandered into stores, lined up at the Orange Julius counter. We moved toward the escalators, and as I scanned the heads of strangers in front of us, one seemed familiar. Even from behind, I felt I recognized the angle at which his ears stuck out, the pink where the light shone through. He was wearing a navy blue shirt, a color I associated with Eric Biersdorfer. My heart started to beat faster at the thought of seeing Eric again. He should know about the affair by now, I thought, and even if he didn't, he would surely be suffering from the same bewildering absence of a parent that Delia and I were. He would be pale, haunted, and confused-looking, unsatisfied with any of the explanations his mother offered about where his father was. If I could pull Eric aside, I could tell him what I knew. My fingertips buzzed. I stared at the back of the boy's head, willing him to turn my way so I could catch more of his profile. I tried to think of what I might say to him when we spotted each other. *Hi, Eric, how are you? It's good to see you. Eric, I've missed you.*

I pushed against the people around me to get closer to him, and when he finally turned toward me, he wasn't Eric at all. His jaw was too heavy, his eyes too small, his lips too round and pursed.

"What's wrong?" my father asked me. "You look upset."

"Nothing," I said.

My father went to an electronics store while Delia and I stayed in the bookstore. I left Delia in the kids' section and looked through the magazine rack for articles about the astronauts. In one, I found a portrait of the crew slated to fly on *Challenger* for the Teacher in Space mission. They wore blue flight suits and held their helmets as if they were about to climb into the shuttle and blast off that very minute. I had seen crew portraits before, but this one had both Judith Resnik and Christa McAuliffe, the teacher who had been chosen to fly in space. All seven of them smiled real smiles, happy smiles. I waited until no one was within earshot, then ripped the page out of the magazine and folded it into my pocket.

Delia appeared at my elbow.

"What?" I demanded, afraid that she'd seen me tear the picture, but she just whispered, "Let's go to the arcade."

The video arcade was a darkened room lined with glowing booths, their screens shielded on both sides by the edges of the boxes. Teenage boys leaned into them, their forearms working, their faces glowing blue. The machines sang in bleeps and single-toned melodies, bleeding into a single discordant song. Delia got a wicked look and started to trot through the arcade, around in a circle. The second time through, she picked up speed. I was too old to run with her, but I could see why she did. I knew how the bleeps and songs of the machines would warp and blend together as she ran, the lights flashing past. Neither of us tried to play the games; it seemed we'd lose right away, that the games were above us.

I saw older kids, teenagers, and they reminded me of the new school year approaching. I spent more and more of my time envisioning high school, the things I would be expected to know. The kids at my new school would possess a sophistication that would make everyone I knew look childish, even Elizabeth Talbot. It was impossible to imagine what this would look like, but I tried anyway: They would use words I didn't know, talk about music I'd never heard. I could never catch up, never join them where they were. They would see my childishness and it would be too late.

My father bought me four cassette tapes, six pairs of socks in bright colors, and a silver heart-shaped locket. He bought Delia a white sundress, a pink zip-up jacket, and a gold heart-shaped locket. In the car on the way home, I went over each of my new possessions in my mind, savoring the precise colors of the socks. These things, it seemed to me, would be everything I would ever need to live a normal life as a high school freshman. The others would never know I was a year younger because I would have the right things, look the right way, know all the bands, all the song names. Though I knew it couldn't possibly be true, I felt that this sense of satisfaction, this fullness, would stay with me forever, that I could never feel deficient in any way again.

When we got home I pulled all of my old clothes out of the closet and spread them across my bed and the floor. I held each item up and asked myself: Will this be acceptable in high school? For most of my clothes, the answer was no. I made a pile to give to Delia. She seemed surprised when I offered it to her and eyed me warily as she picked up a dress and held it to her shoulders. It was way too big. I piled more and more in front of her. She walked back and forth from my bed to hers, her arms stacked high with ruffles and lace, with pinks, yellows, bright blues and greens.

That night, I couldn't sleep; I was too anxious about the first day of school. To calm myself, I read the last entry in my space notebok, written ten days before.

STS 51-I, *Discovery.*
 Launch attempt August 24, 1985, called off 5 minutes before liftoff because of bad weather. Launch attempt August 25 called off due to the failure of one of the on-board computers. Launch attempt August 27 delayed 3 minutes because of a combination of bad weather and an unauthorized ship intruding on the area of the ocean where the Solid Rocket Boosters fall. Launch at 6:58 am.
 The sunshield on one of the three satellites got caught on the Remote Manipulator Arm camera and the satellite had to be deployed one day early. Another satellite failed to function after it reached geosynchronous orbit. Two astronauts, William Fisher and James van Hoften, performed spacewalks totaling 11 hours and 27 minutes including time spent fixing the satellite deployed on mission 51-D.
 My father took me to this launch.

I set down the notebook and closed my eyes. I tried to picture my mother: I saw her in the yellow dress she had bought for work, with a white belt and white shoes. She smiled broadly and opened her arms. She was proud of me, excited for me to start high school. She would have advice for me about what to wear, how to act. She would tell me stories about her high school days. And did she not know, I wondered, that tomorrow was the first day of school? Or was she so busy with her new life wherever she was that she had forgotten something so important?

In my mind, I wandered through Eric's house, floating above the floor, drifting through the living room with its vaulted ceiling. I made myself remember each tile around the fireplace, the precise square shapes of the ultramodern furniture, the black leather chairs facing each other in little clusters, as if the chairs themselves were chatting. The huge vague modern paintings on the wall, just slashes of fuzzy color across the canvases. I passed through the doorway and across the hall to the dining room, where everything matched in shades of burgundy and cream. I measured the precise width of the gold edge of the plates, the exact weight of the silver forks. Behind the chair where Mrs. Biersdorfer had sat, there lurked a tall china cabinet, and though I hadn't looked into it carefully that evening while Eric and I ate our dinners, I catalogued its contents now. Gold-rimmed dishes, rows and rows of them, large plates and smaller plates and dessert dishes. Silver bowls and decanters, a large silver platter, engraved, resting upright. Tiny delicate teacups, each one with a matching saucer, tiny silver spoons laid across each edge. The glass door of the cabinet, clean, free of fingerprints. Cleaned every day by Livvie.

And the wide beige uniform and kind brown eyes of Livvie, the way she had looked away from me as I stared. I decided to imagine her as a loving mother for Eric: I gave her a soft warm lap for him to climb onto, a secret stash of cookies for her to slip into him when Mrs. Biersdorfer wasn't looking. I liked to imagine that it was Livvie who encouraged Eric's love for reading. I imagined after-school snacks at the kitchen table while she asked him to describe what he had read, correcting his pronunciation of the hard words. Eric must have had someone to encourage him, I reasoned, and it comforted me to imagine it was her.

I thought of him. I thought of him growing up in that house with those people, both of them dry as matches, humorless, quick to anger. I thought about Mr. Biersdorfer, and how a boy like Eric was in so many ways a mystery to him: a boy with no aggression, a boy with no desire for power. A boy who takes no values for granted, not the value of spaceflight nor of patriotism, a boy who must think through every blessed thing for himself.

I got out of bed and tiptoed to the kitchen. I didn't want to turn on a light, so I felt the buttons on the phone, counting the squares with my fingers to push the numbers I had memorized.

"Hello, you have reached the medical offices of Dr. Albert Chalmers. Our offices have closed—"

This time, her pauses sounded a little distant, as if she were unhappy about something. It was the same recording I had heard before, of course, but it was unmistakable, this halting sadness, and it was hard not to hear this as a sign that things were going badly with Biersdorfer, that she might change her mind and come back to us.

13.

THE MORNING OF THE FIRST DAY OF SCHOOL, I WOKE UP TO FIND
Delia watching an interview with Christa McAuliffe on TV. I studied
Christa McAuliffe, trying to memorize her: dumpling face, kind eyes,
frizzy hair. She smiled at Bryant Gumbel and told him how excited
she was to be going to space. He asked whether the idea of the space
shuttle frightened her.

"Maybe just a little?" he prodded.

"Not yet," she said. "Maybe when I'm strapped in and those rockets are going off underneath me, I will be. But spaceflight today really
seems safe."

"She shouldn't get to fly," I told Delia. I wanted all astronauts to
have the compact athleticism of Judith Resnik: a daredevil smile, a
pilot's comfort with switches and joysticks and headsets. Christa
looked like a mom, like someone who would have to ask her kids to
help her program the VCR.

Delia didn't answer.

"I think she's pretty," Delia said after a while. "She seems nice."

"I'm sure she's very *nice*," I said, "but that doesn't mean she
should get to go to space. Only astronauts should get to go."

We both watched Christa talk. She spoke excitedly, widening her
eyes and waggling her head back and forth to convey her awe and
gratitude.

"She looks like Mom," Delia observed.

"No, she doesn't," I said.

"She does to me," Delia insisted quietly. She missed our mother, I knew, but she didn't ask about her much anymore. She had decided to believe our father's story, that our mother had gone on a trip, and had set my ugly story aside.

"We should get ready for school," I said. I snapped the TV off.

I took a shower, washing my hair twice, then spent a long time looking at myself in the mirror. My face looked raw, pink, and frightened. Elizabeth Talbot, I thought, would never look like this, not on the worst day of her life. Her skin would always be the color it should be; her expression would always be confident and consistent. I tried to arrange my face into an expression like Elizabeth's, like those of the teenagers at the pool—calm, bored, superior. The clothes I had picked out so carefully the night before now looked childish. I wanted clothes that would shield me from adversity, make me invisible.

I waited for the bus at a new stop, a few blocks away from where Delia and the younger kids in the neighborhood still waited for the grade-school bus. When my bus pulled up, it was mostly full, and the sight of the students on it alarmed me. I had known that I was going to high school, yet I still wasn't entirely prepared to see actual teenagers sitting on the school bus—people so much older than me, so much more developed, possessing darker and more complicated knowledge. I tried not to stare at them as I took an empty seat toward the front. They were sitting alone, one to a seat, and glaring out the windows. Some of them, boys especially, looked vaguely monstrous—swollen and pimply and misshapen. Their bones were growing too fast and stretching their skin.

When the bus reached the school and stopped at the curb, everyone shuffled off reluctantly. The building was a series of cubes, cinderblock, with long slits for windows. The athletic field behind it was surrounded by a chain-link fence, and a few kids leaned against it, their fingers worked through the links, smoking cigarettes while they waited for the bell to ring. I walked past them, avoiding their eyes.

The main hallway on the first floor was packed with bodies. I had to force myself to join the crowd wandering toward classrooms and lockers. Here, as on the bus, everyone looked much older than me. Everything I saw the girls wearing, especially the older girls, had a similar style to it: a preppiness or little-girlishness just at the edge of going haywire: pink and white button-down shirts with the tails flying, or tied into slutty knots over their belly buttons; pleated plaid skirts that showed too much leg; sweaters in primary colors with plunging V-necks revealing tank tops underneath. They wore red and purple and lime green scarves in their hair with the corners sticking up like rabbit ears. They wore bright plastic jewelry. They wore lipstick and eyeliner. I felt conspicuously babyish, a little mouse.

I had allowed myself to imagine that Eric might be here too, that the Gifted and Talented program might have lured him away from his private school. I found myself looking for Eric everywhere. Any boy of vaguely the right build and hair color I studied and followed with my eyes, convincing myself that he might be Eric. Maybe Eric had let his hair grow out like that boy's, I told myself nonsensically; maybe as he's grown his shoulders have gotten broader, or his hair has gotten darker. When I finally saw these boys' faces, they were disgusting, deformed, all wrong for not being Eric's.

When I walked into my first class, physics, about a dozen other kids already sprinkled around the room looked up at me listlessly. No one seemed to know each other, except for two girls who were whispering together. One of them I recognized: the tall girl from the pool with the purple bathing suit. I knew her name was Chiarra, which I thought was an unspeakably cool name. She didn't recognize me.

Waiting for class to begin, I realized that I had no idea what a high school class would be like. I thought back to the hardest things I had ever had to learn in math or science and tried to imagine ideas much harder, much more resistant to understanding. It would be like trying to make a bed with a too-small sheet, I thought; once I had tacked down one corner, the others would come flying off again, and I'd be lost.

The bell rang, and still no teacher had come in to take control. We all looked around at each other briefly. A few kids whispered quietly and looked at the door. Just then, a tall, gawky man with huge blue eyes appeared. He leaned in the doorway, bracing himself with his arms on either side. For a moment he stood there looking at us, swiveling his head back and forth unhurriedly.

We fell silent, watching him, waiting for him to do something. When he finally spoke, it was in quick little yelps of excitement.

"Good afternoon!" he cried. "My name is Dr. Schuler. I'm sorry I wasn't here to greet you as you came in, but I had to use the lavatory. Did you know that teachers have more kidney problems than any other occupation? It's because we're never given a moment in the day to use the lavatory."

We stared at him. He jogged to the front of the room.

Dr. Schuler had a big rubbery face that looked somehow exaggerated, like a cartoon character's. His eyes were topped with wiry and mobile eyebrows that reminded me of a dog's. His mouth was large and loose, his purplish lips parted with happiness. He wore a tie covered with a pattern of Greek symbols.

"Good afternoon!" he said again.

"It's morning," said a boy in the front row.

"So it is," said Dr. Schuler. "Good morning, then." He stood before us, rocking on his heels and looking pleased. He seemed to be waiting for someone else to speak. When no one did, he walked up to the boy who had spoken. He stood toe to toe with him.

"What makes things go down?" Dr. Schuler asked the boy in a conspiratorial tone, but loud enough for all of us to hear. "Why don't they go up? Why don't they go sideways?"

The kid, a skinny boy wearing a rugby shirt, gave a couple of blinks. When it became clear that Dr. Schuler planned to wait for an answer, the boy turned slightly pink. After a long pause, the kid cleared his throat.

"Um," he said. He looked to his left, at his buddy, and smirked quickly before turning back to Dr. Schuler. "Gravity?"

"Oh, because of *gravity*!" Dr. Schuler repeated, then made the exaggerated expression of enlightenment, eyebrows raised, lips curled into an O of wonder.

"And *what,* can you explain to us, Mr. . . . ."

"Doug," the kid answered.

"Can you explain to us, Mr. Doug, what gravity *is* exactly?"

Doug shifted in his chair.

"Oh. Um. Gravity is, uh . . ." He dragged out his groan for effect. More laughs from around the room. "Gravity is the force that makes things go down and not up."

"Ah, a circular answer," said Dr. Schuler. "Scholars, remember this: a circular answer is no better than no answer at all."

Everyone snuck looks at each other. The girl to my left, when I turned to face her, looked at me and rolled her eyes. She had short dark hair, spiky. When she smiled, a sort of wry smile ending in a sneer, I noticed that she wore thick makeup forming a crust over her acne. I smiled back.

"Can *anyone* tell me what gravity is?" Dr. Schuler cried.

I looked up at him, and, horribly, he was looking right at me. The adrenaline crashing through me made it hard to see his face clearly—everything went gray and spotty, pulsing with my heartbeat.

"Can *you* tell us, young lady?" he asked me.

As he had with Doug, Dr. Schuler hovered over me and stared until I spoke.

"Gravity is a force that—" I stammered and had to clear my throat in the middle of my sentence. "That draws objects together."

"Hm," Dr. Schuler grunted, and held a finger up to his lips, contemplating the implications of what I had said.

"*Any* two objects?" he asked. "What about two pencils? Is there a gravitational force between these?" He clasped a pencil in one hand, and with the other he pried my rainbow pencil out of my fingers. He moved our two pencils slowly together like magnets, then pried them apart. Together, apart. Together, apart.

"Yes," I answered. My voice was a tiny dry croak, the sound of a little cricket in the corner. "But . . . the gravitational force depends on the mass. So the force between two pencils is too small to have any effect."

"Too small," he repeated loudly, "to have any effect." He had been bending forward in order to hear me, but now he snapped upright. "Actually, Ms. . . . ?"

"Gray," I squeaked.

"Actually, Ms. Gray, that isn't quite accurate. There *is* a gravitational effect, however small, which can be measured using sensitive instrumentation. Even though there is no effect visible with the naked eye, it would be wrong to conclude that there is no effect at all."

For a second I could hardly breathe. I'd been so sure I was giving him the answer he wanted, an answer he would be impressed with. The girl next to me gave me a sympathetic look, and when Dr. Schuler's back was turned, she stuck out her tongue and flashed a middle finger in his direction. She was clearly expert at this sort of behavior—she knew just when to put the finger away as Dr. Schuler turned back toward the room without seeming to hurry, without losing her cool.

Dr. Schuler spent most of the hour outlining his policies for the class.

"Throughout your school careers, you have undoubtedly become accustomed to a certain paradigm of education. Can anyone tell me what a paradigm is?" He looked around the room hopefully while everyone stared back at him.

"Well, we'll have to work on your vocabularies, I see. My point, scholars, is that until now your education has probably been lax. You have been given credit for trying, even when you have failed. You have been given credit for trying, even when you did not try very hard. Undoubtedly, you have come to believe the underlying assumption that *effort* is all that counts, *effort* defined very loosely as a vague willingness to receive an education.

"This class will be different. Achievement will be measured by empirical evidence of your mastery of the subject, not by my perception of your effort. Standards for achievement will be set high. I believe that students float to the mark I set for them, scholars, and I have set the mark for you very high. No more than one of you will earn an A in this class."

He paused for a long moment to let this sink in. He seemed to relish the horrified whispers running through the room.

"If you want that A, you'll have to compete with your peers to get it. Competition is rather out of vogue these days in educational circles, you may have noticed. But I think you'll find that the motivation of competition will help you achieve much more than you might have otherwise, and in the end that scholar who earns the A will know that he truly deserved it."

While we took this in, Dr. Schuler moved to his desk, which was piled high with textbooks. We approached his desk one by one while he sat inscribing our names and copying the numbers into his record book. When I got to the front of the line, Dr. Schuler said, without looking up, "And what's your first name, Ms. Gray?"

"It's Dolores."

"Hmmm." Dr. Schuler looked up at me while cupping his chin in his hand. "Sorrows."

"Excuse me?"

"Dolores," he pronounced slowly and carefully. "From *Our Lady of Sorrows.* It's a very sad name your parents gave you, Dolores."

"I didn't know that," I said stupidly.

"Well. We'll just have to see what we can do this semester to cheer you up." He added my name to his list. I had time to notice his handwriting was just like my father's, all square capital letters, before he snapped the book closed. He fixed me with a large smile as he handed the book to me. I took it and tried to smile back.

When I turned around, the spiky-haired girl who had been sitting next to me was standing near the door with Chiarra. At the pool, in her bathing suit, Chiarra had been rather nondescript, but here she wore a tight black shirt, jangling bracelets, a hot pink scarf in her hair, and thick black eyeliner. I couldn't tell whether she recognized me or not. Chiarra and the acne girl both watched me, and I became immediately self-conscious that I had been talking to a teacher, practically sucking up to him. Chiarra leveled her eyes at me. I flushed.

"What are *you* looking at?" she asked me.

There was no good answer to this question, so I pushed past them and headed down the hall toward the gym for PE, my next class. The two girls followed me.

"Did he pick out a nice book for ya?" one of them, probably Chiarra, called after me. They both cackled, and I felt sick with regret.

Later that night, I sat on my bed and prepared to do my physics homework: read Chapter 1 and answer the review questions. I examined the book. The title, *Discovering the Physical World,* was splayed across the cover in embarrassing seventies-style letters. The book's pages were thin and glossy, the color photos giving off a foul chemical smell. The pictures were of bright young people in out-of-date clothes smiling oddly as they performed the experiments described in the book—measuring sugar into water, making pulleys out of string, blowing up balloons, balancing needles on water. Someone who had used the book before me had tried to add obscene drawings in pencil, but the marks were hopelessly pale and smudged—the glossy paper wouldn't take the graphite.

Paging through the book, I felt a strange excitement, the consciousness that I was embarking on my career. I saw myself sitting cross-legged on my bed and diligently studying, as if from far away, a scene in a documentary about astronauts. A deep voice narrated the scene: *From the beginning, even before she had shared her dreams of flying in space with anyone, Dolores Gray distinguished herself as a talented and hardworking student of physical science.*

The book offered lists of questions I was supposed to try to answer before reading each chapter: Why do you think you can put your finger into a glass of water but not into a stone? If you dropped a bowling ball and a tennis ball off the roof of your school at the same time, which one do you think would hit the ground first? How do you think a compass knows which way is north? None of these questions seemed adequately explained by the CONCEPTS listed in capital letters in the book: MOLECULES, GRAVITY, MAGNETS.

The material came to her quickly, the voiceover said. *She soon exceeded the abilities of her classmates, then her elders. The first to notice her exceptional talent was her physics teacher, Dr. Schuler.*

Out in the living room, the TV murmured and shouted. My father would be on the couch, Delia beside him, or crouched on the floor so she could look up at the TV, letting its light bathe her. Fake TV laughter rose and fell.

I read the first paragraphs over and over until I had nearly memorized them. I felt Chiarra hovering over me, giggling, mocking me for studying, for trying to please Dr. Schuler. So instead I tried to imagine myself as Eric Biersdorfer—not embarrassed to be smart, not caring what anyone thought of me. I tried to think his thoughts, to inhabit his mannerisms. I even imagined his face as my face, breathing through his nose, seeing through his light gray eyes. As Eric Biersdorfer, I read the first chapter in the physics book slowly, taking notes as I went, and answered the review questions as thoroughly and clearly as I could. Then I did something I'd never done before: I went over my homework again, rewriting some of the sentences, looking up words to make sure I'd spelled them correctly, and checking my math on the problems with calculations in them. Then I copied the whole thing over onto a fresh sheet of paper, free of smudges and crossings-out. I enjoyed the feel of the pencil lead scratching against the white fiber in the paper, seeing my neatest handwriting marching across the page. When I was done, I stared at it for a long time, admiring my work. There was a part of me that wanted to show it to my father; I knew he would admire it, praise me, encourage me. I knew that my good behavior would somehow make him feel better about my mother's absence—he'd think I was telling him that he was doing a good job on his own, that we could do just fine without her. But I wasn't doing fine without her, and I didn't want either of us to feel that I was seeking his approval, that I had done this—or anything—to please him.

Delia and I ate cereal while my father was in the shower. I picked up the phone before I could think about what I was doing and punched the number I had memorized.

The line barely had a chance to ring once before someone picked up at the other end. I heard my mother's voice, the high, formal tone we'd heard her bring home in the earliest days of her job. "Good morning, Dr. Chalmers's office."

Her voice was a shock to me; I'd been expecting the machine again.

"Hello," I said in my best adult voice. "I'd like to make an appointment."

There was a small pause, and I thought for a second that she had recognized my voice. But then I heard a quiet rustle of paper.

"Just a moment, let me check the book," my mother said. At a distance, as if she were holding the phone away from her face, I heard her say, "Good morning. Please fill this out, both sides, and this one only if she hasn't been seen here before. Here you go. And here's a pen."

The distance of her voice and the light clack of pen against clipboard carved out on the other end of the phone a whole scene: my mother at a metal desk, the phone turned down against her shoulder, against the warm fabric of her green dress. Her arm reaching the clipboard out toward a mom with one protective arm around her daughter, a girl of uncertain age with strep throat, or with an earache, or in need of booster shots. Plastic padded chairs around the edges of the room with more moms and children. Magazines and children's books on the table, a box of worn toys. Behind my mother, rows of files kept in alphabetical order. Behind a swinging door, clean white examining rooms; in one of them, Dr. Chalmers bending over a child, a metal instrument in his hand.

"Yes, hello," my mother said directly into the phone. "Thank you for waiting. Are you calling for an urgent need or for a checkup?"

"Checkup," I said, keeping my voice low.

"All righty," my mother said. "Would an afternoon work for you? The earliest I have is the twentieth at three."

Now I didn't know what to say. I'd hoped that my mother would recognize my voice, that her formal tone would dissolve and turn to warmth and surprise, or even annoyance that I was bothering her at work. Most frightening of all was that I could disguise myself as an adult to her, that I could disguise myself as some woman not her daughter.

"Never mind," I said, and instead of trying to push my voice lower, I spoke as myself. Now surely she would know it was me.

"Oh!" My mother's voice sounded a little note of surprise. "All right. Well, do call back if you change your mind."

The phone clacked into its receiver at her end; just before the sound cut off, I could hear her voice again, speaking to the same woman or to someone else, just a friendly snip of a syllable, and then she was gone.

"Who's getting a checkup?" Delia asked warily.

"No one, Delia." I said. "Eat your cereal."

That day in physics, Dr. Schuler marched to the front of the classroom and, clearly trying to demonstrate something, held out at arm's length a sheet of paper in one hand and a dictionary in the other. His head was thrown back oddly; his left shoulder muscles strained against the weight of the dictionary, but he held it out stiffly anyway, for what seemed like a long time.

"Why will this book fall to the floor faster than this sheet of paper?" he shouted suddenly.

We were used to his questioning style now, and everyone spoke up at once. "It's heavier." "It weighs more."

Dr. Schuler let go with both hands, and the book dropped with a bang. Everyone jumped a little in their chairs, then shifted and chuckled, looking at one another, laughing off the embarrassment of having jumped. Long, leisurely seconds went by as the white sheet of paper drifted its way toward the floor, hiccupping to the left and right on its way down.

"Why did the book fall faster than the paper?" Dr. Schuler asked, his eyebrows arching high.

"Because it's *heavier*," someone at the back of the room answered, a boy. He spoke vehemently, as if he were answering an annoying child.

"Because it's *heavier*!" Dr. Schuler repeated, making his way down the aisle toward the kid who had spoken. "Refresh my memory as to your name, Mr. . . . ?"

"Matt," the voice said proudly. I didn't want to turn around in my seat to look at the kid speaking; somehow it would have seemed childish to do so.

"Matt, this book weighs more than a pencil. Do you think the book will fall faster than the pencil as well?"

"Of course," Matt said.

"Well, Mr. Matt," Dr. Schuler said happily, "you'll be happy to know that you're in good company. Many wise men have made the same mistake of observation that you have made today. Aristotle, for example. Aristotle set himself the futile task of explaining why heavier objects fall more quickly toward the Earth. Do you recall the explanation he came up with?"

"Uh—no," Matt said.

"Those who *do* not read, Matt, have no advantage over those who *cannot* read," Dr. Schuler told him gravely. "Think about that." Dr. Schuler left us a silence in which to ponder this before continuing.

"Aristotle hypothesized that heavier objects fall faster because all matter *wants* somehow to return to the Earth. He posited the notion that all matter has some kind of *Earth essence* in it, so that as an object gets closer to the Earth it starts to get *excited* to see the Earth, its old friend, and it speeds up, faster and faster, trying to get home."

Dr. Schuler stepped away from Matt and moved to the front of the room again.

"Of course, he was completely wrong. It's impossible to explain *why* heavier things fall faster because, in fact, heavier things *don't* fall faster." He paused and turned to look at us, a dramatic look, as if he expected some outcry.

"Don't believe me? Good. You shouldn't. Never believe what anyone tells you. But never believe what you were raised to believe either. What you want, scholars, is empirical evidence. Let's go outside."

Ten minutes later, we stood outside in the parking lot in the blazing heat. Dr. Schuler had told us precisely where to stand before disappearing back inside. We stood sweating, looking at each other, waiting. We knew he would reappear on the roof, but somehow it still surprised us when he did. He looked strange up there, small and fragile, his movements tiny and ineffectual, his voice high and weak. A breeze picked up the front of his hair.

"Scholars!" he hollered. No one answered. We all squinted up at him.

"Can you hear me?" he yelled.

We all nodded. A couple of kids groaned, "Yes . . ." in annoyed tones.

"All right, then!" he yelled. "Timekeeper, are you ready?"

He had chosen the girl with the acne and spiky hair, Tina, to hold the stopwatch; she waved back up at him listlessly.

"Drumroll, please!"

Nobody responded, but there was, in fact, an odd feeling of suspense. Everyone was tense, leaning forward slightly, eyes trained on Dr. Schuler.

"Five!" he yelled. "Four! Three! Two! One! Ignition!" The book and the pencil seemed at first not to be moving at all. Then they were floating down softly, all at the wrong sizes and wrong speeds, falling faster and faster until a soft thunk seemed to precede their actually hitting the pavement.

"Which hit first?" Dr. Schuler screamed, jumping up and down. "Which hit first?"

No one had any idea. I'd been so amazed by the falling itself, by the sheer drama of the falling, that I'd forgotten to notice which hit first. It had been difficult to take in both the book and the pencil at once; it was only possible to watch one at a time.

"Which hit first?" Dr. Schuler screamed again. "Timekeeper!"

But Tina shook her head and shrugged sheepishly. She had forgotten to click the stopwatch at the right time. Dr. Schuler turned away and disappeared from the roof.

Back in the classroom, when we still couldn't tell him whether the book or the pencil had reached the ground first, he stormed around and didn't meet anyone's eyes. He refused to give his follow-up talk on gravity. Instead we had to spend the rest of the hour making calculations of how long various objects would take to fall from the roof of our school using the gravitational constant.

"If we can't perform a simple experiment," he fumed, "if we can't establish some basic facts about gravity through empirical study, then I can't see how you can ever gain an understanding of the physical universe. I can stand here and tell you about it, but you know and I know that that doesn't mean anything. You have to see it with your own eyes."

For the rest of the hour, Dr. Schuler sulked at his desk. He thought we had disrespected his experiment, but he was wrong; on the contrary, I had been too interested in it to see what he wanted me to see. It was that very first fraction of a second of motion that had startled me; it had seemed that something had gone wrong. For the tiniest instant, I had thought it was Dr. Schuler himself falling, and not the objects. Dr. Schuler in his tie and his glasses, slipping past the raised lip of the roof and falling, falling toward the Earth.

Tina and Chiarra didn't seem to notice me at all that day, even though Tina sat next to me again in class. But as I left the classroom and headed toward math, I heard Chiarra's voice calling out to me.

"Hey, Miss Physics!" Chiarra called.

I turned around, fearing an attack. The two of them were leaning against a row of lockers. But their faces were smiling, not mocking. They waved me over.

"Hey, what's your name again?" asked Chiarra. "You go to my pool, right?" It was hard to tell whether she was being friendly or just gathering information to taunt me with. Tina tilted her head to one side, examining me from head to toe.

"It's Dolores," I answered.

"Dolores," Chiarra repeated. "What grade are you in?"

"Ninth," I said. I had decided not to mention being Gifted and Talented.

"We're in tenth."

"You're sophomores?" I asked, impressed.

"Yeah. My father said I have to take physics with Dr. Schuler. He's supposed to be this big genius or something. At least that's what my father says."

"Tina's father works for NASA," Chiarra explained.

"Mine too," I said, pleased that this was no longer a lie.

"Oh my God, is your father a physicist?" Chiarra asked. "That must be why you're so good at physics. I can't believe you knew the answer to that thing he was asking yesterday about gravity. I didn't even know what he was talking about, did you, Tina?"

"Not a chance in hell," Tina agreed.

"Did you study beforehand or something?" Chiarra asked.

I gave her a you're-crazy look, and that was the right response—they both smiled.

"My father's always talking about that stuff," I said. "I try not to listen, but I guess some of it sinks in accidentally."

"Ugh, I know what you mean. NASA talk," Tina said.

They both regarded me for a moment, and I waited for their next question, feeling I was being interviewed for a job. But neither of them asked me anything.

"She's so cute," Chiarra said to Tina finally, as if I were no longer there. "Isn't she cute?"

They both looked at me, smiling. Somehow, this did not seem inconsistent with their behavior yesterday—they were like a couple of little girls finding an unfamiliar creature, unsure whether to torture it or mother it. Somehow, without even trying, I had made my first high school friends.

14.

ALTHOUGH WE HADN'T EXPECTED IT TO, THE NEW MALL CHANGED the way we lived. Soon it was where we spent all of our time. When our father was done with work, he'd pull up and idle in the driveway. Delia and I came running out, locking the house behind us, me with my physics book under my arm. The longer my mother was gone, the more we seemed to want to avoid spending time in the house. We'd drive to the mall in silence, park in the acres of parking lot, and when we all walked through the wide set of doors, that cool air and soft music and recessed lighting worked on us like a drug, calming the jumpy feeling we all had. Sometimes we had dinner in a restaurant on the Concourse Level, but more often we ate in the Food Court, where we didn't have to agree on anything, the three of us chewing different fried foods at a plastic table, not bothering to take our things off the plastic trays.

The mall did something to me that I would never recover from. Only the best would be good enough, and the best was to be determined at a national, not a local, level. I begged for the things I saw at the mall, things I hoped would transform me into a better person: tapes of the bands that Tina and Chiarra talked about, glitter nail polish, a princess phone, a portable cassette player, glow-in-the-dark earrings, a set of three lip glosses that smelled like various fruits. I'd start working on my father, still sitting in the Food Court, trying to convince him that I needed these things. In the stores, I begged for things I didn't even want, just so as not to have to leave the mall empty-handed. I saw kids from school in the stores with their parents, begging for new things too. We'd meet eyes, but not talk. We were all playing catch-up, trying to correct our incorrect lives, to replace all the things we owned that we now realized were wrong.

One night soon after school started, my father suggested we try a new restaurant at the mall. We noticed right away that he seemed more purposeful than usual; he kept checking his watch as we parked and walked through the main doors. He led us to the entrance of the Italian restaurant on the first floor, the nicest restaurant in the mall. It was dark inside, red tablecloths and red booths lit by low lamps and a flickering candle on each table. My father lingered in the entryway, looking for something, even though the sign said PLEASE SEAT YOURSELF.

Then I saw why we were here. I spotted her before my father did; she was sitting in a corner booth, smoking. The glass of red wine in front of her was half empty. My mother looked like a stranger, like a woman I'd never seen before, her skin and eyes glossy in the candlelight. I had so rarely seen her when she didn't know she was being watched—it was like having the chance to see her life without me, her life if she hadn't been a mother. Her face was beautiful, I realized, and it was dear to me. Her brown eyes constantly searching, looking for someone to look back at her. Somehow, as she looked around, she kept missing me.

She made another sweep of the bar area to her left, this time bringing her cigarette up to her lips, and it was such a practiced gesture, my heart broke for her. I wondered how many times she had sat in bars and restaurants like this, waiting for Mr. Biersdorfer, looking around with just this expression. It was somehow inviting and confident, while underneath that, just barely visible, an intense hopefulness, desperate and unloved, a look of one just about to give up hope. There was something else in her face too, something maybe only I could see: that undercurrent of growing certainty that she had been stood up, made a fool of. The suspicion that could quickly turn to hurt, then anger.

I knew my father had spotted her when he said quietly, "Oh!" a surprised grunt, as if he hadn't been expecting to see her here, though of course they must have planned this. His face relaxed into a look of happiness—not exactly a smile. He almost seemed to glow, catching sight of her, admiring her across the room. Only when I saw this look did I understand, for the first time, that he had no idea what was going on with Mr. Biersdorfer, that he thought she might come back.

Then Delia spotted her. She gave a cry of happiness, ran down the aisle between tables, and flung herself into my mother's arms. People on either side looked at them and smiled nervously. My mother didn't seem self-conscious—she giggled and hugged Delia hard.

"We didn't see you here," my father announced; then he looked embarrassed as he realized this made no sense. He slid into the booth opposite my mother. I sat next to him; Delia was still in my mother's lap.

I couldn't take my eyes off her. She had changed, though of course she was also exactly the same. She was wearing a dress I had never seen before, a maroon wraparound with a pattern of tan squares. She had straightened her hair recently, and the chemicals had been too strong, as often happened to her; the ends were fried, as though they had drifted too close to a flame. Her face was shiny with makeup, her cheeks pinked and her eyes outlined with pencil. She looked as nervous as she'd been the night the Biersdorfers came to dinner so long ago. I thought about how everything was backward now: Mr. Biersdorfer saw my everyday mother, her real face, while we saw her made-up face and tense smile. Her nervousness was a smell, her perfume and the faint sweet burnt smell of her hair relaxer tinged with the cigarettes she'd had on the way over. I knew she had worked so hard to make everything perfect and matching, but her tan high-heeled shoes didn't quite match the pattern on the dress; neither did the tan purse with the broken strap. I'd thought some-how that Mr. Biersdorfer would have changed her, that she would now have nice things, the expensive sheen that Mrs. Biersdorfer had. It made me angry at him, at Mr. Biersdorfer, not only for taking her away from us, but for failing to make her better, as surely she had hoped he would.

"You're looking well, Deborah," my father said. We all looked at him.

"Thank you," my mother murmured, then cleared her throat. Nobody said anything for a while.

"Delia was just telling us about her field trip to SeaWorld," my father said. This was true; she'd talked about it in the car, and we had both more or less ignored her.

"She was telling us about the sea lions," he added, hoping to prompt her. But Delia said nothing; she was looking up openmouthed at our mother sitting next to her, warm and fragrant, larger than life.

"Ohh, that sounds like fun," my mother enthused, holding the *f* a long time between her teeth. I'd forgotten that about her: the way she pronounced words more crisply when she was wearing lipstick.

"Tell me what the sea lions did, baby." She folded her hands on the table in front of her, a friendly but unfamiliar smile, like an aunt or a babysitter, a childless friend of the family.

"Umm . . ." Delia trailed off. Delia, who was always looking for an audience, was suddenly struck with stage fright. She looked up at our mother, her eyes wide and wary. While we waited for her to answer, my mother changed the interlocking of her fingers, then changed it back again. She wore her diamond engagement ring, but I wasn't sure whether she was wearing her wedding ring stacked under it. I squinted at her finger, leaned forward a bit to get a better look. My mother noticed me and tried to catch my eye.

"And what about you, Dolores?" she asked, still formal, still with that distant-sounding warmth. "What have you been up to?"

I wasn't sure what to say to this, and I sat struggling for a minute. But she didn't seem to notice; she wasn't waiting for an answer anyway. She had already turned back to my father.

"And how have you been, Frank?" she asked him. "How's it going? Have the girls been good for you?"

"Oh, just fine," my father said. "They've been great for me." My father turned his jovial smile on me, looking for affirmation. I glared back at him.

"Umm, we went to SeaWorld?" Delia piped up, raising her little face to my mother.

"We went to SeaWorld? And they had these sea lions there and one of them was named Pinky? And they told him to put his flippers up on the thing and he stood up like this. . . ."

Delia sat up on her knees and put her flippers up on the table. She babbled on, her eyes wide and locked on my mother. For the first time I could remember, we all sat quietly and listened to Delia talk, concentrating on every word she said. She described a show she had seen at SeaWorld in which trained sea lions and sea otters, dressed as pirates, flopped about on a large pirate ship set. She told us about an underwater tank full of dolphins that streaked by the glass, showing the healed scratches and scars on their flanks. She stretched out her little hand to show us how she reached into a shallow tank to stroke a manta ray gliding by. He felt dry, she said, and he circled around the tank a second time to let her touch him again.

Delia talked and talked, mostly watching my mother but turning nervously toward my father and me now and then, to check that we were listening too. She showed no signs of stopping when my mother began to cry, a quiet sniffling at first, but then a single animal sound escaped from her. At first I thought it was a laugh, a helpless squawk at the ridiculousness of this—of Delia's story, of the specta-cle of our sitting here together like strangers, like distant relations with no particular feelings toward one other. But it wasn't a laugh. She put her hand over her mouth, as if trying to catch the sound. People at nearby tables looked over at us.

"Deborah, don't," my father said quietly. She bowed her head for-ward, shoulders trembling, her hand still pressed to her mouth. Delia had trailed off speaking and now just watched our mother, her lips hanging open. We all waited while my mother sniffed wetly and dried her eyes on a napkin.

"It's okay," my mother said to Delia, "it's okay," in her exagger-ated consoling voice, as if it were Delia who was crying, and wrapped her arm around Delia's shoulders. Delia climbed back into my mother's lap, her big feet sticking out into the aisle. Delia promptly began to cry softly into my mother's shoulder, burying her face in the fabric of the new dress.

"She's been brave," my father said, and my mother nodded in agreement. I was outraged that only I could see that she wasn't brave at all, that she was crying like a baby.

My mother fiddled with something in her purse. It was a ball of pink something, a hand-sized doll wearing a gauzy tutu. Delia's mouth dropped open and she stopped crying instantly. This was the kind of thing she loved, tacky and girly. She crawled out of my mother's lap and sat up straight in anticipation of receiving this gift, sniffling. But then my mother seemed to have forgotten what she had brought it for, and played idly with the doll, flipping its skirt up and down obscenely. She was looking at my father.

"Well, the girls have sure missed you," my father said. I wondered if he had planned this line ahead of time, chosen it for its lighthearted sadness, for the way it might move my mother to feel sorry for us without actually trying to direct her sympathy toward him. I pictured him working the sentence out in his mind last night, after they'd made these plans to meet here, mumbling it to the bathroom mirror while he shaved this morning. *The girls have sure missed you, Deborah,* his lips barely moving. *Gosh, they sure have missed you.* And what could she say to that? What could she say but to cry, apologize, explain? But my mother only smiled vaguely at the doll.

"Dr. Chalmers says to say hello," she said. My father nodded gravely, as though this were relevant. He and my mother's boss had never actually met, at least as far as I knew. My mother opened her mouth again, and she seemed to forget what she was going to say, just sat with her mouth open, communicating something to us silently.

My father nodded, as if he heard and understood. When the waitress finally came by, he looked up at her happily.

"I think we're ready to order," he said.

When we got up to leave, we all paused awkwardly at the entrance, the three of us watching my mother to see what she would do.

"It was so nice to see you all," she said formally, in the same tone and cadence that I had heard on the phone when I called her at work. Her hand fluttered up to her hair, and for a moment she looked as though she had something more to say. But then she turned, pivoting slowly on her high heels, and walked off in the opposite direction from where our car was parked, and we all watched her go, fascinated. She was going somewhere we didn't know, without us.

After our mother had left us again, I remembered all the things I had wanted to ask her. Where she had gone, why she had left us, when she planned to come back. Whether she blamed me, whether she ever saw Eric. While she was with us, we had been confused; our thoughts had been jammed in our heads like radios in a thunderstorm. The physical fact of her, the cigarette smell on her hair and the lipstick crumbs at the edges of her mouth, the crackling energy of her, had distracted us. She fidgeted and smiled and cocked her head while she talked to us, and we couldn't take our eyes off her. When asked direct questions, she looked off into a corner and the slightest expressions might cross her face—the eyebrows gently lifted into the tiniest indication of surprise. The lips turned up into the barest smirk. We could see, now that she didn't live with us anymore, that we didn't know a thing about her.

My father drove us home, and it seemed he thought everything was still the same. He gave the same grunt as he plopped himself into the driver's seat of the car. He tapped his ring against the steering wheel, never thinking of his wife's ring, never wondering whether she still wore hers or not. He hummed quietly, a formless song. He asked if we needed anything from the store. We didn't. When he pulled the car into the driveway, he let out a quiet comment he'd clearly been saving up for some time.

"That was nice," he said quietly.

"Yeah," Delia agreed.

"What was nice?" I demanded. I knew what he meant, of course, but I wanted to hear him talk about it.

"Seeing your mother," he answered.

"Yeah," Delia said again. I resisted the urge to tell her to shut up.

"I hope we can do it again soon," he said after a long pause. "Would you like that?" The tone of his voice was happy, nostalgic, hopeful. I realized with a horrible heavy feeling that he had misinterpreted the whole dinner; he thought something had been accomplished, some contact made. Only I knew that he had accomplished nothing, that she wasn't coming back.

"Yeah!" shouted Delia from her corner of the backseat, where she had been busy stripping her new doll. I felt my father turn to look at me. I tried to think of the most hateful and disgusting thing I could say. I felt someone needed to tell the truth about what was happening. My father nodded a quick encouraging nod at me. His face was full of hope.

"Yeah," I said finally. "That would be nice."

STS 51-J, *Atlantis*.

Launch attempt October 3, 1985, delayed 22 minutes and thirty seconds due to a false instrument reading. Launch at 11:15 am.

This was the first launch of the last Orbiter to be built, *Atlantis*. This mission was the second one dedicated to the Department of Defense, so the mission objectives were top secret.

After landing, *Atlantis* was found to have lost a heat tile, which had caused some damage to underlying structures.

My father took me to this launch.

I'd been in high school for a month, and I found everything but physics boring and pointless. I spent the time in my other classes, the classes that weren't physics, thinking about physics. The Emancipation Proclamation; the independent clause and the subordinate clause; the *passé composé:* nothing compared to the hard reality of physics, the pleasurable frustration of its difficulty. I didn't listen when other teachers talked; instead I thought about Dr. Schuler, Dr. Schuler who would explain it all to me, Dr. Schuler who would recognize my talent and send me to Space Camp in Houston, where Judith Resnik would notice me, pick me out of the crowd.

Tina and Chiarra invited me out to the parking lot with them during lunch; this is what the cool kids did, they had explained. When we got outside, the heat was crippling. Kids, mostly juniors and seniors, were sitting on the hoods of cars, eating fast-food lunches or sandwiches from brown bags.

Tina and Chiarra had pointed out cute boys to me, boys they deemed worthy of the label, and under their influence I had started to watch boys more closely myself. I had learned to pick out the common elements among the boys Tina and Chiarra liked—a strong jawline, a heavy brow, full lips, white teeth. Broad shoulders were important, as was height. Of course, they sometimes labeled "cute" boys who lacked all of these qualities if they behaved the right way—funny, mocking, slightly hostile. It seemed that Tina and Chiarra liked confidence, arrogance, aggression. These were boys who, if someone were to embarrass themselves by tripping, would call attention to it rather than pretend it hadn't happened.

But now that I was looking at the boys, I noticed the other kind too. The kind who didn't compete, didn't shout or laugh loudly or hit each other. They were nearly invisible—you had to train yourself to see them, like ghosts. They walked around by themselves, books tucked tightly under their arms, not making any impression on the world around them, just trying to get to the next class, get through the day. I was most fascinated by these boys who didn't seem to have a shred of aggression in them, like Eric. Unlike Tina and Chiarra's "cute" ones, they met my eyes if I looked at them, always with a tinge of shock at finding themselves locking eyes with me. Always a feeling of electric current with these boys, of actual human contact. I didn't understand why Tina and Chiarra chose the ones they did: the boys who were so closed, so hard, the ones who took trouble to make sure you knew that there was nothing special about you, that they barely noticed you at all.

Chiarra found a new boy to talk to this time, a pimply dark-haired boy sitting crossed-legged on the roof of a beat-up old Volvo with a bumper held on by duct tape. Tina and I watched from a respectful distance while she sailed a few comments his way; he answered her, and after a couple more exchanges, he held out a hand and helped her up onto the roof of the car.

"It's amazing," Tina said, dejected. "That guy is a senior. He even has a girlfriend. Chiarra has this weird power with guys. She always gets whatever she wants." I thought of my mother smiling up at Mr. Biersdorfer at the dinner party, everyone's eyes on her. It occurred to me that my mother might have preferred a daughter like Chiarra, a daughter open to the world, daring and confident like herself.

"You could do it too," I said. "You just have to talk to one of them." Then, to comfort her, I added, "You know, you're much cuter than she is."

"What difference does it make? They always like her."

Across the parking lot, I spotted an older boy, broad-shouldered, who looked familiar. It took me a minute to recognize him without his orange board shorts—Josh, the boy from the pool. He was holding a can of Coke in one hand and trying to pick up a blond girl by her waist with the other.

Chiarra returned a few minutes later, flushed with success. "I have a date Saturday," she announced. "How'd you do?"

Tina and I shook our heads. "Not much to pick from out here," Tina said.

"Oh, come on," Chiarra protested, twisting to look back at the parking lot as we headed inside. "Use your imagination. What about you, Dolores? Anything?"

"Maybe next time," I said.

I still felt young compared to Tina and Chiarra, but it occurred to me that if I told Elizabeth and Jocelyn and Abby about the parking lot, that we came out here to meet boys, they would be intimidated. If I offered them a chance to join us, they would back away, saying, *No, thanks, we're too young.* They would go back to their playground gossiping.

I was distantly afraid that Dr. Schuler would come to associate me with Tina and Chiarra and their lack of interest in physics. But he seemed not to notice the social groupings in his class; he seemed to make a point of ignoring such things. I decided to respect him for that.

"On Monday," Dr. Schuler had announced at the end of class that day, "you will come in to find the room hushed with concentration. None of the usual hustle and bustle will take place. You will simply proceed quietly to your places, where you will find a freshly-printed Opportunity to Achieve waiting for you."

"You mean a test?" some kid called from the back.

"No, I do not mean a test. I mean an Opportunity to Achieve. An opportunity to show me—and yourself—what you have learned about physics so far this term, and how you are developing as a problem-solver."

No one had anything to say to that.

"When you come into the room," he continued, "you will take out one pencil"—here he brandished his own yellow pencil—"and nothing else. You will take your OTA silently and thoughtfully. If you finish before the bell rings, which is highly unlikely, you will set down your pencil and think intelligent thoughts about physics until such time as the bell should ring, looking neither to your left nor to your right."

As we shuffled out, everyone around me complained about the OTA.

"'Look neither to your left nor your right,'" Doug said, trying to mimic Dr. Schuler's tone. "It's like living under a Nazi regime."

I laughed with the others, but I was secretly thrilled by Dr. Schuler's speech. I was impressed by the idea of a test being so important that it needed a special name and special instructions.

At home I sat down to study, arranging myself on my bed with my physics book and notepad and pens around me. But once I was flipping through the chapters and looking at the notes I had taken in class, I didn't quite know what to do with them all. Much of the information I felt I knew already, in some commonsense way. And the things I didn't know—for example, the fact that the metal rod that set the standard for the meter was kept in Sèvres, France— seemed unimportant to the study of physics, irrelevant details, the type of maddeningly pointless information that English and history teachers wanted us to know. Dr. Schuler didn't seem like the type of teacher who would test us on facts like that, details that didn't have any bearing on our understanding of the actual subject. At the same time, he did seem like the type of teacher who would make his tests ridiculously hard. He would enjoy including questions that would make kids like Doug and Matt groan—Dr. Schuler would get a satis- fied look on his face and rock back and forth on his heels while those boys complained. I flipped through the book looking for the formulas I would need to memorize.

I looked up to find Delia standing in the doorway, watching me. I wondered whether I had been talking to myself, what I had been doing with my face.

"He's talking to her," she whispered.

"What do you mean?" I shot back at normal volume.

"Mom," Delia said.

Together we crept out to the hallway, where I picked up the phone.

At first I heard just the seashell static of an open phone line, an oceany silence. I was about to say something, just to hear the reverberation of my voice, when I heard the papery sound of someone exhaling into the receiver. I held my breath.

Two seconds went by, then three, then four. Then my father's voice: "Deborah," he said. Then, after another long pause: "Deborah . . ."

Delia looked up at me, smiling. So she did this too, this telephone listening. When I replaced the receiver carefully, they still hadn't said anything more.

"Maybe Mom's coming back," Delia whispered. Her mouth was hanging open with anticipation.

"Don't count on it," I said.

Long after I'd gone to sleep that night, I woke to a warm weight on my bed.

"Go back to sleep, Delia," I mumbled. The weight shifted and remained. But then I recognized the smell of my mother, her perfume and the faint tinge of cigarettes and something else under that, something like new bread. She was biting her nails.

"Mom?" I whispered. "Where are you?"

"I'm right here, duckie," she said. "Right here with you."

What I had meant to ask was, *Where* were *you? Where have you been?* But somehow it would seem rude to ask directly. My mother didn't seem to think her presence required any explanation.

"I want to ask you something," she said, kicking at some of my clothes strewn on the floor. I felt a sudden fear.

"What has your father said?" she asked. As she spoke, she snagged one of my T-shirts with her toe. She lifted it to her hand, sniffed it, and dropped it again.

"About what?" I whispered back.

"About *me,*" she answered, irritated, as if I were being obstinate.

"Nothing," I insisted quickly. It was true: as much as Delia and I were dying to hear him speak of her, as much as we hoped he would slip up and admit that she had left us, he never said a word, never showed a sign. "Nothing." Just too late, I realized my mistake. This was the wrong answer.

"Really. Nothing. I wouldn't have thought—after fourteen years of marriage . . ." She trailed off, gave a shrug, an elaborate gesture of hurt and shucking off that hurt, both at once.

"No, I mean, he *talks* about you," I stumbled. "He talks about you all the time. I just meant he won't say anything bad about you to anyone. He says wherever you've gone, that's your business." I was guessing now, flailing at what she might want to hear.

"Wherever I've *gone,*" she sneered. "Why is he saying that? Does he want people to think he doesn't know where I *am?*"

It had never occurred to me that he might know where to find her. If he did, why wouldn't he have told us? Why wouldn't he have convinced her to come back?

"What else does he say?" she whispered.

"He wants you to come back," I said.

"Does he?" she asked shyly.

"*Yes,*" I said, so relieved to have hit on a right answer. "We all want you to come back. We talk about it all the time." It was an idea she would find appealing, the three of us invoking her name every morning and every night, remembering her, missing her more and more. It occurred to me that this was all she was waiting for. If we could prove to her that we missed her, that we loved her, then she would come back. But for now it wasn't enough, and soon after I spoke, she slipped out again.

In the morning, I watched my father for signs that he had seen my mother. He didn't seem especially upset or exhausted, and there was no physical evidence of a visitor, no glasses on the coffee table, nothing that had been moved. He ate his cereal and sipped his coffee and didn't seem to notice me staring.

"Did you hear anything strange last night?" I asked.

"What?" he grunted, turning the page of the newspaper. "What do you mean, strange?"

"Like the door opening and closing? Anything like that?"

My father looked up.

"Door opening . . . ?" he repeated.

"I saw Mom last night." He didn't respond to me right away, and that was how I knew he had seen her too.

"How often do you see her?" I asked. "How often does she come here in the middle of the night?"

"Your mother and I need to talk together now and then," he said. He moved his cereal around in his bowl as though he'd seen something interesting at the bottom.

"About what?" I asked. "Why can't she come over in the daytime? Why doesn't she want to see all of us?"

"You saw her last night," my father pointed out lightly. Then he got up and rinsed out his dishes. This was true, of course. But I couldn't get past the idea that he should be able to make her come back for good.

It occurred to me that Mr. Biersdorfer hadn't treated her to an expensive hotel after all; maybe she'd had to check herself in somewhere, somewhere cheap, the type of motel not by the beach but by the highway, run by a retired couple, painted garish colors, and eaten away by salt. The kind of motel where on either side of each door squats a metal patio chair, the rivets circled with rust. From each window protruding an air conditioner, its metal gills smashed and bent out of shape.

My mother would be unhappy to find herself there—she would crave marble bathtubs, thick sheets, room service, two champagne flutes side by side on a silver tray. At the highway motel, she would try to make the best of things. Maybe, as she slipped her key into the ill-fitting lock, felt the doorknob give and the thin door swing open, the thought occurred to her: *His wife would never let him get away with a place like this.* It made her feel tired and shabby, a used-up mother, to understand that this was what he thought of her, that she was not a luxury, a rare confection, but a bargain, a compromise, a second choice. She wanted to be his prize, but she must have known, even then, that she was only his respite.

I almost cried for her. It surprised me, the level of emotion I could elicit for her, now that she wasn't here, just by imagining the worst for her.

Each desk had a mimeographed OTA on it when we walked into the room, all of them perfectly lined up. As instructed, we each held a single pencil, sharpened.

"Are you *ready*?" Dr. Schuler said imperiously from the front of the room, his face deadly serious. The room was hushed and tense. I looked to my left and right: the kids on either side of me were tapping their feet, playing with their pencils with trembling fingers. One girl hugged herself and rocked back and forth, very slowly. Somehow, despite all our complaining and mocking, we had been convinced to believe in his OTA. I felt that if I failed to impress Dr. Schuler with what I wrote on this piece of paper, if I didn't Achieve, he would know I wasn't smart enough. I would not be astronaut material. I'd be just another mediocre girl.

The questions on the OTA were just what I should have expected from Dr. Schuler—no fill-in-the-blank, no multiple choice, no true-or-false. There were only word problems: *If you jumped off the Empire State Building and shot a gun due east at the exact same moment, how many seconds would pass between your splat and the bullet's hitting the ground? If you dropped a ten-kilogram weight onto a scale on an elevator moving up one hundred meters at five kilometers per hour, how would the scale's reading change over time? Why does the space shuttle create a double sonic boom when it reenters the Earth's atmosphere?*

Each question was followed by a full page of blank space in which to show our work. I started with the first question, the Empire State Building one, and sketched a diagram. I answered the question in as much detail as possible. I knew Dr. Schuler would want to see not only the right answer, but that we understood the concepts involved—in this case, that motion in the x direction has no effect on motion in the y direction—and all their implications, all the ways motion can be predicted and described, all the laws of the physical world. I dumped everything I knew onto those pages, taking extra time with details I knew he savored especially. My OTA was like a weird valentine from my mind to his, showing him I understood physics the way he wanted us to, in the way that he did. I wrote until the bell rang, long after everyone else had put down their pencils.

15.

STS 61-A, *Challenger.*

Launch October 30, 1985, on schedule at 12:00 noon.

This mission carried eight crew members, more than any other, including two West German astronauts and one from the Netherlands. A German Spacelab carried life sciences experiments.

My father didn't take me to this launch because he couldn't get out of work.

I rode in the car with my father to Elizabeth Talbot's house. When she had called the night before to invite me to a slumber party, I'd been so surprised to hear from her I couldn't think of any excuses not to go. I anticipated a long evening with her and Abby and Jocelyn, listening to them giggle and gossip about people I didn't know, trying to answer their questions about the Gifted program, about high school. I planned to exaggerate my new sophistication with a bored nonchalance. If any of them questioned me or criticized me about anything, I thought, I could always imply that high school kids would find their opinions immature, and that would shut them up.

My father hummed and tapped his wedding ring against the steering wheel.

"Do you need some money?" he asked as he pulled up at Elizabeth's house. He was already contorting himself against the seat to reach his wallet.

"No," I said. "I don't think we're going anywhere."

"Well, just in case," he said, and gave me a ten-dollar bill. "Call tomorrow when you're ready to get picked up." I thanked him, and he kissed me goodbye.

Elizabeth opened the door wearing a bright green minidress. She had cut her hair so short it curled into a bowl, which made her face look fat. She led me through the living room into the kitchen. I remembered the first time I'd seen her house, the way all the fussy furnishings, the wicker and chintz, had seemed so delicate and unapproachable, like museum pieces. Now that I wasn't afraid of Elizabeth, the room seemed girly and busy, too many things crammed together, too many patterns and curlicues.

Abby and Jocelyn were nowhere in sight.

"So what's your Gifted program like?" Elizabeth asked politely, perching on the couch. "Our class is so boring. It's just like seventh grade, except the guys are taller."

I didn't know what to say. I thought of telling her about Tina and Chiarra, Dr. Schuler, the parking lot.

"Oh, school is good, I guess," I said. "I mean, it's fun being in high school. Everyone is much more mature." She nodded and murmured appreciatively. When I had anticipated bragging about my new school, it had been for the purpose of taking Elizabeth down a notch, but I wouldn't be able to do that if she refused to try to act superior. I was surprised by how much this disappointed me.

"When are Jocelyn and Abby getting here?" I asked.

"Oh," Elizabeth said carefully, "they're not coming." Her round face didn't change or register any emotion. I felt an unexpected surge of annoyance. As much as I wasn't looking forward to an evening with the three of them, an evening with just Elizabeth was even less appealing.

"Jocelyn and Abby and those guys have been kind of mean to me lately," she said quietly. "I don't really know why. Actually, they don't seem to like me at all anymore." A large tear welled out of one of her eyes and plopped onto her raised knee. She rubbed it in with her thumb. I knew I should ask a question, but I wasn't sure what.

"Do you still sit with them at lunch?" I asked.

"I still sit at that *table,* yeah. But they don't *include* me. I mean, they don't do anything to stop me from sitting with them, but they don't really talk to me either. They sort of talk around me."

Elizabeth took a tissue from a box on the side table and blew her nose daintily. I found it hard to imagine Jocelyn and Abby daring to ostracize Elizabeth, daring to take control. But maybe they had seen enough to understand how Elizabeth's power only existed if everyone agreed to believe in it. I hadn't understood that myself until I got away from her.

"But we don't have to talk about that," she said. "What's new with you?"

"Actually, I have a boyfriend," I said. This lie popped out without warning.

"You do?" Elizabeth said. "What's his name?"

"Josh. He's a senior. He's so cute. I wish I had a picture of him to show you."

"God, Dolores," Elizabeth breathed. "A *senior.* I can't believe it. Does he drive?"

"Yeah," I said modestly.

"Wow," she said. "There aren't even any *eighth*-graders who like me."

"Oh, I'm sure there's lots of boys in your class who like you," I said. "You just have to find them."

"I don't think so," she said quietly. I wished she would pretend, as I was, for the sake of making this evening go more smoothly.

"Well, what should we do?" Elizabeth asked, sniffing. "Are you hungry?"

Elizabeth's parents were out for the evening, so we helped ourselves to the dinner her mother had left for us, spaghetti and meatballs, which we ate cold, right out of the serving dish. I felt trapped. My father wouldn't be picking me up until the next day. After we had watched two movies and dutifully consumed all the popcorn and candy, we went to bed. Elizabeth's mother had made up the trundle bed with fresh sheets for me. They had a strange flowery smell and felt coarse, unfamiliar. For the first time I could remember, I felt homesick.

"Did you want to use the phone before we go to bed?" Elizabeth asked suddenly.

"No," I said. "That's okay."

"I thought you might want to call your boyfriend to say good-night."

"We don't really do that. We don't talk on the phone that much. We see each other after school."

"Oh," Elizabeth said. "You probably think I'm so lame, I don't even know how you're supposed to act with a boyfriend."

"You can act any way you want," I said in a wise and reassuring tone. "The important thing is to be yourself."

"I've *been* being myself," Elizabeth pointed out. "Do you know I've never even been kissed?"

"It's not that big of a deal," I said knowingly. "I mean, when it happens, it happens."

"I know I shouldn't worry about it, but I can't help it. I know if it ever happens, I'll screw it up. I won't know what to do."

"Sure you will," I said confidently. "You don't have to do anything. He just kisses you, and you kiss back."

"Will you show me?" she asked, sitting up in bed.

"What, you mean like this?" I kissed the back of my hand. "It's just a kiss. Just like that."

"No, on the lips," she said shyly. "I mean, unless you think it's gross."

"No, I'll show you," I said, and sat up. I had come this far; I couldn't drop my confident act now. But I wasn't doing it just to save face—I actually wanted to show Elizabeth how to kiss, even though I didn't know myself.

"I'll be the boy," I announced, and without any hesitation or awk-wardness, I took her round face in my hands and kissed her, firmly, on the lips. At first she pursed her lips against mine, a false kiss, but then her mouth relaxed, and I could feel the square edge of her teeth under her lip, the moisture of her mouth. I tasted her toothpaste and, faintly under that, the organic taste of her breath, different from my own.

"There," I said decisively as I let go. "Now you've been kissed." Elizabeth smiled at me, a tranquil smile, the first real smile I'd seen on her all evening. We both lay back in our beds.

"You're right," she said. "It's not that big a deal. Did I do it right?"

"Of course," I reassured her. "You're a pro."

"Thanks, Dolores," she said after a few minutes. "I wish you were still in our class. You're my only real friend." We were both quiet for a long time. I could tell she was still awake.

"Dolores," she whispered, very quietly. I didn't answer. Soon I heard her breathing become louder and more regular.

I lay on the trundle bed for a long time, nowhere near sleeping. At some point in the night, I heard Elizabeth's parents come in, quietly take their turns in the bathroom, then close their bedroom door. Soon I sensed they were asleep too. I got up to dress quietly in the dark.

While I waited for the cab to arrive, I wrote Elizabeth a note. *I couldn't sleep and I didn't want to bother you. I'm going home to sleep in my own bed. I'll call you tomorrow. Thanks for everything. Dolores.*

I was waiting on the front steps when the cab pulled up. I gave the driver the address, and it was only about fifteen minutes later when we arrived at the Biersdorfers' house.

"This is it?" I asked. I remembered the house being much farther away.

"This is it," the driver said. He turned around in his seat to look back at me, and the vinyl squeaked loudly. "You want me to wait?"

"No," I said. I paid him with the money my father had given me.

The house looked even bigger than I remembered. Floodlights bathed tall exotic plants on the lawn. The houses on either side were set far away, so I could barely make out their shapes. Not like in my neighborhood, where we could hear the neighbors' air conditioners whirring as loudly as our own. All of the windows were dark.

In the back yard, a swimming pool that I didn't remember being there before shimmered palely, sending up waves of light over the back of the house. White wrought-iron furniture was grouped in clumps by the side of the pool, and I decided to sit in one of the chairs.

I watched the back of the house and thought of Eric sleeping inside. I thought about whether he had grown, whether he had changed. He might have become someone unrecognizable to me by now, the way some boys at school had decided, seemingly overnight, to become more aggressive, to stop smiling or showing any kindness. I tried to picture Eric with a hard look, his hair gelled, muscles bulked from working out. I couldn't actually imagine it. My thoughts of him would keep him pure, I hoped, my fantasies of how we would come together again. There were ten windows on the back of the house, and one hundred ninety-seven bricks across. Somehow I'd imagined once that Mr. Biersdorfer had brought my mother here. This was a ridiculous idea, childish, something Delia would imagine.

Toward morning a thin blue sunlight began to show itself through the trees. I imagined I could feel Eric's dreams, his dreams seeping out to wash over me in the back yard and disappear into the pool. I thought I could feel his love for me as he slept, a big reluctant love, alive and permanent. I enjoyed the feeling that no one knew where I was and no one was looking for me. I could go anywhere. People thought they knew where I was and what I was doing, but really, it was up to me.

"I have your OTAs," Dr. Schuler announced when we took our seats on Monday. "Most of you"—and now he was back to his old self, strutting and smirking—"most of you did not make full use of this opportunity to achieve. Most of you chose to remain largely ignorant of the workings of the physical world. The median grade for this class was fifty-eight."

He paused, looking out over us with a bemused look, while an outraged exhalation traveled around the room.

"A few of you, a sadly small number of you, took this opportunity to achieve according to even the most modest definition of the word. And only one of you"—and here he raised a single crooked finger—"*one* of you chose to seize this opportunity to actually achieve in a real way." He lifted above his head an OTA with the score marked in huge red numbers: 102. He was too far away for anyone to make out the name.

"Only one among you chose to acquaint herself with the workings of the physical world and to try to master the mathematical descriptions of those workings."

I heard annoyed hisses and groans from around the room as boys noted the *herself.* I started to flush then, imagining that he might mean me.

"This scholar not only demonstrated her thorough grasp of all the concepts we have explored thus far, she also distinguished herself by being the only student to correctly answer the extra-credit question on the gravitational constant."

"Cunt," a low voice said clearly from somewhere behind me. Everyone watched Dr. Schuler closely for a reaction. He hadn't heard, or else chose to pretend not to have heard.

"Are you still going to grade on a curve?" someone asked.

"What do you mean, still?" Dr. Schuler asked, perplexed. "This *is* the curve." He brandished the paper over his head again. With one bony finger of his free hand, he tapped the red circled number.

"One. Oh. Two. *That's the curve.* That is what a young mind from one of your peers is capable of. What one of you is capable of, all of you are capable of. I firmly believe that, scholars. This person, Miss One Oh Two, has set a standard. She has, as you say, ruined the curve."

Now I felt desperate for the OTA to be mine, even while I hoped not to be the person everyone else hated. I hoped that, if the 102 were mine, Dr. Schuler would wink at me as he handed me my OTA, facedown; we would share a knowing look before he worked his way down the row of desks. I was still lost in this scene, imagining exactly how Dr. Schuler would word his praise of my abilities later in private, when the actual Dr. Schuler took three quick steps forward and, with a lunge and a flourish, placed the OTA on my desk.

"Dolores Gray," he shouted. Every head in the room swiveled to stare at me. The blood rushed to my skin so quickly I felt my pulse thudding in my earlobes. My whole body shuddered with embarrassment, trying to shiver myself out of existence. I snatched the OTA from the top of my desk and shoved it into my notebook, as if by removing the evidence I could divert everyone's attention from me. For the rest of the class period, even as we started on new material, I still felt them all staring.

As I got up to leave after class, Dr. Schuler gestured me over to him.

"I hope you don't mind me making an example of you," he said in a low voice. Up close, his eyebrows looked even more wild.

"Young people often become very good at making excuses for themselves," he said, making a gesture to encompass the room behind me. He affected a lazy, whiny tone: "'I couldn't.' 'It was too hard.' 'It was impossible.' They start to believe their own excuses, you see. It's important for the others to know that it *is* possible to succeed."

I felt myself blushing horribly all over again.

"Tell me, Dolores. Are you interested in a career in science?" Dr. Schuler asked, raising his eyebrows. I wasn't sure what to say. No one had ever asked me what I wanted to do when I grew up in a way that didn't seem patronizing, half mocking. Dr. Schuler was studying me seriously, his eyes darting all over my face, the front of my shirt, my fingers on the strap of my backpack.

"I'm going to be an astronaut," I said, so quietly that he leaned forward to hear me.

"The astronaut corps!" he said warmly. "Well. That's quite an aspiration. The odds are certainly against you, but I admire your confidence. We'll have to talk about that sometime."

Tina and Chiarra drifted close to us, waiting for me to finish.

"Well, thanks," I said quickly. "I'll talk to you about that later," and hurried out of the room before he could answer.

"Well, Miss One Oh Two!" Chiarra crowed as soon as we got out into the hall. "'This is what a young mind is capable of!'"

"Shut *up,*" I said, grateful that Chiarra's tone was warm and affectionate. The other kids who were still filing out stopped to listen to our exchange.

"You got that extra-credit question?" Tina asked. "What the hell was that?"

"Oh, I don't remember," I said. "Some crap about Sir Isaac Newton."

Doug came shuffling dejectedly out to the hallway, and when he heard us discussing the test, he paused to listen, holding an OTA marked 79 under his arm.

"I can't believe you got those extra-credit points," he said. "I didn't even understand the question."

"She's so smart," Tina said, gazing at me.

"I wish you'd tell us your secret before the next OTA," Doug said. "I really have to do well in this class and so far I'm sucking at it."

"Her father is a physicist for NASA," Chiarra explained. "It's genetic or something."

"Jeez," Doug said. "How am I supposed to compete with that?" The look he gave me was not spiteful or condescending but friendly, even admiring.

STS 61-B, *Atlantis.*
Launch November 26, 1985, on schedule at 7:29 pm.
The crew deployed three satellites and conducted two six-hour spacewalks to demonstrate space station construction techniques. They were in space on Thanksgiving and ate a special turkey dinner.
My father took me to this launch.

"What do you think of this Teacher in Space?" my father asked Delia and me while we got settled in to wait for the launch. It was unseasonably cold for November, in the forties, so we huddled in the car with the heat on rather than get out and wait on the hood as we often did.

The next mission would be launching in only three weeks; the mission after that, 51-L, was scheduled for January 22 and would carry Christa McAuliffe, Judith Resnik, and five others.

"Not a real astronaut," I said dismissively. The day before, Delia and I had watched a TV special about Christa McAuliffe—Christa standing up at the chalkboard teaching her students with a broad smile, Christa trying out safety equipment in a swimming pool. Christa training for her upcoming mission in the KC-135, the plane that flies up and then plunges down again, simulating the weightlessness the astronauts will experience on *Challenger*. She stretched her arms out like a bird, kicked her legs up under her, and hovered in the padded cabin, a gleeful smile on her face. This is why they chose her, I thought, because she doesn't seem to think she's better than other people.

"I like her," said Delia distinctly now, in answer to my father's question. "I wish she was my teacher."

"I'm sure she's a fine *teacher*," I said, annoyed. "But she's not a real *astronaut*. Some people work all their lives to get to go to space, and she just gets picked. The way they pick Miss America." Delia listened, her face blank. "She doesn't even have a degree in science. It's not fair."

"I think she's nice," Delia said. "She'll teach kids about space."

"Delia likes her, Dolores doesn't," my father summed up. I knew he agreed with me.

"It's not that I don't *like* her, it's that she doesn't know what she's *doing*," I said, exasperated. "She'll jeopardize the mission." I could imagine Christa pushing the wrong buttons, asking stupid questions, getting in the astronauts' way.

But in the footage I'd seen of her training, I had to admit she did seem just as competent as the real astronauts. She floated in a pool wearing her flight suit and helmet, learning safety procedures, what to do in case of a water landing. She thrashed through the water with the same combination of determination and self-mocking as the others, wearing a huge smile all the while.

16.

DR. SCHULER KEPT ADMINISTERING HIS OTAS AS COMPETITIONS with a single winner, and I kept winning. I had gained a special awareness in the eyes of Dr. Schuler; when he asked a difficult question in class and no one else answered it, he saved me for last, a right answer he knew he could count on, and he called on me with a flourish.

"Ms. Gray!" he shouted, waving his chalk in the air with his impossibly long arm. "Perhaps you can settle this for us!"

I enjoyed answering in a calm, almost bored voice. I feared the effect this might have on my social standing, but I loved being right. I loved understanding what the others didn't; I loved seeing Dr. Schuler's smirk as he turned back to the blackboard to inscribe my words in large block letters. Then he turned to repeat them in a satisfied shout.

"The coefficient of FRICTION! THANK you, Ms. Gray."

Everyone looked at me in those moments, and I know I always blushed. But Tina and Chiarra made clear they didn't judge me for it; they claimed to find my ability in physics "cute." It was a decision I kept making, over and over again; I made it every night when I opened my physics book again and studied hard the way I did, learning not just all the terms and formulas but the derivations, the logic behind them.

It wasn't just that I wanted to please Dr. Schuler. When I turned a page and saw equations that didn't mean anything to me yet, impenetrable symbols, my heart gave a little skip with the anticipation of knowing I would soon understand them all. The wall of incomprehensibility would slowly dissolve. It wasn't anything as benign as intellectual curiosity. It felt more like arrogance, egotism, competitiveness pure and simple. I didn't just want to understand; I wanted to understand better than anyone else. I knew it must be the same for Eric. Even though it had been many months now since I'd seen him, I felt closest to him when I studied this way, felt almost that he was looking over my shoulder. I missed him most feeling that almost-understanding, that resistance, giving way in a warm rush of knowledge.

Then came my birthday and Christmas, our first without our mother. I turned thirteen on December 11, and my father bought and wrapped the things I'd written down for him: hair curlers, a Prince tape, a calculator.

For Christmas, my father tried to prepare all the foods my mother traditionally made, and we tried to enact all the normal activities—decorating the tree, cutting out white paper doilies to simulate snowflakes, watching the ancient animated Rudolph on TV. My father overcooked the turkey and undercooked the potatoes, and for the first time I could remember since my mother had left us, Delia cried for her.

"It's okay, D," my father murmured. "Hey, look at Dolores. She's not crying. She's having a nice Christmas."

But I felt the bleakness of everything too, the bleakness of our dim empty house, of the semi-apologetic way my father had of doing everything—looking in cookbooks for help cooking even the simplest foods, perching the sparkly star at the top of the Christmas tree at not quite the right angle.

"It's okay, Delia," I said. My father got up to clear the table. Delia, still weeping, struggled to finish her potatoes before he could take her plate away.

"She'll calm down when we open the presents," he told me quietly as we did the dishes together. And he was right: while we finished up in the kitchen, Delia opened her first present, a Barbie. She squealed with a rapture I could never remember having felt myself over any toy, over anything. My father must have stood in the girl aisles of the toy store, studying the shiny hot pink boxes of Barbies, laboring to discern the fine differences between the Barbies in order to pick the right one for Delia. He might have brought me with him to help, but he probably bought my presents on the same trip, and imagining what he might have bought me, what pains he might have gone to for me, I teared up.

"Oh, not you too," my father said good-naturedly. He shook off the pot he was washing and slung the dish towel over his shoulder to give me a hug.

"I'm fine," I said, and it was true. In the living room, Delia had fully recovered and was singing "O Christmas Tree" at the top of her lungs, lifting her Barbie over her head. We opened the rest of our presents, and my father had bought me a portable stereo for my room, just what I wanted.

STS 61-C, *Columbia*.

Launch attempt December 18, 1985, delayed one day to finish closing out *Columbia*'s payload bay.

Launch attempt December 19 scrubbed at T minus 14 seconds due to a problem with the right Solid Rocket Booster.

After an eighteen-day delay so the crew and workers could celebrate Christmas, a launch attempt January 6, 1986, was scrubbed at T minus 34 seconds. 4,000 pounds of liquid oxygen were accidentally drained from the External Tank. Two more delays due to weather and one more due to a problem in the Main Engine.

Launch January 12, 1986, at 6:55 am.

Congressman Bill Nelson flew on this mission. His district covers the Kennedy Space Center. My father says it was inappropriate for him to fly and that he will not vote for him again.

My father took me to the first and second launch attempts.

STS 61-C went through more attempts than any other mission had. We were all used to delays due to technical problems and weather, sometimes two or three delays stacking up together until visitors went from exasperated to angry and newscasters started to snicker and joke on the nightly news. I had thought I was above this, but 61-C was delayed so many times, for so many different reasons, that I started to feel the desperate frustration myself. When the fourth launch attempt was called off only nine seconds before liftoff because of bad weather at an abort site, my father and I threw our hands up and groaned like the tourists. *Bad weather in Africa!* We heard people yell at each other in disbelief. Part of the frustration came from the fact that this mission was meant to study Halley's Comet, and with every passing launch attempt, the window for pho-tographing the comet narrowed. The mission finally launched at the last possible moment to catch the comet, but once in orbit, the cam-era had battery problems and didn't work anyway.

Then it turned colder. Only a few times in my life had I felt true cold outside, a cold that made me huddle and shiver no matter how many sweaters I piled on, one over the other. A cold with a smell, narrow and sharp, so that when the cold would finally leave and the normal Florida smell came back, the air would taste broad and generous in the back of my throat, the smell of warmth and murky water and decaying green plants.

The mission with the schoolteacher, STS 51-L, was next and had been assigned a new launch date later in January. Everyone started talking about that mission, about Christa McAuliffe. TV crews, which had in recent years stopped showing up for launches, came out again to examine the shuttle and champion the astronauts, all because of the Teacher in Space. The area was swarmed with space tourists again, as it had been in the early days of the shuttle.

We watched a segment on TV together about the upcoming mis-sion: brief snippets of interviews with the crew members. Judith Resnik, wearing a nice dress and makeup, answered questions about traveling with the Teacher in Space.

Then we saw Christa—a piece from her appearance on *The Tonight Show.* She leaned toward Johnny Carson, laughing at some-thing he had said.

"I had a couple of teachers in school I wouldn't mind being sent into outer space," Johnny Carson deadpanned, and Ed McMahon shouted laughter. Christa smiled politely.

"I wonder how they picked her," my father said without interest. "Out of all the teachers in America."

"She won a contest," I said. "She's a social studies teacher. She teaches about the pioneers. Apparently she's going to keep a diary about being a pioneer in space. That's her big project: a diary. I bet she's never flown a plane. She probably can't even drive a stick shift."

My father chuckled, but something dark passed over his face. "That's not very nice," he said. "You shouldn't talk that way."

"Delia thinks she looks like Mom," I told him, watching closely for his reaction. His expression didn't change.

"I don't really see it," he said finally.

In physics, Dr. Schuler talked about the upcoming Teacher in Space mission nearly every day. I would have thought he would take an attitude toward it similar to my father's, but Dr. Schuler had applied to the Teacher in Space program himself and had made it to the semifinals, and as a result he found the mission to be of historic significance. He had written essays explaining why he should be the Teacher in Space and a proposal describing his project: a study on fluid dynamics in microgravity. Probably his project had been too scientifically rigorous, he told us; probably that was why he hadn't been chosen. Once Christa McAuliffe won with her diary proposal, Dr. Schuler said, he realized that he should have dumbed it down.

"You'll be able to tell your grandchildren that you were there when the first civilian astronaut was launched into space," he said in his documentary voice-over tone.

"She won't be the first civilian," Doug pointed out. Dr. Schuler looked surprised, and a bit annoyed, to hear from Doug. I was surprised too—I had thought I was the only one who knew that.

"Last year," Doug said. "A Saudi prince flew on 51-G."

"Is that true?" Dr. Schuler asked, screwing up his face to show his skepticism. Doug nodded.

"Just on the last mission, 61-C, they sent a congressman from Florida," I mentioned.

"And a year or so ago, they sent a senator from Utah. He got really space sick," Doug added.

"A senator? Why would that be?" Dr. Schuler asked.

"He's on the Space Appropriations Committee," I answered.

Dr. Schuler clearly felt he was losing control of the discussion.

"Well, it appears that NASA has previously sent some nonastronauts into space, for what sound like fundraising purposes. But this remains an historic occasion, the first time a civilian will fly for the purpose of instructing young people about spaceflight."

But once civilians started flying, I thought, how could we separate fundraising purposes from other purposes? Reagan had started talking about the Teacher in Space idea while he was running for his second term as President—Walter Mondale had pointed out his terrible record on education, and this had been Reagan's response, send a teacher into space. My father was horrified that NASA had gone along with the plan, but even more embarrassing was that everyone else had bought into it too.

The morning of the scheduled launch date for the Teacher in Space mission, Dr. Schuler dragged the TV on wheels into the classroom. We fell silent while he flipped through the channels, trying to find the local station broadcasting a feed from the Cape. We watched boring live footage for half an hour—the countdown clock running, people milling around in the VIP bleachers, the Launch Vehicle steaming against the launch tower.

The announcement finally came only a few minutes before the planned liftoff time: the launch had been scrubbed until the next day. Shots of spectators shouting with annoyance, packing up their things, shaking their heads at the Launch Control Building, their fists on their hips. Vice President Bush, the newscaster mentioned, must be annoyed; he'd made the trip all the way from Washington for nothing. The weather had turned in Senegal again. A cancellation due to bad weather, the newscaster intoned in his how's-that-for-irony voice, while in Florida it was a beautiful day.

Delay time began. I knew the schedule that had been planned for the mission: had it launched on time, by now the astronauts would be unpacking in weightlessness, preparing for Christa's first broadcast lesson. Instead, the launch was rescheduled for the next day. But that morning, before we even settled down in physics class, Dr. Schuler told us that the launch had been postponed yet again because the ground crews hadn't had time to prepare overnight.

Bad weather was predicted for Sunday, so the launch was postponed yet again, for Monday, January 27. But, as it turned out, they should have launched on the twenty-sixth after all; that turned out to be a beautiful day, cool and clear, not a cloud in the sky. My family watched the news that night while we ate dinner. The newscaster smirked; footage showed people out on the Cape looking up at the sky, shaking their heads, bewildered.

"Can't launch if the forecast says not to," my father pointed out to the TV.

"That's true," I said.

"So," my father said with such exaggerated nonchalance that I knew exactly what he was about to ask, "what have you been learning in physics class lately?"

I didn't know what to say. I thought again of Dr. Schuler brandishing my OTA over his head, Dr. Schuler crying, "Ms. Gray!" when he needed the right answer to a hard question. My father would be immensely proud if he knew how well I was doing in such a competitive class, but he would also miss the point. He didn't feel the desire to be better than everyone else, and I was just starting to understand that this was one difference between us.

"I don't know," I mumbled. "Just the basics, I guess."

"Hmm," my father said thoughtfully, as if I'd just told him something interesting and mildly surprising. "Have you gotten to ballistics yet?"

"Yes," I sighed.

"That's great. In one dimension or two?"

I put down my fork, letting it clatter onto my plate. Because he had always asked for so little, those rare times when he pushed me for more, some bratty force took over me. He always backed off from conversations with my mother whenever she warned him in her usual ways, through her tone, her expression, her movements. If she banged one pan down on the stove, he left her alone for the rest of the evening. Why didn't he respect the same signals when they came from me?

"What is it?" my father asked carefully.

"I'm done," I said.

"You haven't finished your dinner yet," he said in a quiet, defeated voice.

"Well, I have a stomachache now," I said. "I don't want any more."

I went into the living room to lie on the couch. After he and Delia finished eating and he cleared the table, he came and sat down next to me. I'd been hoping he would; that was why I lay there and not in my room. For a minute or two I heard him breathing.

"Hey, D?" he finally asked. "Can I get you anything?"

"No," I said, not as hostile as before. He waited another long minute.

"Why does it bother you when I ask you about school?" he asked, making his voice gentle. "I'm not trying to *test* you, I'm just . . ." He breathed heavily, and I felt the shift of weight as he raised his hands in a helpless gesture.

"I'm just curious about what you're learning. Okay?" his voice was weak and raspy. I didn't answer.

"I just think it's important, what you're learning at this stage in your life. I remember it was right around your age that I started doing badly in school. I didn't do anything terrible, I didn't fail any classes, but I started goofing off. I started making excuses for myself. I guess I didn't take it very seriously, because I didn't know how important it would be later. And I want you to have the chance to do everything I was never able to do."

I felt a disorienting shift in my ideas about my father. He had this story about failure, locked away in some drawer labeled FAILURE in his mind, and he had waited my whole life to tell me about it. I didn't know how to answer him, so I didn't. I kept my breathing soft and even so he would think I was asleep. But he sat there for a long time before he finally left.

––––––––

I woke from a dream about my mother. She was sitting in the passenger seat of our car; I was in the backseat. We were flying down the road, but no one was behind the wheel.

"It was nice to see you," she said, but not to me; she was looking sadly through the windshield. I knew somehow that she was talking only to my father.

Then the dream changed and I was lying on my stomach while my father rubbed my back the way he used to when I was little and had trouble sleeping. Slowly, I became aware of him, his weight on the bed, the sleepy smell of him in his pajamas.

"You awake, D?" he finally asked. I was. I turned over to look at him.

"What's wrong?" I asked. "What time is it?"

"Nothing's wrong," he said. "Do you want to go out and see the launch this morning?" I stalled for time by rubbing my eyes and looking at the clock.

"We don't have to," he added. "It's up to you."

"When is it going to launch?"

"Nine thirty-eight."

"I have school."

"You'd just miss the first couple of classes. I'll get you there by eleven."

I was tired, and I didn't want to miss physics. But I loved seeing the launches, and this was a special one. I knew that later I would want to be able to say that I had been there.

"Okay," I said, and rolled out of bed. I woke Delia and coaxed her into her clothes.

We drove out to the Cape in silence. Red taillights gathered in the dark—more cars than I had seen for a launch since the first test flights. People milled around talking, shouting, eating, blasting music out of their car radios.

My father and I got out of the car, leaving Delia to sleep in the backseat, and we sat on the hood with a blanket over us. The hood was still warm from the engine, and the combination of this warmth and the unseasonably cold air was pleasant. Across the river, the stack was lit up dramatically; as always, it was hard to imagine that soon it would actually lift off the ground.

"Great day for a launch," my father said. A meaningless claim, he had taught me long ago: if the launch hadn't been called off, then by definition it was a great day for a launch.

"Nice and clear," he added when I didn't answer. "That's one thing about the cold. It's always nice and clear. Good launch weather."

I watched the countdown clock—the same big orange numbers that Eric and I had watched together at the *Discovery* launch. The hundredths of a second skittered by too fast to read.

"January twenty-seventh," he said. "Did you know the Mercury accident was nineteen years ago today?" I knew all about the Mercury accident; he'd told me about it a million times. I also knew what he wanted from me now: he wanted me to ask him questions so he could tell about it again. I thought of the reporter from Ohio he'd met here six months ago, the fascinated attention he'd paid my father. I said nothing.

"Sure doesn't seem like that long ago," he continued. He paused, looked at me out of the corner of his eye. "It was a fire, you know, during a launch rehearsal on the pad. The hatch wouldn't open from the outside. Can you believe that?" He shook his head in wonder, as if just hearing the news for the first time. "The hatch. Just . . . a *door.* Maybe the simplest part on the whole spacecraft. Some people said we should have ended manned spaceflight right then, that it wasn't worth the risk." He waited again, a polite moment, for me to respond. When I didn't, he went on.

"We lost three astronauts that day. Including the one I liked best."

"The one you liked best?" I echoed, surprised. "Which one?" My father had never mentioned having a favorite astronaut before.

"Gus Grissom."

I could picture Gus Grissom; his portrait was in some of my astronaut books. He had a sad face—full downturned lips, big soulful lidded eyes.

"Did you know him?" I asked.

"No, never met him. In those days, the astronauts spent some of their time in the VAB, leading tours of politicians and journalists. So I saw him sometimes. He was educated as an engineer. I guess I liked that about him, that he was an engineer and not just a thrill jockey like some of them. He was just more shy and reserved."

"He looked just like you," I said, and once I'd said it I realized how uncannily true that was—my father had those same drooping lids, the same tragic-yet-bemused look, even the same crew cut. My father gave a smile.

"Really," I said. "You look just like him. You should have been an astronaut too."

My father gave a little laugh.

"I never wanted to be an astronaut," my father said quietly. "Most men my age did, you know. But I wanted to work on it. That was more important to me than flying.

"I hope you can grow up to do more than I did," he said. "You've got the brain for it. You might grow up to design a better engine. You might solve the liquid fuel problem. You might design the Mars transport. It's going to be your generation, D, that goes to Mars."

I could have kept quiet. I could have agreed.

"I'm not going to be an engineer," I announced. "I'm going to be an astronaut."

"That's what you said when you were a kid. But as you get older, you're going to see what it would mean to be an engineer. You're going to want the intellectual challenge."

"Why would I work my whole life just so someone *else* gets to go to space?" I spat. "*I'm* going to Mars. I'm not going to be a stupid engineer, and I'm *certainly* not going to be a sucker technician, getting laid off for no reason after years of work."

My father nodded, his face neutral, and folded his hands in front of him. I watched him as he looked out toward the launchpad and listened to the calls of Launch Control, waiting patiently for the launch to start and change the subject for us.

When the announcement came over the speakers that the launch had been scrubbed yet again, I felt the decision to be somehow passing judgment on us, on our family.

My father dropped Delia off at her school, but then he forgot to take me to mine, or else he had decided not to. When we got home, I fell asleep on the couch, all the long blank afternoon with the TV burbling in the back of my consciousness. I woke up when Delia got home from school. The sun was setting, and my father was sitting next to me on the couch. I watched his profile, tired and blank, while the news made fun of NASA. His face looked the way it always had in the blue light, tired but falling in all its normal shapes and folds. He smiled at me when he saw my eyes were open.

"Let's go to the mall," my father whispered, his voice quiet like a dream.

We ate dinner in the Food Court. My father told me what he'd heard on the news about the scrubbed launch: a tool used to close the hatch to the crew capsule had broken off, like a key breaking in a lock. After hours of struggle with a hand saw, an electric drill had finally been authorized for use, but all of the batteries in all of the drills on the pad were close to dead. By the time the hatch handle was extracted, the weather had turned windy and the launch had to be scrubbed. I knew my father was remembering our conversation about the hatch and the Mercury accident, that he thought the similarity was eerie. I kept my face blank.

"Why didn't they just use an electric drill in the first place?"

"Well, it seems simple enough that you should use a drill, but when you have tons of rocket fuel sitting out there, you don't want to fire up an electrical device right next to it unless you have to."

He stopped to take a breath and shove some french fries into his mouth.

"And the thing with the batteries! Did you hear that on the news, saying that we sent up eight batteries for the hand drill, all of them dead? As if all these guys working on the Mobile Launch Platform show up for work with bad equipment? They forgot to mention that when it's freezing cold, batteries have a tendency to die."

"Can we go again tomorrow?" I asked. My father looked confused for a second, woken out of his story.

"I don't think so," he said.

The three of us walked slowly through the mall to get back to our car. There was something about the mall that I resisted now, something that ran counter to physics and the hard, sterile comfort of the space shuttle. Judith Resnik wouldn't spend all of her time in a mall;

she was somewhere real, reading about physics, practicing the piano, doing sit-ups; every thought, every action, pointed toward the future.

My father took Delia into a clothing store while I sat on a bench outside reading my physics book. I pretended to be sulking; otherwise, he might not feel he had to balance things by buying something for me too. I finished the chapter we were working on in physics; then I had the idea to flip back to the first chapter to read it again. *Gravity,* the book said, *is what keeps everything—houses, trees, your school, even you—from flying off the face of the Earth and into outer space.* The fake trees in the mall were hung with white lights left over from Christmas. Faraway music played. Suddenly the air around me felt cold. I shivered and closed the book.

My father and Delia were at the back of the store, lined up at the counter. My father stood frozen with his credit card outstretched toward the frozen cashier. My sister rested her chin on the glass counter and the rest of her body drooped away from it as if she'd been shot with a tranquilizer. The two of them stood fixed; somehow I had frozen them like that. Fake violins played on as my father and sister stood motionless. But then they moved: Delia kicked her foot against the floor, the cashier finally took the credit card from my father's hand, which he dropped nervously to his side. But the chill remained, and as we pushed our way out the ten glass doors, we felt the cold wind blowing outside, colder than I'd ever felt, and we all huddled together as we ran out to our car. The cold felt like something menacing, like something that meant us harm. My father put on the heat in the car. It blew unfamiliar in our faces, hot and dry.

That night, I wrote up the launch attempts for this mission so far in my space notebook.

STS 51-L, *Challenger.*
Launch attempt January 22, 1986, slipped to January 23, then January 24, due to delays on the previous mission, 61-C.
January 24 attempt delayed one day due to bad weather at transoceanic abort site.

January 25 attempt postponed one day to let launch processing crews at Kennedy prepare.

January 26 attempt postponed to January 27 because of predicted bad weather.

January 27 attempt scrubbed when hatch closing handle could not be removed from the hatch.

My father took me to the fifth attempt.

17.

DR. SCHULER PULLED THE TV ON ITS CART INTO THE ROOM AND positioned it up at the blackboard where he usually stood. He drew the blinds so we could see the TV better, but light leaked in pink at the edges of the windows. We watched the astronauts emerge into the day, waving, single-file. We knew they had eaten a breakfast of steak and eggs together while photographers snapped their pictures. We watched the seven of them emerge from the Operations and Check-out Building for the ceremonial walkout to a rising cheer and the flashes of cameras. We watched them climb into their strange silver van, one by one, ducking their heads to get in, flashes punctuating their smiling and their awkward gestures.

We all knew about the elevator they rode up to the top of the stack, the White Room where they waited their turns to climb through the hatch. The astronauts are tipped onto their backs for launch, the entire crew cabin pointing toward the sky. We knew about the white-coated technicians whose job it was to strap them violently into their seats, then wish them godspeed and seal the hatch.

The planned launch time of 9:38 came and went. This was the hardest part, the waiting. I imagined myself as Judith Resnik: for a mission specialist, there was nothing to do during the wait—no sensors to monitor, no controls to adjust, no plans to review. She sat tipped on her back, wiggling her feet now and then to keep them awake, talking with the crew and the ground. Sitting on the mid-deck and wearing a helmet, she couldn't see any of the others, and if they all fell silent for too long, it became weirdly possible to imagine that she was entirely alone up there, miles from any other living soul, the empty static in her headset loud as swimming underwater. Judith Resnik was always the one to break the silences—she'd complain about the wait, crack some joke. She was reassured by the sound of her own voice echoing back through the headset. And then the warm responses of the others, their voices layering over one another, and all was well.

We counted down along with the NASA announcer, and when the countdown reached T minus six seconds, we saw the Main Engines ignite, the Launch Vehicle bucking in place against its restraints. We held our breaths at the moment of ignition, that strange fire and shudder. At *one, liftoff,* the bolts detached and I felt the thunderous force of the rockets.

After so many delays, it was finally happening. We saw the ship struggle against gravity and lift itself slowly, clearing the tip of the launch tower. For one long minute, the shuttle rose on a fat column of puffy smoke, rising and gradually tilting itself, executing its slow, lazy roll. We knew it to be moving, but it appeared to be stationary, jiggling only slightly in the camera's frame.

The explosion was subtle but unmistakable to people who had seen previous launches, and we had seen many of them. The rising exhaust trail popped into a ball of smoke; then two contrails arched away, carving a white Y onto the cloudless sky. Then there was nothing.

The Solid Rocket Boosters were supposed to jettison at T plus two minutes, but the elapsed time was only seventy-three seconds. A tiny confused cheer went up on the TV at the moment of the puff of smoke—those people thought the boosters had dropped off early. But we knew better.

I wondered what this would feel like to Judith Resnik—an unexpected bang and shudder, then a low thrum as the Main Engines take over and the vehicle slows. The pilot would have to do an RTLS,

Return to Launch Site, circling the vehicle around and landing it on the runway at Kennedy. This had never been attempted.

But then where was the shuttle? The camera searched and searched the sky, crazily panning and tilting, picking up bits of building, the ocean at the edge of Merritt Island, a palmetto tree, a bird flying low over the causeway.

I thought of Eric, the way we had stood together at the launch site and watched *Discovery* tear into the sky. I wondered where Eric was watching this now, and wondered whether he thought of me.

The announcer spoke again in his authoritative, noncommittal voice: "Flight controllers here looking very carefully at the situation . . . obviously a major malfunction."

A rustle went through the physics room at these words. None of us had ever seen a major malfunction. That was an old term, left over from Apollo, when major malfunction was purely hypothetical. Launch Control had never lost sight of a ship at launch.

The camera, not finding the shuttle, searched the people in the bleachers. Acres of faces tipped up, squinting against the sun, shivering in the cold. Christa McAuliffe's son Scott had brought his whole third-grade class to the launch. The kids all looked up at the sky, confused, then at their teacher. She was young and blond. She had her hand over her mouth. The loudspeaker crackled something, and the NASA announcer repeated it: "We have no downlink . . ."

Now Christa's parents were in the camera's frame. Bundled against the cold, they weren't sure what they were being told, and their fixed, proud smiles were becoming crossed with confusion. They spoke to each other briefly without taking their eyes off the sky, inclining their heads together.

The announcer's voice came on again: "We have a report from the flight dynamics officer that the vehicle *has* exploded," he said in the same tone he had used to report the wind speed. "Flight director confirms that. We are looking at checking with the recovery forces to see what can be done at this point." Christa's father took off his hat and clutched it to his chest.

Some kids around me said, "Oh!" a shock like someone had poured cold water over them. Dr. Schuler still stood with his back to us, never taking his eyes off the TV. We all watched the edge of his face for some reaction. He only flexed his jaw muscle; we could see the shadow of it standing out in the glow of the screen. I looked around the room at the other kids, their eyes sparkling, their cheeks flushed with the euphoria of disaster. The TV was still on when we ran outside. We got up, leaving our books and notebooks and pencils behind, and ran past the teachers, ran down the hall, and banged out the double doors to the athletic field, where other classes already stood in clumps out in the cold, their heads tipped back. We stopped, dizzy, to look up. The accident was all over the sky.

I'd forgotten that it was cold outside; the smell and feel of it kept shocking me. I stood on the grass and looked up, feeling as though I had been out there looking up all day, as though I had been born and raised only to look up. It made me dizzy to see it. On TV, the explosion had been such a neat and tidy Y shape, white against blue, simple to understand, but out here it was distorted and misshapen, sickeningly three-dimensional—the arms arced out away from us, raining debris into the ocean. A kid behind me said he could see one of the astronaut's bodies falling, that he could make out a speck with arms and legs, but we knew he was lying. It was too far away.

The teachers shivered out on the athletic field, pulling their cardigans tighter around themselves. We stood a distance from one another and planted our feet wide, as people do on unstable ground. It felt like entering a strange room in a dream, everything's place unknown and sickeningly familiar. The monkey bars in the playground across the street stood out against the sky, and it was embarrassing how I had played on them, laughing stupidly as if everything would always be for the best. Behind them now were vertical streaks, hundreds of them, white and crazed, and we followed the streaks up to where they met the Y. Each piece took forever to make its way crookedly down to the horizon, trailing a bright white ribbon of smoke. We stood and watched them all until only the trails were left melting. No one told us to go back to class.

Some time later, I found myself crouching with my head between my knees. I could see the steam of my breath gathering and then drifting away. Sets of shoes walked through the grass. Some of them approached me, then politely steered around me. One pair stopped, large black men's shoes. A hand dropped onto my head.

"Feeling faint?" Dr. Schuler's low voice said. He sounded strangely muffled because my knees were pressed against my ears. I made no move to answer.

"You should go to the nurse's office if you feel you might pass out," he said. His voice was distant, authoritative. The warm print of his hand weighed like a secret thought on my head. I waited, crouching silently, until he slowly pulled it away and I heard the shoes scuffle across the grass, back to the open door of the school.

I wasn't thinking about the astronauts then, or about technical causes or the public reactions, the inevitable layoffs, not until later. Instead, I remembered my first memory, which was of lying on the floor watching TV with my father and not understanding anything I saw. It was a memory I often used to soothe myself: the warm light and the burbling voices, my father's steady concentration, his steady breathing. My mother would be in and out of rooms, a snarl of smoke. I remembered the grim gaiety of the children's shows, animated, the bits of color and sound. The old movies from the fifties with their black and white laugh tracks, the women always wearing dark lipstick, their lacquered hair. Game shows, late night, music and glum enthusiasm, applause, applause, and a man in a blue suit all in garish color, standing on a stage with his hands in his pockets. The safety of knowing that even if this was meaningless to me, it made sense to my father.

I worried about how I must look squatting down like that, a little ball of a girl curled on the ground. I could imagine my curved back, shoulder blades protruding, my brown ponytail curling around my neck, my thin arms wrapped around my knees. I was not Judith Resnik. I felt the dullness of being, again and forever, myself—breathing my own breath, thinking my own thoughts. There was no escaping it. Again I thought of Eric, of his breath and his thoughts, and this time I felt sure he was thinking of me too, right at that moment, and that we could achieve some telepathy this way. *I miss you,* I tried to send him. *No one sees me but you.*

More feet walked toward me, then around. I wondered what people must think of me. Perhaps they thought I just wanted attention, that I was exaggerating my own reactions the way some girls did, to make a general disaster into something about themselves. I stood up and dusted myself off.

Inside, I found the hallways filled with students. Kids stood together in groups, their arms crossed, talking about launch criteria, budget cuts, whether the astronauts had been killed instantly or not, whether the shuttle had been sabotaged by the Iranians or not. From a row of three pay phones snaked three lines of kids waiting to talk to their parents. I walked down the hall to the lunchroom, where more kids huddled around a TV that someone had rolled in from one of the classrooms. A shot of the bleachers, now nearly empty of spectators, and beyond it, the countdown clock still running, oblivious, its huge orange numbers still counting the elapsed minutes of the mission. T plus one hour seven minutes. An anchorman who had sweat through his makeup was saying over and over that there had been an explosion of the space shuttle *Challenger,* that all seven astronauts were missing and feared dead. We stood for a long time and watched him talk, listened with care to every word he told us, though he didn't know a thing we didn't.

18.

THE BUS JERKED AND SWAYED US AS IT ALWAYS HAD ON THE RIDE home. We leaned with it, this way and that. We were almost completely silent. The sound of the bus's gears grinding, an old and familiar sound, was now new and dangerous, the sound of impending mechanical failure. One kid in the back kept yelling, "They blew it up, they blew it up!" Everyone turned to look at him, and he looked giddy, clutching the seat in front of him as though on a roller coaster cresting the highest peak. His friends laughed as quietly as they could, frantically shushing him.

I let myself into the house and walked around it aimlessly, unable to settle down anywhere. The living room looked strange to me now, all our furniture squatting in its usual places on the carpet. It seemed a million years since I'd seen it that morning, back when the shuttle was still safe and ordinary. I walked around the house as if it were someone else's.

I found my space notebook and opened it to the picture I had torn from a magazine before the launch, before its subjects' faces became famous for being the faces of the dead. It was a formal NASA portrait showing the seven astronauts in their blue jumpsuits, posing at a draped table with a plastic model of the ship. An American flag huddled discreetly in the corner. The astronauts smiled in the photo, and there was something strange about their smiles; not posed or awkward, they were real smiles, slightly goofy. It seemed the seven of them were amused by the prospect of going on this journey together, like a long car ride. They wore patches bearing their last names and held their space helmets in front of them.

In the eternal present of the photo, McNair holds his helmet gingerly on both sides, slightly away from his body, like it's a full fishbowl. Jarvis, wearing a gleeful smile, grips his as if it's a helium balloon that may get away from him. McAuliffe holds hers to one side, a little awkwardly, smiling distantly, like it's somebody else's baby. Resnik smiles a smile so pleased it's smug. She holds hers out to us balanced on her straightened fingers, like it's a gift.

I flipped through the notebook, moving backward through all the launches, back to the very first. I saw dozens of times launches had been delayed or scrubbed due to problems with the Main Engines, Solid Rocket Boosters, heat tiles, the External Tank, the onboard computers, safety contingencies, payload, launchpad facilities. Every mission was a list of possible failures. Somehow, the constant presence of those failures had made it seem that nothing could ever really go wrong.

I went into my parents' room. It had a warm, musty smell with traces of my mother's perfume. I sat on their unmade bed for a while looking around to see whether any of her things had moved, whether anything had been taken or put back. Nothing had.

I looked in my mother's bottom bureau drawer; the carton of cigarettes was still there. I selected a pack and turned it over in my hands, not sure yet whether I was going to take it. The cellophane was dry and satiny in a way that plastic is for only a short time, until the touch of hands makes it greasy. Something about the shape and size of the pack comforted me. I took it and hid it at the bottom of my desk drawer.

By the time Delia got home, I was switching from channel to channel, looking for new information. Delia's teacher had told her class that the space shuttle was "missing," a euphemism that had confused Delia thoroughly.

"Probably they'll find it today," she assured herself, going into the kitchen to look for a snack.

"I think they know where it *is*," I said. The rescue planes had had to wait over an hour for debris to stop falling before they could move into the area to search. By that time, heat tiles and lighter pieces of debris were already washing up onto beaches.

Delia stopped in her tracks, turned, and asked, "Where is it?"

"You're so stupid, Delia," I said. "Never mind."

On the TV, a local newscaster insisted that, compared to other launches, *Challenger* had risen significantly more slowly. He speculated that maybe the External Tank hadn't held enough fuel. Experts offered other theories: the computers had malfunctioned; the heat tiles had been damaged by ice; a breach inside the External Tank had allowed the two fuels to mix; Christa McAuliffe had panicked and pressed the wrong button; some malicious person had committed sabotage. Computer experts expressed concern that none of the onboard computers had corrected the problem, whatever it had been, or even picked up on it. NASA denied any connection between the explosion and the unusual cold.

Again and again, the white trail of smoke climbed jumpily, then popped and split into two trails. That image would later become iconic of the disaster, overexposed into cliché, drained of horror, but in its first moments and days, it was still a shock each time to see it, still the experience of watching failure, watching people's deaths. Each time, as *Challenger* muscled its way toward the top of the screen, it seemed that everything would be normal this time, and each time I was shocked all over again to see it explode.

Over and over, the camera zoomed in on different pieces of debris, zoomed in on the Solid Rocket Booster that broke off and shot to the right, painting its white trail against the blue sky. I watched the right-hand rocket, the white casing that I had seen up close, that my father had touched and assembled. That rocket broke off and arced crazily, traced a new, wrong trail, then popped into a cloud, its self-destruct explosives having been triggered by a signal from the ground. The camera zoomed in and in, trying to find some telling detail, and the picture became blurred, white pixels and gray pixels and pink pixels separating themselves and blurring into one.

The walkout repeated over and over, the shot of the seven astronauts leaving Operations and Checkout that morning and waving for the cameras—Delia and I studied that moment each time we saw it, as if we hadn't already seen the same thing a million times before. We wanted to see the astronauts waving and smiling optimistically; it made us feel that they were still all right.

Over and over again, the Y in the sky, the "If you are just joining us," the "Authorities are still unsure." The summaries were the same each time, but each time we listened closely, hoping to catch some word, some intonation that would betray some new piece of information. The news anchors looked gravely into our eyes, their voices and expressions communicating their displeasure with us, with our accidents, with our failure. They were like stern parents; they were sympathetic for our loss, but they could not condone this oversight. We had been far too careless this time.

President Reagan appeared, sitting at his desk in the Oval Office. I got out my space notebook to take notes.

"He's nice," Delia said preemptively. She loved the President fiercely and got upset when our mother had called him names. Reagan adjusted himself at his desk, refolded his hands. He spoke, warm and firm. The astronauts were heroes, he told us; we had to carry on in their names.

"And I want to say something to the schoolchildren of America," he said, his voice smooth and brown as gravy. He gazed right into the camera, his face lined with concern. As always, his cheeks were oddly rosy.

"I know it's hard to understand," Reagan said, "but sometimes painful things like this happen."

"You are aware that he's cut NASA's funding every year he's been President?" I asked Delia. She and Reagan ignored me.

"The future doesn't belong to the fainthearted," Reagan said slowly. "It belongs to the brave."

"The future doesn't belong to the faint-farted," I said for Delia's benefit.

She smiled warily. "He's nice," she repeated. "He's my favorite President."

"You can't remember any other President," I reminded her. I had only a dim recollection of Jimmy Carter myself, a slow-talking man with a big smile and a wide tie.

"The crew of the space shuttle *Challenger* honored us by the manner in which they lived their lives. We will never forget them, nor the last time we saw them, as they prepared for their journey and slipped the surly bonds of Earth to touch the face of God."

"'The face of God'?" I yelled at the TV. "What's *that* supposed to mean?"

Delia looked up at me, worried. I was surprised by my sudden anger at Reagan for implying the astronauts' being vaporized in a fireball was a good thing, like they were lucky to have died that way.

"'The face of God,'" Delia repeated.

Delia and I watched TV for six hours that night, never moving, as the sun set and our father didn't come home. Everything in the living room turned redder, then grayer, then faded until it was dark. Every channel announced that the State of the Union address, scheduled for that evening, had been canceled due to the national tragedy.

"Do you know what happened, Delia?" I asked her once it was so dark I couldn't see her face clearly, just the white of her cheeks in the reflected light of the television.

I could feel her looking toward me, wondering whether I was somehow tricking her. "There was an accident," she said carefully.

"That's right," I said. "An accident."

"An explosion," she added. "Something went wrong with Daddy's space shuttle."

"That's right," I said.

A while later, she asked, "Are they dead?"

"Who?" I asked, though of course I knew who she meant.

"The people," Delia said. It seemed such a childish word to use. *Here is the church and here is the steeple.* On TV, we had seen footage of Coast Guard boats on the ocean, searching for survivors. We had seen the water moving with a layer of twisted debris, smashed pieces of the ship, heat tiles floating.

"I think so," I said. "I'm pretty sure they're dead."

Long after dark, we heard the front door open. Delia looked at me, her eyes wide. We knew it was my mother even before she appeared

in the glow of the TV; we recognized her way of opening the front
door, her way of jingling her keys. We heard her in the entryway,
fumbling with her coat and then her shoes, one clunking onto the
floor after the other. She crept into the living room, and we could
make out only the nimbus of her hair, the shiny material of her dress
where it fell across her shoulder, the swishing of her skirt. She moved
as quietly as she could, heel to toe, as if someone were sleeping or
sick, and she did not turn on a light.

"Girls," she whispered.

"Yeah," Delia whispered back.

Our mother knelt in front of us where we sat on the sofa. She
looked pink and youthful; her eyes sparkled as she turned her face
quickly from me to Delia and back again. "Girls," she said again. "I've
missed you."

Neither of us said a thing; we just watched her.

"Your dad asked me to come over tonight," she said. It felt odd to
hear her explain, as if we would challenge her right to be there. "He'll
have to be at work a long time tonight. Maybe all night. Do you
know about what happened today?"

I felt a surge of anger. Were we not sitting in front of the television, upon which the space shuttle blew up repeatedly?

"Yeah," whispered Delia again.

My mother looked at me, her eyes darting back and forth, searching mine.

"Did your dad take you out to see the launch today?" my mother
whispered to me.

Somehow, it hadn't occurred to me that I could have been at the
launch, could have seen it live and in person on NASA grounds. I was
infuriated anew that, after driving out for two failed attempts, after
sitting through dozens of failed attempts over the years, I had missed
the only one I really needed to see firsthand.

I got up and left the room, feeling my mother and Delia watching
me go. I paused in the hallway, listening to hear what they would say
about me. But neither of them spoke. I heard only the rustle of my
mother's dress as she reached out to Delia, the quiet creak as she
rocked her on the couch. I stayed in my room until my mother called
me in to eat. She had found some pizza in the fridge and warmed it

up, and she and Delia sat eating in front of the TV. She smiled shyly at me as I sat down, a smear of grease on the corner of her mouth. I made an effort not to smile back.

As we ate, the phone rang. Delia and I looked at each other, but my mother sprang up to get it. I could tell by her voice that she was talking to my father. She asked him rushed, breathless questions.

"Do they think that's what it was, Frank?" my mother asked after a long pause. Her voice was hard with fear. "Do they think it was the rockets? *Your* thing?" She listened for a long time, nodding. I watched her face, waiting for some clue. The worst of all explanations would be the Solid Rocket Boosters. Then my father would not only be affected, he might actually be blamed.

"Okay," she said many times with pauses in between. "Okay. Okay."

"There's no reason to believe it had anything to do with the rockets," my mother repeated to Delia and me once she had hung up. "It was most likely the Main Engines."

"It could have been anything," I corrected. "The Main Engines, Solid Rocket Boosters, External Tank, fuel lines, anything. They really have no idea what happened."

"But your father said the Main Engines were most likely. He said they've had the most problems from the beginning, and that the way it exploded . . ." I could see her trying to reconstruct his exact words. "The way it exploded, it looks to him like Main Engine failure. He said if it had been the rockets, the shuttle would have exploded on the launchpad."

"That doesn't really prove anything," I said. "There are plenty of ways a rocket failure could develop after launch."

"Your father knows more about this than you do, D," she said, and smiled tightly. She sat on the couch again. She looked uncomfortable, I noticed; she couldn't change out of her work clothes. "We'll wait and see."

Wait and see sounded strange in her mouth. It was my father's phrase, not hers.

"So how have things been at the new school?" she asked me brightly. "We haven't really had a chance to talk about it."

"Fabulous," I said quietly. It was my new favorite word.

"Really?" My mother smiled uncertainly. She waited for me to say something more. I just glared.

"And you're keeping up with your classes and making friends?"

"Yeah, everything's great. The space shuttle blew up and now Dad will probably lose his job along with everyone else in central Florida. I don't know where my mother lives. Oh, and I'm failing English."

For a moment she stared at me, horrified. Even Delia sat up to look at me. My mother opened and closed her mouth a couple of times. I knew my mother wished my father were here now, to help her respond to my behavior. He would react appropriately, angry but not hysterical. He would send me to my room, then comfort her.

"Do*lores*," she said slowly, her voice low with hurt.

"What," I said evenly. I'd figured it out: all I had to do was not care what she thought of me. That easily, I had undone her.

Later, as I was getting into bed, I noticed movement in the dark. I'd thought Delia was asleep, but I could make out her standing outline, her fidgeting silhouette. I watched her hover by her bed, moving from foot to foot, trying to balance and thumping down. The voices on the TV reached us from the living room, although we couldn't make out what they were saying. We could hear our mother's voice as well—she was making phone calls every few minutes, murmuring with concern.

"Go to sleep, Delia," I hissed.

"Okay," she agreed, and she crawled into her bed, but I could hear her there, fidgeting and breathing loudly.

A while later, my mother came in and crept over to Delia's bed.

"Hey, duckie," she whispered. "Are you having trouble sleeping?"

"Yeah," Delia whispered back.

"How come?"

"They're missing," Delia said. "Are they going to be okay?"

My mother breathed in and out before she answered. "They might," she said, "We'll see." And then she sang a tuneless lullaby, just la-la-la. It was so dark I could hear the liquid clicking sounds inside her mouth while she sang.

"Dolores said they're dead," Delia said. I felt a jolt at hearing my name.

"Well, Dolores is probably right," my mother said. "But, you know, Delia, we can hope if we want to. She's probably right, but we can hope."

"Can we say a prayer for them?" Delia asked. I rolled my eyes in the dark. Delia had never set foot in a church in her life.

"Where did you get that idea, baby?" my mother asked. Delia didn't answer. I knew: from TV. People prayed all the time on TV, when they were worried about someone. The whole family praying together, clasping hands, heads bowed. That was the sort of thing Delia loved, just the look of it, even though she didn't understand the meaning.

"You can pray if you want to, Delia," my mother said finally. "You know what? It's good to have hope. It's good to think positive thoughts because sometimes that helps good things happen." It was just like the two of them, I thought, to believe that, even on a day like today.

I woke again in the middle of the night from busy dreams, plumes of smoke rising from playgrounds. For hours I'd been hearing through sleep the strange, familiar sound of my mother's voice, whether on the phone or talking to someone in the house, I couldn't tell. Now all was silent; she had finally gone to bed. (In the bed she used to share with my father? Would he sleep on the couch?) I took the pack of cigarettes from its hiding place in my desk and crept down the hallway. In the living room, my mother had left a mess of food and ashtrays. I took a lighter from the coffee table and slipped on a jacket before letting myself out the front door.

I'd thought about taking a cab to Eric's house again—thinking of him earlier in the day, I'd become almost convinced that he wanted to see me again too—but I couldn't risk leaving the house with my mother here. Out on the stoop, the cold air was oddly quiet. The cicadas sang their drifting song, but the usual thrum of air conditioners was missing; people had turned them off because of the cold. My fingers grew numb quickly, making it difficult to open the cellophane wrapper on the pack. I opened one edge, and the cellophane lifted off in a perfect box shape, the plastic clinging to my fingers. The top cracked open to reveal the cigarettes lined up in there, in two perfect rows, their ends snow white and marred by a few crumbs of tobacco. I drew out a cigarette slowly; it was surprisingly light, weighed almost nothing at all. Smokers somehow held them as if they had more substance to them, but the cigarette I held was light as air. I held it between my index finger and middle finger as my mother always did, as all women did.

It took me a few tries to get the lighter to work, and even when I had a pale yellow flame, I couldn't get the cigarette to light. I tried again a few more times before I figured out that I had to suck in at the same time. All this business of smoking was harder than it looked, and I thought of my mother's easy gestures, the fast click of her lighter, her quick suck of breath.

I had nearly finished the cigarette when my father's car pulled up slowly at the curb. He shut off the engine and turned off the headlights; I waved, still holding the cigarette, but he didn't seem to see me. He stared straight forward, his hands resting lightly on the inside of the steering wheel. My father was gathering himself before getting out of the car, waiting for something to settle. I had never seen him do this before. He seemed to be staring at a high branch that dipped toward the street, nodding vehemently in a sudden breeze. When he finally opened the car door, setting off the dome light and a faint pinging sound, he squinted at my left hand, looking at the cigarette for so long that I looked down at it myself, curious to see what it looked like. I flicked off a bit of ash.

"Dolores, what is that?" my father asked, his voice weary. As he stepped into the light, I saw that the bags under his eyes were heavier than usual, swollen and purplish. The skin hung on his face in exhausted folds.

"What, this?" I asked, holding it up for both of us to inspect. "Oh, don't worry about this. It's nothing." I was almost giddy. While he watched, I lifted the cigarette to my lips and took a drag. My father closed his eyes for a second and breathed a jagged breath as though the sight caused him pain.

"D, what are you doing?" He slumped against the side of the car, resigning himself to the fact that this conversation might take a while.

"Smokin'," I answered happily.

"This isn't like you," he said.

I didn't say anything, just examined the end of my cigarette and ashed carefully onto the grass.

"Should we go in?" he asked. "It's freezing."

"Mom is here," I said. He raised his eyes to the roof for a moment, then looked back down at his shoes. He nodded, a weak nod, a gesture without any authority. She was here, tomorrow she might be gone, back to wherever she had been, and he would do nothing to try to make her stay.

And for that, I decided to hate him. Like a key turning in a lock, I turned against my father. I dropped my cigarette into an old pile of my mother's butts behind a bush, stamped it out with a single twist of the toe as my mother did. Once I took my foot off it, I couldn't tell mine from hers, and that pleased me. My father nodded at it once, a nod that meant he wouldn't say anything to my mother about this if I didn't. We would agree to forget about it. I felt a premonition for the rest of my teenage years: whatever I did, he would find a way to absorb my hostility, cover it up. He would rather do that than have to react.

"How did you know where to find Mom?" I asked. "Have you known where she was all this time?"

"Your mother needs some time to herself," he said vaguely. "I try to respect her privacy."

"Where is she sleeping tonight?" I asked. "Are you sleeping in your room together? Or did she kick you out of your bed?" He opened his mouth, struggling to find a response.

"Are you just . . . maybe you're just upset, D. About what happened today. And you're just . . . expressing. . . . Maybe that's normal. But let me tell you, D, this isn't going to help."

"Why do you keep saying, 'what happened today'?" I demanded. "Why don't you just say 'the space shuttle exploded'?" He didn't react.

"What difference does it make?" he said. "You know what happened."

"Not really," I corrected. "I don't really know what happened. I saw the Launch Vehicle explode. And I assume the astronauts are dead. But it's *not* clear what happened. Maybe it was the Main Engines. Maybe it was a crack in the fuel line. Maybe it was the Libyans." I gathered my courage before saying the last piece: "Maybe it was your Solid Rocket Boosters. Your *joint rotation.*"

His eyes flicked to me for a second, and he opened his mouth as if to speak. But then he just rubbed his hand across his mouth and looked back down at his feet.

"So no, I don't know what happened. And how will they ever find out, with everything in pieces, burnt up on the bottom of the ocean?"

He had nothing to say to that, and his silence scared me so much I lost my nerve. I was ready to take everything back, apologize, beg to start over. But it was too late. He had finally shut himself off to me.

"Goodnight, Dolores," he said, and his stooped figure behind the screen didn't pause, but kept moving slowly, toward his bed.

I didn't sleep that night. I sat up paging through my space notebook again. The saddest pages were the early pictures of the first test launches, my childish handwriting and childish enthusiasm. *Launch attempt delayed,* I'd written. And, *Judith Resnik became the second woman in space.* And, *We met a reporter from Ohio.* And, *I saw this launch with my father, Eric Biersdorfer, and Mr. Biersdorfer, the Director of Launch Safety.* And, *My father took me to this launch.* Every launch was there, every astronaut to fly, every mission objective. Every time I made my way through the notebook, it was a surprise to turn the last page and find the picture of the seven *Challenger* astronauts, wearing their sky blue suits and smiling hard, looking for all the world like they were alive and well, up in space and playing a joke on us all.

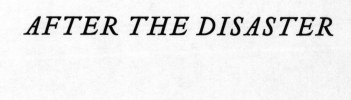
AFTER THE DISASTER

19.

WHEN I WOKE UP, THE HOUSE WAS QUIET. AT FIRST I FELT ONLY a vague impression of worry, but then I remembered that Y in the sky. The memory of it had the weird power of a dream, as did everything I remembered from the day before—my mother's face glowing in the light of the TV, Dr. Schuler's working jaw, the cackling kid on the bus, the chunks of grass under me where I had crouched, dizzy.

I got up and stumbled out to the living room. Delia sat at the kitchen table, quietly crunching cereal. When she saw I was awake, she picked up a note from the table and held it out to me, its ink bleeding in places where she had dripped milk onto it.

Dear D and D, it began.

My mother's handwriting showed that she had been agitated when she wrote it, the blue pen clenched in her fingers so hard her knuckles were stiff and drained of blood. My mother had always had trouble writing, even simple things like notes or lists; her words looked wrong to her written down; she got frustrated and forgot what she wanted to say. Delia looked over my shoulder, mouthed the words of the note as I read, but didn't speak them.

I was so happy to get to see my precious girls last night.
I am going to be away for a bit more and I hope that you

can understand. Take care of each other and I'll see you just as soon as I can. Love and kisses to you both,
    Mommy.

I read the note again. Her handwriting looked different on each line, sometimes cursive, sometimes print.

"Where did she go?" Delia asked after a while.

"Shh," I said. I was still reading, though by that time I had already read the note through four or five times. *Away for a bit more. My precious girls.* The last word was strange; we had never in our lives called her Mommy, only Mom. It seemed in her hurry to leave us again, she didn't quite remember us, only a vague impression of children.

"But she came *back,*" Delia pointed out with a faint note of protest.

"I know," I said. I understood how she felt. When a mother goes missing for six months and then comes back, we assume she's come back for good.

"She was only here because of the explosion," I said. "She only came back because it was an emergency."

"Oh," Delia said.

But where was she now? The more time that had gone by, the harder it was to keep her in any of the places I had chosen for her—hotels, motels, the Biersdorfers' spare room—none of it actually made any sense. And now that I'd seen her, remembered the specific sound of her voice and planes of her face, now it was even harder to imagine where she might be.

When Delia and I walked outside to catch our school buses, we found that the air had warmed ten degrees. We smelled the dirt smell of thawing, a spring smell. I wondered whether Eric was smelling this smell right now too, whether he was on his way to school and thinking about whether *Challenger* might still be fine if his father had decided to wait one more day. There was a weird Saturday feeling in the air, as if it wasn't really a school day, and I was almost surprised when the bus pulled up. The long ride to school was unusually silent; kids acknowledged each other with quick nods, then sat together without talking.

———

At school it was the same—everyone moved through the halls quietly, their conversations hushed, the words *Challenger, McAuliffe, NASA* muffled in their mouths. Everyone offered theories and dismissed theories with equal conviction.

"They said it wasn't the cold."

"But how could it have *not* been the cold?"

"Except they wouldn't have launched if the cold was a danger."

"I heard Greg Jarvis's father had a heart attack when it happened."

"I heard the Vice President is here."

"They should have sent the President."

"It had to have been the External Tank. All it would take is a breach in the wall and a spark. The thing is like a huge bomb."

"Sure, but no one's talking about how easy it would be to trip the remote self-destruct. All you'd have to do is crack the code."

I went to my locker and spun the combination. The familiarity of the motion comforted me. The scratched army green surface of the steel, the deep click when the lock disengaged, the way the door shivered in its hinges when it first stood open. My things, inside, just as I'd left them the day before. My limp jacket, unread books, crumpled old homework papers, all of them innocent of the disaster.

Tina and Chiarra came up behind me.

"My mother said I looked like a whore this morning," Chiarra drawled, examining herself in the magnetized mirror in my locker. She ran a fingernail under her eye, removing a green smudge. Then she turned to us and clapped her hands together in a businesslike way.

"Okay. So what have you guys heard about the accident? Tina?"

"Well, my dad was on telemetry?" Tina started. "He works in Launch Control. He wasn't watching the monitors right then, so he didn't know that anything had gone wrong? Some guy was, like, yelling, 'Where'd it go? Where's the bird?' But my dad didn't get what they were talking about? Because the telemetry was normal." With her finger, Tina traced the normal trajectory of the shuttle through the air, a gentle skyward lift.

"What the hell's telemetry?" Chiarra demanded. "And why would it still be normal? The space shuttle blew *up*."

"The debris," I guessed. "The pieces still had some momentum on them, so the sensors would show them still moving in the right direction."

"Wow," Chiarra said perfunctorily. "Did you guys hear that this launch was going more slowly than the others or something?"

"I heard that, but then I heard it actually wasn't true. Dolores, what have you got? What did your dad say?"

"I don't know, I haven't talked to him yet," I lied. I didn't want to talk about my father or his Solid Rocket Boosters. "He didn't come home last night."

Tina and Chiarra nodded gravely at this.

"Your dad must have a more important job than mine," Tina observed. "Mine came home at four in the morning or something." I didn't mention that my mother had come home, of course; they didn't know that she had been gone in the first place. I wondered whether Mr. Biersdorfer had been at the Space Center all night like my father, whether Eric had waited for him to come home.

I looked around Dr. Schuler's classroom, waiting for class to begin. Like my house, it looked different now somehow, bright and bare. Only twenty-four hours earlier we had sat right here, innocent and bored, waiting for the launch, assuming the adults would take care of everything. We'd been stupid to believe it, and now the room felt tainted with our stupidity. All around me, I heard kids having the same conversations, comparing what their parents had reported, gathering data, offering theories, dismissing theories.

Dr. Schuler came in and moved slowly to the front of the room. He'd dressed up for today in a tie and jacket, as if he expected someone to take his picture. He cleared his throat and bent forward slightly from the waist, to signal that he was ready to speak, but then he didn't. We stared and waited.

"Would anyone like to share their thoughts or feelings or observations about what occurred yesterday?"

No one moved or reacted. Dr. Schuler knit his fingers together and waited. Time went by. Finally he spoke.

"Well, for me . . ." he said reluctantly. "For me, I had a very difficult day yesterday. For me, personally, it's very difficult to see something like this happen. The people involved—the seven of them—they were very brave and very young. I know they probably don't seem young to you, but they were. And to think that we lost them like this . . ." Dr. Schuler looked off into the corner.

"Well, it's a tragedy. And I know that in your young lives there are many things that *feel* like tragedies. Maybe you don't make the team, or so-and-so doesn't want to go to the prom with you, or you fail an OTA, or you have a disagreement with your parents. But these—you need to understand—these are not tragedies. A young person in his thirties, at the prime of his life, with a couple of kids at home, never coming back from this mission—" Dr. Schuler got a fake-sounding hitch in his throat and stopped talking. He laid an index finger across his lips, begging our patience.

"Scholars," he said when he'd composed himself. "I want you to consider the future of manned spaceflight. There are going to be those who suggest that we react to this event by ending the shuttle program altogether right now. I'm sure a number of your parents are concerned about just such an eventuality. I want you to consider whether that would be an appropriate remedy to this disaster, whether this makes sense. And I want you to consider whether that kind of step, taken perhaps out of shock and anger, is really what the *Challenger* crew would have wanted.

"As an applicant for the Teacher in Space program myself," Dr. Schuler said with a false offhandedness, "I feel this concern. And I know that if it had been me yesterday, I would want manned spaceflight to go on."

This was the first time I'd heard anyone refer to what the astronauts would have wanted, and I suspected it wouldn't be the last. Rodney, a kid in the back who rarely spoke up, exhaled loudly and raised his hand. Dr. Schuler pointed in his direction with an open palm, his face expectant.

"Are we going to have class today?" Rodney asked.

Dr. Schuler's face fell, and he squinted angrily at Rodney. "I'm not sure what you mean," he said coldly. "The bell rang five minutes ago. We are currently in class."

"I mean, are we going to go over the homework from chapter six? Are we going to do physics?" A quiet rustle went up around the room as everyone turned to look at Rodney. For once, Dr. Schuler seemed unsure of how to answer.

"In a sense . . ." he said in the same slow and thoughtful tone he'd been using, "in a sense, we *are* talking about physics. We are talking about the future of manned spaceflight in America, which is an important application of the field of physics." Rodney threw up his hands and closed his textbook with a loud thump. Everyone watched him as he crossed his arms in front of him, staring at Dr. Schuler belligerently.

"So does this mean we have no OTA on Monday?" Rodney asked.

Dr. Schuler looked shocked by the question. "As far as I am aware," he said calmly, "we still have an OTA scheduled for Monday."

"Will it only cover chapter five, then?" asked Rodney. "Because if we're not going to start on chapter six today, I don't think it's fair we should be tested on it on Monday."

Dr. Schuler nodded to himself, as if to say that something he had long suspected had just been confirmed.

"This is a difficult time for all of you," he said. "It's a difficult time for your parents, I'm sure, if they work for the space agency in some capacity. I'm sure it's a difficult time at home." He looked around the room with a cold and appraising look. His eyes caught on me for a second, and I stared back, keeping my face blank.

"When a disaster occurs, a national tragedy with relevance to our own lives and relevance to the field of physics, I would think that you would want to take a class period to discuss it."

He looked out at us again as if someone were about to answer him. No one did.

"But if you'd rather not discuss it," he said, "that is fine. We can sit here in silence for the next forty minutes until the bell rings." His voice had taken on a certain edge that I recognized from my mother. Something had shut down within him, had gone cold, and there would be no way to bring it back.

So we sat in silence for the next forty minutes. Some kids pulled out books or homework from other classes, and Dr. Schuler did nothing to stop them. Chiarra put her head down and went to sleep; some kids doodled on their notebooks or looked off into the air.

When the bell rang, everyone got up to leave, watching Dr. Schuler to see whether he might say anything more. I slipped out, avoiding his gaze.

All the students congregated in the cafeteria at lunchtime. Several TVs were switched to the news. Tina, Chiarra, and I drifted toward the back of the room and stood at the edge of a clump of people talking together. A kid I didn't know was describing excitedly how he had found something washed up on the beach near his house. NASA had warned people not to touch any debris they might come across, especially the small tanks filled with rocket fuel to power the shuttles' maneuvering thrusters. The tanks could blow up spontaneously, the papers said.

"I swear to God, when I went out there in the morning, there were a bunch of heat tiles, and a whole chunk of External Tank," he said. "But the weirdest thing was—there was a *glove*."

"Did you keep any of it?" Tina asked him.

"No, my mom called NASA like you're supposed to."

"A glove?" someone repeated. "Like from a space suit?"

"Like from a space suit," the kid confirmed. "It was white and silver. You know, with the rubber fingertips. I was so sicked out, I like almost lost my lunch."

"You should call Channel Seven," a girl near him said. Some of the news stations had featured local residents who found interesting debris. I thought again of the reporter my father had met at the launch of 51-F, the way he'd told my father to call him if he learned anything new. I hadn't understood at the time what he might have meant.

"Was there a *hand* in it?" Chiarra called. Only Tina and I could tell that she didn't believe him.

"I didn't look!" the kid cried. "My mom called NASA and they came and picked it all up. All I know is, the NASA guys who showed up made everyone leave the area, and I saw them with one of those boxes that said CAUTION: HUMAN REMAINS on it."

"Oh my God," squealed a girl sitting near him, holding her hands up against her mouth.

"Oh please," I scoffed quietly. I'd meant to speak only for Tina and Chiarra's benefit, but everyone turned to look at me, including the beach house kid.

"What did you say?" he asked.

"Well, it's just that there couldn't have *been* a hand in it," I explained, feeling myself blush harder and harder.

"Why not?" asked the girl who had put her hands over her mouth.

"The astronauts don't wear space suits for launch anymore," I explained. "They just wear those blue flight suits. No gloves."

Everyone looked at the beach house kid. He was working his mouth back and forth, looking at me with hatred. Everyone remembered the walkout, the seven astronauts strutting out of Operations and Checkout wearing those blue suits. We'd seen it a million times since then.

"They carry pressure suits on board for the spacewalks," I offered him. "Maybe the glove was from one of those."

But now that the glove was empty, no one cared what the beach house kid had found anymore. I felt unaccountably sorry for him, for his simple desire to own something that the rest of us would want to crowd around and examine with him, poke at with our toes. Everyone else seemed annoyed with me too; they knew I was right, but they would rather have been allowed to go on believing him. I decided to keep my mouth shut for the rest of the day, and I did, through other implausible debris stories and theories about the accident's cause that denied the laws of physics.

As Tina and Chiarra and I left the building and drifted toward our buses, I lit another cigarette from my mother's pack. I'd worried I would look stupid doing it, but I lit it smoothly and inhaled easily while they watched; it was like I'd been doing it all my life. Everything about it seemed familiar: the match catching the crispy ends of tobacco at the cigarette's tip, the rich dirty feeling of the smoke pulling into my lungs. Tina and Chiarra exclaimed briefly over my smoking, but not as much as I had expected. They each took one, and then we were smoking together, the three of us.

I could see already how yesterday's events would become shaped and smoothed over. Sitting on the afternoon bus, I heard my first *Challenger* jokes: What does NASA stand for? *Need Another Seven Astronauts.* What were Christa McAuliffe's last words? *"What's this button do?"* It's hard to imagine laughing at such jokes, but I did—not the way I laughed at things that were actually funny, but I laughed all the same. I opened my mouth and out came a sort of dry, sarcastic, incredulous sound.

My father's note lay on the kitchen table, on top of the one our mother had left, in his familiar blocky capitals. His handwriting always looked exactly the same.

DEAR GIRLS, the note said. *I AM GOING TO HAVE TO WORK LATE TONIGHT. I'LL PICK YOU UP AT 8 TO GO TO DINNER, BUT THEN I WILL PROBABLY HAVE TO GO TO WORK AGAIN. PLEASE BE READY WITH YOUR SHOES ON. LOVE, DAD.*

He must have known that our mother wouldn't stay; they must have discussed it. Apparently they made all kinds of plans between them without bothering to inform Delia or me of the simplest of facts.

"What did you do in school today?" I asked Delia.

"I don't know," she said. "Jennifer threw up."

"Didn't your teacher talk about the space shuttle? Didn't she mention that at all?"

"Mrs. Givings said, 'How many children are sad today because of the space shuttle?'"

"Yeah? And what did you say?"

Delia dug into her backpack for something, then fished out a drawing. It showed a crude outline of the space shuttle, several disproportionately large children clustered around it. *We are sad for the shettle,* she had written across the bottom, and signed it, extravagantly, *Delia Gray.*

"It's a nice picture, Delia," I told her. "And it's *shuttle,* not *shettle,*" I couldn't resist adding. "But you did a good job."

Delia nodded and put the picture on the fridge where our father would see it. We watched TV again all evening as the living room grew dark. Right at eight we heard a honk: our father had pulled in the driveway, and we ran out. The dome light illuminated the top of my father's head and the trash on the floor of the car, crumpled homework papers, old fast-food wrappers, a lost sock.

"Hi, Daddy!" chirped Delia.

"Hi, D," said my father to Delia, and, "Hi, D," to me. His eyes were red and puffy.

"How are you doing?" he asked in a weary voice.

"Good," said Delia. She was back to being normal and chipper. It seemed there was nothing that could happen to Delia that would bother her for more than fifteen minutes. "A girl threw up. And we made igloos. Out of sugar cubes." I had hoped that Delia would ask the questions she had asked me that morning about our mother—where she was, why she had come back only to leave us again. I wanted to see my father struggle to answer them. But Delia seemed to have forgotten about all of that.

"Igloos, huh?" my father echoed, craning his neck to look at Delia in the backseat. "That sounds great. What about you, D? How was your day?"

"Fabulous," I said flatly. I wanted to know what had happened at his work, but I knew he wanted to tell me, and I didn't want to give him the satisfaction.

The radio was playing low, a song I couldn't quite make out, as we drove along the freeway, slowing, turning, finally stopping in the vast landscape of parking lot. We walked into the mall, and it seemed ages since I'd been there now, a different place, busy and more substantial. The multicolored lights looked lurid reflected in the beige tiles of the floor, and tinny music echoed oddly off the walls.

"Well, the investigation's gotten started," my father said once we were all settled at a plastic table with our trays in the Food Court.

"I've had to fill out a lot of reports, more than you would have thought possible," he said. "There's a lot of data, a lot of notes we took, that we have to straighten out while we can still remember all the details, write everything up clearly for the investigators."

"Do they think something went wrong with the SRBs?" I asked.

"Not necessarily. They just want to be very thorough and get every scrap of information about every single component." He paused, chewing, for a few minutes.

"But if I had to guess, I'd look at the Main Engines. A cracked turbine blade in a Main Engine."

We left the mall and walked to our car. The sun had gone down, letting the cold reassert itself. The wind on our faces felt cruel, intentional. NASA had already denied the possibility of any connection between the accident and the cold, but I felt certain that a cold like this must have had effects they couldn't have predicted. According to my physics book, there was actually no such thing as cold, only the absence of heat. But I felt the cold, even if it didn't exist: the cold like a substance, like a force of its own with a menace to it, a hostility.

My father pulled into the driveway and sat back with an exhausted sigh. He didn't shut off the motor. Delia and I both waited.

"Do you have your key?" he asked me.

"Why?" I asked, suspicious. "Where are you going?" I felt cheated that he wasn't even going to come in with us.

"I'll be back soon," he answered placidly, with a small fake smile. "There's some more things I've got to take care of at work. Make sure you and Delia both brush your teeth."

"I want to go with you," I said. I thought of Eric, the way he would demand to know everything his father knew, the way he would stand, arms crossed and scowling, asking relentlessly for the truth. Maybe if I went to the Space Center, I thought, I could see him.

My father just smiled sadly, didn't bother to say no; it was obvious my request was unreasonable. I sat for a few more minutes, waiting him out, and Delia waited too. My father tapped his fingers against the steering wheel, waiting for us to get tired of waiting.

"Don't cry, D," he said after a few minutes. I looked at Delia, surprised—she had been so calm and happy all day. But Delia was dry-eyed, staring back at me with a look of concern. My father was looking at me too. Then I felt it, my eyes stinging, and then, a second later, the sadness. I sniffed hard. My father pulled out the tissue he always kept in his pocket and handed it to me.

"Where is Mom?" I demanded. "Why would she come back and then just leave again?"

"It was an emergency," he said. "I asked her to come back just for the evening because it was an emergency."

"Why don't you ask her to come back for good, then? If that's the way it works?"

He shook his head sadly.

"That's not the way it works," he said.

We both thought about this for a minute before he spoke again.

"I want you to know that no one has said anything about layoffs," he told me. "They're taking this one step at a time. Once the cause is determined, everything is going to get back to normal. No one has said anything about laying anyone off, or about any budget cuts."

"It's still too early for that," I pointed out.

"Well, we'll see," he said. "But in the meantime, don't worry."

I blew my nose and continued to sit, waiting for him to say something more.

"Dolores," my father said heavily to the steering wheel, "I don't want you to blame yourself. I don't want you to think that any of this is your fault."

"Why would it be my fault?" I asked. I was thinking of the disaster. But then I thought of my mother, that maybe he meant her leaving, that I might blame myself for that. And, of course, I could.

Delia popped her door open, and in the sudden light of the car, my father patted my knee and gave me an uncomfortable smile.

"Goodnight," he said, and kissed us both. We got out of the car and watched him drive away.

"You shouldn't have said that," Delia told me once we were alone.

"Shouldn't have said what?" I asked.

"About Mom," Delia said. "That just makes him feel bad."

"I think he could do more than he does," I said. "That's all."

"He does everything he can," Delia said. She spoke in a fake grown-up tone, like something she had heard on TV.

I read all the articles about the disaster from the newspaper. One long piece was about the possibility of terrorism: each shuttle was equipped with explosives that could be activated from the ground; this signal was protected by a restricted frequency, but the code could have been stolen by the Iranians, the Libyans, the Soviets.

Another article wondered whether unseasonable cold could affect the performance of the External Tank; it also raised the possibility that the failure of a Solid Rocket Booster might have pierced the tank, causing it to explode.

Another article described my father's favorite theory, the problems with the Main Engines that had persisted since the development of the shuttle. The engineers and technicians quoted were convinced that one of the Main Engine's turbine blades had cracked, starting an explosion from within. Another detailed the possibility of pilot error—it was conceivable, an engineer said, that the pilot or commander could have pressed the button to detach the External Tank a full minute too early. If he had, the fuel still in the severed lines would have ignited, causing an explosion like the one we saw.

It seemed there was no end to the things that could have gone wrong. Already, I looked back with contempt at my younger self, when I had believed the space shuttle to be indestructible, when I had dreamt of flying on it and assumed that everything would work when I flipped the switch. Now it seemed like one big mechanical flaw, barely held together by explosive bolts. Now I knew they'd just gotten lucky all along.

20.

EVERY DAY THAT WEEK, NEW PICTURES OF THE SMOKE TRAILS appeared, new angles of that Y in the sky. I cut them out, though by that time I already had dozens. Each one was slightly different—a different angle, different lengths of time elapsed from the explosion, and I rearranged them over and over. I developed a ritualistic way of examining each new photo, starting from the top, the branches of the Y, each tip capped with a puff of smoke showing where the Solid Rocket Boosters had detonated. Follow the branches down, to the point where they meet the thicker root, the point where all the pieces had diverged. A larger ball of smoke there, marking where the External Tank exploded and took the Orbiter with it. And below that, most fascinating of all, the seam between disaster and the time when things were normal, nominal, operational, the column of smoke that marked where all had been one, all had been on course, the astronauts living, and *Challenger* had been on a perfect mathematical trajectory, unknowing of what lay just ahead.

Saturday afternoon, I was flipping between channels and saw a new image: an extreme close-up of the rising Launch Vehicle, thirteen seconds before the explosion, showing a plume of fire emerging from the right Solid Rocket Booster. "A plume of fire" was how the newscaster described it, but to me, squinting at the screen, it wasn't exactly a plume, just a finger of brighter pixels emerging from the side of the rocket, getting bigger and bigger frame by frame until the whole thing was engulfed in flame. I called my father over to see it. He looked gravely at the TV, and I studied his face for any change. There was none.

"Why did it take so long for this to come out?" I wondered aloud.

"It's only been four days," my father said.

"That's the right SRB," I said. "At about the level of the aft field joint."

"It is," my father agreed evenly. "But if the joint failed, we wouldn't see the problem for the first time a minute into the flight."

"It would have blown up on the launchpad, right?"

My father winced and nodded.

"At any rate," he said a few minutes later, "that picture doesn't prove anything."

After only four days, I had so many articles and notes in my notebook that I had to divide it into sections. My dividers were labeled: COLD/ICE, MAIN ENGINES, EXTERNAL TANK, SOLID ROCKET BOOSTERS, REAGAN/STATE OF THE UNION, TERRORISM, ASTRONAUT ERROR, and MISCELLANEOUS. The thicker my notebook grew, the more carefully I hid it. I didn't want my father to find it and ask questions. *What's this you've got here?* I could imagine him asking as he paged through it.

I cut out all of the articles I could find. I knew the theories already, but it was the details I wanted to save, the exact language, for future reference. Exact times and exact temperatures. Names and quotes. I read these articles obsessively, hoping to find a definite answer about what had happened, while at the same time mentally correcting everything I read. Most of the so-called experts on the space shuttle knew less than I did. This was even more true on the TV news: somehow, the networks continued to scrape up new speculations, side notes, irrelevancies. They hyped each piece of trivia to sound like breaking news, like a revelation. I was drawn in every time, shushing Delia and turning up the volume to hear whatever it was they had dragged out. Every time, they told me only things I already knew.

A few times we saw Mr. Biersdorfer squinting into a camera. He always spoke vaguely. "We will get to the bottom of this accident," he said. "A full investigation is being conducted." I searched Mr. Biersdorfer's face for some resemblance to Eric, some echo of him, but there was nothing.

On Monday, six days after the disaster, Chiarra and I skipped class together. She was skipping math; I was supposed to be in English. After a quick head check for teachers, we slipped into an unused classroom full of broken furniture and scrambled under a desk. A few older girls were already crouched in a corner, chatting and doing their nails. They looked up briefly and said, "Hey," as we found our own corner.

We still talked about *Challenger* in the hallways between classes, but most of our teachers were trying to return us to a normal schedule. I'd thought by now I would be ready to go back to afternoon classes, but the chapters we'd been studying last Monday, before any of this had happened, seemed so far away as to be theoretical, no more familiar or urgent than the things I had studied in sixth grade. When the bell rang again, I told Chiarra I planned to skip French as well.

"Dolores, I'm already on the verge of failing half these classes, but you're a really good student. You should go."

"I'm not a *really good student*," I sneered, looking at the girls in the corner to see whether they had heard. "No one will miss me. I'll go to everything Tuesday or Wednesday."

It seemed like a logical enough plan—the week of the disaster, I figured, none of us was really expected to concentrate on our schoolwork. I would make a fresh start once a full week had gone by.

Soon after the next bell rang, a new batch of upperclassmen snuck into the skipping room, which was now full to capacity; nearly every desk had a kid or two under it. There were so many of us I didn't notice right away that Josh had come in with Doug from my physics class; the two of them hunkered under a desk a few feet away from me. Josh wore a bright green polo shirt with the collar up—a style that Tina and Chiarra and I generally mocked—but it seemed to me that Josh wore his collar this way ironically, that he meant it as a joke. He had let his hair grow since the summer, and now it was a shaggy surfer mop that I found appealing. Though he wasn't as tan as he had been during the summer, I thought he still looked heart-stoppingly cute in that nonchalant way he had, as if he were assuming both that everyone was watching him and that no one paid him any attention, that it didn't matter what he did.

"Hey," Chiarra hissed at Doug. "What are you losers doing?"

Doug introduced us casually ("Chiarra, Dolores, you know Josh?"), then asked Chiarra something about the class the two of them were skipping that hour. I felt Josh looking at me.

"Dolores, right?" he said. I nodded, trying not to blush.

"What class are you skipping now?"

"French."

"With Madame Davis? Ugh. You made the right choice."

I had claimed to Elizabeth Talbot that Josh was my boyfriend, and I feared that now he would somehow sense this lie, smell it on me. I couldn't tell whether he remembered me from the pool the previous summer, and I wasn't sure I wanted him to. It seemed I had been a kid then, and he had seen me as a kid. But he seemed to take me seriously enough now.

Soon Josh and I were crouched under the same desk whispering to each other—Josh, the boy I had been admiring since I first laid eyes on him at the pool, alone with me, talking to me. At first I had trouble focusing on what he was saying; he was talking about the disaster, but in the closeness of his face, even the smell of his shampoo, my own crippling self-consciousness about how I must look and smell, I could barely follow what he said.

"Did you hear that the President appointed a commission to report on the accident?" Doug asked from under an adjacent table.

"When did that happen?" I asked, annoyed that he knew this before I did.

"It was just announced. I heard it in Spanish."

"What do you mean, a commission?" Chiarra asked. "What does that mean exactly?"

"To figure out what went wrong, I guess," Doug said.

"NASA already has an investigation board working on the accident," I pointed out. "Why do they need a commission too?"

Doug shrugged slowly, clearly enjoying the attention. I wanted to be hearing this from some official source, someone who would use the right terminology and adequately reflect the import of this event. I thought of my notebook at home and longed to be alone with it, flipping between the channels for news coverage and taking notes on what I learned.

"My dad might have to testify for the investigation," Josh added.

"Really?" I asked, impressed. "Was he involved somehow?"

"I guess," he said.

"What exactly does he do for NASA?"

"I have absolutely no idea. Every time he tries to tell me I, like, fall asleep. It has to do with getting money from the government or something like that. Why, like, what does your dad do?"

"He's a physicist," I said. I'd gotten so used to this lie that I no longer felt I was lying at all. "He works on the Solid Rocket Boosters. He had nothing to do with *Challenger*."

"Well, he's safe, then, right? Besides, they'd never fire my dad, anyway," Josh said with a note of false modesty. "He's, like, too high up."

I didn't say anything, but even then I knew that his logic was wrong. Being high up was no protection; in fact, quite the opposite. When a disaster happened, everyone wanted to see the leaders fall, top men, the higher the better. I thought again of Mr. Biersdorfer. If he were fired, what would happen to Eric? And would that mean my mother would come home?

"My dad says ice," Josh said. "There was ice all over the Mobile Launch Platform. That's what did it for sure."

"It wasn't the ice," I said. I hadn't expected to hear my own voice sounding so confident, and I immediately felt conscious of having contradicted Josh.

"Why couldn't it have been the ice?" he asked after a minute.

"Well, with ice," I said, "the danger isn't during the launch. If ice had damaged the tiles, the shuttle would have launched fine, but then it would have burnt up coming back into the atmosphere."

"Why, what do *you* think caused the accident?" Josh asked.

"It could have been a lot of things," I answered. "The ice just doesn't make any sense."

"Right, but what do you *think* it was?" There was a new note of deference in his voice. I paused for a moment before speaking, but I already knew what I was going to say. I was so glad to have Josh's attention, I would have said anything to keep it.

"It could have been the Solid Rocket Boosters," I said. "There's been a problem with them for a long time."

Doug hunched in closer. "What kind of problem?"

"The joints between the pieces," I said. "They don't seal right. Sometimes hot gas gets through." I wished that I could be smoking during this conversation, that I could blow a plume of smoke for punctuation the way my mother did. If Josh could see me smoking, I felt sure, he would know that I wasn't a child.

"Wouldn't that have meant it would blow up on the launchpad?" Doug pointed out. He was clearly well versed in the leading theories.

"Well, yeah," I admitted. "That would have been more likely."

"How do you know all this?" Josh asked me. He was looking at me with something like awe.

"My father," I said. "My father works on the Solid Rocket Boosters."

The article appeared on Tuesday, exactly one week after the disaster. Reagan had appointed an independent commission to investigate the causes of the accident. The chairman would be William P. Rogers, former Secretary of State. The commission would be made up of scientists, engineers, generals, and two astronauts: Neil Armstrong and Sally Ride. I was glad to see the astronauts' names on the list; they would get to the bottom of this, and if in the end they felt it was safe to fly, I would trust them. I clipped the article carefully.

"Not a good sign," my father said.

I knew what he meant: the message was that NASA couldn't be trusted to investigate itself.

"What does this mean about the SRBs?" I asked.

He looked at me quizzically. "What do you mean?" he asked.

"What does this mean for *you*?"

"Nothing," he answered. "It doesn't necessarily mean anything."

My notebook grew so fat with articles about the disaster it wouldn't close properly. I set it under weights overnight—a heavy dictionary, the leg of my bed. In the morning, the binding sprang open again, the edges of its ugly facts peeking out. I knew every technical detail of the explosion, every call and response from ship to ground, how many nautical miles downrange, wind at how many knots, from moment to moment. I still clipped stories about cracked turbine blades, about remote destruct malfunction, about astronaut error, but more and more the articles were focusing on the Solid Rocket Boosters. There were many possible problems with them: flawed casings, badly fitted seams, improperly packed fuel.

"Is that for school?" Delia asked one afternoon as I took notes from a newspaper article.

"Not exactly," I said. Delia had asked about my space notebook a few times, both before and after the disaster, but she had always accepted the vague explanations I gave her.

"Well, what is it, then? You're always writing in it."

"It's an investigation notebook," I said.

"And you're investigating the *Challenger*?"

"That's right."

Delia thought about that for a minute. "Why are you writing everything down?"

"It's the only way to understand what happened."

"So now you understand what happened?" she asked.

"Well . . . no. But before you can understand you have to have all the information." Delia nodded, and I thought she might be satisfied, but then she spoke again.

"Mom said we can never understand."

I felt a flash of anger at my mother again for the way she'd spoken to Delia that night, for the clichés of hope she had given her. She couldn't know how Delia carried them around, how they confused her.

"Delia, she meant we can never understand why people die. We can never understand *that*. But we can understand what went wrong with the space shuttle. We can figure that out."

"Oh," Delia said, nodding. She went back to her snack. I knew she didn't understand why anyone would want to know what went wrong just for the sake of knowing. If it wouldn't bring back the people, then what was the point?

Late at night, after my father put us to bed, I slipped out to the darkened living room and picked up the phone as quietly as I could. I heard my mother's voice.

"I've been following things on the news," she said in a low voice.

"Oh yeah?" My father spoke enthusiastically, as though she had paid him a compliment. "Well, this commission is just getting started, but I can tell you that they're going to be very thorough."

I couldn't imagine how he would know such a thing, but my mother murmured, "Oh, I see."

"They've been all over the country," he said. "Houston, Marshall, Utah—they're going around getting a solid foundation on how the whole system works before they start to make any judgments. Of course, they've spent a fair amount of time in my department," he added modestly.

"So they're checking out the whole thing? Do they have any idea yet what it might have been?"

"Well, there have been plenty of issues with those SRB joints," he said. "I mean, among other possibilities. They seem to be most interested in that segment we used on 51-L that was out of round," he told her. "They're interested in the way we fixed it. I've had quite a few interviews on that topic."

"*You* did that booster," she pointed out, her voice tensing. "*Your* thing? Do they think that's what it was?"

"Oh, we didn't do anything *wrong* in assembling it," my father tried to assure her. "We followed specifications down to the letter. We didn't do anything wrong at all."

"But the rockets, those segments, are your *thing*," she insisted. I could hear the way her throat was tightening, the growing worry that could lead to anger.

"That's not for sure yet," my father pointed out. "But even if it was the SRBs that caused it, Deborah, the design was to blame, not the assembly. Not the work I did."

This wouldn't mean a thing to my mother, I knew. I heard the soft static of her exhaling into the phone.

"Do you see that they're setting you up to blame you," my mother said quietly, more of a statement than a question.

A long silence went by, with only the faint sounds of static and breathing. The sharp intake of breath on my mother's end of the phone was the sound of her smoking. That sound made me crave a cigarette too, to feel that quick dirty gasp of maturity.

I hung up the phone as quietly as I could and sat on the couch. I felt sorry for my father; he loved talking to the investigators, and now my mother was spoiling that pleasure for him. I imagined him being called into a series of offices and asked to describe, over and over, what he did when assembling that booster joint. He could go into as much detail as he liked—the more detail, the better. My father was packed tight with information about his job: triumphs, complaints, stories that would take background explanations in order to under-stand the explanations. I thought again of the way he'd talked to the reporter from Ohio we met at the launch of 51-F, the pleasure it had given him to explain what he knew. My father spoke to the investiga-tors on the clock, but he would have done it for free. He never would have thought to try to protect himself.

Meanwhile, his wife was with the Director of Launch Safety. And if she was with him, she might have access to information that we didn't. For the first time, it occurred to me that she had probably been with Biersdorfer the night before the disaster; he had probably con-fided his worries to her in bed, told her about all the delays and the pressure to launch the Teacher in Space mission. She had probably pursed her lips at him soothingly, told him everything was going to be okay, wearing the peach nightgown that was missing from her room.

I sat for a long time, until I was sure that my father had hung up and gone to sleep. Then I called a cab, put on a sweater and a jacket, took my cigarettes and house keys, and looked in on Delia—she was sleeping on her side, her mouth open. I locked the front door carefully behind me before I slipped out. This time I knew just where I was going and how long it would take. After the cab dropped me off and pulled away, I went straight around to the poolside, to the same wrought-iron chair I had sat in before. In a square window adjacent to the back door, a warm yellow light illuminated a single head: Livvie's. She moved slowly through the kitchen from left to right, then she stopped and moved back again in the other direction. I found it calming to watch her finish straightening up in the kitchen; then that light snapped off too, and I was alone.

I sat in their back yard for a long time smoking, watching the dark and closed house, the blank brick face of the Biersdorfers'. The serene movie-set lights on their landscaping, the impassive heaving of the pool. Every few minutes a car drove by, and every time I waited for its sound to slow and stop, but it never did.

Suddenly the back door opened. The screen door hung ajar for a moment. I couldn't see who was there because the doorway was in shadows. The screen closed again, and for a second I thought I must not have been spotted. But then a tall stooping figure crept down the three steps to the poolside, stepping carefully with his long feet turned sideways on the stairs. Eric emerged into the light slowly, still holding the screen door with one hand, leaning forward to peer at me. He was at least a foot taller than the last time I had seen him, but unmistakably Eric, his new lankiness dressed in a pair of cotton pajamas and a down vest.

"Dolores?" he whispered loudly.

I felt that everything up to that moment had happened just to allow me to come here. Not only the phone call I had eavesdropped on, but even my mother's leaving—even the explosion itself—had occurred for no other reason than to guide me here, to this back yard, in the middle of the night, so I could see Eric again.

21.

ERIC WASN'T WEARING HIS GLASSES. HE MOVED TOWARD ME and stopped about three feet away, still leaning forward to get a better look at my face.

"Hey," I said, trying to sound nonchalant. "You're about a foot taller." He looked embarrassed, as though I'd pointed out something disgusting he'd done. He must be looking at me the same way, I thought, cataloguing my differences. I must have grown too; maybe my hair had changed color, my face restructured like his. I wished I could see myself as he saw me then, to know what I really looked like.

"How did you know I was here?" I asked.

"I heard that chair scraping on the concrete," he said. "You're lucky my mom didn't wake up and call the cops." His voice had not exactly deepened but had somehow widened; it sounded slightly trumpety.

"Do you think she heard?" I asked.

Eric shook his head. "I listened a few minutes outside her door. I don't think she woke up."

Eric shivered and pulled his vest tighter around him. I expected him to ask me what I was doing here, but he just looked out over his back yard.

"Is this pool new?" I asked. "I don't remember it being here."

He looked at it disdainfully over his shoulder. "Yeah. It was my mom's idea. She thinks my father should swim every day, for his heart. She talked him into having the pool dug, but she can't talk him into using it."

Eric lifted another chair and set it silently on the concrete next to mine. He sat and crossed his legs ankle over knee. In the light of the pool, I could see him more clearly. I had forgotten that his face was lightly dusted with freckles, that he had a large freckle just under his left eye, an orange dot along the eyelash line. That he had pores amazed me, that he had hair on his face—not real facial hair, but fuzz on his cheeks, thick, like a bee. I was surprised by the reality of him, by the very face-ness of his face, its tiny details.

"It's a nice pool, though," I said. "It's pretty."

"It's obscene," he said. "It's bad enough we live in a house big enough for twenty people and there's only four of us." He looked over at me, as if noticing me for the first time. "How did you get here?"

"Took a cab," I said.

"A cab?" he repeated. "All the way from your house to here?"

"Yeah. It's not that far." I decided not to mention that I had been here before. "Actually, I got the idea from you. Remember?"

He gave me a puzzled look.

"You told me once that you took a cab to run away to your old school."

"Why?" he asked.

"I don't know, you didn't say. I guess you wanted to run away, and that seemed like the best place to go."

"No, I mean—why did *you* come *here*?"

"Oh. That." I ran my thumbs along the arms of the chair, which were shaped like ivy curling around a branch. I considered telling him the truth—that I thought of him all the time, that when I wasn't thinking of him, I was thinking about the affair between my mother and his father. I wondered how much of this Eric might know. Probably nothing.

"I . . . I just wondered what you thought," I stammered. "About the accident and everything."

"I don't use the word *accident*," Eric said a bit imperiously. "That term implies that no one could have possibly seen this coming, that it was completely unavoidable. *Accident* means it was no one's fault."

"Your father used the word *accident*," I pointed out. I'd seen him quoted in the paper. "And he's the Director of Launch Safety." Mentioning his father gave me a little shiver. I had started to feel that I had made up Mr. Biersdorfer.

"He did?"

"He said something about 'this tragic accident.'"

"I've only heard him call it a 'tragedy.'"

"What has your father told you about *Challenger*?" I asked.

"He hasn't been home much," Eric said. "I don't know what he thinks it was. I assume he couldn't tell me even if he knew."

"He hasn't been home? Do you know where he's been?" I leaned forward, waiting for some crucial piece of information about my mother to drop.

Eric gave me a look. "Well, he's been at work. He's been at NASA."

"Right," I said. How could Eric know where his father had been? "What about *disaster*? Do you like that word better?"

Eric considered, then nodded. "*Disaster* is a better word. Though it still has some implications of bad luck rather than bad decision-making."

"What do *you* think happened?" I asked him.

"Whatever it was, it was probably something simple," he said. "It was something small and normal and routine."

"I think it was the cold," I announced. I wanted to be on record as having predicted that correctly.

"Is that what your father thinks it was?" Eric asked.

"No. He wants it to be the Main Engines, because that way he and his whole department will be blameless. He'd be happiest of all if it was hit by a meteor." I had never talked about my father this way before, so judgmentally. But saying it made it seem true. Eric was quiet and looked at me gravely.

"Well," he said. "It'll come out in the end."

"What'll come out?" I asked.

"The truth," he said.

I remembered his father and mine sitting in my family's living room, talking about problems with the backup flight system, laughing, assuming that everything broken would always be fixed.

"I was thinking of you when it happened," Eric said. "I was wondering if you still wanted to be an astronaut."

Nobody had asked me this, not my mother or father, not Dr. Schuler. I wondered now whether they assumed that I still did or that I didn't.

"Of course I do," I said. "Of course I do." Even knowing the risk, seeing that risk vividly illustrated in the sky, what else was there for me to want? What other fantasy could I fantasize for myself to get me through these long years until I could leave the Space Coast?

Eric was gazing back at me steadily, curiously. In the time that we had been separated, I had always imagined Eric this way, talking with me, leaning toward me, waiting with furrowed brow as if what I had to say were more important to him than anything else. He looked away and watched the surface of the pool.

"I thought of you too," I said. "I wanted to see you."

"Why?" he asked, furrowing his brow. "*I* never wanted to be an astronaut."

"I know. I just thought of you."

"I still sneak out sometimes at night," Eric confessed. I knew he had heard what I said. "I go out to the Cape—you know, to the viewing area, and sit in the stands."

"You mean where we sat for that *Discovery* launch?" I asked. He nodded.

"Even when there's nothing going up?"

"Sure. Sometimes you can see the stack on the pad, all lit up. *Challenger* was out there for a long time, because of all the delays. Most of the time there's nothing out there at all."

"You just sit out there?"

"Sure. It's nice. You can hear the alligators."

I felt a shiver of recognition for Eric then, for his type of daring. For most people, a stunt like trespassing at the Kennedy Space Center in the middle of the night would be intended to impress others, but if Eric did a risky thing, it was for no other reason than that he wanted to.

"I've missed you," I said, and the words reverberated in the air, embarrassing. I wasn't sure why I'd said it. It sounded fake, but it was true.

Eric looked at me for a long time with his steady gray eyes. The pool lapped quietly.

"I don't really like you, Dolores," he said, his brow furrowed. "I don't trust you. Do you understand that?"

"Sure," I said. And I did understand. "But you've missed me anyway, right?"

I had wanted to speak with Judith Resnik's voice then, to feel her daring, but this wasn't her voice. I tried to think of whose it was—not Chiarra's, not Elizabeth Talbot's. Then I heard it, felt it in my throat: it was my mother's. This was how she must have felt when she did this, offering herself to men, trying to cajole them into wanting her, this desperate flirting gesture. Maybe she had said such things to Mr. Biersdorfer, maybe feeling the way I did at that very moment: Watched by a man with both desire and judgment; trapped into doing something that he could scorn. Trapped into doing something so that he wouldn't have to.

"Yeah," Eric finally admitted. "I guess I have missed you."

He reminded me so much of himself in seventh grade. He spoke so much the way Eric would speak, his words, his pauses, his expression. I felt nostalgic for everything I'd forgotten about him.

We didn't say much more, just sat watching the back of his house. We didn't talk about the disaster, or about our parents, or about what I'd done to him in the seventh grade. I thought about his body, how strange it was that he wore his tallness in exactly the same way he'd worn his tininess when we were younger. When it was time for me to go, Eric lifted a long bony hand that both resembled and didn't resemble the Eric hand I remembered lying between us on the back seat of his parents' Oldsmobile, on the way home from a shuttle launch a long time ago, and waved goodbye.

I got home at dawn and snuck in before anyone was awake. I opened my notebook and pulled out the picture of the astronauts again—I still had the feeling that the picture held some sort of evidence if I could just find it. But something was missing: something I had forgotten to think about.

I knew right where that paper napkin was, stuck into my science folder from seventh grade. I found it quickly: a diagram in ballpoint pen, labeled and cross-hatched, drafted carefully months ago. Most of the words were unfamiliar—CLEVIS, PRIMARY O-RING, SECONDARY O-RING, ZINC CHROMIUM PUTTY. The entire diagram was neatly labeled SRB FIELD JOINT with the date, *7/29/85,* in my father's square handwriting. My hands trembled as I studied it. The napkin seemed to glow with the force of evidence. I could show it to people, and they would pay attention to it, take it seriously, and believe they were being shown something secret and therefore significant. I hid it in my notebook and went to sleep.

22.

As soon as I got home from school that day, I went for the phone book before I lost my nerve. The Biersdorfers' number was listed.

"H'lo?" Eric mumbled on the first ring. It sounded like he had something in his mouth, his voice flattened and altered by the phone's speakers. I'd never spoken to him on the phone before. He said hello again before I could gather my voice.

"Eric? Hey, it's me. Dolores."

Then there was a silence, an oceany emptiness that reminded me of my parents' conversation the night before.

"Uh—hi," Eric said eventually.

"So," I said. "You didn't get caught last night, did you?"

"What? Oh . . . no, I don't think so," Eric said. "I'm pretty sure no one woke up."

"Good," I said. "I would feel really bad if you got into trouble for hanging out with me in your back yard."

Eric was quiet again, except for a faint sound that might have been him chewing.

"Is that why you called?" he asked. "To find out if I got in any trouble?"

"Well, also to see if you wanted to get together again."

"Oh," Eric said. He didn't seem to feel any need to answer.

"I wanted to show you something," I said. "If you can meet."

"What is it?" At least he sounded curious.

"Oh, I'll wait until we see each other," I said coyly. "It's pretty top secret."

Eric breathed loudly into the phone.

"I don't think I can," he said. "I mean, where would we go? We don't really have any way of getting together."

"Well, we could meet at the mall," I suggested. "We could both get rides there. Or maybe take cabs, if we didn't want our parents to know."

"The *mall?*" he repeated, in a tone that suggested that he had never been there and would never go under any circumstances. "Why don't you just tell me what it is you want to show me?"

"You know what?" I snapped. "Never mind. I'll show it to someone else." I spoke in what I hoped was a chilly tone and not a babyish whine.

"Okay," Eric said neutrally. "'Bye." The sound of the phone hanging up on his end was slow, a series of muffled clicks as if he were having trouble getting the receiver to stay on the hook. I held on at my end, listening, until the dial tone broke in, moaning its steady indifference.

I watched the salvage operation continue on TV that night, the ships with cranes on them pulling torn pieces of the shuttle out of the ocean. I watched a long flank of the Orbiter being hoisted up through the surface of the ocean, sheets of gray water reluctantly pouring off, its black heat tiles soaked and warping white at the edges. It was daunting to see, impressive in a way completely different from watching a shuttle launch. The piece of ruined broken ship, huge as a whale, dangled from metal cables. And where were the astronauts?

The presidential commission investigating the accident held its first televised hearing, much to the delight of my father and me. We watched it for hours, both of us making an effort to be companionable, nodding at each other's remarks. The hearing took place in a large room, the commissioners sitting on two tiers, nameplates on

the tables identifying them. The witnesses—managers and engineers, mostly—spoke into a silver microphone, explaining slowly
and carefully everything they knew about *Challenger*. The chairman, William Rogers, asked most of the questions, but the commissioners all felt free to interrupt the witnesses to ask follow-up
questions.

While my father and I watched, a thin man with light red hair testified. He wore a dark suit and sat back easily, toyed with a pen,
paused for a long time before answering each question. He clearly
felt himself to be immune; I immediately hoped he would be blamed
for something egregious and be fired. The witnesses I had seen who
looked nervous, looked sorry, wiped their brows, and hunkered forward into the microphone—those men I sympathized with and
assumed were telling the truth.

"He's lying," I said of the thin man. My father raised his eyebrows
and swayed his head from side to side, a gesture that meant, *Maybe,
we'll see.*

"The chairman is really grilling him," my father assented. "I don't
think he likes this guy one bit."

"That's because he's obviously lying," I said. "Who is he?"

But before my father could answer, the man's name and title
popped up in white text at the bottom of the screen. WILLIAM
FITZGERALD, NASA ACCOUNTING OFFICE. I opened my mouth to wonder
aloud why an accountant had been called to testify, but before I
could, I realized that this man must be Josh Fitzgerald's father—he
had Josh's height, his eyes. The father Josh assumed couldn't be fired.

Mr. Fitzgerald was nodding vigorously at something a commissioner was saying to him, a knowing look on his face. He leaned in
toward the microphone.

"I did write a memo to that effect at that time," he said. "I indi-
cated those concerns to the best of my ability."

"I know that guy," I said. "I mean, that guy's son. I know his son."

"He goes to your school?" my father asked. "Is he in the Gifted
and Talented?"

"I don't think so. He's a senior."

My father said nothing more, and I knew he couldn't understand the import of what I had told him. What it meant for me to see, on television, the man who had raised Josh, who lived with him, to see that man interact with the commissioners who by now were celebrities to me—my father could never understand that.

"Why do you say he's lying?" my father asked after we watched Mr. Fitzgerald drone on for a few more minutes.

"He seems arrogant. He seems like he thinks nothing can happen to him."

The commissioners reached the end of their questions and thanked Mr. Fitzgerald.

My father shook his head gently. "No one will be immune," he said.

"What about someone like the Director of Launch Safety?" I asked, trying to sound casual.

"Biersdorfer?" my father said. It sent a little shiver through me. I was tempted to tell my father I'd spoken to Eric only a few hours before, but he would ask too many questions. "Well, that depends on what the cause is found to have been, whether it's something the director should have known about. For instance, if it was the ice—the commission might feel that he should have seen that as a risk and scrubbed the launch."

"What could they find that *wouldn't* be his fault?" I asked. "What is outside his responsibility? He's Director of Launch Safety."

"I see what you mean," my father said. He fell silent, and I thought he wasn't going to answer me, but a few minutes later he said, "Astronaut error, maybe. That wouldn't be his fault. Or if there was some problem he was never informed of. That's possible."

"Mr. Biersdorfer should take the blame," I said, suddenly angry that our lives could be changed so much while Mr. Biersdorfer continued on in his job.

"Not necessarily," my father said in the same neutral voice. "Not if the cause was something he didn't know about."

"If he didn't know about it, then he should have," I said. "That's his job." The anger I felt was so sudden it threatened to choke me. "Better that he take the blame than someone like you."

"It's not a question of who to blame," my father said patiently.

"It's a question of finding the truth."

I wanted my father to be right, and as recently as yesterday I'd thought the same way: something had caused the explosion; we could find the cause, then fix it. But now I saw the way this would really work. Blame would be placed as low on the chain of command as it would stick. And that might be on my father.

23.

My father and I watched on TV the next evening as Mr. Biersdorfer, fat, pink, and arrogant, performed for the commission. He answered the questions, said all the right kinds of things. I didn't want him to be fired if it would mean Eric would move away, but I still found it satisfying to watch him pinned to that seat, trapped by the edges of the camera's frame.

We listened while Mr. Biersdorfer denied knowing anything about possible problems associated with cold weather. He lowered his eyebrows as he spoke, shook his head. I was impressed by his acting. I leaned forward to study his face more closely, looking for some sign of my mother—some smudge of her, a mark, a clue as to where he had hidden her. Maybe my mother was waiting somewhere for him right now.

"There's also the possibility," Mr. Biersdorfer said, looking up woefully, "that the assembly procedures at Kennedy were not properly followed. That is, the question now becomes, to what extent did the engineers draw up faulty procedures, and to what extent did workers at the Cape not properly follow those procedures?"

"Oh my God!" I yelled. My father looked at me warily.

"He's blaming you," I told him, pointing at the TV. I studied my father's face, trying to find his reaction, but he was blank. He stared at the TV for another moment, then nodded at me reassuringly.

"It wasn't my team," my father said. "It was the contractor. They know that."

"Biersdorfer just said, 'improper assembly at the Cape.' Were you listening to that? That's *you*." My father shook his head.

"I don't think that's going to be the official position," he said. "They investigated it, but there's just no evidence." He wandered into the kitchen again. I'd never seen him like this, turning his back on new information, not wanting to know. Except, of course, where my mother was concerned.

"Mom was right about you," I said. "They're blaming you and you're just going to let them." He appeared in the doorway again, a dishcloth over his shoulder.

"Dolores, you do know that I assembled that joint, right? I packed that O-ring and the putty and did the leak check. You know that, don't you?"

"But you did it the way they *told* you to," I protested. "You did it *right*."

"Well, of course," he said. "But it's hard for people to understand what that means. I'm the one who had my hands on it." He held his hands up with their backs to me, his fingers wilting, like a doctor on his way into surgery.

"I know I'm not to blame," he said finally. "It was a faulty design. We knew that almost from the beginning. But it's hard not to think maybe there was something I could have done different. I could have spoken up more."

"You're going to *let* him put this on you?" I demanded. I sounded like my mother then, and I knew he heard it too. He shook his head and tried to explain, tried to calm me, but I wasn't listening. I went to the table near the front door where my father kept his wallet and picked it up.

"What are you doing, D?" he asked listlessly. "Do you need some money?"

I opened his wallet, old brown leather shiny with use. I went past his bills and credit card receipts and pulled out the business card I knew would still be there: Rick Landry, National Desk, Cincinnati *Observer.*

"What have you got there?" my father asked. He couldn't see the card from across the room; maybe he had forgotten that he even had it.

I stepped closer and showed him the card. He still looked confused, until I went to the phone and dialed long distance.

My father did nothing to stop me. He sat down heavily on the couch to listen, the yellow dishcloth still on his shoulder.

Rick Landry picked up on the first ring and said his name. He didn't seem surprised to hear from me. I reminded him where we had met, and he remembered. He didn't ask why I was calling or where I had found his number, just asked calmly what he could do for me. Maybe thirteen-year-old girls called him all the time, spilling out their fathers' secrets.

I told him, calmly and thoroughly, everything I knew about the field joint. I described the napkin with the diagram, all the parts labeled. I told him what my father had told me long ago, that the engineers wanted to call off the launches until the rocket joint was fixed, but that the managers weren't showing a lot of urgency about it. This phrase seemed to snag Rick Landry's attention.

"'Not a lot of urgency'?" he repeated. "Were those your father's exact words, Dolores?"

"Yes," I said, even though I wasn't sure. But I was relieved to have caught his interest. Up to that point, he hadn't offered any reaction to anything I'd said.

"Is there anything else he told you?" Landry asked.

"No," I said. "Just that there was this problem with the rockets all along. Especially on cold days. And they knew about it."

"Did your father tell you anything about *who* was in charge of the decision to launch in spite of that? Whose decision it was to keep the problem quiet?"

I wasn't sure how to answer this question, because the question didn't make any sense. No one had made a decision to hide the problem; they had just failed to pass the knowledge up the chain of command. Even I knew that.

"I don't know," I said.

"Are you sure, Dolores?" he implored. "Think. Did your dad ever mention who was responsible? Maybe you don't remember the name, but the position? The title?"

I looked at the TV, where Biersdorfer's mouth still opened and closed. The look on his face was the same self-satisfied expression he had worn at the launch the year before, lecturing my father and Eric and me on things we already knew about. It was the same smug look he wore while eating my mother's cooking, sitting at the head of our dining room table. He must have worn that look as he stroked my mother's arm in the evening over drinks, assuring her that everything would return to normal soon, meaning that he would survive this disaster and my father might not.

"Director of Launch Safety," I said.

I could swear I heard the sound of Rick Landry's mouth dropping open. At the same moment, my father's eyes flicked to me, alarmed. The shock of finally having gotten my father's attention made my stomach lurch.

"Are you sure about that, Dolores?" Rick Landry asked.

My father's expression was not angry. His face looked like a delicate gray bag full of something heavy. His eyes settled on me blankly—he looked at me as if to say, *You are doing what you are doing. You are who you are.* It was a look of recognition.

"Actually, no, I'm not sure about that," I said into the phone. "I might be mixed up."

"Okay," he said calmly. "I have one more question for you. I'm wondering if you could fax me that napkin."

"Fax?" I repeated. I had only a vague idea of what that meant—something used in offices.

"Is there a fax machine you can use? Or maybe you could photocopy it and send it to me?"

"I don't know," I said. "I'll try." I felt unreasonably disappointed that Landry didn't show more appreciation for what I had done. Rather than thanking me, he was demanding that I find access to obscure office machines.

I took down the fax number and address he gave me and hung up the phone. I had no intention of sending him anything.

"I hope you understand what you've just done," my father said, back in the kitchen, as soon as I hung up. He started fixing Delia's lunch for school the next day.

"Nothing's going to happen," I said curtly. I was just a kid, after all; no one would take seriously what I reported.

"*You* know what's going to happen," my father said calmly. He cut my sister's sandwich into the shape of a letter D. My mother had done this for both of us when we were little, which now seemed like a hundred years ago. I had asked her to stop when I was in fourth grade, because I was afraid the other kids would think it was babyish. I started to cry.

"You wouldn't have done this if you didn't know what would happen," my father reasoned. He didn't react to my crying at all. He opened Delia's thermos, sniffed inside, and went to the sink to wash it out.

"You're a smart girl," he added. "You must know. You must have your reasons."

I felt disoriented, like I'd been dropped into this scene from somewhere else and didn't know what I had done just moments before.

"But I *don't* know," I insisted. "Really."

He didn't respond.

"What will happen?" I asked. "Daddy? *What* will happen?" I followed him around the kitchen, frantic, waiting for him to answer. "Daddy? What's going to happen?"

He finally turned around, the dishcloth suspended in his hand.

"Dolores, the newspapers have been trying to get this kind of leak since the moment of the explosion. So far, no one has given them anything. Until . . ." He gestured at the phone rather than finishing his sentence.

"What you told him will be in his newspaper tomorrow morning. Joint rotation. O-rings. Cover-up." He ticked off the steps on his fingers. "The big papers will pick it up. It will look like there was a conspiracy to cover up the real cause. Bob Biersdorfer, since you named him, will definitely be fired."

"Good," I choked. "At least you won't be fired for his mistake." This had been my motivation, I reminded myself. To protect my father.

"Oh, honey," my father said. He turned off the water and dried his hands. He snapped Delia's lunchbox closed with a solid metal click. "Don't you know? I'm going to be fired no matter what."

It took only two days for the story to make its way into the national news. My father threw the newspaper into my lap the morning the story appeared, then sat at the table finishing his breakfast with the sports section.

"What is this?" I asked, though I could see the headline: *NASA Had Warning of a Disaster Risk Posed by Booster.*

"I thought you might be interested in that," he said. The story was not under Rick Landry's byline, and of course my name was never mentioned. Reputable sources were quoted, from inside and outside NASA, and just as my father had predicted, the story took the form of an exposé, accusing NASA of a cover-up of the problem with the Solid Rocket Boosters.

"Did you read this?" I asked.

"Skimmed it," he said.

"What did you think?"

He took several more bites of his cereal and drained his coffee cup before he answered.

"There's not much *to* think," he said finally. "It's just what I expected."

He was right: just as he had predicted, the article exaggerated the possibility of wrongdoing and took a slight tone of outrage. I told myself that the article wasn't exactly inaccurate: the joints in the rockets *did* have a history of failing, especially in cold weather. Managers *did* know about it and allowed the shuttle to continue to fly. A new design to fix the joint rotation problem had been agreed upon, even as *Challenger* launched.

But the story didn't feel true either. Its tone implied outrage that anything on the space shuttle had been found to be unsafe. There was no reflection of the fact that the shuttle was an experimental vehicle, that every part of it was being used for the first time. Reading the article, I was surprised to find myself feeling defensive for the engineers. They found problems all the time, and they had to make decisions about whether those problems were serious enough to stop flying. They chose as well as they could, and up until now their decisions had resulted in safe flights. What the article missed was that the same story could have been told about the shuttle's Main Engines, or the heat tiles, or the space suits, or the outdated computers, or a thousand other things. The space shuttle was neither safe nor reliable, nor was it supposed to be. The surprise was that it worked at all.

"Do you think anything will happen from this?" I asked when I had finished the article. My father answered me in the same neutral voice he had been using since the day Biersdorfer testified and I called Rick Landry.

"We'll see," he said. By which he meant: *Yes, everything will change because of what you have done.*

And it would. The facts about the faulty joint design would have come out even if Landry had never written his article. But this news might not have been characterized as a conspiracy, and everything that followed might have been different had the evidence emerged piecemeal, on its own.

The next day, the presidential commission held an emergency closed-door session to discuss the issues revealed by the newspaper article. Only then did they learn of the late-night teleconference the night before the launch, when engineers, experts on Solid Rocket Booster joints, had advised against launching in cold weather. They had pointed out that the O-rings in the joints had shown signs of erosion in cool weather in the past. But managers had pressured them to change their minds—one manager was quoted as having said, "My God, when do you want us to launch, April?"

By the end of the day, the commission issued a statement: because there was a possibility that the decision-making process itself had been to blame, their investigation would no longer work in tandem with NASA's, but would replace it entirely. No one who had been involved with the decision to launch would be invited to take part in the investigation.

My father exhaled loudly at the news. "It's been taken from us completely," he said. "Now heads are really going to roll."

As horrified as I was by what I had done, by the way it might have hurt my father, I couldn't help feeling a warm flush of pride then, that something I had done was now changing the course of history.

24.

FOR THE FIRST TIME IN MY LIFE, THERE WAS NO SCHEDULED launch date in the future, and we had to face the possibility that the shuttles would never launch again. It seemed now that all the delays to the *Challenger* launch and the one before were just practice for this ultimate delay, which could no longer be accurately called a delay because it had no foreseeable end.

Through February and early March, I collected evidence in my notebooks and felt the cigarettes I smoked accumulating in my chest as a sticky yellow film of sophistication. The investigation was still dominating the news, and since the story about the joint rotation had appeared, the commission found more and more evidence that NASA had known about the problem, that O-rings had partially burnt on previous flights, and that engineers had tried to raise alarms about the danger of continuing to fly with this design. A new theory had emerged, which appealed to me immensely because it blamed the President: if Reagan had planned to talk to the astronauts live during his State of the Union address that night, the White House might have put pressure on NASA to launch that day, despite the freezing weather. If this were found to be true, NASA would take less of the blame, my father wouldn't lose his job, the shuttle program would continue, and I could still become an astronaut. But no evidence had emerged for this theory, while more and more evidence against the O-rings piled up.

I watched one afternoon as Commissioner Feynman, a physicist with a sense of showmanship, soaked a piece of O-ring in his ice water, then held it up for the cameras to show how brittle it had become. The tape was replayed on the news again and again: Professor Feynman's smirk as he fished the C-clamp out of his glass, unscrewed it to reveal the flattened O-ring, then held it up in two fingers.

"I think this might have something to do with your problem," he said wryly.

My father shook his head at the professor's demonstration—"a little dramatic," he complained—but of course Feynman was right. When cold, rubber loses its flexibility. My father would have preferred that the commission talk about something else altogether—the Main Engines, for instance—but Feynman endeared himself to me by focusing the attention where it belonged: on the design of the booster itself, not on the work my father had done assembling it.

Tourists swarmed to central Florida to visit the site of the disaster, more than had come to see the launch itself. They pointed up toward where the smoke formation had hung in the sky; they traced with outstretched arms the path the short flight had taken. After some discussion and agreement, they solemnly snapped pictures of the horizon, then got back into their cars and returned to where they came from.

I watched my father those days even more closely than before, monitoring him for signs. After being at the Cape day and night for the first weeks after the disaster, now he stayed home from work most days. There was nothing for him to do, since all missions had been canceled for at least a year. Many workers at the Cape had been laid off already, and rumors predicted more. Delia loved coming home from school to find him there, ready to fix her a snack and hear about her day. To me he was still distant but polite.

Things had gone almost completely back to normal at school. No one cried in class anymore, and no teachers, not even the softest ones, let us discuss the disaster rather than having class. But the habit of skipping classes I had started the week of the disaster had proved impossible to shake once I'd discovered that teachers didn't care. I still went to physics and math every day and still did well in those two classes, but the others—English, history, French, and physical education—I skipped often, experimenting to see how much I could miss without affecting my grade and without the teachers calling my father.

I had kept my reputation as the star physics student. I made a habit of getting to class early in order to help other kids with the hardest homework problems. One Monday morning as we waited for Dr. Schuler to arrive, after I had helped Doug and Tina with a tough problem on buoyancy, we discussed where we might have to move if our fathers were laid off. It was all over the papers, the number of workers at the Cape who would have to find work elsewhere. As a physicist, my father would have had a good chance of keeping his job, so I acted nonchalant. Tina was convinced we would all be sent to Houston. On the other side of her, Doug was talking to Chiarra, and at first he seemed to be telling her of other jobs his father would be qualified for, but then he was telling her something that caused her to bring both hands up to her face, moaning, "Oh my God, oh my God," over and over in a low drone.

"What?" Tina demanded. Chiarra turned to us, hands still on her mouth.

The look on Doug's face as he pulled his chair closer to Tina and me was a look common to people bearing bad news that doesn't affect them—self-importance straining at the seams of a thin humility.

"Okay," Doug said, his head bowed, his voice quiet to keep others from hearing. "Okay. So you know my dad works on accident reconstruction," he began. "Well, he told me that yesterday they finally dragged up . . ." and here Doug looked around again and lowered his voice even more. "They dragged up the *crew cabin*."

He paused to let this sink in.

"Why wasn't this in the news?" I asked. I kept such careful notes on the coverage, I found it hard to believe that something as momentous as this could have escaped my monitoring.

"It was recovered in the middle of the night," Doug explained. "It'll probably be in the news tomorrow."

"Why would they pull it up in the middle of the night?" I challenged him.

"Because NASA didn't want it to be seen. *Any*way," Doug said with a sideways look to Tina. It was clear I was ruining his fun. "They recovered the crew cabin in the middle of the night. And you'll never guess what they found." He waited, as though we might actually take a guess.

"Dead astronauts?" Tina offered.

"Well, yeah," Doug whispered. "But you'll never guess what *about* them."

In the seconds that ticked by while Doug paused to let the suspense build, I tried to imagine what he might say about the astronauts that I didn't already know. I knew everything about them—where they had grown up and gone to school, their military training and specialties. I knew their hobbies and their children's names. I knew how they had smiled and how they had touched their helmets. For Judith Resnik I knew even more, the inner life I had imagined for her, the daring and intelligence I wanted for myself.

"What?" Tina begged. "What *is* it?"

"The astronauts survived the explosion," Doug said. "After the shuttle blew up, they were still alive."

We sat back in our seats, taking this in.

"How is that possible?" Tina demanded. "The shuttle was a *fireball.*"

"Yeah, there was a huge explosion, but the crew capsule didn't blow up," Doug said. "It's, like, separate from the rest of the shuttle, and it's pressurized. It was blown free. The astronauts almost certainly survived the explosion."

I watched Doug's face then, the way he tried to watch all three of us at once, savoring our reactions to what he'd told us. It was hard not to start hating him a little for it, the way I'd started hating my father.

"Were they *awake*? Did they know what happened?" Chiarra asked.

"It probably depressurized," I put in. "Maybe they were still alive, but they probably blacked out instantly."

Doug shook his head, trying to suppress a smile. "They wore

emergency oxygen packs that have to be turned on by hand. They've found three of the packs so far in the debris, and all of them had been turned on."

"So they were awake and falling," Tina said gravely. We sat silently for a minute, imagining this.

"So they drowned?" Tina asked.

"No, they would have died from the impact," I corrected. "They would have hit the surface going really fast."

"How long did it take?" Chiarra asked. "I mean, how long did they fall?"

They all looked at me.

I pulled out a piece of notebook paper and sketched out the variables. It was simple ballistics: $y = v_{0_y} t + \frac{1}{2} a_y t^2$. They watched over my shoulder as I sketched in the numbers, then worked through the math. I didn't know how to correct for air resistance, so I had to estimate that.

The others watched as my pencil scratched over the paper, holding their breaths, Tina and Chiarra covering their mouths. I had never felt so powerful, not even when I called Rick Landry. I felt as though I were determining our fates; if I could somehow find that this equation made no sense, then it would not be true that they had fallen, and maybe they could still be saved.

I started to cry a bit as I worked through the last of the math. I was embarrassed and tried to hide my tears, but no one seemed to notice; they were still watching my pencil.

"About two and a half minutes," I said when I reached the end. We all pondered this for a moment.

"I guess that's not all that long," Doug said.

"Are you kidding?" Chiarra spat. "If you jumped off the Empire State Building, that's like *eight seconds*." We all knew this because it was a popular example on Dr. Schuler's OTAs. "They fell, like, *twenty times* that long."

We were all quiet, counting silently in our heads, for eight seconds, then more. Long before we reached two minutes, Dr. Schuler arrived and class began.

I couldn't concentrate after that; my mind was singing a high note of horror, imagining that long fall. All this time, I had assumed for the astronauts instant death, painless. Standing outside and watching the explosion rain down the sky, I had thought they were already dead. That was the mystery I had pondered: living one moment, gone the next. It was terrible to imagine that they had not been dead yet as I watched, that while I stood out there, they were still falling. Somehow, every tiny comfort was being eroded for me, even the comfort of assuming that their deaths had been painless. As soon as class was over, I cornered Chiarra.

"We've got to get out of here," I told her.

She put on a serious face. "Where are we going to go?" she asked.

"We'll go to the mall," I said. "Tell Tina."

Chiarra's mouth fell open into a pink little O.

"The MALL," she repeated. "But how would we get there?"

"Hitch," I said in a high voice, as if it were obvious. Hitch. Just one little throwaway syllable. I had never hitchhiked anywhere, and had never known anyone who had.

We found Tina and told her the plan.

"Good," she said, slamming her locker. "If I have to hear Mrs. Nichols tell us one more time how inspiring it was to watch fucking John Glenn walk on the moon, I'm going to puke myself."

"Is she still talking about that?" I asked. "It's been two months. And it was Neil Armstrong," I added. We marched down the hallway, pushing past the tide of kids headed the other way.

"What*ever*," Tina responded as we pushed out the side door. "Why do teachers think that stuff is relevant? Or one more story about how they *thought* about applying to be the Teacher in Space, and now they're aware of their own mortality."

"Yeah. I *wish* Dr. Schuler had been the Teacher in Space," Chiarra said.

"Wow," Tina observed. "That's harsh."

We ran across the athletic field as fast as we could so we wouldn't be spotted by a teacher looking out the window. The weather was warmer than it had been the week before, but still cold, in the fifties. When we reached the road, there were no cars. We trudged along the shoulder in the direction of the mall. Scrubby grass grew up to the edge of the thin gravel, and a fine layer of trash was strewn everywhere, bits of glass, bottle tops, straw wrappers, pieces of plastic. It seemed so depressing that this road should look like this, that this wind should blow so cold on us, that nothing could ever just be clean and perfect.

We heard the low whine of a car approaching. Tina and Chiarra watched me, waiting to see what I would do. I stuck out my thumb, feeling like an idiot. The drivers of approaching cars glanced at me, surprised. In one car, a woman about my mother's age leaned forward to squint at us, her face a ball of worry. But she didn't pull over. Another car approached, a huge station wagon stuffed full of redheaded kids, and it rolled to a stop. We stamped out our cigarettes and ran toward it. The driver was a smiling fat woman with the same red hair as the kids. She was turning herself in her seat to greet us as we piled into the back.

"Well, hello!" she cried. "Aren't you three adorable!"

The children squeezed over against the door to make room for us and stared at us, openmouthed.

"What are you girls doing out in the middle of the day?" the mother called from the front seat. "Don't you have school?"

"We got let out early," Chiarra lied as the mother piloted the car back into traffic. "Special recess."

"Oh, sure," the mom agreed in a happy voice. "That must be fun." Something in her voice made me think she knew we were lying, but she felt no need to let us know that she knew. I was moved by her generosity; most of the adults I knew would have started questioning, narrowing in on details, exposing the lie.

Pulling up to the mall entrance, the redheaded mother made us promise never to hitchhike again, because of the perverts, she said, and we promised happily, knowing that we would.

"Now, do you girls have a way to get home?" she asked, rummaging through her giant purse.

"Yeah," Chiarra lied as the lady handed her a quarter.

"Just in case you need to call home," the mom said. "Do you have any money in case you get hungry?"

"No, thank you, we'll be fine!" Tina called as we all clambered out. "Thanks for the ride!"

The kids in the back turned to wave through the rear window as the station wagon pulled away.

"That was nice of her," Tina observed, waving back. "My *parents* never give me money."

"Should have taken it," Chiarra said. "She'll just spend it on food."

I laughed with them, but there was something about the fat lady that I loved, the way she fussed over us as if we were her own. Even with so many children demanding her love and money, she still had more to give us, strange girls she'd never see again. She cheered me and made me feel hope for the day. But as we walked around in the mall, I quickly forgot her face and her voice, and everything seemed bleak again. The only people in the mall at this hour were the employees and a few old people who sat on the benches full-time. I remembered how it had felt to walk into this mall when it had first opened, the shivering sense of elegance and possibility. Now the mall seemed grubby; its surfaces had worn thin, like a strong wind could blow everything away. All the merchandise on the tables looked flimsy, too brightly colored, and I didn't feel the old lust for the things I saw. I could already see how they would change when I got them home, how the clothes would look after they had been worn a few times, pilly and thinned and misshapen, how nothing would ever quite make me better. I thought of my mother, the way she fixated on things, thinking if she only had a certain lipstick or pair of shoes that her life would be changed forever.

We headed to the Food Court and sat down at a plastic table near the entrance to eat our fries and Cokes.

"What class are you supposed to have now?" asked Chiarra. The question was strange to me—I'd adjusted so quickly to the idea of being here and not at school.

"French," I said, and imagined my empty chair in the middle of the room. All around it, kids were chanting sentences after the pudgy Madame Davis: *"Elle porte un chapeau rouge." "Il faut que je fasse mes devoirs."*

Tina looked over my shoulder at something far away.

"Oh my God," she said in a low voice. "Don't look."

Chiarra and I turned to look. A clump of boys from the soccer team was moving toward us, among them Doug and Josh. They didn't show any outward signs of noticing us, but, seemingly by accident, they walked directly to our table and surrounded it.

"Shouldn't you girls be in school at this hour?" Josh asked, crossing his arms over his chest. He was wearing a shell necklace that emphasized his tan. I admired him for wearing the necklace; I could imagine the other boys giving him a hard time about it, and somehow his taking that risk made me like him even more.

"Hey, thanks for offering us a ride," Chiarra said nastily. "We had to risk getting raped and killed just to hitch a ride here."

"You hitched?" repeated Josh. "I can't believe you guys hitchhiked to the mall. I figured you, like, rode your little bikes or something."

"It was Dolores's idea," Tina supplied, and the boys all looked at me.

"Innocent little Dolores?" Josh asked. "Girl, where'd you learn to hitchhike?"

"What's to learn?" I said. "You just stick out your thumb and a car stops."

For some reason, everyone thought that was hilarious. The laughter went on for a long time, and Josh gave me his special sneering smile.

Some of the other boys drifted downstairs toward the arcade. Tina and Chiarra exchanged a look and got up to join them. Josh slid into the plastic seat next to mine, giving me his most mischievous smile.

"We'll catch up with you," Josh said, looping a tanned arm around the back of my chair. I wasn't sure what he meant by this, but everyone else seemed to, and a long low hooting rose from the crowd as they walked away. I felt a happiness crossed with panic, a privileged terror as I let my bag slump back to the floor. Neither of us spoke until our friends had disappeared over the lip of the escalator.

"I can't believe you hitched," Josh said again. I felt I should answer, but I had no idea what to say to this. Now that we were alone, I had lost the power of speech.

"You are so unbelievably cute," Josh said. He didn't look at me as he said this, but instead showed me his handsome profile, his jutting chin and blond mop of hair grazing the top of his nose. I blushed hard, feeling I should provide some response, but I had no idea what.

You're cute too? Thanks? But he didn't seem to expect a response; he just smiled at me. Something had been decided by his paying me this compliment, by his first nonsarcastic statement in my presence.

Josh and I sat in the Food Court for a long time, and he held my hand under the table. The big warm ball of his thumb kept tracing a circle on the palm of my hand, around and around. I tried to cultivate an air of mystery by not saying anything at all. Every once in a while, Josh looked at me and laughed, but it didn't seem that he was mocking me, only that he couldn't contain his amusement at noticing me, finding me here with him, over and over again. I thought about Delia—my father had been at work again this week, organizing files, so Delia would be coming home right about now to an empty house.

After a while, we got up to join the others at the arcade. At the top of the escalator, Josh slipped his arm around my waist. His touch was surprising, and I jumped a bit. His usual smirk faded into a closed-down look, concern or annoyance, I couldn't be sure which.

"What's wrong?" Josh said quietly. His voice sounded strange, lowered like that.

"Nothing," I said. I panicked, sure I had just revealed to him that I was only thirteen, younger than everyone else, too young to be with a senior. Josh took my hand then, but he didn't try to put his arm around me again.

In the arcade, I stood at his elbow, watching him wiggle and jerk a series of colored knobs violently. On the screen, he controlled a tiny white triangle, which shot rows and rows of blobs out of a black sky. He was good, but it didn't seem to matter—as soon as he cleared one screen, another appeared in its place.

"You try it," he said after a while, and held out a quarter to me. I watched the quarter and shook my head. I didn't want to play in front of him, for him to see how bad I was. I thought of how the quarter would be warm from his pocket if I were to touch it.

"Come on," he said. "Have you ever played this game?"

"No," I answered. "I'm not very good at video games."

"Well, give it a try," he said. "My treat." He put the quarter in the slot and stepped back. The game blinked to life, playing its song and flashing information on the screen. My heart beat fast in my throat. I couldn't let him see me play. I couldn't stand the idea of struggling to figure out the controls, screwing up, with him watching me. He would know I was just a child.

"No, really," I said. "You play it."

"I've just played five games," he said reasonably. "I want to see *you* try."

"Well, I don't *want* to try," I said, trying to keep the panic out of my voice. The result was that I sounded cold and angry. Josh was still smiling at me, waiting for me to take the controls.

"You're going to die," he warned, looking at the screen. "Lookit, the bad guys are coming to get you."

On the screen, rows of alien spaceships marched back and forth, dropping bombs at the white triangle.

"You're going to die!" Josh cried, his voice rising to a shriek. "Come on!" At the last minute, he couldn't stand to watch and grabbed the controls himself. He struggled for a few seconds, but it was too late; the white triangle was trapped and exploded under bombs from above.

"Aw, man, look at that," he said quietly. "You let him die. I can't believe you did that."

He went on to play the next two lives of the game. When it was over, he moved on to another machine without mentioning what I had done.

Josh never asked, so I never mentioned that I was thirteen. Before we met up with the others, he pulled me into a deserted corridor lined with pay phones and lockers, and I read the messages on the emergency exit door over and over while he kissed me carefully, as if conscious of violating something with every move he made. His mouth felt different from Elizabeth's, his lips rubbery and moist. What satisfied me most, even more than having a boyfriend or becoming suddenly, unquestionably popular, was that my lies about him were no longer lies.

He kissed me for so long, I had time to think about how far I had come in the months since the disaster, since January, when I'd hoped to fly in the space shuttle and felt proud that my father worked on its rockets, or even since this morning, when I'd thought the astronauts had died instantly. I thought about my home, far away, and Delia there by herself, waiting for me. Delia was old enough to be home alone, I told myself. She would be fine.

Josh dropped me off at home in his rattling Datsun. I'd been embarrassed to let him see where I lived, but he showed no reaction when I announced, "This is it." He took a quick glance at the house, then slung an arm around me.

"Can I have a kiss goodbye?" he asked in a falsely formal tone. Without waiting for an answer, he leaned in. This time it was a quick kiss, almost perfunctory. As I climbed out of the car, I looked around at the neighbors' houses, afraid that someone might have seen us, that someone might describe this scene to my father. But the street was silent, all the adults still at work.

Delia was watching a special about Judith Resnik on TV with all the lights off when I went inside. In the darkened room, the interior of the space shuttle glowed white, its walls covered with drawers and switches and handles and unidentifiable white gadgets. Judith Resnik, alive, flying on her first shuttle mission, STS 41-D, drifted into the frame, her curls floating. She was tanned and beautiful in her shorts and socks; she smiled wryly at the camera, then executed a somersault.

Delia looked up at me.

"Where were you?" she asked.

"The mall," I said.

"The *mall?*" she repeated, incredulous. "How did you get there?"

"I went with my friends. What did you tell Dad?"

"He didn't call," Delia answered. She looked back at the TV. Judith Resnik floated to a window and looked out at the turning Earth.

"But you were okay, right?" I asked. "You were okay by yourself."

She didn't answer.

"Delia, look at me," I said. Delia turned her little face up to me.

On the TV behind her, the astronauts were floating candy across the crew cabin to each other, trying to catch it in their mouths.

"You were okay, right, Delia?"

"Yeah," she admitted. She hadn't been in any kind of danger—she had a key of her own, she knew the rules. She knew not to open the door to anyone, not to use the stove or the toaster, not to open the drapes. Someone looking in might see there were no adults, my mother had taught us long ago.

That night, I dreamt of falling.

The newspapers the next morning verified Doug's story. The crew cabin had been found along with some of the crew remains, though there was no reference to the emergency oxygen packs. The article did mention a cockpit recorder, which might have been damaged by salt water, but if it could be restored NASA could listen to the crew communications after the explosion, establishing how long the astronauts had lived and how much they had known.

I cut out the article but didn't bother pasting it into my space notebook. Of all the questions I'd thought I was interested in—the precise technical causes, which part of the Launch Vehicle had malfunctioned and why, who had known what and when—it seemed now that all I really wanted to know was this. How they had died, what I might have experienced if I had been Judith Resnik. I'd thought I wanted much more, but now that I knew about that two and a half minutes, it was hard to imagine what more I could possibly want to know.

25.

THE SECOND TIME I WOKE UP TO FIND MY MOTHER SITTING ON
my bed, I wasn't as surprised as I had been the first time. When I
opened my eyes, she was humming to herself quietly, kicking
through a pile of clothes and books next to my bed. She picked up a
tape, turned it sideways to read the case, then let it fall back to the
floor.

"Mom," I whispered.

"Hi, D," she said. "You shouldn't be wearing these jeans anymore.
They're too short. Or is that the way the kids are wearing them?"

"That's the way they're wearing them," I whispered.

"Well, still," she said. "Tell your father to get you some new
things. You're in high school now, and clothes are important. I
remember how it is."

"Okay," I said.

"I missed Delia's birthday," she told me, as if confiding something
I didn't know. Delia had turned six a few days before.

"It was fine," I said. "We had a special dinner for her."

"Does he ever talk about me?" she asked, turning her face away
shyly.

"Who?"

"Your father. What does he say about me?"

I didn't know what to say. My father never mentioned her. He seemed to believe that if he avoided talking about her, Delia and I wouldn't be hurt by her absence.

"He says he misses you," I lied. "He says he hopes you come back."

"He says he *hopes*?" she asked, suddenly enraged. "Is that what he's been saying to people? That he *hopes* I come back?" I didn't know what to say. She shook her head, picking at a loose thread in the hem of her dress.

"What else does he say?" she whispered. This time I knew what she wanted to hear.

"We all miss you, Mom," I said.

"Yes," she said, tilting her head modestly. "I know that. I've known that for quite a while now."

"Are you coming back?"

"Oh, that depends, baby," she said finally.

"That's what everyone always says," I said. "But on what? What does it depend on?"

She looked at me for the first time. She seemed surprised that I'd asked.

"Well, baby. It all depends on you."

The TV news had shown Coast Guard ships pulling up still more of the wreckage. The salvage operation had become the largest in naval history. My father and I watched together as a crane hauled up a long flank of the Orbiter, the words UNITED STATES and a small emblem of the flag still barely visible, washed translucent by their weeks underwater.

My father had nodded gravely at these images on the news.

"You know, they've found almost all of the debris," he said quietly. He told me about the warehouse where the wreckage was being catalogued and laid out in a grid on the floor, each piece of the Launch Vehicle painstakingly reconstructed.

"Can we go see it?" I asked.

"Why would you want to see it?"

I didn't answer. A few minutes later, he added, "It's probably restricted."

I watched the news for mention of what Doug had told me about the emergency oxygen tanks, the astronauts' long fall, and every day that no mention appeared, I only became angrier. I didn't know who I resented more—the journalists for not finding out, or NASA for keeping it a secret.

Every afternoon that week at lunch, Josh waited for me in the parking lot where everyone could see us, lying on the hood of his Datsun. I came to look forward to seeing him in the middle of the day. I started to notice that I felt something for him other than curiosity—a surprisingly sharp affection for his goofy gestures, his sunburned nose, his immature sense of humor, his generosity in not pretending nonchalance with me.

I skipped afternoon classes with Josh. Missing class didn't make me anxious anymore. I felt only relief, a simple pleasure at being able to get out of school, at not caring about the consequences. He always took me to the mall. The time was our own, so we wasted it. We didn't need to do anything at the mall but walk around holding hands, letting people see us, laughing conspiratorially together and basking in the warmth of their watching. I let Josh buy me a silver necklace, and he stood behind me in the Food Court, right in front of everyone, to clasp it around my neck.

On Friday Josh picked me up at lunchtime, which meant that I would be missing all my afternoon classes again. I assumed we were heading toward the mall, as we always did, but instead of turning right at the end of the road, he turned left.

"I thought we'd do something different for a change," he explained before I had a chance to ask. "I'm getting tired of that place. It's always the same."

"Sure," I said. "Whatever you want to do." But I felt mildly alarmed. I loved going to the mall, seeing the same things and the same people every day. At the mall I could forget about the accident; I could forget about my mother's absence. It was only at the mall that I felt the full force of what I had accomplished with Josh, the way I had successfully changed myself into a different kind of person.

"You've never seen my house," he said a few moments later.

"True," I agreed.

He hadn't seen the inside of mine either, and I hoped to keep it that way. So far, I'd been successful at keeping him from knowing anything about my family.

Josh's house was much bigger than mine, though not as big as Eric's. I was used to this, though; nearly everyone's house was bigger than mine. I looked around, taking in the white carpet, high ceilings, leather furniture, huge patio, landscaped yard.

"You want something to drink?" Josh asked, disappearing into the kitchen.

"Sure," I said. I sat at one end of a robin's-egg blue leather couch. It was as long as a car. He returned with two cans of Coke and jumped over the back of the couch to sit next to me.

"What do you want to do?" he asked, flipping on the TV.

"I don't know," I said. "Whatever." Unlike my family's TV, Josh's had cable, so he cycled through eighty channels before coming back to the ones we'd seen first. A few of them still showed images of the disaster—the walkout, the split cloud formation in the sky. Those images were as familiar to me now as my own face, but I still watched them closely when they appeared, hoping somehow to see something new in them. When Josh reached the channel showing the commission's hearings, he stopped. A middle-aged white man with glasses sat in the same chair Mr. Biersdorfer had sat in, the same chair Josh's father had sat in. This man leaned forward to speak into the microphone. He was sweating, a stricken apologetic look on his face. He described inspecting the Mobile Launch Platform for ice.

"My dad had to testify for this," Josh said with false offhandedness.

"I saw him," I said.

"Really? What did you think?"

I remembered my instant decision that Josh's father was arrogant and guilty. I remembered my father saying, "The commission is really grilling him," and feeling satisfied that we agreed on something.

"He did fine," I said. "I only watched for a few minutes."

"He said they might call him back, you know, like, to ask follow-up questions."

Josh's talking made it hard for me to hear the testimony about the ice, and for the briefest moment I wished I were home to watch in peace with Delia. Josh soon grew bored and leaned in to kiss me. I'd become accustomed to the feeling of kissing him, the weird muscular movement of his tongue, the taste of spit not my own. I had even come to enjoy it now that I understood what the pattern of it was, the way he would kiss me for a while with his head pointing in one direction, then in the other. He had never tried to go any further. But, it occurred to me now, we had always been in the school building or in the mall; we had only ever made out in hidden corners of public places. But now we were in his house by ourselves. Before long, I found myself pinned on the couch with him halfway on top of me, his kissing becoming faster and more desperate, his breath rasping in his nose.

So this was why we had come to his house, I thought calmly. I couldn't see the TV, so instead I listened to the voices: a man with an exaggeratedly grave voice ran through the evidence indicating whether or not the astronauts had known anything had gone wrong before they died. The man assured us that they hadn't known a thing. I felt a shock of anger at his lying, or his ignorance. The image of the astronauts awake, alive, strapped into their seats and falling, came back to me like a remembered bad dream. Josh was surprisingly heavy, and his weight made breathing difficult. I felt only mild alarm when I realized that he was fumbling with my shirt. I sat up.

Josh's face was flushed and his bottom lip hung open, crimson and heavy. I studied him: his eyes were lowered into a look that I knew was meant to convey some sort of longing, but instead looked like a drugged stupor. I resisted the urge to look toward the TV, where something bright was flashing. Probably the explosion again.

"I want you," Josh groaned. This struck me as the funniest thing I had ever heard, and the nervous giggle that came out of me felt like someone else's, high and light.

"What?" he said angrily.

"I'm sorry," I said. "You're funny."

He glowered. "Why is that fucking funny?"

His look, his tone, should have intimidated me—the thought of angering Josh, causing Josh to think I was immature, normally would have filled me with horror. But I had been infused with a strange sense of confidence.

"What do you mean, that's funny?" Josh asked, his brow creasing. He picked up the remote and clicked off the TV without looking at it; his eyes flicked back and forth between mine as he tried to figure out whether he had been insulted.

"Nothing," I assured him. "Really."

I had finally understood that I was something he wanted, and not the other way around.

"When do your parents come home?" I asked.

"Late," he grunted, to show me he was still put out. "Like, nine."

"Good," I said.

Josh's eyes widened in disbelief when I peeled off my shirt, the same shirt he had been fumbling with for long minutes. I was wearing a bra that I'd stolen from my mother's drawer, pink with lace edging.

"Come here," I said, and he did. He moved toward me in a low crouch. He was smiling again, my laughing at him forgotten now.

"Are you sure about this?" he asked a short while later. He was looking up at me then, his expression hopeful. I smiled and took him by the hand. His room was at the end of a long hallway, twice the size of Delia's and my room. All the furniture matched, a pale wood, but it all seemed too small, things bought for a little boy and never replaced. A single bed with blue plaid sheets, unmade, a chest of drawers, a small desk covered with dirty clothes. This room, like everything else about Josh, could have intimidated and confused me before today, but now the room felt suffused with my new power, my new understanding, which stood in the air like dust motes as he drew the curtains against the reddening afternoon light.

"Are you sure about this?" he asked again, and I thought it was sweet that he didn't want to take advantage of me, didn't want to be that kind of boy. I didn't answer him, just crawled into his unmade bed. His sheets had a simple boy smell, a mild stink, like a puppy. When he undressed in front of me, I saw that his fingers were shaking. All this time, he had been an impenetrable figure of cool, never

had shown the slightest emotion or vulnerability. But look: I had con-
quered him, this easily. I had never seen a naked boy before, but
what I focused on were his big red hands dangling by his thighs, limp
and obedient. He was waiting to be told what to do.

"Comeer," I said. And just like that, everything had changed.
Now I was in charge. I wished I'd figured this out a long time before.
I told him what to do, when to stop and when to start again, and he
complied, struggled to please me.

I knew from Tina and Chiarra more or less what to expect from
sex—"It's *nasty*," Chiarra had emphasized—but the pain was sharper
than I'd imagined. At one moment, I'd almost pulled back, almost
changed my mind, but I had something to prove to myself now, and
to Josh too. It was no different from jumping off the high dive at the
pool, I told myself; no different from skipping school, no different
from hitchhiking. You stick out your thumb and a car stops.

"Are you okay?" Josh asked when I betrayed signs of pain. I nodded, motioned for him to continue.

"Is this your first time?" he asked.

"Shut up," I hissed low, and he did. The look on his flushed face
was doggedly obedient, wanting only to placate me, to please me so
that I might allow him to continue, so that I might come here and do
this again. In one afternoon, I had changed him into a boy just like
any other.

I didn't think of my sister at all until afterward, until after I cleaned
myself up in Josh's bathroom, endured his long grateful kisses and his
guilty questioning as to whether I was okay, until after he pulled his
car up at the curb in front of my house. I climbed out after still more
kisses and endearments, slammed his car door behind me. I didn't
think of Delia until I was walking up our weedy front walk; only
then I remembered that I had left her alone for hours, much longer
than usual. As I unlocked the door, I felt for the first time how sore
and uncomfortable I was, as though something unnatural had been
done to me. But it wasn't unnatural, I reminded myself as I unlocked
the door, and it hadn't been done to me. I had chosen it myself, every
bit of it.

Delia wasn't at her usual spot in front of the TV, and I stood in the living room for a minute, still thinking my own thoughts, while her absence slowly dawned on me. She wasn't in the kitchen or the bathroom. I ran to our room. It was empty too. I stood in the reverberating silence of our messy beds. The room smelled of us.

The whole house pulsated with Delia's absence. I had lost my sister. I pictured myself on the evening news, crying, *I came home and she was gone.* The color of the walls was sickening; what I had done earlier in the afternoon was sickening. I never should have left Delia alone for so long, never should have pushed my luck this far. Then I saw a flash of something outside our bedroom window. It was Delia, running in a circle around the palmetto tree in our back yard, her hand never losing contact with the green skin, her other arm stretched out like a wing. She was such a spaz, I thought in my sudden flash of anger. Weirdo, retard, moron—I called her every insult I could think of in my mind, even as my eyes filled with tears of love for her. On her next pass around the tree, Delia saw me and waved, then ran inside.

"What?" she asked, confused, when she saw my face. Delia stared at me with those green eyes, her round face and missing teeth and disheveled play clothes suddenly dear to me.

"I just didn't know where you were," I said finally. "I was worried about you."

"I'm okay," she said. "I'm right here."

In the Food Court that night, my father ordered Chinese; I got a baked potato with ham and cheese. Delia couldn't decide what she wanted.

"Chicken McNuggets?" my father prodded her. Delia shook her head.

"Egg roll?"

"No."

"Fried chicken? Spaghetti? Taco?"

"No," Delia said, her face going soft in the red glow of the Arby's sign. "No, no, no."

"Delia," said our father patiently, always patiently. "You have to eat something. What do you want?" Delia looked around as if she didn't know where she was, starting to cry. Her eyes fixed on me and she regarded me hatefully, her green eyes narrowed. I had never seen her this way before, none of the many times when I'd been cruel or thoughtless toward her. Delia cried and cried, moaning softly.

I looked to my father, and for the tiniest moment our eyes met; each of us was hoping the other would handle this. He was the first to speak.

"Delia, what is it? What's wrong?" he asked her soothingly. He reached out to stroke her back.

"Nothing's wrong with her," I snapped. "She's just being a brat."

Delia's eyes flashed up at me, surprised. Too late, I realized my mistake.

"Dolores left me alone," Delia said to my father, dropping her voice to a whisper, though she knew she couldn't keep me from hearing. "She didn't come home after school."

My father looked from Delia to me. His face was a smear of confusion just as it had been the time I told him my mother and I hadn't been shopping. It was the same bewilderment crossed with weariness, with a hope that whatever we were talking about, it would be resolved soon without his intervention. But Delia was crying openly now, big salty tears running down her face and plopping onto the table.

I thought about where I'd been earlier that day, about the red afternoon light in Josh's room, the gratitude in his gestures when he touched me, the noises that had escaped him even though he tried to hold them back.

"What's going on?" my father asked me. "What is this about?"

I ignored him and watched Delia. I wanted to hate her, to believe that she was an incorrigible brat, but I couldn't. It was horrible now to think of her sitting alone at home—no mother, no sister, her father at work trying to piece together an accident he might have helped to cause.

"I'm sorry, Delia," I said. I'd spoken the words before, but I'd never really meant them. "Hey, Delia? I'm sorry, okay?"

She wouldn't look at me.

"What's going on?" my father asked again, alarmed now. Delia didn't answer him.

"Nothing," I told him. "It's okay. We're both okay."

"Dolores, you have to look after your sister while I'm gone," he said. "With your mom away, I need to be able to depend on you to help out."

We both stared at him. He almost never mentioned my mother, and he certainly had never referred to her absence as a hardship. He took a sip of his coffee and checked his watch. To him, this discussion was over.

"When is she coming home?" Delia asked him.

"She'll come home," he assured her. "When she's ready."

"Mom said the astronauts might be okay," Delia announced, as if this had been what she had meant to say all along.

"When did she say that?" my father asked, the surprise lifting his voice.

"The night of the accident," I explained. "Delia, she said you could *hope*, right? She said you could *hope* they were okay."

"Yeah," Delia said. She didn't seem surprised that I knew this. "We can hope."

"Delia, I don't think—" my father started. But I caught his eye and shook my head no. Delia should be allowed to keep talking about hope if she wanted, even if in some way she had to know there was no hope. Delia heaved a sigh and looked as relieved as we were that her crying was over.

As always, distant music played. My father bought us ice-cream cones, soft serve, and he let Delia have one even though she hadn't eaten any dinner. He stroked her hair while she ate it, still sniffing.

26.

THAT NIGHT, I SNUCK OUT AGAIN AFTER DARK. THE WARMTH and humidity had come back, so when I looked up I no longer saw the crisp field of stars, only the brightest ones peeking through the murk, faint and few.

I walked twenty minutes or so along the main road, then waited for a car to come by. The first thing to pull over was an eighteen-wheeler. It grumbled to a stop at the shoulder, then the passenger-side door, far above me, popped open.

"Are you lost, honey?" the driver called. I could tell from his voice that I could trust him, that he had kids of his own.

"I'm not lost!" I yelled up at him. "I know where I'm going."

I climbed up into the cab and pulled the door closed behind me. The driver was a small, slight man, a few years older than my father, neatly dressed in khaki pants and a cardigan sweater. He was going in my direction, toward the Space Center; he didn't ask me why I was going there. On his dashboard, I saw a picture of a girl and a boy smiling.

"How old are they?" I asked.

"Oh, that's out of date," he said, smiling at the picture. "My oldest just started college." He pulled the truck back out onto the road, bumping and jostling, and I found it pleasant to ride so far above the surface of the street.

When we pulled up to the gates at the first checkpoint, everything was closed and locked, the guard station empty.

"Are you sure this is the right place?" the driver asked, hunching over to scan the horizon, his chin almost touching his huge steering wheel.

"I know where I'm going," I insisted. "My dad works here."

"How old are you, honey?" he asked. I could tell he didn't quite believe me about my father. He didn't stop looking around.

"Sixteen," I said. I'd been experimenting with lying about my age. So far, I'd always gotten away with fourteen and fifteen; sixteen only sometimes. The driver sized me up and didn't blink an eye. He nodded, then turned to search the horizon again.

"You should get your license so you can drive yourself," he offered happily.

"Oh, I have my license," I assured him. "I just don't have a car."

"A car. Sure," he agreed quickly. "That's half the battle, isn't it?" He continued to look around as we talked, hoping to see some responsible adult presence before he let me go.

"I'm going to wait for you here," he announced when he saw none. "Just in case. You go run make sure your father's here. I don't want to leave you with no way to get home."

"Oh—oh no, really, that's okay," I stammered. "He's working late. He was supposed to pick me up but he got stuck working."

"It's dark out here. There's alligators," the trucker insisted, half kidding.

"My dad has me come out here and meet him all the time," I said. This sounded ridiculous, even to me. But I didn't want this kind trucker waiting for me; knowing he was here waiting and worrying about me would ruin everything. I tried to give a reassuring smile while I opened the door.

"Okay, thanks! 'Bye!" I yelled.

"You run back and tell me when you've found your dad," the driver called after me as I got out. I pretended not to hear him.

Outside, I was struck by the warm swampy smell, a wilderness smell. The heat was hotter in the dark, the sound of the truck's door slamming behind me oddly muffled by the humidity. Far away and all around me, the low sounds of insects and reptiles pulsed. I ducked under the metal checkpoint gate—now I was officially trespassing on restricted land—and walked along the road toward Launch Control and the spectators' stands.

The road was long, longer than I remembered. Everything at the Cape was separated from everything else by miles of nature, and though in a car this made for a pleasant drive, I had no idea how long it would take to reach Launch Control on foot. Maybe all night. I walked through pools of light from the sodium lamps above, each of them bending their heads over me protectively.

I walked and walked. For a long time, I could still hear the low hum of the truck; the driver was waiting for me after all. I had thought I would find his waiting intrusive, but actually it was comforting, a sound I could go back to, a presence like my father's, waiting without impatience for as long as I might take.

I walked until I no longer heard the low thrumming sound of the truck's engine; I couldn't be sure whether he had turned it off or if he had finally given up waiting for me and driven away. Everything out here was far away on the horizon, and nothing seemed to draw any closer as I walked. I'd thought I would be afraid to be alone out here at night, but even in the dark, this place was familiar. I had seen it enough times to imagine it: rolling green rises, not hills exactly, but gentle swells, ditches filled with water and lurking alligators. The wide beige crawlerway bisecting the landscape. The Banana River lapping against its banks, a wild beach, and past that, another narrow strip of land where the two main launchpads stood, 39-A and 39-B, from which *Challenger* had launched. And past that, the ocean into which it had crashed.

I reached the Launch Control Building, with its narrow row of windows facing the launchpads. Until I recognized it, I had started to doubt I was anywhere near the right place. I recognized the VIP stands, the white bleachers where I'd sat with Eric and our fathers to see the launch. I started climbing up the stands, recalling for the millionth time our awkward conversation that day, the way I'd cried, the way Eric had looked at me with such shy concern.

About halfway up, I saw something on the top row of bleachers, a long object disturbing the even rows, maybe a blanket someone had left behind after the *Challenger* launch. It was farther away than

I'd first thought, and when I got closer, I saw that it was a person lying across the seats, a man with his arms folded under his head, looking up at the stars.

Though I'd been thinking of Eric, though it was Eric who had told me about coming to the Cape at night, I didn't allow myself to even suspect that strange form could be him until he sat up and looked at me, until I could see his squinting face. His dear pale face thrust forward, struggling to recognize me too.

Eric's face was studiously blank, his eyebrows lifted only slightly. He didn't acknowledge me at all except to pick himself up and shift over a bit, as if there might not be room here for both of us. I settled down next to him, remembering that day on the school bus in seventh grade when we had swayed next to each other, struggling not to touch.

"Did you take another cab?" he asked by way of greeting.

"Nope," I said proudly. "Hitchhiked."

"Hitchhiked," he repeated. "You're going to get killed." His voice was flat, but I still felt a weird satisfaction that he was concerned for my safety.

"Why, how did *you* get here?"

"Drove," Eric said simply.

"*Drove,*" I repeated, feeling inexplicably annoyed with him for always one-upping me. "You're only thir*teen,*" I informed him. "You can't *drive.*"

"It's against the law," Eric said smugly. "It's not a physical impossibility."

"Where did you learn to *drive?*"

"My father used to try to teach me. I wasn't very good at it, so he stopped. But I picked up the basics." I could imagine Mr. Biersdorfer yelling at Eric from the passenger seat, turning redder and redder as Eric rode the brakes, stalled out the motor.

"He started when I was about ten. I couldn't even reach the pedals. He learned young, I guess, because he grew up on a farm."

"I see. And *what* do you drive?"

"My mother's car," he said.

"Doesn't she know you take it?"

"If she does, she doesn't say anything about it. She probably doesn't know, though. Her room is on the other side of the house from the garage."

"How often do you come out here?" I asked.

"I don't know," he answered. "Depends." I could imagine him driving here every night, doing his homework by the light of a flashlight, eating a picnic dinner.

I wanted to tell him everything then, everything that had happened—my mother's trips to the strip mall to see Eric's father, my mother's leaving us, my afternoon with Josh. The phone call I'd made to Rick Landry, which had a weird way of disappearing and then presenting itself again in my mind. Each time, I felt anew the shock of what I'd done.

"My dad's going to be in a lot of trouble," Eric said matter-of-factly.

"Why?" I asked quickly.

"Well, he's Director of Launch Safety," Eric said carefully. "He's responsible for—"

"I *know* what your father does," I interrupted him. "Believe me."

"Okay."

"He won't necessarily take the blame. Depending on what kind of evidence they find, he might be able to wiggle out of it."

Eric shook his head. "Even if they find the cause and it's something he couldn't have prevented, they'll still fire him. They basically have to."

"Do you think he knew something?"

Eric shrugged off the question.

"He knew about a million problems before every launch. A lot of problems he never even heard about. He listened to what the engineers said and he made a decision."

We sat silently for a long time, listening to the faraway sounds of alligators croaking.

"Do you remember when we came here with our dads?" I asked.

Eric was quiet for so long that I feared he had stopped speaking to me for some reason, but then he answered.

"Of course I do," he said.

"I was so embarrassed when I cried. I thought you'd think I was stupid."

Eric shook his head. "No," he said. And this seemed such a generous word from him. Just, *No: not stupid. No, don't be embarrassed.*

"I wanted you to like me again so badly," I said.

He was silent again.

"Did you hear what I said?" I asked.

"Yeah," he admitted. "I knew that. I knew you wanted me to like you again."

"But you didn't."

Eric sighed. It was a sigh I've come to know well from boys and men, the sigh of being asked for more than they want to give. I thought of that time at Eric's house, when my mother talked and laughed in the Biersdorfers' living room while Eric and I whispered together in his room. I knew now that that had been the closest I'd ever felt to anyone, just talking quietly together, offering bits of fear and history. I would never have that again.

"Your father and my mother are having an affair," I said. I hadn't known I would say it until I did. Eric didn't answer, just watched me steadily with his gray eyes.

"They have been for about eight months now. My mother moved out in the summer, and I don't know where she is exactly, but I think she's been staying someplace where she can be with your father." As I spoke, I watched Eric for a reaction, but he was perfectly still until he was sure I was finished speaking.

"I don't think that can be true," he said finally.

"But it is," I said. "That's what I'm telling you. I've *seen* them. My mother used to take me with her to go and meet him."

"Why would she do that?" he asked. The light evenness of his tone was maddening.

"For cover. She used to tell my father she was taking me shopping and go meet your father instead."

Only then did Eric really react. He cracked a grin, a little warily, the way my father smiled at my mother when he thought she was wrong but didn't want to say so.

"Okay, well, let's look at the facts." He peeled a pinky finger away from its fist. "You saw them together—once?"

I hadn't anticipated that Eric would instigate an Eric-style argument over this. His flat arguing voice was familiar, his irritating arguing face with its expression of calm superiority.

"It was more than once," I corrected. "It happened on several distinct occasions."

This wasn't entirely true, actually. I knew I'd seen my mother and Mr. Biersdorfer together once, but the other times, my mother had dropped me off and disappeared for the rest of the afternoon. I'd assumed she was meeting him, but it was true that I hadn't actually seen Mr. Biersdorfer except that once.

"Second"—now Eric peeled the ring finger back—"your mother left. Okay. That's a hard thing. But you can't assume it has anything to do with my father. It doesn't make much sense that she would leave to be with him, honestly, because he's still living in his own house with his wife and his son."

"Eric, have you ever heard of a thing called having a mistress? Married men put up their girlfriends in a nice apartment where they can go visit anytime."

"But *when* does he go?" he demanded. "Even before this *Challenger* thing happened, he was working all the time. If he's home, he's locked away in his study. I mean, *all* the time—nights, weekends, holidays. Do you know, my family has *never* been on a vacation? And since *Challenger*, he's been working even more. In fact, he's working in his study at home right now. Where would an affair with your mom fit into all this?"

"Did it ever occur to you," I asked triumphantly, "that your father might not *always* be where he says he is? Like tonight. You think he's working in his study, your mom thinks he's working in his study." I leaned forward and lowered my voice for effect. "Maybe he's with my mother right now."

"What, you think he went into his study and then snuck out when no one was looking?"

"Why not?" I pointed out. "We did."

Eric didn't answer right away. I felt pleased with myself for having presented an argument he couldn't immediately dismiss. He sat and thought for a minute. Then he took in a breath, let it out heavily, and smacked his palms against his knees, a gesture that reminded me of my father.

"Let's find out," he said.

"What do you mean?"

He stood up and pulled a key ring from his pocket, jingling it. "Let's go," he said.

"Go where?"

He was already walking, and I had to hustle in order to catch up with him. "My house," Eric said. "If you're right, he won't be there."

We walked to the west entrance of the Space Center, closer than the entrance I had used. Eric led me to the car, parked a bit up the road. It was a newer version of the Oldsmobile I had known in seventh grade. Eric slipped into the driver's seat and fit the key into the ignition.

"What?" he said to my exaggerated openmouthed look of shock at his driving. "What's the big deal?" But Eric couldn't help showing me his real smile then, quick and devilish, with a lift of the eyebrows. I felt a sudden jealousy for the girls at his school, the girls who got to see this smile every day.

Eric pulled out onto the road. He made little adjustments with the wheel, slowing steadily before stop signs and accelerating away from them smoothly.

"You can drive," I marveled.

"That's what I told you," Eric answered. "I wouldn't lie to you."

Twenty minutes later, we pulled up at Eric's house, lit up as always with landscaping lights. He took me around to a side door.

"Okay, you're going to have to be really quiet," Eric said. He looked me up and down. "Um, take off your shoes."

"They're sneakers," I protested, but I slipped them off while he watched.

"Okay, you'll have to follow me and step exactly where I step," Eric whispered. We climbed up two flights, Eric pausing on each landing to let me catch up with him. I watched the backs of Eric's sneakers until they faded and disappeared, and then I could see nothing, felt nothing but the smothering airlessness of absolute dark. I reached out in front of me to feel for invisible obstacles.

"Eric," I whispered as quietly as I could. I felt him stop walking.

"Yeah," he whispered back. He had moved very close to me, our faces almost touching, so we could hear each other.

"I can't see."

"Yeah, well, the lights are off."

"No, I mean . . ." I tried to keep the panic out of my voice. "I can't *see*. I can't see where to go."

"Okay, hold out your hand," he commanded. I did, waving my arm slowly from side to side until I felt our fingers brush together. His skin was warm and surprisingly soft. The fingers gripped my hand delicately. I squeezed back. Holding hands, we walked up the last flight of stairs, and Eric flipped on the hallway light.

"We still have to be quiet," Eric whispered. "My mother's room is right under us." Our hands were still joined; I wasn't sure whether Eric had forgotten or if he meant to hold my hand, and if so, what that meant. I looked up at him: his profile was set and unreadable.

"Okay, it's right here," he whispered outside a closed door. He pressed his ear to the door for a long time, his face registering nothing.

I could imagine Mr. Biersdorfer in there working late, his white shirtsleeves folded up, paging through reports and memos detailing theories and data from the investigation, all stamped CONFIDENTIAL in red. He would be scowling and sweating, dictating brief angry memos into a machine. When he found us here, he would go into a rage. He would call my father, who would be horrified.

"I don't think he's in there," Eric whispered. I could tell by how slowly he spoke that he wasn't sure. He dropped my hand suddenly and reached for the doorknob.

"What are you *doing*?" I breathed.

"I just want to be sure," Eric said.

"Eric, *no*," I whispered, but he was already swinging the door open and stepping into the room. A dim light was on in the office, but after a few seconds of silence, I stepped forward and saw Eric standing in the middle of the room, his hands against his hips. I followed him in.

A huge desk of dark wood faced the door, covered with books

and files. A dim gold lamp sat on the desk, spilling a circle of light onto the papers. All of the walls were lined with dark wood shelving, interrupted here and there by plaques, framed photographs of Mercury and Apollo vehicles and astronauts, and a calendar identical to the one Mr. Biersdorfer had given to our seventh-grade class. The room had a vague smell that seemed to come partly from the wood, but that was also made up of paper, old coffee, and a warm tinge of cologne. The room was in some ways exactly what I would expect, but at the same time its sense of habitation was surprising. The fact of Mr. Biersdorfer's physical presence in this room, the fact of his breathing here, sitting and moving around here for so many hours over the years, was palpable in the roughness of the papers' piles, in the quality of the yellow light on the desk, as if everything were waiting for him to return in just a moment.

I stepped closer to the wall to see the NASA memorabilia. There were signed photographs of the Mercury seven, Neil Armstrong planting the flag, the shot of the whole Earth, the blue marble from Apollo 17, taken the week I was born.

"Well," Eric said, looking around the office in a businesslike way, "this could mean a lot of different things." He still stood with his hands on his hips. "He might have gone to bed, for one thing. He might be in his office at work. He doesn't usually go there this late, but it's possible."

Eric stood quietly then, and I could practically hear the activity of his mind, trying to come up with more possibilities.

"This doesn't prove anything," Eric said, but now he was looking at me, searching my face for an answer or some reassurance.

"No, of course not," I said. "The absence of evidence is not the evidence of absence." I had learned this from Dr. Schuler.

Eric nodded. "Right. I mean, he could be anywhere. My father and your mother. Really. It's absurd. I suppose you think this started that time your family had us over for dinner?"

"He *was* flirting with her an awful lot that night," I pointed out.

"But it would be so *stupid*. This would be the worst time for something like this to happen. Even if he was doing something like this before the disaster—which I'm not saying he was—but now he's under so much scrutiny. It would be insane."

I reached out and took Eric's elbow. At first he stood more rigidly, almost about to pull away. But still I wasn't surprised when Eric crumpled against me, his back rounding as he stooped over to slip his arms around my neck. His head hung on my shoulder awkwardly; I could tell he didn't know what to do, but he didn't let go.

"We should get out of here," I whispered after a long time. I still felt nervous that his father could return at any minute and unravel everything. But Eric was ready to kiss me then, and he wanted to do it there, in his father's study. What I felt then was so different from what I had experienced with Josh any of the times he had kissed me, especially that afternoon in his room, that afternoon which had so quickly shrunk in my mind to the image of Josh sweating over me, laboring at something private, something only he could know. Eric's kiss was trembling, unpracticed, but it was entirely for me, and we stood kissing for a long time in that room with the dark wood smell and the faces of old-style astronauts smiling all around us, just outside that yellow circle of light.

27.

I KNEW I LOVED ERIC BIERSDORFER THEN, SO IT WAS A STRANGE feeling to climb off the bus on Monday morning and see Tina and Chiarra lounging in the grass, sleepy and smiling, sneaking a smoke before homeroom, and to think they knew nothing of Eric and would only want to hear about Josh.

"Hey, what happened to you on Friday?" Chiarra called. "We went to the mall, but you guys weren't there. Did you sneak off somewhere?"

"You'll never guess," I began, and they fell silent as I told them about Josh picking me up and turning left instead of right. By the time I got to the two of us climbing into Josh's bed, Tina and Chiarra were clutching each other for support.

"Oh my God, you *let* him?" Tina demanded. I felt as though I were lying to them, because really I had barely thought of Josh since Friday; I had been thinking only of Eric. I felt as though Josh were something I had accomplished, like work—he was a permanent shield I had constructed for myself. But Eric was what I had wanted to find all along.

As I spoke, we saw Josh approaching us from across the parking lot. He sidled up to me, and I felt aware of Tina and Chiarra's attention, the way they scrutinized the two of us—they were just as curious as I was to see how people are supposed to act together after they've had sex.

"Ready for some new *Challenger* jokes?" Josh asked.

"Oh God, no," Tina moaned, but then we all listened expectantly.

"How do they know that Christa McAuliffe had dandruff?"

"How?"

I studied Josh's expression—lighthearted, amused, only slightly mean. For the first time, I realized the *Challenger* explosion hadn't really affected him, not the way it had affected Eric or me.

"They found her head and shoulders on the beach," Josh said, then opened his mouth wide and squinted in a parody of helpless laughter.

"Josh, that is disgusting," Tina moaned, covering her face with her hands. "Did they really find her head and shoulders on the beach?" she asked a moment later, her voice rising in panic. Josh burst out laughing for real.

"Ugh, I don't want to hear any more," Tina said. She and Chiarra gathered their things.

"We'll leave you two lovers alone," Chiarra said.

As soon as they were gone, Josh pulled me to him and slipped an arm around my shoulders.

"I've missed you," he whispered, his breath hot on my neck. I resisted the urge to flinch away. Josh didn't seem to notice; he was nuzzling my cheek.

"I've been thinking about you," he added. "I haven't been able to get you out of my mind." He didn't seem to expect answers to any of these statements. He played with my hair, traced the outline of my jaw, a child excitedly exploring a new toy.

I marveled at his transformation, at the way sex can make the hardest, most sarcastic character into a pile of unabashed mushy clichés. Did he mean any of these things he was saying? It hardly mattered. He would say anything in the world to ensure I would come over to his house again this afternoon. Or maybe he meant every word of it, maybe he *had* been thinking of me, missing me, dreaming of me. I tried to imagine what this would be like, tried to conjure his image of me: a silent brown-haired thing, a tiny package, skinny arms and legs, pink unpracticed lips. I tried to see myself as he had seen me, pulling my shirt over my head and smiling mischievously. I couldn't imagine it.

"So, um—are you doing okay?" Josh asked, and now there was an edge of nervousness in his voice. I wasn't sure at first what he meant. Why wouldn't I be okay? But then I understood—he meant the sex. He was trying to ask delicately whether I had been damaged.

"I don't know," I lied. "It still hurts pretty bad." Just at that moment, I had decided to be cruel. The first bell rang, a five-minute warning to get to class.

"Still?" he said, blanching. "I'm sorry. Do you think—"

"Plus," I added, "I think I may be pregnant."

Josh's eyes bugged. "You mean you're *late*?" Even as he spoke, I could see his brow furrowing, counting the days as the illogic of this claim set in.

"But it's too early," he said. "I mean, you wouldn't know something like that for at least a couple of weeks, right?"

"Oh, I know. I'm just kidding," I said quickly. I gave a little giggle. "Joke." Josh's face went from white to red.

"Joke," he echoed. "Okay, just a note for future reference?" His sarcasm was back in full force. "That? Is *not* a good joke."

He bared his teeth and tried to give a laugh, a low *heh-heh,* to show that he could laugh at himself.

"But it sounds like you know a lot about it," I pointed out. "Sounds like you know what you're talking about."

"Whatever," Josh said vaguely, looking up at the main doors, where the other kids were hurrying in. "Health class." But I was surprised by how deeply I felt the pain of this possibility, that Josh had experienced previous pregnancy scares, the idea of Josh having done this before, many times, with lots of other girls. Maybe he chose a freshman girl every fall; maybe he made a hobby of it. Maybe everyone knew but me.

"I have to go to physics," I said.

"But can you come over again after school?" his voice was high, almost squeaking. "Meet you in the parking lot?"

"I have to take care of my sister," I said.

"I'll get you home before she gets there," he offered.

His expression was beseeching, and it was somehow embarrassing to see it, even obscene, his eyes shining and his mouth open, completely unself-conscious. He was exposed, much more than when I'd seen him without his clothes. I had no intention of ever going to Josh's house again, to his puppy-smelling bed. But I said, "Okay."

Josh smiled broadly, relieved, and that smile reminded me again of the Josh I'd once admired from afar, the Josh of such effortless cuteness, such easy grace. As he kissed me, I felt surprised that he couldn't see the change in me, the mark of Eric. I could feel Eric as a cloud hovering around me, Eric as a part of my body, another organ. He could see everything I did, hear everything I said and thought, and I felt I could commune with him this way, glance at him sideways under my eyelids and share an invisible look, even when he was miles away.

After my last class, I slipped onto the bus early. I knew that Josh was waiting for me, that he had pulled his car up to the curb where everyone could see him, lounging on the hood. I had never before considered the effort that must have gone into Josh's performances, but now I could see that he had worked hard to impress me. Josh waited on his Datsun, first with anticipation, then with impatience, then with annoyance. He watched everyone else he knew stream out the doors. He greeted them, yelled friendly things to them, turned down their offers of other places to go. He told them he was waiting for me. I know he must have waited a long time, until after everyone had driven away and the yellow buses had rumbled off in a long parade of diesel fumes. Only then would he have given up and turned the key.

28.

ERIC AND I MET IN HIS BACK YARD THE NEXT NIGHT. WE WERE awkward together, but we found things to talk about. School, classes, good teachers and bad teachers. I wanted to ask Eric about the girls at his school, whether he had made friends with any of them, or even a girlfriend. But I decided not to; it was none of my business, and besides, I wouldn't have wanted him to ask me similar questions.

Toward morning, as we sat in the pool chairs behind his house holding hands, we talked about the disaster again. I told him what I had done, about my call to Rick Landry; I told him about the long fall, about the napkin and the joint rotation, about his father's attempts to blame the workers at the Cape. Eric listened quietly, taking everything in and staring at the pool. I watched his profile, waiting for some change in expression.

He shook his head. "I can see why you think this whole thing in the news happened because of what you did," he said carefully. "But it didn't, necessarily. The same information could have come from another source at the same time."

"That would be an awfully big coincidence, don't you think?" I asked. "The same information on the same day coming from two different sources?"

"Well, if you think about the number of people who know stuff, the amount of different kinds of information, it's possible. It probably happens all the time," Eric said. "Like Watergate. Those guys at the *Washington Post* broke the story, but there was another reporter at another paper who was figuring out the exact same thing, just a few days behind. It probably happens all the time." Part of me felt annoyed that Eric couldn't just be impressed by something I told him, that ever since we were little, he had never just said, *Oh, really?* or *Wow, I didn't know that.* He always had to have a new interpretation, something I hadn't thought of.

But at the same time I found it comforting that Eric could hear my story and imagine that I wasn't to blame. I almost felt absolved.

"Thanks, Eric," I said.

"For what?" He dropped my hand to scratch his nose. Then he flashed a smile at me as he took my hand again, that smile I'd seen as we snuck into his father's study. It seemed all I'd wanted all along was for that smile to be for me.

Eric drove me home near dawn, and I watched him drive, the easy swing of his arm as he turned the wheel.

"Maybe we can meet again tomorrow," he said as he pulled up at my house. "Or maybe Saturday." I felt a thrill of anticipation for the days to come when I could see Eric and know he wanted to see me too. It seemed we could do whatever we wanted now.

As I climbed out of the car, I didn't notice at first that our house was the only one without a newspaper on the stoop, the only one with a light on in a living room window. I had become so accustomed to sneaking out at night, I was capable of silence, and so as I unlocked the front door and stepped in as quietly as I could, I didn't cry out when I saw a hulking human shape on the couch. My father.

He must have woken up and found me gone. Or maybe I had made some sound on my way out. Maybe he had lain awake in his bed fighting the impulse to get up and check, and when he finally did, he must have been horrified to find me missing. Now he'd been sitting here in his pajamas and robe, drinking coffee and waiting for me to return.

He stared at me for a long time. My father had never yelled at me, and I knew he wouldn't yell now. I looked back at him, at the exhaustion etched into the lines of his face, the faint stain on the lapel of his pajamas where he had dripped coffee on himself.

"Where in God's name have you been?" he asked, only once it was clear that I wasn't going to speak.

"With my boyfriend," I said. A terrible silence ticked by as my father stared at me. "I'm sorry," I added lamely.

"With your *boyfriend*?" my father repeated. "Dolores, you are thirteen years old. Who is your boyfriend?"

And what would my father say, I wondered, if I spoke the name Eric Biersdorfer? His wife lost to the father, his daughter lost to the son. I would have happily said it a month or two ago, just to watch his reaction. Just after the disaster, I would have announced it without hesitation, looking for a way to hurt him. But not now.

"Josh Fitzgerald," I said. My father thought for a second, scanning his memory for the name.

"That accountant we saw testify? His son?"

I nodded.

"How old is he?"

"Seventeen, I think. He's a senior."

My father winced and shook his head.

"I had no idea," he said. "What would your mother think of me? I do the best I can with you girls, I do the laundry and feed you and drive you where you need to go, and meanwhile my thirteen-year-old is sneaking off in the middle of the night with a boy who is nearly an adult."

"You shouldn't worry what she would think," I told him. "This is more her fault than yours."

"Don't say that," he said. Even now he was trying to defend her from any criticism.

"Do you know where she is?" I asked.

He looked at me, confused. "Who? Your mother? Not at this very minute."

"No, I mean—do you know where she's staying? Since she left us?"

He nodded. "Of course. She's staying with Carol. Her friend from work."

"Did you know that all along?"

He nodded again.

"Why didn't you tell me?"

"It was never a secret," my father answered.

The image of Mr. Biersdorfer's broad white back as he sat across from my mother came to me, the jingling of the ice in his glass.

"I'm sorry," I said again. After months of never apologizing to him for anything, now I couldn't stop. The truth was that he didn't know what my mother's relationship with Biersdorfer had been, and I didn't either. Maybe she had left us to be with him, and maybe she hadn't.

"She just wants to be wanted," I told him. "Maybe if you just told her that you really want her back."

My father smiled sadly, the kind of smile he gave Delia and me whenever we asked him for something unreasonable. I knew he was about to end this, tell me everything was all right, tell me to go to bed. "It's very complicated," he said. "It's not that simple."

"Oh, I know," I said. "But . . . do you love her?"

He didn't answer.

"I'm sorry," I said. "It's none of my business."

"No, it's not," my father said. "But I do. I do love her, very much."

I stood alone in the living room for a few minutes after he went to bed, then walked around turning out the lights. He'd said that it was complicated between him and my mother, that it wasn't that simple. *But wasn't it?* I wondered as I climbed into my cool bed, listening to Delia's soft snores. I knew that some things were complicated—I'd learned that, I thought, as well as any adult. But weren't some things, in fact, that simple?

The space notebook stayed at the bottom of my desk drawer under a dictionary. I'd stopped adding to it or studying it, though new articles about the flaws in the Solid Rocket Booster design kept appearing every day. Now my desire to know all the details seemed childish anyway. I thought of telling Eric what I'd learned when I saw him that night, that people can't hurt you if you decide not to care what they think. But it occurred to me he'd just nod and say, *Of course.* He'd known that all along.

I rode the bus home the next afternoon, sitting alone although the bus was crowded. I watched the trees through the scratched school bus windows, and I was moved by the way something so ugly could make everything outside look so beautiful: the shiny green leaves lit up white by the sun; the smudges of people dressed in white, pink, blue; hanging Spanish moss like brushstrokes. The bus stopped at my corner, and as I climbed down the three steps, I sensed something different about my house—it held itself tensed, pulsed slightly with energy, the way *Columbia* had seemed to glow with fate as it stood on the launchpad at the very first test launch. The way my house had looked so different from the others the night my mother and I had walked, swinging our two hands between us. I fit my key into the door, and I swear I was so prescient then, so sharpened by all that had gone before, I knew already what I would see. The door creaked open slowly to reveal my mother's battered plaid suitcase, her kicked-off shoes, and her limp jacket over a chair. And in the middle of the room, the pillar of my two parents, just as I remembered from when I was a tiny girl and used to put my two hands on their knees to stop them, my two parents standing in the middle of the living room, in the middle of their house, embracing.

EPILOGUE

I STILL THINK ABOUT THAT O-RING. I'VE LEARNED THAT IT WAS manufactured in 1985 in Brigham City, Utah, cleaned off like a newborn, inspected and measured and inspected again before being packed and shipped to Florida. That O-ring made an American journey by railway, across deserts and mountains, across the width of the American South to arrive at the coast of central Florida on October 11, 1985, at the marshy wildlife refuge, the improbable spaceport. There it waited to be unloaded into the Vehicle Assembly Building, unpacked and reinspected and remeasured and reinspected again, by Frank Gray. By my father.

I can see my father turning that O-ring back and forth across his square fingers, peering at it through his square glasses. In the moments when I have hated my father most, this is how I have pictured him, so fixed in his concentration, his gaze so focused he is nearly blinded, looking for flaws but missing the point. When I have loved my father most, I picture him this way too.

After my mother came home, she was different; being away from us had changed her. She seemed more solid, more sure of herself, as if she too had grown up during those months she'd been gone. Sometimes I've wanted to ask her where she was, just to know whether any of the scenarios I'd imagined for her had been accurate. Sometimes I've wished we could go through my memories together piece by piece like photos in an album, so she could explain to me what each image had really meant: Mr. Biersdorfer watching her at the dinner party, our mysterious trips to the strip mall, our midnight walk. When I was younger—when I was as young as I'd been before she came back—I would have pursued the truth relentlessly. But now I could admit to myself that this was one truth that didn't need to be exposed. Everything I'd suspected might have been true, or she may not have been with Biersdorfer at all. And nothing would be changed if I never knew.

In June, the presidential commission released its findings. The technical cause for the disaster was found to be a burnt O-ring; the larger cause was faulty management. Mr. Biersdorfer resigned as Director of Launch Safety and took a job in Colorado, moving his family with him. Eric and I wrote letters for a few years, but we never saw each other again. My father, to everyone's surprise, was cleared of wrongdoing in connection with the failed Solid Rocket Booster, but he was laid off again anyway, for the last time, along with thousands of workers at Kennedy.

The details of the astronauts' deaths are only alluded to in the commission's report, buried in an appendix. What Doug had told me was true—partly used emergency oxygen packs had been among the debris found in the crew cabin. NASA had recovered the tape of crew communications from the cockpit and, miraculously, experts had been able to restore the tape despite its being soaked in seawater for months. To this day NASA will not release the recording or a transcript, citing the privacy of the families.

I read those pages in the report over and over that summer when my father brought it home, analyzing the language for some glimmer of the long fall. The reality of the astronauts' deaths is neither present nor absent, neither confirmed nor denied. We are asked simply to look away. Most people today have no idea that the seven of them survived the explosion.

On January 28, 1986, seven astronauts are awakened at 6:20 A.M. exactly. They eat their breakfasts together, steak and eggs. They are served a cake before the photographers, smiling so hard they grit their teeth. They climb into their spacecraft, wait for the countdown, and finally launch. The feeling of launching cannot be described. They tear into the sky.

The first thing that happens after the explosion is a blinking light and buzzer alerting the pilot to a drop in cabin pressure. As they have been trained to do, they activate their emergency oxygen packs. Mike Smith cannot reach his, so Judith Resnik, seated behind him, reaches forward to switch his on. They all breathe. They have six minutes of air. Five men and two women, all in the prime of health, sit strapped into their seats, breathing, refusing to panic. They have been trained to respond to malfunctions, accidents, and emergencies of every kind with calm and logic. And so it is with calm and logic that they scan their sensors and readouts to understand what has happened.

Attached to nothing, the crew cabin flies free, trailing its comet tail of wires and hoses. So powerful was the thrust exerted by the two rockets and three Main Engines that the crew cabin continues to climb. They travel skyward for another sixty long seconds. After the unbearable noise and vibration of the launch, then the crushing pressure of the explosion, this quiet is a relief, a blissful silence except for the distant hiss of wind. The cabin sails smoothly and silently, still traveling up and up, pointing its nose at the clear cold sky.

Then there is a moment of equilibrium, of weightlessness. The women's hair lifts, their bodies rise against their seat restraints. Just for a second, they feel the weightlessness they had anticipated and trained for. They float. It seems that they could go anywhere they want now. It feels as though they are finally free.

Then, slowly, gravity gathers itself in their stomachs; then, gradually, they begin to fall.

The front-heavy cabin points its windows at the ocean. At first they are still so high up—over eight miles—that the sea and sky are indistinguishable, the coast they left not three minutes earlier a fuzzy green and brown map. They can easily make out the Cape, that strip of land from which every American astronaut has been launched.

They have plenty of time to think. They fall for so long that falling starts to seem a natural state of being; they start to feel that they could live normal lives this way. They have time to observe the blue of the bright sky separate itself from the blue of the wide blue Atlantic. They don't panic, not one of them. They have time to review what they will miss most about being alive. Those with children will miss their children; those with loves will miss their loves. They already miss the simple pleasures of this mission they had trained so long for, so looked forward to. The simple pleasure of hovering by the window, watching the turning world.

They also think they will probably survive this. They remind themselves of the fact that every single American astronaut on every mission has returned to Earth alive. Experimental orbits, unstable rockets, multistage moon shots. Every one! Why should they be different? They consider the spectacular redundancy of NASA safety: surely someone has anticipated the minuscule possibility of this situation and created a contingency plan. That plan is, at this very moment, being activated in Houston or at the Cape. Their minds reel with the possibilities—parachutes built into the crew cabin, as they were on Apollo capsules? Ejection seats? Thrusters to dampen their fall? In the time they have, they can imagine quite a few. Even as the water draws close, as the waves develop wavelets, whitecaps, birds, the astronauts do not panic. They are not dying; they can't be. They feel fine. In fact, they feel wonderful, full of energy and optimism. They have never felt better.

They fall for two minutes and forty-five seconds, longer than anyone else has ever fallen unfettered. They have more time to contemplate their impending deaths than anyone ever to feel the acceleration of thirty-two feet per second per second. But—and this is the odd thing about falling—no matter how far they fall, no matter how long they wait and how certain they are now that no parachute, no net, nothing can save them, in the moment just before impact, they are still perfectly whole, breathing, living, and in that state it is impossible, impossible, to believe in their own deaths.

ACKNOWLEDGMENTS

ALTHOUGH THIS NOVEL IS BASED ON TRUE EVENTS IN NASA'S history, all of the main characters and their actions are fictional.

Several books were especially important to my research for this book. Claus Jensen's *No Downlink*, Richard Feynman's *What Do You Care What Other People Think?*, and Gene Gurney and Jeff Forte's *Space Shuttle Log* all provided important details. Diane Vaughan's *The Challenger Launch Decision* deserves special mention for changing my thinking about the cause of the disaster.

Special thanks are due to my professors and classmates at the University of Michigan MFA program. While I was a student, this book, then a novel-in-progress, was the recipient of a Hopwood award; I'm also grateful to the English department for funding a research trip to Florida and to the Davis family for their hospitality.

For their wisdom, good humor, and tireless efforts, I'm indebted to Julie Barer and Marysue Rucci. I'd also like to thank my friends and family for their love and support.

And finally, most of all, thank you to Chris Hebert, who is on every page.

ABOUT THE AUTHOR

Margaret Lazarus Dean was born in 1972. She grew up in St. Paul, Minnesota, and received a BA in Anthropology from Wellesley College and an MFA from the University of Michigan. She is currently a lecturer at the University of Michigan and lives in Ann Arbor.